A Tangle of Tails

3 Books in 1

Also by Liz Kessler

Philippa Fisher's Fairy Godsister

Emily Windsnap

A Tangle of Tails

3 Books in 1

LIZ KESSLER

Orion
Children's Books

This omnibus edition first published in Great Britain in 2008
by Orion Children's Books
a division of the Orion Publishing Group Ltd
Orion House
5 Upper St Martin's Lane
London WC2H 9EA
An Hachette Livre UK Company

5 7 9 10 8 6 4

Originally published in three separate volumes:
The Tail of Emily Windsnap
First published in Great Britain in 2003
Emily Windsnap and the Monster from the Deep
First published in Great Britain in 2004
Emily Windsnap and the Castle in the Mist
First published in Great Britain in 2006
All by Orion Children's Books

The Orion Publishing Group's policy is to use papers that
are natural, renewable and recyclable products and made from
wood grown in sustainable forests. The logging and manufacturing
processes are expected to conform to the environmental regulations
of the country of origin.

A catalogue record for this book is
available from the British Library.

Printed in Great Britain by
Clays Ltd, St Ives plc

ISBN 978 1 84255 685 6

www.orionbooks.co.uk

Contents

The Tail of Emily Windsnap   1

Emily Windsnap and the Monster from the Deep   209

Emily Windsnap and the Castle in the Mist   399

The Tail of Emily Windsnap

Decorations by Sarah Gibb

For Frankie, Lucy and Emily
And for Dad

Come, dear children, let us away;
Down and away below.
Now my brothers call from the bay;
Now the great winds shoreward blow;
Now the salt tides seaward flow;
Now the wild white horses play,
Champ and chafe and toss in the spray.
Children dear, let us away.
This way, this way!

from The Forsaken Merman,
by Matthew Arnold

Chapter One

Can you keep a secret?
I know everyone has secrets but mine's different. Kind of weird. Sometimes I have nightmares where I get found out and locked up in a zoo or a scientist's laboratory.

It all started in Year Seven when swimming lessons began. It was the first Wednesday afternoon at my new school and I was so looking forward to it. Mum hates swimming and always used to change the subject when I asked why I couldn't learn.

'But we live on a boat!' I'd say. 'We're surrounded by water!'

'You're not getting me in there,' she'd reply. 'Just look at all the pollution. You know what it's like when the day cruises have been in. Now stop arguing and come and help me with the vegetables.'

She even kept me out of swimming lessons all the way through primary school. Said it was unhealthy. 'All those bodies mixing in the same water,' she'd shudder, 'not for *us* thank you very much.'

And that would be that: end of discussion. I finally wore her down the summer before I started secondary school. 'All right, all right,' she sighed, eventually. 'I give in. Just don't start trying to get *me* in there with you.'

I'd never been in the sea. I'd never even had a bath. I'm not dirty or anything – I have a shower every night. But there isn't enough room for a bath on the boat, so I'd never been totally *immersed* in water.

Till the first Wednesday afternoon of Year Seven.

Mum bought me a new bag especially for my costume and towel. On the side, it had a picture of a woman doing front crawl. I looked at the picture and dreamed about winning Olympic races, with a Speedo costume and black goggles just like hers.

Only it didn't quite happen like that.

When we got to the baths, a man with a whistle and white shorts and a red T-shirt told the girls to go in one room and the boys to go in the other.

I changed quickly in the corner. I didn't want anyone to see my skinny body. My legs are like sticks and they're usually covered in scabs and grazes from getting on and off *The King of the Sea*. That's our boat. Which is a bit of a grand title for a little sailing boat with mouldy ropes, peeling paint and beds the width of a ruler. But anyway. We usually just call it *King*.

Julie Crossens smiled at me as she put her clothes in her locker. 'I like your cozzy,' she said. It's just plain black with a white stripe across the middle.

'I like your hat,' I smiled back as she squashed her hair into her tight, pink swimming cap. I squeezed my ponytail under mine. I usually wear my hair loose; Mum made me put it in a bobble today. It's mousy brown and used to be short but I'm growing it at the moment. It's a bit longer than shoulder length so far.

Julie and I sit next to each other sometimes. We're not best friends. Sharon Matterson used to be my best friend but she went to Our Lady. I'm at Brightport High. Julie's the only person I might want to be best friends with. I think she wants to be Mandy Rushton's, though. They hang out together at break.

I don't mind. Not really. Except when I can't find my way to the canteen – or to some of the classes. It might be nice to have someone to get lost with.

Brightport High is about ten times bigger than my primary school! It's like an enormous maze, with MILLIONS of boys and girls who all seem to know what they're doing.

'You coming, Julie?' Mandy Rushton stood between us with her back to me. She gave me a quick look, then she whispered something in Julie's ear and laughed. Julie didn't look up as they passed me.

Mandy lives on the pier, like me. Her parents run the amusement arcade and they've got a flat above it. We used to be quite friendly till last year when I accidentally told my mum that Mandy had showed me how to win free goes on the one-armed bandit. I didn't *mean* to get her in trouble but – well, let's just say I'm not exactly welcome in the amusements any more. In fact, she hasn't spoken to me ever since.

And now we've ended up in the same class at Brightport High. Brilliant. As if starting a new school the size of a city isn't bad enough.

I finished getting ready on my own.

'OK, listen up, 7C,' the man with the whistle said. He told us to call him Bob. 'Any of you kids totally confident to swim on your own?'

'Course we can – we're not babies!' Mandy sneered under her breath.

Bob turned to face her. 'All right then. Do you

want to start us off? Let's see what you can do.'

Mandy stepped towards the pool. She stuck her thumb in her mouth. 'Ooh, look at me. I'm a baby. I can't swim!' Then she dropped herself sideways into the water. Her thumb still in her mouth, she pretended to slip under as she did this really over the top kind of doggy paddle across the pool.

Half the class were laughing by the time she reached the end.

Bob wasn't. His face reddened. 'Do you think that's funny? Get out! Now!' he shouted. Mandy pulled herself out and grinned as she bowed to the class.

'You *silly* girl,' Bob handed her a towel. 'You can sit on the side and watch.'

'*What?*' Mandy stopped grinning. 'That's not fair! What did I do?'

Bob turned his back on her. 'Now, we'll start again. Who's happy to swim confidently *and* sensibly?'

About three-quarters of the class raised their hands. I was desperate to get in the pool but didn't dare put mine up. Not after that.

'Right then.' Bob nodded at them. 'You can get in if you want – but just in the shallow end, mind.'

He turned back to the rest of the class who were lined up and shivering by the side of the pool. 'I'll start with this lot.'

Once his back was turned, I couldn't stop myself. I sneaked in with the group making their way round to the shallow end! I'd never swum before so I shouldn't have, but I just knew I could do it. And the water looked *so* beautiful lying there, still and calm, as though it was holding its breath waiting for someone to jump in and set it alive with splashes and ripples.

There were five big steps that led gradually into the water. I stepped onto the first one and warm water tickled over my toes. Another step and the water wobbled over my knees. Two more, then I pushed myself into the water.

I ducked my head under, reaching wide with my arms. As I held my breath and swam deeper, the silence of the water surrounded me and called to me, drawing my body through its creamy calm. It was as if I'd found a new home.

'Now THAT is more like it!' Bob shouted when I came up for air. 'You're a natural!'

Then he turned back to the others, squinting and staring at me with open mouths. Mandy's eyes fired hatred at me as Bob said, 'That's what I'd like to see you *all* doing by the end of the term.'

And then it happened.

One minute, I was skimming along like a flying fish. The next, my legs suddenly seized up. It felt as though someone had glued my thighs together and strapped a splint on my shins! I tried to smile as I paddled to the side but my legs had turned to a block of stone! I couldn't feel my knees, my feet, my toes. *What was happening?*

A second later, I almost went under completely and I screamed. Bob dived in, in his shorts and T-shirt, and swam over to me.

'It's my legs,' I gasped. 'I can't feel them!'

He cupped my chin in his big hand and back-stroked us to the side. 'Don't worry,' he said, looking behind us as he swam. 'It's just cramp. Happens to everyone.'

We reached the big steps at the side of the pool and sat down on the top one. As soon as I was halfway out of the water, the weird feeling started to go away.

'Now, let's have a look at those legs.' Bob lifted me onto the side of the pool. 'Can you lift your left one up?' I did.

'And your right?' Easy.

'Any pain?'

'It's gone,' I said.

'Just a bit of cramp, then. Why don't you have a rest here for a few minutes? Get in again when you're ready?'

I nodded and he went back to the others.

But I'd felt something that he hadn't seen. And I'd seen something that he hadn't felt. And I didn't have a *clue* what it was but I knew one thing for sure – you wouldn't get me back in that pool for a million pounds.

I sat by the side for a long time. All the rest of the class eventually got in and started splashing about. Even Mandy was allowed back in. But I didn't want to sit too near in case I got splashed and it happened again. I was even nervous when I went home after school in case I fell off the jetty into the sea.

The jetties are all along one side of the pier. There are three other boats on ours. A posh white speed-boat and a couple of bigger yachts. None of the others have people living on them though.

I stepped onto the jetty. We've got this old plank of wood that we put across to the boat. Mum used to carry me over it when I was little but I'd been doing it on my own for ages. Only, I couldn't that day. I called her from the jetty.

'I can't get across,' I shouted when she came up from below deck.

She had a towel wrapped round her head and a satin dressing-gown on. 'I'm getting ready for my book group.'

I stood frozen on the jetty. Around me, the boats melted into a wobbly mass of poles and sails. I stared at *King*. The sail was down. The mast rocked with the boat, the wooden deck shiny with sea spray. My eyes blurred as I focused on the row of portholes along the side of the boat; the thin metal bar running round the edge. 'I'm scared,' I said.

Eventually, Mum pulled the dressing-gown cord tighter round her waist and reached her skinny arm out to me. 'Come on then, let's have you.'

When I got across, she grabbed me and gave me a hug. 'Dingbat,' she said, ruffling my hair. Then she went back inside to get ready for her group.

Mum's always got some group or other on the go. Last year it was pilates; now it's her book group. She works at the secondhand bookshop on the promenade. That's where they meet. It's pretty cool, actually. They've just opened up a café bar where you can get thick milkshakes with real fruit in them and huge wodges of chocolate flapjack. I reckon the book group is just her latest excuse to meet up and gossip with her friends – but at least it keeps her off my back.

Mystic Millie who does Palms on the Pier comes and sits with me. Millie's all right. Sometimes she practises reiki or shiatsu on me. She brought her tarot cards round once. Said I was about to achieve academic success and win praise from all quarters. The next day I came bottom in the spelling test and was given three lunchtime detentions to catch up. But that's Millie for you.

Luckily, *Emmerdale* and *EastEnders* were both on tonight so I knew she wouldn't bother me. Just as well because I wanted to be left alone. I needed time to think about what to do. There were two things I knew for sure. One: I had to work out what had happened to me in the pool. And two: I needed to get out of swimming lessons before it happened again.

I could hear Mum in her cabin while I paced up and down in the front room. *'Do ya really love me? Do ya wanna stay?'* she was singing louder than her CD. She always sings when she's getting ready to go out. I don't mind too much – except when she starts on the actions. Tonight, I hardly noticed.

I'd already tried asking her if I had to go swimming again and she went mad. 'I hope you're joking,' she'd said in that voice that means *she* isn't. 'After the fuss you created – *no way* are you giving up now!'

I paced up to the gas fire in the corner of the saloon. That's what we call the living room. I usually get my best ideas when I pace but nothing was coming to me. I paced past the tatty old sofa with a big orange blanket. Pace, pace, left, right, creak, squeak, think, think. Nothing.

'Better tell me soon, baby I ain't got all day.' Mum's voice warbled out from her room.

I tried extending my pacing to the kitchen. It's called a galley, really. It's got a sink, a tiny fridge and a cooking surface that's always covered in empty cartons and bottles. Mum makes us recycle *everything*. The galley's in the middle of the boat with the main door and a couple of wooden steps opposite. You've got to be careful on these when you come in, because the bottom step comes loose. I usually jump down from the top one.

I paced through the kitchen and along the corridor that leads to the bathroom and our cabins.

'How do I look?' Mum appeared at the end of the corridor. She was wearing a new pair of Levis and a white T-shirt with 'BABE' in sparkly letters across the middle. I wouldn't mind but I bought a similar one myself at the same time – and it looks better on her!

'Great.' A familiar sharp rap on the roof stopped me saying any more. The side door opened and Mr Beeston poked his head through. 'Only me,' he called, peering round the boat.

Mr Beeston's the lighthouse keeper. He comes round all the time. He gives me the creeps – he kind of looks at you out of the corner of his eyes when he's talking to you. And they're different colours: one's blue, one's green. Mum says he probably gets lonely in his lighthouse, sitting around looking out to sea, switching the light on, only having contact with people by radio. That's why he's always popping in. She says we have to be friendly to him.

'Oh, Mr Beeston, I'm just off out to my book group. We're waiting for Millie to turn up. Come in a sec. I'll walk down with you.' Mum disappeared down the corridor to get her coat as he clambered through the door.

'And how are we?' he asked, staring sideways into my eyes. His mouth was crooked like his tie. His shirt was missing a button, his mouth missing a tooth. I shivered. I wish Mum wouldn't leave me on my own with him.

'Fine, thanks.'

He narrowed his eyes, still staring at me. 'Good, good.'

Thankfully, Millie arrived a minute later and Mum and Mr Beeston went out.

'I won't be late, darling,' Mum said, kissing my cheek then wiping it with her thumb. 'There's shepherd's pie in the oven. Help yourselves.'

'Hi Emily.' Millie looked at me intensely for a moment. She always does that. 'You're feeling anxious and confused,' she said with alarming accuracy for once. 'I can see it in your aura.'

Then she swept her black cape over her shoulder and put the kettle on.

I waved goodbye as Mum and Mr Beeston headed down the pier. At the bottom, Mr Beeston turned left to walk round the bay, back to his lighthouse. The streetlamps lining the prom were already on, pale yellow spots against an orangey-pink sky. Mum turned right for the bookshop.

I watched till they'd gone out of sight before joining Millie on the sofa. We had the shepherd's pie on our knees and laughed together at the weatherman when he fluffed his lines. Then *Emmerdale* started and she shushed me and went all serious.

I had an hour.

I cleared the plates, then raided the pen jam jar, got

a sheet of Mum's posh purple writing paper from the living room cupboard and shut myself in my cabin.

This is what I wrote:

Dear Mrs Partington
Please can you let Emily off her swimming lessons. We have been to the doctor and he says she has a bad allergy and MUST NOT go near water. At all. EVER.
Kindest wishes
Mary Penelope Windsnap

I pretended to be asleep when I heard Mum come in. She tiptoed into my room, kissed me on top of my head and smoothed the hair off my forehead. She always does that. I wish she wouldn't. I hate having my fringe pushed off my forehead but I stopped myself from pulling it back till she'd gone.

I lay awake for hours. I've got some fluorescent stars and a crescent moon on my ceiling and I looked up at them, trying to make sense of what had happened.

All I really wanted to think about was the silkiness of the water as I sliced through it – before everything went wrong. I could still hear its silence pulling me, playing with me as though we shared a secret. But every time I started to lose myself to the feeling of its creamy warmth on my skin, Mandy's face broke into the picture. Glaring at me. A couple of times I almost fell asleep. Drifting into panicky half-dreams – me inside a huge tank, all the class around me, pointing, staring, chanting: 'Freak! Freak!'

I could *never* go in the water again!

But the questions wouldn't leave me alone. What had *happened* to me in there? Would it happen again?

And no matter how much I dreaded the idea of putting myself through that terror again, I knew I would never be happy until I had the answers. More than that, something was simply pulling me back to the water. It was like I didn't have a choice. I HAD to find out – however scary it might be.

By the time I heard Mum's gentle snores coming from her room, I was determined to get to the bottom of it – before anyone else did.

I crept out of bed and slipped into my swimming costume. It was still damp and I winced and pulled my denim jacket over the top. Then I tiptoed out of the boat and looked round. The pier was totally deserted. Along the prom, guesthouses and shops stood in a silent row of silhouettes against the night sky. They could have been a stage set.

A great big full moon shone a spotlight across the sea. I felt sick as I looked at the plank of wood, stretching across to the jetty. *Come on, just a couple of steps.*

I clenched my teeth and my fists – and tiptoed across.

I ran to the bollards at the end of the pier and looked down at the rope ladder stretching into the darkness of the water. The sea glinted coldly at me; I shivered in reply. Why was I doing this?

I wound my fingers round my hair. I always do that when I'm trying to think – if I don't feel like pacing. And then I pushed the questions and the doubts – and Mandy's sneering face – out of my mind. I *had* to do it, had to know the truth.

I buttoned up my jacket. I wasn't getting in there without it on! Holding my breath, I stepped onto the rope ladder and looked out at the deserted pier one last time. I could hear the gentle chatter of masts clinking in the bay as I carefully made my way down into the darkness.

The last step of the rope ladder was still quite a way from the sea because the tide was out. *It's now or never*, I said to myself.

Then, before I had time to think another thought, I pinched my nose between my thumb and forefinger – and jumped.

I landed in the water with a heavy splash and gasped for breath as soon as I came up. At first I couldn't feel anything, except the freezing cold water. *What on earth was I doing?*

Then I remembered what I was there for and started kicking my legs. A bit frantically at first. But seconds later, the cold melted away and so did my worries. Instead, a feeling of calm washed over me with the waves. Salt on my lips, hair flat against my head, I darted under the surface, cutting through the water as though I lived there.

And then – IT – happened. I swam straight back to the pier, terrified. NO! I didn't want this – I'd changed my mind!

I reached out but couldn't get hold of the ladder. *What had I done?* My legs were joining together again, turning to stone! I gasped and threw my arms about uselessly, clutching at nothing. *Just cramp, just cramp*, I told myself, not daring to look as my legs disappeared altogether.

But then, as rapidly as it had started, something changed; I stopped fighting it.

OK, so my legs had joined together. And fine, now they had disappeared completely. So what? It was good. It was . . . right.

As soon as I stopped worrying, my head stopped slipping below the surface. My arms stopped flailing about everywhere. Suddenly I was an eagle, an aeroplane – a dolphin, gliding through the water for the sheer pleasure of it.

Right, this is it. You might have guessed by now or you might not. It doesn't matter. All that matters is that you promise never to tell anyone.

I had become a mermaid.

Chapter Two

It's not exactly the kind of thing that happens every day, is it? It doesn't happen *at all* to most people. But it happened to me. I was a mermaid. A mermaid! How did it happen? Why? Would I always be one? Questions filled my head, but I couldn't answer a single one. All I knew was that I'd discovered a whole new part of myself and nothing I'd ever done in my life had felt so good.

So there I was, swimming like – well, like a fish! And in a way, I *was* a fish. My top half was the same as usual; skinny little arms, my fringe plastered to my forehead with seawater, black Speedo cozzy.

But then, just below the white line that goes across my tummy, I was someone else; something else. My costume melted away and, instead, I had shiny scales. My legs narrowed into a long, gleaming, purple and green tail, waving gracefully as I skimmed along in the water. I'd never done anything gracefully in my life so it was a bit of a shock! When I flicked my tail above the surface, it flashed an arc of rainbow colours in the moonlight. I could zoom through the water with the tiniest movement, going deeper and deeper with every flick of my tail.

It reminded me of the time we went to World of Water with school. We were in a tunnel under the water with sea life all around us. It felt as if we were really in the sea. Only, this time I was! I could reach out and touch the weeds floating up through the water, upside-down beaded curtains. I could race along with the fat grey fish grouped together in gangs, weaving around each other as though they were dancing.

I laughed with pleasure and a line of bubbles escaped from my mouth, climbing up to the surface.

It seemed as though I'd only been swimming for five minutes when I realised the sky was starting to grow pink. I panicked as a new thought hit me: *what if I couldn't turn back?*

But the second I'd pulled myself out of the water, my tail softened. I dangled on the rope ladder and watched, fascinated, as the shiny scales melted away, one by one. As my legs returned, they felt odd, like when your mouth goes numb after you've had a filling.

I wiggled my toes to get rid of the pins and needles in my feet. Then I headed home with a promise to myself that I would be back – soon.

Bob, the swimming instructor, was standing in front of me, talking into a mobile phone. I couldn't hear what he was saying. Someone grabbed my shoulders.

'This the one, is it?' a snarling voice growled behind my ear. Bob nodded.

I tried to wriggle free from the man's clutches but he was holding my shoulders too firmly. 'What do you want?' a voice squeaked from my mouth.

'As if you didn't know,' the snarly voice snapped at me. 'You're the freak.' He shook my shoulders.

'I'm not a freak,' I shouted. 'I'm not!'

'Stop pretending,' a woman's voice replied.

'I'm not pretending,' I wriggled under the hands holding my shoulders. 'I'm not a freak!'

'Emily, for pete's sake,' the woman's voice said. 'I know you're not really asleep.'

My eyes snapped open to see Mum's face inches from mine, her hands on my shoulders, shaking me gently. I bolted upright in my bed. 'What's happening?'

Mum let go of me. 'What's happening, dozy drawers, is that you're going to be late for school. Now get a move on.' She parted the curtain in the doorway. 'And don't forget to brush your teeth,' she said without turning round.

Over breakfast, I tried to remember my dream and

the things I'd been shouting. It had felt so real: the capture, the voices. Had I said anything out loud? I didn't dare ask so I ate in silence.

It was on the third mouthful that things went seriously wrong.

Mum was fussing around as usual, shuffling through the huge pile of papers stuffed behind the mixer. 'What did I do with it?'

'What is it this time?'

'My shopping list. I'm sure I put it down here somewhere.' She leaned across to a pile of papers on the table. 'Ah, here it is.'

I looked up in horror as she picked up a piece of paper. Not just any piece of paper. A SHEET OF POSH PURPLE WRITING PAPER!

'No-o-o-o!' I yelped, spitting half a mouthful of cereal across the table and leaping forward to grab the paper. Too late. She was unfolding it.

Her eyes narrowed as she scanned the sheet and I held my breath.

'No, that's not it.' Mum started to fold the paper up. I breathed out and swallowed the rest of my mouthful.

But then she opened it again. 'Hang on a sec. That's my name there.'

'No, no, it's not. It's someone else, it's not you at all!' I snatched at the paper.

Mum ignored me. 'Where are my reading glasses?' They were round her neck – as they usually are when she's looking for them.

'Why don't I read it to you?' I said, in my best Perfect Daughter voice. But as I was speaking, she found her glasses and put them on. She studied the note.

I tried to edge away from the table but she looked up on my second step. '*Emily*?'

'Hm?'

She took her glasses off and waved the note in front of my face. 'Want to explain this to me?'

'Ah, well, hm, ah, er, let's see now.' I examined the note with what I hoped was an I've-never-seen-it-in-my-life-before-but-I'll-see-if-I-can-help kind of expression on my face.

She didn't say anything and I kept staring at the note, pretending I was reading it. Anything to avoid meeting her eyes while I waited for my telling off.

But then she did something even worse than tell me off. She put the piece of paper down, lifted my chin up with her hand and said, 'I understand, Emily. I know what it's about.'

'You do?' I squeaked, terrified.

'All those things you were saying in your sleep about being a freak. I should have realised.'

'You should?'

She let go of my chin and shook her head sadly. 'I've been an idiot not to realise before now.'

'You have?'

Then she took my hand between her palms and said, 'You're like me. You're afraid of water.'

'I am?' I squealed. Then I cleared my throat and

straightened my school tie. 'I mean, I *am*,' I said seriously. 'Of course I am! I'm scared of water. That's exactly what I am. That's what this has all been about. Just that, nothing more than –'

'Why didn't you tell me?'

I looked down at my lap and closed my eyes tight, trying to squeeze a bit of moisture out of them. 'I was ashamed,' I said quietly. 'I didn't want to let you down.'

Mum pressed my hand harder between hers and looked into my eyes. Hers were a bit wet, too. 'It's all my fault,' she said. 'I'm the one who's let *you* down. I stopped you from learning to swim and now you've inherited my fear.'

'Yes,' I nodded sadly. 'I suppose I have. But you mustn't blame yourself. It's OK. I don't mind, honestly.'

She let go of my hand and shook her head. 'But we live on a boat,' she said. 'We're surrounded by water.'

I almost laughed, but stopped myself when I saw the serious expression on her face. Then a thought occurred to me. 'Mum, why exactly *do* we live on a boat if you're so afraid of water?'

She screwed up her eyes, stared into mine as if she was looking for something. 'I know,' she whispered. 'I can't explain it, but it's such a deep feeling – I could *never* leave *King*.'

'But it doesn't make any sense. I mean, you're scared of water and we live on a boat in a seaside town!'

'I know, I know!'

'We're miles from anywhere. Even Nan and Grandad live at the other end of the country.'

Mum's face hardened. 'Nan and Grandad? What have they got to do with it?'

'I've never even seen them! Two cards a year and that's it.'

'I've told you before, Em. They're a long way away. And we're not – we don't get on too well.'

'But why not?'

'We fell out. A long time ago.' She laughed nervously. 'So long ago, I can't even remember why.'

We sat in silence for a moment. Then Mum got up and looked out of the porthole. 'This isn't right; it shouldn't be like this for you,' she murmured as she wiped the porthole with her sleeve.

Then she suddenly twirled round so her skirt flowed out around her. 'I've got it!' she said. 'I know what we'll do.'

'Do? What d'you mean, "do"? I'll just take the note to school, or you could write one, yourself. No one will ever know.'

'Of course they will! No, we can't do that.'

'Yes we can. I'll just –'

'Now Emily, don't start with your arguing. I haven't got the patience for it.' Her mouth tightened into a determined line. 'I cannot allow you to live your life like that.'

'But *you* don't –'

'What I do is my own business,' she snapped. 'Now

please stop answering me back.' She paused for a second before opening her address book. 'No, there's nothing for it. You need to conquer your fear.'

'What are you going to do?' I fiddled with a button on my blouse.

She turned away from me as she picked up the phone. 'I'm going to take you to a hypnotist.'

'All right, Emily. Now, I want you to breathe nice and deeply. Good.'

I was sitting in an armchair in Mystic Millie's back room. I didn't know she did hypnotism but according to Sandra Castle she worked wonders on Charlie Piggot's twitch, and that was good enough for Mum.

'Try to relax,' Millie intoned, before taking a very loud, deep breath. Mum was sitting in a plastic seat in the corner of the room. She wanted to be there, 'just in case'. In case of what, she didn't exactly say.

'You're going to have a little sleep,' Millie drawled. 'When you wake up, your fear of water will have completely gone. Vanished. Floated away . . .'

I had to stay awake! If I fell into a trance and started babbling about everything, the whole plan would be ruined. Not that I had a plan, as such, but you know what I mean. What would Millie think if she found out? What would she do? Visions of nets and cages and scientists' laboratories swam into my mind.

I forced them away.

'Very good,' Millie breathed in a husky voice. 'Now, I'm going to count down from ten to one. As I do, I'd like you to close your eyes and imagine you are on an escalator, gradually travelling down, lower and lower, deeper and deeper. Make yourself as comfortable as you can.'

I shuffled in my seat.

'Ten . . . nine . . . eight . . .' Millie said softly. I closed my eyes and waited nervously for the drowsy feeling to come.

'Seven . . . six . . . five . . .' I pictured myself on an escalator like the one in the precinct in town. I was running the wrong way, scrambling up against the downward motion. I waited.

'Four . . . three . . . two . . . You're feeling very drowsy . . .'

I waited a bit more.

That's when I realised I wasn't feeling drowsy at all. In fact . . .

'One.'

. . . I was wide awake! I'd done it – hooray! Millie *was* a phoney! The 'aura' thing had been a fluke after all!

She didn't say anything for ages and I was starting to get fidgety when a familiar noise broke the silence. I opened my eyes the tiniest crack to see Mum in the opposite corner – fast asleep and snoring like a horse! I snapped my eyes quickly shut again and fought the urge to giggle.

'Now, visualise yourself next to some water,' Millie said in a low voice. 'Think about how you feel about the water. Are you scared? What emotions are you experiencing?'

The only thing I was experiencing was a pain in my side from trying not to laugh.

'And now think of somewhere that you have felt safe. Somewhere you felt happy.' I pictured myself swimming in the sea. I thought about the way my legs became a beautiful tail and about the feeling of zooming along with the fish. I was on the verge of drifting into a happy dream world of my own when – 'Nnnnnuuurrrggggghhhh!' – Mum let out a huge snore that made me jump out of my chair.

I kept my eyes closed tight and pretended I'd jumped in my sleep. Mum shuffled in her chair and whispered, 'Sorry.'

'Not to worry,' Millie whispered back. 'She's completely under. Just twitching.'

After that, I let my mind drift back to the sea. I couldn't wait to get out there again. Millie's voice carried on in the background and Mum soon started snoring softly again. By the time Millie counted up to seven to wake me up, I was so relieved I hugged her.

'What's that for?' she asked.

'Just a thank you, for curing my fear,' I lied.

She blushed as she slipped Mum's £20 note into her purse. 'Think nothing of it, pet. It's a labour of love.'

Mum was quiet on the way home. Did she know I hadn't been asleep? Did she suspect anything? I didn't dare ask. We made our way through the town's narrow streets down to the prom. As we waited to cross the road, she pointed to a bench facing out to sea. 'Let's go and sit down over there,' she said.

'You OK, Mum?' I asked as casually as I could while we sat on the bench. The tide was out, little pools dotted about in the ripply sand it had left behind.

She peered out towards the horizon. 'I had a dream,' she said without turning round. 'It felt so real. It was beautiful.'

'When? What felt real?'

She looked at me for a second, blinked and turned back to the sea. 'It was out there, somewhere. I can almost feel it.'

'Mum, what are you on about?'

'Promise you won't think I'm crazy.'

'Course I won't.'

She smiled and ruffled my hair. I smoothed it back down. 'When we were at Millie's...' She closed her eyes. 'I dreamed about a shipwreck, under the water. A huge golden boat with a marble mast. A ceiling of amber, a pavement of pearl . . .'

'Huh?'

'It's a line from a poem. I think. I can't remember the rest . . .' She gazed at the sea. 'And the rocks. They weren't like any rocks you've ever seen. They used to glisten every colour you could imagine –'

'*Used* to? What do you mean?'

'Did I say that? I mean they did – in my dream. They shone like a rainbow in water. It's just, it felt so *real*. So familiar...' Her voice trailed away and she gave me a quick sideways look. 'But I suppose it's sometimes like that, isn't it? We all have dreams that feel real. I mean, *you* do. Don't you?'

I was trying to work out what to say when she started waving. 'Oh look,' she said briskly, 'there's Mr Beeston.' I glanced up to see him marching towards the pier. He comes round for afternoon tea every Sunday. Three o'clock on the dot. Mum makes tea; he brings iced buns or doughnuts or caramel slices. I usually scoff mine quickly and leave them to it. I don't know what it is about him. He makes the boat feel smaller, somehow. Darker.

Mum put her fingers in the edges of her mouth and let out a sharp whistle. Mr Beeston turned round. He smiled awkwardly and gave us a quick wave.

Mum stood up. 'Come on. Better get back and put the kettle on.' And before I could ask her anything else, she was marching back to the boat. I had to run to keep up.

28

Chapter Three

I sneaked out again that night. I couldn't keep away. I swam further this time. The sea was grimy with oil and rubbish in the harbour and I wanted to explore the cleaner, deeper water further out.

Looking back across the water, Brightport looked so small. A cluster of buildings all huddled round a tiny horseshoe bay; a lighthouse at one end, a harbour at the other.

A hazy glow hovered over the town. Blurry yellow street lamps with an occasional white light moving along between them.

As I swam round the rocks at the end of the bay, the water became clearer and softer. It was like switching from grainy black and white into colour. The fat grey fish were replaced by stripy yellow and blue ones with floppy silver tails; long thin green ones with spiky antennae and angry mouths; orange ones with spotty black fins – all darting about purposefully around me.

Every now and then, I swam across a shallow sandy stretch. Wispy little stick-like creatures as thin as paper wriggled along beneath me, almost see-through against the sand. Then the water would suddenly get colder and deeper as I went over a rocky bit. I swished myself across these carefully. They were covered in prickly black sea urchins and I didn't fancy getting one of those stuck on my tail.

Soon the water got warmer again as I came to another shallow bit. I was getting tired. I came up for breath and realised I was miles from home; further away than I'd ever been on my own. I tried to flick myself along but my tail flapped lazily and started to ache. Eventually, I made it to a big, smooth rock with a low shelf. I pulled myself out of the water, my tail resting on some pebbles in the sea. A minute later, it went numb. I wiggled my toes and shivered as I watched my legs come back. That bit was still *really* creepy!

Sitting back against a larger rock, I caught my breath. Then I heard something. Like singing, but without words. The wet rocks shimmered in the moonlight but there was no one around. Had I imagined it? The water lapped against the pebbles, making them jangle as it sucked its breath away from the shore. There it was again - the singing.

Where was it coming from? I clambered up a

jagged rock and looked down the other side. That's when I saw her. I rubbed my eyes. Surely it couldn't be . . . but it was! It was a mermaid! A real one! The kind you read about in kids' stories. Long blonde hair all the way down her back, which she was brushing while she sang. She was perched on the edge of a rock, shuffling about as if she was trying to get comfortable. Her tail was longer and thinner than mine. Silvery green and shimmering in the moon-light, it flapped against the rock as she sang.

She kept singing the same song. When she got to the end, she started again. A couple of times, she was in the middle of a really high bit when she stopped and hit her tail with the brush. 'Come on, Shona,' she said sharply. 'Get it right!'

I stared for ages, opening and closing my mouth. Like a fish! I wanted to talk to her. But what exactly do you say to a singing mermaid perched on a rock in the middle of the night? Funnily enough, no one's ever told me.

In the end, I coughed gently and she looked up straight away.

'Oh!' she said. She gawped open-mouthed at my legs for a second. And then with a twist and a splash, she was gone.

I picked my way back down the rocks to the water's edge. 'Wait!' I shouted as she swam away from me. 'I want to talk to you.'

She turned in the water and looked at me suspi-ciously. 'I'm a mermaid too!' I shouted. Yeah right, with my skinny legs and my Speedo cozzy – she'd *really* believe that! 'Wait, I'll prove it.'

I jumped into the water and started swimming towards her. There was still a moment of panic as my legs stuck together and stiffened. But then they relaxed into their new shape and I relaxed too as I swished my tail and sped through the water.

The mermaid was swimming away from me again. 'Hang on,' I called. 'Watch!' I waited for her to turn back, then dived under and flicked my tail upwards. I waved it as high as I could.

When I came back up, she was staring at me as though she couldn't believe what she'd seen. I smiled but she ducked her head under the water. 'Don't go!' I called. A second later, *her* tail was sticking up. Not twisting around madly like mine did; more as if she was dancing or doing gymnastics. In the moonlight, her tail glinted like diamonds.

When she came back up, I clapped. Tried to anyway, but I slipped back under when I lifted both arms out and got water up my nose.

She was laughing as she swam towards me. 'I haven't seen you before,' she said. 'How old are you?'

'Twelve.'

'Me too. But you're not at my school, are you?'

'Brightport High,' I said. 'Just started.'

'Oh.' She looked worried and moved away from me again.

'What's wrong with that?'

'It's just . . . I haven't heard of it. Is it a mermaid school?'

'You go to a mermaid school?' The idea sounded like something out of a fairy tale, and even though I've *totally* grown out of fairy tales, I had to admit it sounded pretty cool.

She folded her arms – how did she do that without sinking? – and said quite crossly, 'And what's so wrong with that? What kind of school do you *expect* me to go to?'

'No, it sounds great!' I said. 'I wish I did, too.'

I found myself wanting to tell her everything. 'It's just . . . I haven't been a mermaid for long. Or I didn't know I was, or something.' My words jumbled and tumbled out of me. 'I've never really been in water – properly – and then when I did, it happened and I was scared, but I'm not now and I wish I'd found out years ago.'

I looked up to see her staring at me as though I was something from outer space that had got washed up on the beach. I stared back and tried folding my arms, too. I found that if I kept flicking my tail a little, I could stay upright. So I flicked and folded and stared for a bit and she did the same. Then I noticed the side of her mouth flutter a bit and I felt the dimple below my left eye twitching. A second later, we were both laughing like maniacs.

'What are we laughing at?' I said when I managed to catch my breath.

'I don't know!' she answered – and we both burst out laughing again.

'What's your name?' she said once we'd stopped laughing. 'I'm Shona Silkfin.'

'Emily,' I said. 'Emily Windsnap.'

Shona stopped smiling. 'Windsnap? *Really*?'

'Why? What's wrong with that?'

'Nothing – it's just . . .'

'What?'

'No, it's nothing. I thought I'd heard it before but I can't have done. I must be thinking of something else. You haven't been round here before, have you?'

I laughed. 'I'd never even been swimming a couple of weeks ago!'

Shona looked serious for a second. 'How did you do that thing just now?' she asked.

'What thing?'

'With your tail.'

'You mean the handstand? You want me to do it again?'

'No, I mean the other thing.' She pointed under the water. 'How did you make it change?'

'I don't know. It just happens. When I go in water, my legs kind of disappear.'

'I've never seen someone with legs before. Not in real life. I've read about it. What's it like?'

'What's it like having legs?'

Shona nodded.

'Well it's – it's cool. You can walk about, and run. And climb things, or jump or skip.'

Shona gazed at me as if I was talking a foreign language. 'You can't do this with legs,' she said as she dived under again. This time her tail twisted round and round, faster and faster like an upside-down pirouette. Water spun off as she turned, spraying tiny rainbow arcs over the water.

'That was brilliant!' I said when she came back up.

'We've been doing it in Diving and Dance. We're doing a display at the Inter-Bay competition in a couple of weeks. This is the first time I've been in the squad.'

'Diving and dance?'

'Yes,' she went on breathlessly. 'Last year, I was in the choir. Mrs Highwave said that FIVE fishermen were seen wandering aimlessly towards the rocks during my solo performance.' Shona smiled proudly, her earlier shyness totally vanished. 'No one at Shiprock School has *ever* had that many before.'

'And that's – that's good, is it?'

'Good? It's brilliant! I want to be a siren when I grow up.'

I stared at her. 'So all that stuff in fairy tales about mermaids luring fishermen to watery graves – it's all *true*?'

Shona shrugged. 'It's not like we *want* them to die. Not necessarily. Usually, we just hypnotise them into changing their ways and then wipe their memories so they move away and forget they saw us.'

'Wipe their memories?'

'Usually, yes. It's our best defence. Not everyone

35

knows how to do it. Mainly just sirens and people close to the king. We just use it to stop them stealing all our fish, or finding out about our world.' She leaned in closer. 'Sometimes, they fall in love.'

'The mermaids and the fishermen?'

Shona nodded excitedly. 'There're loads of stories about it. It's *totally* illegal – but so romantic. Don't you think?'

'Well, I guess so. Is that why you were singing just now?'

'Oh, that. No, I was practising for Beauty and Deportment,' she said, as if I had the faintest clue what she was on about. 'We've got a test tomorrow and I can't get my posture right. You have to sit perfectly, tilt your head exactly right and brush your hair in a hundred smooth strokes. It's a pain in the gills trying to remember everything all at once.'

She paused and I guessed it was my turn to say something. 'Mmm, yeah, I know what you mean,' I said, hoping I sounded convincing.

'I came top in last term's test, but that was just hair brushing. This is the lot.'

'That must be difficult.'

'B & D is my favourite subject,' she went on. 'I wanted to be hairbrush monitor but Cynthia Smoothflick got it.' She lowered her voice. 'But Mrs Sharptail told me that if I do well in this test, maybe they'll give it to me next term.'

What was I meant to say to that?

'You think I'm a real goody-goody, don't you?'

She started to swim away again. 'Like everyone else.'

'No, of course not,' I said. 'You're . . . you're . . . ' I struggled to find the right words. 'You're . . . interesting.'

'You're pretty swishy, too,' she said and inched back.

'How come you're out at this time anyway?' I asked.

'These rocks are the best ones around for B & D but you can't really come here in the day. Too dangerous.' She stuck a thumb out towards the coast. 'I usually sneak out on Sunday nights. Or Wednesdays. Mum's always out like a tide by nine o'clock on a Sunday. She likes to be fresh for the week ahead. And she has her aquarobics on Wednesdays and always sleeps more soundly after that. Dad sleeps like a whale every night!' Shona laughed. 'Anyway, I'm glad I came tonight.'

I smiled. 'Me too.' The moon had moved round and was shining down on me, a tiny chink missing from its side. 'But I'll have to get going soon,' I added, yawning.

Shona frowned. 'Are you going to come back another time?'

'Yeah, I'd like that.' She might be a bit strange, but she was a *mermaid!* The only one I'd ever met. She was like me. 'When?'

'Wednesday?'

'Excellent,' I grinned. 'And good luck in your test.'

'Thanks.' And with another flick of her tail, she was gone.

As I swam round Brightport Bay in the darkness, the beam from the lighthouse flashed steady rays across the water. I stopped for a moment to watch. Each beam slowly scanned the water before disappearing round the back of the lighthouse. It was almost hypnotic. A large ship silently made its way across the horizon, a silhouette briefly visible with each slow beam of light.

But then I noticed something else. Someone was standing on the rocks at the bottom of the lighthouse. Mr Beeston! What was he doing? He seemed to be looking out at the horizon – following the ship's progress?

I ducked under the water as another beam came round. What if he'd seen me? I stayed underwater until the light had passed. When I came up again, I looked back at the lighthouse. No one there.

And then the light went off. I waited. It didn't come back on.

I tried to imagine Mr Beeston inside. Just him, all on his own, rattling around in a big empty lighthouse. Footsteps echoing with emptiness whenever he climbed up and down the stone spiral stairs. Sitting alone, looking out at the sea. Watching the light. What kind of a life was that? What kind of a person could live that life? *Why hadn't the light come back on?*

Dark questions followed me home.

By the time I reached the pier, it was nearly morning. Shivering, I pulled myself up the rope ladder.

I sneaked back onto the boat, hung my jacket over the fire. It would be dry by morning. Mum likes the place to be like a sauna at night.

As I crept into bed, I thanked the lucky stars on my ceiling that I'd got home with my secret still safe. For now.

Chapter Four

'Don't forget your things.' Mum reached through the side door, holding an object that filled me with dread.

'Right.' I took my swimming bag from her.

'Get a move on, then. You don't want to be late, do you?'

'No. Course not.' I looked down at the rippled sand between the wooden slats of the jetty. 'Mum?' I said quietly.

'What, sweetheart?'

'Do I have to go to school?'

'Have to go? Of course you have to go. What cock-eyed notions have you got in your head now?'

'I don't feel well.' I clutched my tummy and tried to look as if I was in pain.

Mum pulled herself through the door and

crouched on the jetty in front of me. She cupped my chin in her hand and lifted my face up to look at hers. I *hate* it when she does that. The only way I can avoid her eyes is by closing my own, and then I feel like an idiot.

'What's this about?' she asked. 'Is it your new school? Don't you like it?'

'School's fine,' I said quickly. 'On the whole.'

'What, then? Is it the swimming?'

I tried to move my head away but she held on tight. 'No,' I lied, looking as far to the side as I could, my head still trapped in her hand.

'I thought we had that all fixed,' she said. 'Are you worried in case it hasn't worked?'

Now, why hadn't I thought of that? How could I have been so stupid! I should have realised that if I was cured I'd have to go swimming again!

'I've got a bad stomach,' I said weakly.

Mum let go of my chin. 'Come on, sausage, there's nothing wrong with you, and you know it. Now, scoot.' She patted my leg and stood up. 'You'll be fine,' she added, more gently.

'Hm,' I replied, and sloped up the jetty to wait for the bus on the promenade.

I slunk into school and got to my class just as Mrs Partington was closing the registration book. She looked at her watch and said, 'I'll turn a blind eye, just this once.'

She always says that. Everyone laughs when she does because she actually has got a blind eye. It's bright blue, just like her other one, but it doesn't move. Just stares at you, even when she's looking away. Freaky. You don't know where to look when she's talking to you, so we all try not to get told off. She always has the best-behaved class in the school.

I didn't laugh with the others this time, though. Just said, 'Sorry,' and went to sit down, pushing my hateful bag under the table.

The morning was a disaster. I couldn't concentrate at all. We were doing long division and I kept putting the numbers in the wrong place. I was really cross because I can do long division *easily*. Mrs Partington kept giving me sideways looks out of her good eye.

When the bell rang for break, I actually did start to feel ill. We had to line up for the coach to take us to the baths. Everyone ran out of the room but I took ages putting my pens and ruler away in my pencil case.

Mrs Partington was wiping the board. 'Come on, Emily,' she said without turning round. 'It might be nice to get to *something* on time today.'

'Yes, Mrs Partington,' I said and crawled out of the classroom, reluctantly dragging my bag behind me.

I walked to the coach like a zombie. It crossed my mind just to keep walking and not get on the coach at all. I'd got as far as the school gate when Philip Northwood called me back. 'Oi – teacher's pet!' he yelled. Everyone turned to see who he was talking to.

'Teacher's pet? What are you on about?'

'Come on, we all saw you showing off last week in the pool. Bob couldn't stop going on about how *amazing* you were and how we should all try and be like *you*.'

'Yeah. We all heard what he said.' Mandy Rushton came up behind Philip. 'And we *saw* you.'

I glared at her, speechless. She saw me? Saw *what*? My tail? She couldn't have! It hadn't even formed – *had it*?

'I can't help it,' I said, eventually.

'Yeah, right. *Show-off*,' Mandy sneered.

'Shut up.'

Mr Bird, the PE teacher, turned up then. 'Right, come on, you lot,' he said. 'Let's have you all on this coach.'

I found a seat on my own. Julie sat across the aisle from me. 'He's such a pig, that Philip,' she said, putting her bag on her knee. I smiled at her. 'And he's only jealous because he doesn't know how to swim.'

'Thanks Ju– '

'Shift up, Jules.' Mandy plonked herself down next to Julie and flashed me a smarmy smile. 'Unless you want to sit with *fish girl*.'

Julie went red and I turned to look out of the window as the coach bumped and bounced down the road. Mandy's words swirled round and round in my head as if they were in a cement mixer. *Fish girl*? What did she mean?

The coach stopped in the car park. 'You coming?' Julie hung back while Mandy pushed and shoved to the front with the rest.

'Won't be a sec.' I pretended to be doing up my shoelaces. Perhaps I could hide under the seat till everyone came back, say I'd fainted or fallen over or something.

I could hear chattering outside the window, then it went quiet. A moment later, there was a huge groan, people shouting.

'But *sir*, that's not *fair*,' I heard Philip whine. I chanced a quick look out of the window. Bob was there, talking to Mr Bird. The class were all standing around; some had thrown their bags on the ground.

Next thing I knew, someone had got on the coach. I ducked down again, held my breath. But the footsteps came all the way to the back.

'You're not still doing your laces up, are you?' It was Julie.

'Huh?' I looked up.

'What are you doing?'

'I'm just –'

'Doesn't matter anyway.' She sat down. 'Swimming's off.'

'*What*?'

'Staff are on strike. Council cuts. They forgot to tell the school.'

'You're joking?'

'Do I look as though I'm joking?'

I looked at her face; totally miserable. I stared down at my lap and shook my head. 'God, it's just not fair, is it?' I said, trying hard not to grin. 'Wonder what they'll make us do instead.'

'That's what Mr Bird's talking about now with Bob. They're going to send us on a nature trail, apparently.'

'Duh – boring,' I folded my arms, hoping I looked in as much of a huff as Julie. The coach soon set off again and Mr Bird announced with a smile that we were going to Macefin Wood.

Mandy glared at me as she sat down across the aisle. I had to sit on my hands to stop myself punching the air and shouting, 'Ye-e-e-s!'

I went to bed really early so I could get a few hours' sleep before sneaking out to meet Shona. I found my way to the rocks easily and got there first this time. A familiar flick of a tail spreading rainbow droplets over the water told me she'd arrived.

'Hello!' I waved as soon as she surfaced.

'Hi!' She waved back. 'Come on.'

'Where are we going?'

'You'll see.' She splashed rainbow water in my face with her tail as she dived under.

We seemed to swim for ages. The water reminded me of those adverts where they pour a load of melted chocolate into the bar. Silky smooth. I felt as if I was melting with it as we swam.

Shona was ahead of me, gliding through the water and glancing back from time to time to check I was still there. Every now and then, she'd point to the left or right. I'd follow her hand to see a hundred tiny fish swimming in formation like a gymnastics display, or a yellow piece of seaweed climbing up towards the surface like a sunflower. A line of grey fish swam alongside us for a while; fast, smart and pinstriped like city businessmen.

It was only when we stopped and came up for air that I realised we'd been swimming underwater the whole time.

'How did I do that?' I gasped, breathless.

'Do what?' Shona looked puzzled.

I looked back at the rocks. They were tiny pebbles in the distance. 'We must have swum a mile.'

'Mile and a quarter, actually.' Shona looked apologetic. 'My dad bought me a splishometer for my last birthday.'

'A *what*?'

'Sorry. I keep forgetting you've not been a mermaid very long. It shows how far you've swum. I measured the distance from Rainbow Rocks yesterday.'

'Rainbow what?'

'You know. Where we met.'

'Oh, right.' I suddenly realised I was out of my depth – in more ways than one.

46

'I wasn't sure if it would be too far for you but I wanted to bring you here.'

I looked round. Sea everywhere. What was so special about this particular spot? 'Why here?' I asked. 'And anyway, you haven't answered my question. How did we do all that underwater?'

Shona shrugged. 'We're mermaids,' she said simply. 'Come on, I want to show you something.' And with that, she disappeared again and I dived under the water after her.

The lower we went, the colder the water grew. Fish flashed by in the darkness.

A huge grey bruiser with black dots slid slowly past, its mouth slightly open in a moody frown. Pink jellyfish danced and trampolined around us.

'Look.' Shona pointed to our left as a slow-motion tornado of thin black fish came towards us, whirling and spiralling as it passed us by.

I shivered as we swam deeper still. Eventually, Shona grabbed my hand and pointed down. All I could see was what looked like the biggest rug I'd ever seen in my life – made out of seaweed!

'What's that? I gurgled.

'I'll show you.' And with that, Shona pulled me lower. Seaweed slipped and slid along my body, creaking and popping as we swam through it. What was she *doing* with me? Where was she taking me?

I was about to say I'd had enough, but then the weeds became thinner. It was as though we'd been stuck in a wood and finally made our way out. Or to a clearing in the centre of it, anyway. We'd come to a patch of sand in the middle of the seaweed forest.

'What is it?' I asked.

'What d'you think?'

I looked around me. A huge steel tube lay along the ground; next to it, metres of fishing nets sprawled across the sand, reaching up into the weeds. A couple of old bicycles were propped up on huge rusty springs. 'I have absolutely no idea,' I said.

'It's our playground. We're not really meant to come out here. But everyone does.'

'Why can't you come here?'

'You're meant to stick to your own area – it's too dangerous otherwise. Too easy to get spotted.' Shona swam over to the tube and disappeared. 'Come on,' her voice bubbled out from inside it, echoing spookily around the clearing.

I followed her into the tube, sliding along the cold steel to the other end. By the time I came out, Shona was already flipping herself up the fishing net. I scrambled up behind her.

'Like it?' Shona asked when we came back down.

'Yeah, it's wicked.'

Shona looked at me blankly. 'It's wicked?'

'Wicked . . . cool, top. You know –'

'You mean like swishy?'

'I guess so.' I looked around me. 'Where's all this stuff from?'

'Things fall into the sea – or get thrown away. We make use of it,' she said as she pulled herself onto one

48

of the bikes. She perched sideways on it, letting herself sway backwards and forwards as the spring swung to and fro. 'Nice to have someone to share it with,' she added.

I looped my tail over the other one and turned to face her. 'How d'you mean? What about your friends?'

'Well, I've got *friends*. Just not a *best* friend. I think the others think I'm too busy swotting to be anyone's best friend.'

'Well, you do seem to work pretty hard,' I said. 'I mean, sneaking out at night to revise for a test!'

'Yeah, I know. Do you think I'm really dull?'

'Not at all! I think you're . . . I think you're swishy!'

Shona smiled shyly.

'How come there's no one else around?' I asked. 'It's kind of creepy.'

'It's the middle of the night, gill-brain!'

'Oh yeah. Of course.' I held onto the handlebars as I swayed forwards and back on my swing. 'I wish I could meet some other mermaids,' I said after a while.

'Why don't you, then? You could come to my school!'

'How? You don't have extra lessons in the middle of the night, do you?'

'Come in the day. Come on Saturday.'

'*Saturday?*'

'We have school Saturday mornings. Why not come with me this Saturday? I'll tell them you're my long-lost cousin. It'd be evil.'

'Evil?'

'Wicked. Sorry.'

I thought about it. I'd been invited to Julie's on Saturday. I could easily tell Mum I was going there and then tell Julie I couldn't make it. But I was only just getting to know Julie – she might not ask me again. *Then* who would I have? Apart from Shona! And Shona *was* a mermaid. She was going to take me to mermaid school! When else would I get a chance to do *that*?

'OK,' I said. 'Let's do it!'

'Great! Will your parents mind?'

'You're joking aren't you? No one knows about me being a mermaid.'

'You mean apart from your mum and dad? If you're a mermaid, they must be –'

'I haven't got a dad,' I said.

'Oh. Sorry.'

'It's OK. I never had one. He left us when I was a baby.'

'Sharks! How awful.'

'Yeah, well, I don't want to know about him anyway. He never even said he was leaving, you know. Just disappeared. Mum's never got over it.'

Shona didn't reply. She'd gone all rigid and was staring at me.

'What?'

'Your dad left when you were a baby?'

'Yes.'

'And you don't know why he went?'

I shook my head.

'Or where?'

'Nope. But after what he did to Mum, he can stay there as far as I'm –'

'But what if something happened to him?'

'Like what?'

'Like – like – maybe he got taken away, or he couldn't come back to you or something.'

'He left us. And we're fine without him.'

'But what if he didn't –'

'Shona! I don't want to talk about it. I haven't got a dad, OK? End of subject.' I watched a shoal of long white fish swim across the clearing and disappear into the weeds. Seaweed swayed gently behind them.

'Sorry,' Shona said. 'Are you still going to come on Saturday?'

I pulled a face. 'If you still want me to.'

'Of course I do!' She swung off her bike. 'Come on. We need to be heading back.'

We swam silently back to Rainbow Rocks, my head filled with sadness stirred up by Shona's questions. Not so different from the ones I'd asked myself a hundred times. Why *did* my dad disappear? Didn't he love me? Didn't he want me? Was it my fault?

Would I ever, *ever* see him?

Chapter Five

I waved to Mum as I made my way down the pier. 'Bye darling, have a lovely day,' she called.

Go back in, go back in, I thought. 'Bye,' I smiled back at her. I walked woodenly along the pier, glancing behind me every few seconds. She was smiling and waving every time I looked.

Eventually, she went inside and closed the side door behind her. I carried on to the top of the pier, checked behind me one last time, just to be sure – then, instead of turning onto the promenade, I ran down the steps onto the beach and sneaked under the pier. I pulled off my jeans and shoes and shoved them under a rock. I already had my cozzy on underneath.

The tide was in so I only had to creep a short way under the pier. A few people were milling about on the beach, but no one looked my way. What if they did? For a second, I pictured them all pointing at me: 'Fish girl! Fish girl!' Laughing; chasing me with a net.

I couldn't do it!

But Shona! And mermaid school! I *had* to do it. I'd swim underwater all the way to Rainbow Rocks. No one would see my tail.

Before I could change my mind, I ran into the freezing cold water. One last look round, then I took a breath, dived forward – and was on my way.

I made my way to Rainbow Rocks and hung around at the edge of the water, keeping hidden from the shore. A minute later, Shona arrived.

'You're here!' she grinned and we dived under. She took me in a new direction, out across Shiprock Bay. When we came to the furthest tip of the bay, Shona turned to me. 'Are you ready for this?' she asked.

'Are you joking? I can't wait!'

She flipped herself over and started swimming downwards. I copied her moves, scaling the rocks as we dived deeper and deeper.

Shoals of fish darted out from gaps in rocks that I hadn't even noticed. Sea urchins clung to the sides in thick black crowds. The water grew colder.

And then Shona disappeared.

I flicked my tail and sped down. There was a gap in

the rock. A huge hole, in fact. Big enough for a whale to get through! Shona's face appeared from inside.

'Come on,' she grinned.

'Into the rock?'

She swam back out and grabbed my hand. We went through together. It was a dark tunnel, bending and twisting. Eventually, we turned a corner and a glimmer of light appeared, growing bigger and bigger until eventually we came out of the tunnel. I stared around me, my jaw wide open.

We were in a massive hole in the rock. It must have been the size of a football pitch. Bigger! Tunnels and caves led off in all directions, around the edges, above us, below. A giant underwater rabbit warren!

Everywhere I looked, people were swimming this way and that. And they all had tails! Merpeople! Hundreds of them! There were mermaids with gold chains round slinky long tails, swimming along with little merchildren. One had a merbaby on her back, the tiniest little pink tail sticking out from under its sling. A group of mermaids huddled outside one passageway, talking and laughing together, bags made from fishing nets on their arms. Three old mermen sat outside another, their tails faded and wrinkled, their faces full of lines and their eyes sparkling as they talked and laughed.

'Welcome to Shiprock – merfolk style!' Shona said.

'Come on, Shona. Don't want to be late.' A

mermaid with her hair in a tall bun appeared beside us. 'Five minutes to the bell.' Then she flicked her dark green tail and zoomed off ahead.

'That's Mrs Tailspin,' Shona said. 'History teacher. We've got her first thing.'

We followed her along a tube-like channel in the rock. At the other end, where it opened up again, mergirls and boys were swimming together in groups, swishing tails in a hundred different shades of blue and green and purple and silver as they milled about, waiting for school to start. A group of girls were playing a kind of skipping game with a long piece of ship's rope.

Then a noise like a foghorn surrounded us. Everyone suddenly swam into lines. Boys on one side, girls on another. Shona pulled me along to a line at the far end. 'You OK?'

I nodded, still unable to speak as we filed down yet another tunnel with the rest of our line.

We each took our seats on smooth round rocks dotted about the circular room. It reminded me of the 360 degree dome at the fair where they show films of daredevil flights and crazy downhill skiing. Only this wasn't a film – it was real!

Shona grabbed an extra rock and pulled it next to hers. A few of the other girls smiled at me.

'Are you new?' one asked. She was little and plump with a thick, dark green tail. It shimmered and sparkled as she spoke.

'She's my cousin,' Shona answered quickly. The

girl smiled and went to sit on her rock.

The walls were covered with collages made from shells and seaweed. Light filtered in through tiny cracks in the ceiling. Then Mrs Tailspin came in and we all jumped off our rocks to say good morning.

Shona put her hand up straight away. 'Is it all right if my cousin sits in with us, please miss?'

Mrs Tailspin looked me up and down. 'If she's good.'

Then she clapped her hands. 'Right, let's get started. Shipwrecks. Today, we're doing the nineteenth century.'

Shipwrecks! That beats long division!

Mrs Tailspin passed various objects around the room. 'These are all from *The Voyager*,' she said as she passed a huge plank of wood to a girl at the front. 'One of our proudest sinkings.'

Proudest sinkings – what did *that* mean?

'Not a huge amount is known for sure about *The Voyager*, but what we do know is that a group of mermaids who called themselves the Siren Sisters were responsible for its great sinking. Through skilful manipulation and careful luring, they managed to distract the entire crew for long enough to bring the great ship down.'

Shona passed me a couple of interlocked pieces of chain. I examined them and passed them on.

'Now, the only problem with this sinking was the actions of one or two of the Siren Sisters. Can anyone think what they might have done?'

Shona thrust her hand in the air.

'Yes, Shona?'

'Miss, did they fall in love?'

'Now, how did I know you were going to say that? Ever the romantic, aren't you Shona?'

A giggle went round the room.

'Well, as a matter of fact, Shona is right,' Mrs Tailspin went on. 'Some of these sisters let down the entire operation. Instead of dispersing the crew, they chose to run away with them! Never to be seen again. It's not known whether they attempted to return once they discovered the inevitable disappointments of life ashore . . .'

I shuffled uncomfortably on my rock.

'. . . although as you know,' Mrs Tailspin continued, 'Neptune takes a *very* dim view of those who do.'

'Who's Neptune?' I whispered to Shona.

'The king,' she whispered back. 'And you don't want to get on the wrong side of him, believe me! He's got a terrible temper – he makes thunderstorms and all sorts when he gets in a bad mood. Or unleashes sea monsters! But he can calm the roughest seas with a blink. *Very* powerful. And *very* rich, too. Lives in this huge palace, all made of coral and gems and gold –'

'Shona, are you talking?' Mrs Tailspin was looking our way.

'Sorry, miss.' Shona blushed.

Mrs Tailspin shook her head. 'Now, one rather

sorry piece of *The Voyager*'s legacy,' she went on, 'is that it has become somewhat of a symbol for those who choose to follow their Siren Sisters' doomed path. Instances are rare, but merfolk and humans *have* been caught together here. I needn't tell you that the punishments have been harsh. Our prison is home to a number of those traitors who have attempted to endanger our population in this way.'

'You have a prison?' I whispered.

'Of course,' Shona replied. 'Really scary, from the pictures I've seen. A huge labyrinth of caves out beyond the Great Mermer Reef, near Neptune's palace.'

I couldn't concentrate for the rest of the morning. What if they found out I wasn't a real mermaid and *I* ended up in that prison?

Shona grabbed me as soon as lessons finished.

'I've had an amazing thought,' she said. 'Let's go to the shipwreck. Let's find it!'

'What? How?'

'Mrs Tailspin told us the exact location.'

She ran her hand along the side of her tail. Then she did this totally weird thing. Put her hand inside her scales. Felt around for a bit, then pulled something out of them! It looked like a cross between a compass and a calculator. Her scales closed up as she pulled her hand out.

'What was *that*?' I screeched.

'What?' Shona looked baffled.

I pointed to her tail, where her hand had disappeared.

peared.

'My pocket?'

'*Pocket*?'

'Course. You have pockets.'

'In my denim jacket, yeah. Not in my *body*.'

'Really? Are you sure?'

I fumbled round the sides of my tail. My hand slipped through a gap. Pockets! I did have them!

Shona held up the object she'd pulled out. 'We'll find the shipwreck with my splishometer.'

Mum wasn't expecting me home till four o' clock. Should we?

'Come on Emily; it must be *such* a romantic place!'

I thought for a second. 'OK, let's do it – let's go this afternoon!'

We made our way slowly out to sea, Shona checking her splishometer every few metres. After a while, we came up to the surface to look around. A lone line of seagulls skimmed the surface. Ahead of us, seabirds like white arrows shot into the water.

We ducked under again. Rays of sun shone in dusty beams under the water. Moments later, Shona's splishometer beeped. 'We're getting close,' she breathed as we dived lower.

As we swam deeper, the sea life became weirder. Something that looked like a peach with tentacles turned slowly round in the water, scanning its surroundings with beady black eyes. Further down, a see-through jellyfish bounced away from us - a slow motion space hopper. A rubbery gold crown floated silently upwards. Everywhere I looked, fish that could have passed for cartoon aliens bounced and twirled and spun.

Shona grabbed my arm. 'Come on,' she said, pointing ahead and swimming away again. Lower and lower, the sea grew darker and darker. As we pressed forward, something came into view. I couldn't make out the shape but it was surrounded by a hazy, golden light. The light grew stronger as we carried on swimming towards it; and bigger. It was everywhere, all around us. We'd found it! *The Voyager!*

We darted along its length, tracing the row of portholes all the way from the back end to its pointy front, then swam away again to take it all in. Long and sleek, the ship lay on a tilt in the sand: still, silent, majestic.

'That is so-o-o amazing.' My words gurgled away from me like a speech bubble in a comic strip. It made me laugh, which sent more bubbles floating out of my mouth, up into the darkness.

I couldn't stop staring at the ship. It was like something out of a film – not real life. *My* life! It shone as if it had the sun inside it, as though it was made of gold.

Made of gold? A shipwreck made of gold? A queasy feeling clutched at my insides.

'Shona, the masts –'

'You OK?' Shona asked.

'I need to see a mast!'

Shona pointed up into the darkness again. 'Come on.'

Neither of us spoke as we skirted round the hundreds of tiny fish pecking away at its sides, and up to the deck. Metre after metre of wooden slats: some shiny, almost new looking, others dark and rotting. We swam upwards, circled one of the masts, wrapping our tails round it like snakes slithering up a tree, my heart hammering loud and fast.

'What is it?'

'What?'

'What's it made of?'

Shona moved back to examine the mast. 'Well, it looks like marble, but that's –'

'Marble? Are you sure?'

A golden boat with a marble mast. No!

I let go of the mast and pushed myself away, scattering a shoal of blue fish as I raced back down to the hull. I had to get away! It wasn't right! It didn't make sense!

'What's wrong?' Shona was behind me.

'It's – it's –' *What?* What could I say? How could I explain this awful panic inside me? It didn't make sense. I was being ridiculous. It *couldn't* be – of course it couldn't! I pushed the thought from my mind. Just a coincidence.

'It's nothing,' I said, laughing off my unease. 'Come on, let's go inside!'

Shona slithered along the hull. Fish nibbled at its sides next to her. I shivered as a silky plant brushed against my arm, swaying with the motion of the sea.

'Found one!' She flapped her tail excitedly.

I slithered over to join her and found myself in front of a broken porthole.

She looked at me for a second, her bright face reflecting the boat's light. 'I've never had a real adventure before,' she said quietly. Then she disappeared through the empty window. I forced the fear out of my mind. There was nothing to be afraid of. Then I held my arms tight against my sides, flicked the end of my tail and followed Shona through the porthole.

We were in a narrow corridor. Bits of wallpaper dripped from the ceiling in watery stalactites, swaying with the movement of the sea. Below us, the slanted floor was completely rotten: black and mouldy with the odd floorboard missing. The walls were lined with plankton.

'Come on.' Shona led the way. Long thin fish silently skirted the walls and ceiling. Portholes lined the corridor on our left; doors with paint peeling and cracking all the way down faced them on our right. We tried every one.

'They're all locked,' Shona said, wiggling another rotting doorknob and pushing her weight against another stubborn door. Then she raced ahead to the end of the corridor and disappeared. I followed her round the corner. Right in front of our eyes, a white door seemed to be challenging us. It was bigger than the others, shining and glowing, its brass round handle begging to be turned. A big fat fish hovered in front of it, beady-eyed like a goalkeeper. Shona tossed her head as she leant forward to try the handle, her hair flowing out in the water. The fish darted away.

The door swung open.

'Swishing heck!' she breathed.

I joined her in the doorway. 'Wow!' Bubbles danced out of my mouth as I stared.

It was the grandest room I'd ever seen – and the biggest! Easily as big as a tennis court. At one end, carpet made out of maroon weeds swayed gently with the sea's rhythm. At the other, a hard white floor.

'Pearl,' Shona said, gliding across its shiny surface.

I swam into a corner and circled one of the golden pillars shining bright light across the room. With every movement, rainbow colours flickered around the walls and ceiling. Bright blue and yellow fish danced in the light.

Below huge round windows, benches with velvet seats and high wooden backs lined the walls, large iron tables dotted about in front of them. I picked up a goblet from one of the tables. Golden and heavy, its base was a long skirt, the cup a deep well waiting to be filled with magic.

Above us, a shoal of fish writhed and spun along the yellow ceiling. The ceiling!

'Shona, what's the ceiling made out of?'

She swam up to its surface. 'Amber, by the looks of it.'

I backed out of the room, flicking my tail as hard as I could. *A ceiling of amber, a pavement of pearl.* No! It couldn't be! It was impossible!

But I couldn't brush the truth away this time.

It was the boat from Mum's dream.

Chapter Six

'*S*hona, we've got to get out of here!' I pulled at her hand. My fingers shook.

'But don't you want to –'

'We have to get away!'

'What is it?'

'I don't know. Something's not right. *Please, Shona.*'

She looked at my face and for a moment I saw shock – or recognition. 'Come on,' she said.

We didn't speak as we slithered back down the narrow corridor in silence, Shona following as I raced ahead. I swam back in such a panic I went straight past the broken porthole and almost all the way to the other end of the boat! I turned and was about to start swimming back when Shona tugged at my arm.

'Look,' she said, pointing at the floor.

'What?'

'Can't you see?'

I looked closer and noticed a shiny section of wood, newer than the other floorboards, the size of a manhole. It had a handle on it shaped like a giant pair of pliers.

Shona pulled at the trapdoor. 'Give me a hand.'

'Shona, I've got a really weird feeling about all this. I have to – '

'Just a quick look. *Please*. Then we'll go – I promise.'

Reluctantly, I pulled at the handle with her, flipping my tail to propel myself backwards. Seconds later, it creaked open. A swarm of tiny fish darted out from the gap, shimmering in a flash of silver before disappearing down the corridor.

Shona flipped herself upside down and poked her head into the hole, swishing her tail in my face. 'What can you see?' I asked.

'It's a tunnel!' Shona flipped back up and grabbed my hand. 'Have a look.'

'But you said we could – '

'*Five* minutes.' And she disappeared down the hole.

As soon as we got into the tunnel, the golden light virtually disappeared. Just tiny rays peeping through the odd crack. We felt our way along the sides – which wasn't exactly pleasant. Slimy, rubbery things lined the walls. I decided not to think about what they might be. An occasional fish passed by in the shadows: slow and solitary. The silence seemed to deepen. Inside it, my unease grew and grew. *How could it be? How could it?*

'Look!' Shona's voice echoed in front of me.

I peered ahead. We'd reached another door, facing us at the end of the tunnel. 'Locked,' Shona said quietly. 'Hey, but look at – '

Suddenly a luminous fish with a huge wide-open jaw sprang out of the darkness, almost swimming into my face.

I screamed and grabbed Shona's arm. 'I'm getting out of here!' I burst out, forgetting about the ball-room, the slimy rubbery walls, the trapdoor. All that mattered was getting away from that ship.

We sat on Rainbow Rocks, low down by the water's edge, out of sight from the coast. Water lapped gently against the stones. Shona's tail glistened in the chilly light. Mine had disappeared again and I rubbed my goosepimply legs dry with my jacket. Shona stared. She obviously found the transformation as weird as I did!

'Do you want to tell me what this is about?' She broke the silence.

'What?'

'What happened to you back there?'

I threw a pebble into the water and watched the circle around it grow bigger and wider until it disappeared. 'I can't.'

'Don't want to?'

'No, I mean I really, actually can't! I don't even know what it's about, myself.'

Shona fell quiet again. 'I understand if you don't trust me,' she said after a while. 'I mean, it's not as if I'm your best friend or anything.'

'I haven't got a best friend at the moment.'

'Like me.' Shona smiled shyly, her tail flapping on the rock as she spoke.

Then we fell quiet again. 'Look, it's not that I don't trust you,' I said after a while. 'I do. It's just . . . you might think I'm mad.'

'Course I won't. Apart from the fact that you're a human half the time and a mermaid who sneaks out to play at night, I haven't met anyone as normal as you in ages!'

I smiled.

'Try me,' she said.

So I did. I told her everything; I told her about the swimming lesson and Mystic Millie and about Mum's dream and the ship being exactly the same. I even told her about seeing Mr Beeston on my way home that first night. Once I'd started, I couldn't seem to stop.

When I'd finished, Shona stared at me without speaking.

'What?'

She looked away.

'*What?*'

'I don't want to say. You might get cross, like last time.'

'What d'you mean? Do you know something? You've *got* to tell me.'

Shona shook her head. 'I don't know anything, not for sure.'

'What is it? *Tell* me.'

'You remember when we first met, and I thought I'd heard your name before?'

'You said you'd got it wrong.'

'I know. But I don't think I had.'

'You *had* heard it?'

She nodded. 'I think so.'

'Where?'

'It was at school.'

'At *school*?'

'I think it was in a book. I never knew if it was true, or just an ocean-myth. We did it in history.'

'Did *what* in history?'

Shona paused before saying in a quiet voice, 'Illegal marriages.'

'Illegal? You mean –'

'Between merpeople and humans.'

I tried to take her words in. What did she mean? What was she trying to tell me? That my parents –

'There'll be something at the library in school. Let's go back.' Shona slid down off her rock.

'I thought school finished at lunch time.'

'There are clubs and societies in the afternoon. Come on, I'm sure we can find out more.'

I slipped into the water and followed her back to mermaid school, my thoughts as tangled as a heap of washed up fishing nets.

Back through the hole in the rock; back along the caves and tunnels and tubes until we came to the school playground. It was empty.

'This way.' Shona pointed to a rocky structure standing on its own. Spiral-shaped and full of giant holes and crevices. We swam inside through a thick crack and slithered up through the swirls, coming out into a circular room with jagged rocky edges. A few mergirls and boys sat on mushroom-shaped spongy seats in front of long pieces of scratchy paper that hung from the ceiling. They wound the paper up or down, silently moving their heads from side to side as they examined the sheets.

'What are they doing?' I whispered.

Shona gawped at me. 'Reading! What d'you think they're doing?'

I shrugged. 'Where are the books?'

'It's easier to find stuff on scrolls. Everything's

stored here. Come on.' She led me to the opposite side of the room and swam up to the ceiling. We looked through different headings at the top of each scroll: *Shipwrecks, Treasures, Fishermen, Sirens.*

'Sirens – it might be this one,' Shona said, pulling on the end of a thick roll. 'Give me a hand.'

We pulled the scroll down to the floor, hooked it in place on a roller, then wound an old wooden handle round and round, working our way through facts and figures, dates and events. Stories about mermaids luring fishermen into the ocean with songs so beautiful they were almost impossible to hear; of fishermen going mad, throwing themselves into the sea to follow their hearts' desires; mermaids winning praise and riches for their success; ships brought down. We searched the whole scroll. Nothing about illegal marriages.

'We'll never find anything,' I said. 'I don't even know what we're looking for.'

Shona was swimming around above me. 'There must be something,' she muttered.

'Why is it so illegal, anyway? Why can't people marry who they want?'

'It's the one thing that makes Neptune *really* angry. Some say it's because he once married a human and then she left him.'

'Neptune's married?' I swam up to join her.

'Oh, he's got loads of wives, and hundreds of children! But this one was special, and he's never forgiven her – or the rest of the human race!'

'Shona Silkfin – what are you doing here?' A voice boomed from behind us. We both spun round to see someone swimming towards us. The history teacher!

'Oh, Mrs Tailspin. I was just, we were –'

'Shona was just trying to help me with my home-work,' I said with an innocent smile.

'Homework?' Mrs Tailspin looked at us doubtfully.

'At my school, in – in –'

'Shallowpool,' Shona said quickly. 'That's where my cousin's from.'

'And we've got to do a project on illegal mar-riages,' I continued as an idea came to me. Maybe she'd know something! After all, Shona did say she heard my name in a history lesson. 'Shona said that she'd studied them. She was trying to help me.'

Mrs Tailspin swam down to a mushroomy sponge-seat and beckoned us to do the same. 'What do you want to know?'

I paused, glancing at Shona. What *did* I want to know? Did I want to know at all?

'Emily's doing her project on Shiprock,' Shona said, picking up my thread. 'That's why she's here. We needed to find out if there had been any round here.'

'Indeed there has been one,' Mrs Tailspin said, patting the bun on her head. 'Rather a well-known incident. Do you remember, Shona? We covered it last term.' She frowned. 'Or were you too busy chat-ting at the time?'

'Can you tell me about it?' I asked.

72

Mrs Tailspin turned back to me. 'Very well.'

I tried to keep still on my sponge while I waited for her to carry on.

'A group of humans once found out a little too much about the merfolk world,' she began. 'There'd been a yacht race nearby. A couple of the boats went off course and capsized. Some mermen found them and helped them. They had to have their memories wiped afterwards.' She paused. 'But one was missed.'

'And?'

'And she didn't forget. Word spread, both in her world and our own. They started meeting up. Humans and merfolk. At one point, there was talk of them all going off to a desert island to live together. The rumour was that there was even a place where it was already happening.'

'*Really*?' Shona said.

'Like I said, it was a rumour. I don't believe for one moment that it exists. But they kept meeting. As I'm sure you can imagine, Neptune was *not* pleased.'

'What happened?' I asked.

'There were storms for weeks. He said that if he caught anyone, they would be imprisoned for life. He visited every merfolk area personally.'

'He hardly ever does that!' Shona said. 'He always stays in his palace, except when he goes on exotic holidays, or visits his other palaces. He's got them all over the world, hasn't he?'

'That's right, Shona.'

'So he came to Shiprock?' I asked.

73

'He did indeed.'

Shona bounced off her seat. 'Did you meet him?'

Mrs Tailspin nodded.

'Really? What's he like?'

'Angry, loud, covered in gold – but with a certain charisma.'

'Wow!' Shona gazed at Mrs Tailspin.

'The preparation took weeks,' she continued. 'As you know, Neptune can become most unhappy if he is not presented with adequate jewels and crystals when he visits. Our menfolk went on daily searches under the rocks. We made him a new sceptre as a present.'

'Was he pleased?'

'Very. He gave the town a dolphin as a thank you.'

'So, did the meetings stop?' I asked. 'Between the merpeople and the humans?'

'Sadly, no. They continued to meet in secret. I don't know how they lived with themselves, defying Neptune like that.'

'And the marriage...?' I asked, holding my breath.

'Yes, there was a merman. A poet. Jake. He married one of the women, at Rainbow Rocks –'

Something stirred in the back of my mind; thoughts that I couldn't quite grasp, like bubbles that burst as soon as you touch them.

Shona didn't look at me. 'What was his last name?' she asked, her voice jagged like the library walls.

Mrs Tailspin patted her bun again. Tutted. Squinted. 'Whirlstand? Whichmap? Wisplatch? No, I can't remember.'

Looking down, I closed my eyes. 'Was it Wind-snap?' I asked.

'Windsnap! Yes, that might have been it.'

The bubbles turned to rocks and started clogging up my throat.

'And they had a daughter,' she continued. 'That was when they were caught.'

'When exactly was this?' I managed to squeeze out.

'Let's see...twelve or thirteen years ago.'

I nodded, not trusting myself to speak.

'Gave themselves away with that. The silly woman brought the child to Rainbow Rocks and that was when we got him.'

'*Got* him? What did they do to him?' Shona asked.

'Prison,' Mrs Tailspin said with a proud smile. 'Neptune decided to make an example of him. He said Jake would be locked up for life.'

'What about the baby?' I asked, swallowing hard while I waited for her to reply.

'Baby? Goodness knows. But we stopped that one.' Mrs Tailspin smiled again. 'That's what you'll be doing when you're a siren, Shona. You'll be as good as that.'

Shona reddened. 'I haven't completely decided what I want to be yet,' she said.

'Very well.' Mrs Tailspin glanced round the room. Mergirls and boys were still reading. Some were talking quietly in groups. 'Now, girls, if there's nothing else, I must check on my library group.'

'Yes. Thanks,' I managed to say. I don't know how.

We sat in silence after she'd gone.

'It's me, isn't it,' I said eventually, staring ahead of me at nothing.

'Do you want it to be?'

'I don't know *what* I want. I don't even know who I *am* any more.'

Shona swam in front of me and made me look at her. 'Emily, maybe we can find out more. He's still alive! He's out there somewhere!'

'Yeah, in prison. For life.'

'But at least he didn't want to leave you!'

Perhaps he still thought about me. Perhaps I *could* find out more.

'I think we should go back to the shipwreck,' Shona said.

'*What?* No way!'

'Think about it! Your mum's dream, what Mrs Tailspin said in the lesson. They might have gone there together!'

Maybe she was right. I didn't have any better ideas. 'I'll think about it,' I said. 'Give me a few days.'

'Wednesday, then.'

'OK.'

'Look, I'd better be heading back.' I slithered over to the spirally tube.

'Will you be all right?'

'Yeah.' I tried to smile. Would I? That was anyone's guess.

I swam home through the silent water, my thoughts as crowded and unfathomable as the sea.

Chapter Seven

'A re you eating that or playing with it?' Mum asked over the top of her glasses as I stirred my cereal, watching the milk turn brown and the flakes fade into a soggy beige.

'What? Huh? Oh, sorry.' I took a mouthful, then stirred some more.

Mum had the *Observer* spread out in front of her. She flicked through the pages, tutting every now and then, or frowning and pushing her glasses further up her nose.

How was I ever going to find out what was going on? It's not exactly the kind of thing that crops up over your Sunday breakfast: 'Oh, by the way, Mum, I've been meaning to ask. I don't suppose you married a merman, had his child and then never saw him again? OR THOUGHT TO TELL YOUR DAUGHTER ABOUT IT? *HUH???*'

I squelched my cereal against the side of the bowl, splashing milk onto the table.

'Careful, love.' Mum wiped the edge of her paper with her hand. Then she looked at me. 'Are you all right? It's not like you not to eat your breakfast.'

'I'm fine.' I got up and emptied my bowl into the sink.

'Emily?'

I ignored her as I sat back down at the table and pulled at my hair, winding it round in my fingers.

Mum took her glasses off. That meant it was serious. Then she folded her arms. Double serious. 'I'm waiting,' she said, her mouth tight, her eyes small. '*Emily*, I said I'm —'

'Why do you never talk about my dad?'

Mum jerked in her seat as though I'd punched her. '*What?*'

'You never talk about my father,' I said, my voice coming out quieter this time. 'I don't know anything about him. It's as though he never existed.'

Mum put her glasses back on; then she took them off again and got up. She lit a gas ring, put the kettle on it and gazed at the flickering flame. 'I don't know what to *say*,' she muttered eventually.

'Why not start by telling me something about him?'

'I want to. Darling, of course I want to.'

'So how come you never have done?'

Her eyes had gone all watery and she rubbed them with the sleeve of her cardigan. 'I don't know. I just can't – I can't do it.'

If there's one thing I can't *bear*, it's Mum crying. 'Look, it's OK. I'm sorry.' I got out of my seat and put my arms round her shoulders. 'It doesn't matter.'

'But it *does*.' She wiped her nose with the edge of the tablecloth. 'I want to tell you. But I can't, I can't, I – '

'It's OK, Mum, honest. You don't have to tell me.'

'But I want to,' she sobbed. 'I just can't remember!'

'You can't *remember?*' I let go and stared at her. 'You don't remember the man you married?'

She looked at me through bloodshot eyes. 'Well, yes – no. I mean, sometimes I think I remember things. But then it goes again. Disappears.'

'Disappears.'

'Just like he did,' she said quietly, her body shaking, her head in her hands. 'I can't even remember my own husband. Your father. Oh, I'm a terrible mother.'

'Don't start that,' I sighed. 'You're a brilliant mother. The best.'

'Really?' She smoothed down her skirt against her lap. I forced myself to smile. She looked up and stroked my cheek with her thumb. 'I must have done something right to get you, eh?' she said weakly.

I stood up. 'Look. Just forget it. It doesn't matter. OK?'

'You deserve better than –'

'Come on, Mum. It's all right,' I said firmly. 'Hey, how about some pocket money?'

She pinched my cheek. 'Munchkin,' she sniffed. 'Pass me my purse then.'

She handed me two pound coins and I headed down the pier.

I dawdled as I made my way past the amusement arcade. Not fair. Nothing was fair. I couldn't even have a go on the penny roll. I didn't need Mandy turning up and having a go at me on top of everything else.

I bought some candyfloss from the end of the pier and wandered down to the prom, my head filled with thoughts and questions. I didn't notice Mr Beeston coming towards me.

'Watch yourself,' he said as I nearly walked into him.

'Sorry. Miles away.'

He smiled at me in that way that always gives me weird shivers in my neck and arms. One side of his mouth turned up, the other reaching down and his crooked teeth poking out through the dark gap in between.

'How's Mum?' he asked.

That's when I had a thought. Mr Beeston had been around a long time. He was kind of friendly with

Mum. Maybe he'd know something.

'She's not all that great, actually,' I said as I bit into the top of my candyfloss, warm fluff melting into sugar in my mouth.

'Oh? Why so?'

'She's a bit sad about . . . some things.'

'Things? What "*things*"?' he said quickly, his smile gone.

'Just . . .'

'Is she ill? What's the matter?' Mr Beeston's face turned hard as he narrowed his eyes at me.

'Well, my father . . .' I pulled at my candyfloss and a long piece came away like a loose thread from a fluffy pink jumper. I folded it over into my mouth.

'Your *what*?' Mr Beeston burst out. What *was* his problem?

'I was asking her about my father and she got upset.'

He lowered his voice. 'What did she tell you?'

'That's just it, you see. She didn't tell me anything.'

'Nothing at all?'

'She said she couldn't remember anything. Then she started crying.'

'Couldn't remember anything? That's what she said?'

I nodded.

'You're quite sure now? Nothing at all?'

'Yes. Nothing.'

'Right then.' Mr Beeston breathed out hard through his nose. It made a low whistling sound.

'So, I wondered if you could help me.'

'Me? How on earth can *I* help you?' he snapped.

'I just wondered if she'd ever talked to you about him. With you being her friend and everything.'

He examined my face, squeezing his eyes down to narrow slits as he stared. I wanted to run away. Of course he wouldn't know anything. Why would she talk to him and not me? I tried to hold his eyes but he was staring at me so hard I had to look away.

He took hold of me by my elbow and pointed up the promenade with his other hand. 'I think it's time you and I had a little chat,' he said.

I tried to shake my elbow away as we walked but he held it tighter and paced faster. We'd got all the way to the end of the promenade before he let go and motioned for me to sit down on a bench.

'Now listen to me and listen well because I'll tell you this once and once only.'

I waited.

'And I don't want you bothering your mother with it. You've upset her enough already.'

'But I –'

'Never mind, never mind,' he raised his hand to stop me. 'You weren't to know.'

He wiped his forehead with a hanky. 'Now then,' he said, shifting his weight onto his side as he put his hanky away. His trousers had a hole just below the pocket. 'Your father and I, we used to be friends. Best friends. Even thought we were brothers, some folk did; that's how close we were.'

Brothers? Surely Mr Beeston was loads older than my father? I opened my mouth to speak.

'Like my kid brother he was. Did everything together.'

'Like what?'

'What?'

'What things did you do? I want to know what he was like.'

'All the things young lads get up to,' he snapped. 'We went fishing together. Went out on our bikes – '

'Motorbikes?'

'Yes, yes, motorbikes, pushbikes – the lot. Did it together. Best friends, we were. Chased the girls together, too.'

Mr Beeston chasing girls. I shuddered.

He cleared his throat. 'Then of course, he met your mother and things changed.'

'Changed? How?'

'Well, one might say they fell in love. At least, she did. Very much so.'

'And what about my dad?'

'He did a very good impression of love. For a while. He certainly didn't want to fool around with cars any more.'

'I thought it was bikes.'

83

'Cars, bikes — whatever. He wasn't interested. Spent all their time together.'

Mr Beeston stared into the distance, his hands in his pockets. He looked as though he was struggling with something. Then he jingled his coins and said, 'But of course it didn't last. Your father turned out not to be the gentleman he'd had us believe he was.'

'What do you mean?'

'This is a rather delicate matter. But I shall tell you. Let us say he wasn't the most *responsible* person. He was happy enough to lead your mother up the garden path, but not prepared to stay by her side when they got to the gate.'

'Huh?'

His face reddened. 'He was content to sow but not reap.'

'Mr Beeston, I don't know what you're going on about.'

'Good grief, child. I'm talking about responsibility,' he snapped. 'Where do you think *you* came from?'

'D'you mean he got my mum pregnant with me and then ran off?'

'Yes, yes, that is what I mean.'

Why didn't you say so then? I wanted to say — but didn't dare. Mr Beeston looked so angry. 'So he left her?' I asked, just to make sure I'd got it right.

'Yes, he left her,' he replied through tight lips.

'Where did he go?'

'That's just it. No one ever heard from him again.

84

The strain was obviously too much for him,' he said sarcastically.

'What strain?'

'Fatherhood. Good for nothing layabout, he was. Never willing to grow up and take responsibility.' Mr Beeston looked away. 'What he did – it was despicable,' he said, his voice becoming raspy. 'I shall never forgive him.' He got up from the bench, his face hard and set. 'Never,' he repeated. Something about the way he said it made me hope I'd never get on his wrong side.

I followed him as we carried on along the prom. 'Didn't anyone try to find him?'

'Find him?' Mr Beeston looked at me, but it was as though he was seeing through me. His eyes wouldn't meet mine. 'Find him?' he repeated. 'Yes – of course we tried. No one could have done more than I did. Travelled the country for weeks, put up posters. We even had a message on the radio, begging him to come home and meet his – well, his . . .'

'His daughter?'

Mr Beeston didn't reply.

'So he never even saw me?'

'We did everything we could.'

I looked down the promenade, trying to take in what I'd heard. It *couldn't* be true. Could it? A young couple ambled towards us, the man holding a baby up in the air, the woman laughing, a spaniel jumping up between them. Further down, an elderly couple were walking slowly against the wind, arms linked.

'I think I need to go now,' I said. We'd walked all the way round to the lighthouse.

Mr Beeston pulled me back by my arm. 'You're not to talk to your mother about this, do you hear me?'

'Why not?'

'You saw what happened. It's far too painful for her.' He tightened his grip, his fingers biting into my arm. 'Promise me you won't mention it.'

I didn't say anything.

Mr Beeston looked hard into my eyes. 'People can block things out completely if the memory is too much to cope with. That's a scientific fact. There'll be all sorts of trouble if you try and make her talk about this.' He pulled on my arm, his face inches from mine. 'And you don't want trouble – do you?' he said in a whisper.

I shook my head.

'*Do* you?' he repeated with another yank on my arm.

'No – of course not,' my voice wobbled.

He smiled his wonky smile at me and let go of my arm. 'Good,' he said. 'Good. Now, am I seeing you this afternoon?'

'I'm going out,' I said quickly. I'd think of something to do. I couldn't cope with Sunday tea with Mum and Mr Beeston. Especially now.

'Very well. Tell your mother I'll be round at three o'clock.'

'Yeah.'

We stood by the lighthouse. For a moment, I had a vision of him throwing me inside and locking me in! Why would he do that? He'd never done anything to hurt me – before today. I rubbed my arm. I could still feel the pinch of his fingers digging into my skin. But it was nothing compared with the disappointment I felt in my chest. Jake *wasn't* my father, after all, if Mr Beeston was to be believed. And he had no reason to lie – did he? Nothing made sense any more.

'Now, let's see, where's the, hm . . .' Mr Beeston talked to himself as he fumbled with his keys. He had about five keyrings rattling on a long chain. But then he gasped. 'What the – where's my . . .'

'What's wrong?'

He ignored me. 'It can't be missing. It can't be.' He felt in his trouser pockets, pulling the insides out and shaking his hanky. 'It was here. I'm sure it was.'

'The lighthouse key?'

'No, not the lighthouse key, the – ' He stopped fumbling and looked up at me, as if he'd only just remembered I was there, his eyes dark and hard. 'You're still here,' he said. 'Go on. Leave me be. But don't forget our chat. It's between you and me. Remember, you don't want to cause any *trouble*.' Then he unlocked the lighthouse door. 'I've got some important things to do,' he said. Squinting into my eyes, he added, 'I'll see you again soon.' For some reason, it sounded like a threat.

Before I had a chance to say anything else, he'd slipped inside and shut the door behind him. A second later, a bolt slid across.

As I turned to leave, I kicked something up in the dust. It glinted at me. A keyring. I picked it up. A brass plate with crystals round the edges. There was a picture engraved on one side. A pitchfork or something.

Two keys hung from the ring: one big chunky one, the other a little metal one the same as Mum has for our suitcase. A tiny gold chain hung from the plate, a clasp at its other end open and broken.

I banged on the lighthouse door and waited. 'Mr Beeston!' I called. I banged once more.

Nothing.

I looked at the keyring again, running my fingers over its crystal edge. Oh well. I could always give it back another time.

I buttoned the keyring into my pocket and headed home.

Chapter Eight

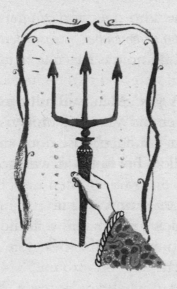

This was it. The moment I'd been dreading. I stepped through the trough of icy cold water on the way to the pool. I'd tried telling Mr Bird I had a verruca but he just gave me a couple of white rubber socks to put on my feet. So now the game was up *and* I looked ridiculous. Great. What was I going to *do*? Five more minutes and my secret would be revealed. Everyone would know I was a *freak*!

'Come on people; we haven't got all day.' Bob clapped his hands together as I walked slowly to the side of the pool and joined the rest of the class. 'It'll be time to get out again before you set foot in the water.'

My heart thumped so loud I could feel it in my ears.

'Right, those who can swim can get on with it,' he said. *Please don't remember, please don't remember*, I prayed silently. Time was running out; I *had* to think of something.

'That means *you*.' Mandy Rushton elbowed Julie and pointed to me. 'What's up, *fish girl*?' she sneered. 'Gone shy all of a sudden?'

I tried to ignore her but Bob was looking our way. 'What's going on over –' Then he spotted me. 'Ah yes. One that got cramp, isn't it?'

I stepped back towards the wall, hoping it might swallow me up and I'd disappear forever. I couldn't do it – I *couldn't!*

'You can get in when you're ready.' *Yeah, right – no way.* 'Take it easy, though. Don't want the same thing to happen.' He turned back to the others. 'Right, you guys. Let's get on with it, shall we?'

'Go on then – let's all see how the *fish girl* does it!' Mandy said loudly and everyone around us turned to look. Then she pushed me forward and I lost my footing. Tripping on the slippy floor, I went flying into the pool with a loud SPLASH!

For the tiniest moment, I forgot all about Mandy. She wasn't important. All that mattered was that I was in the water again, losing myself to its creamy smoothness, wrapping myself up in it as if it was my favourite dressing-gown, keeping me safe and warm.

Then I remembered where I was!

I swam to the surface and looked up to see thirty pairs of eyes facing my way – at least one of them glinting nastily at me, waiting for my FREAKNESS to be revealed!

I had to fight it – I had to! But it was starting already! My legs were going numb, joining together. And, like an idiot, I'd swum halfway across the pool!

I heaved myself through the water, splashing and dragging my body along, keeping my legs as still as possible to try and stop my tail from forming. Bit by bit, I propelled myself to the side, my arms working like a windmill. I *had* to get there before it happened. Hurry, hurry!

Gasping and panting, I finally heaved myself out of the pool – JUST in time! The second I dragged my body over the side, my legs started to relax. Wheezing and breathless, I pulled myself out of the pool and sat on the side.

Bob was over in a second. 'Have you hurt yourself?' He stared down at me and I suddenly had an idea. I grabbed my foot.

'It's my ankle,' I said. 'I think I've sprained it.'

Bob narrowed his eyes. 'How did this happen?'

I was about to say I'd fallen in when I saw Mandy's face. Sneering and jeering at me. Why should I let her off? 'Mandy pushed me,' I said.

'Right, well there'll be no swimming for either of you this week,' he said. 'You can sit in the corner for the rest of the lesson,' he said crossly to Mandy. Then he turned to me. 'And you'd better get that ankle rested.'

He clapped his hands as he went back to the class. 'Right, people, show's over. Let's do some swimming, shall we?'

It wasn't the cold that made me shiver as I limped back to the changing room. It was more to do with Mandy's words, hissed at me through clenched teeth so quietly no one else could hear.

'I'll get you back for this, fish girl,' she said. 'Just you wait.'

I hung back while Shona swam ahead, my tail flapping as we drew nearer to the shipwreck. The night was crunchy with a million stars. No moon.

'Nearly there.' Shona dived under the water. I followed her, trailing a few metres behind.

Soon, the golden light was filtering through weeds and rocks, pulling us towards the ship.

'Shona, we can't do it!' I blurted out. 'There's no point.'

Shona swam back to me. 'But you agreed – '

'It's no good. He's not my father.'

She stared at me.

'My father left us. Just like I thought he had.' I told

her what Mr Beeston had said – and about his strange veiled threat.

'Are you sure?' she asked when I'd finished.

Why would he lie? I'd asked myself that question so many times over the last three days. I still wasn't sure I believed him – but it was better than building up false hopes.

'I was so certain . . .' Shona looked over her shoulder at the ship. 'Look – why don't we go anyway? We're nearly there.'

'What's the use?'

'What have we got to lose? And there was something I wanted to show you. Something about the door in that passageway.'

What did it matter? The ship didn't have anything to do with me. There was nothing to fear. 'OK,' I said.

We slithered down the dark corridor, feeling our way back down those slimy walls. I tried hard not to make eye contact with the open-jawed fish that had followed us down.

'So what did you want to show me?' I asked as we swam.

'There was a symbol on the door. I completely forgot about it after everything that happened.'

'What symbol?'

'A trident.'

'What's one of those?'

'Neptune's symbol. He carries it everywhere with him. It's what he uses to create thunderstorms – or islands.'

'*Islands?* He can create whole islands?'

'Well, that's only when he's in a good mood – so it doesn't happen much. More often he makes the *biggest* storms out at sea!' Shona's eyes had that wide shiny look they always did when she talked about Neptune.

'Some merfolk say he can turn you to stone with his trident. His palace is filled with stone animals. I heard that they were all animals who had disobeyed him at one time. And he can make ships disappear, just by waving it at them – or produce a feast for a hundred merpeople, or create volcanoes out of thin air.'

'Cool!'

We'd arrived at the door. 'Look.' She pointed at the top corner of the door. A brass plate. An engraving. Quite faint – but there was no mistaking what I was looking at.

The picture from Mr Beeston's keyring.

'But – but that's – ' I pulled at my pocket. 'It's impossible. It *can't* be!'

'What?' Shona swam up to my side. I handed her the keyring. 'Where did you get this?' she asked.

'It's Mr Beeston's.' But it *couldn't* be! I'd made a mistake. I must have done!

'Sharks!' Shona breathed. 'So d'you think . . .' Her

words trailed away into the watery darkness. What *did* I think? I didn't think anything any more.

'Shall we try it?' Shona took the key from me.

I watched in amazement as it turned smoothly in the lock.

The door slid open.

Silently, we slithered inside. We were in a small office. It had a desk stacked about a metre high with laminated folders and papers held down by rocks, and a stool nailed to the floor in front of it. Shona swam to the desk and pulled on something. A second later, an orange glow burst out above me. I blinked as I got used to the sudden glare, then looked up to see where the light had come from. A long slimy creature with a piece of string on its tail clung to the ceiling.

'Electric eel,' she explained.

We looked at each other in silence. 'What about the other key?' she said eventually, swimming over to a metal filing cabinet in the corner. I tried the drawers but they wouldn't pull out. I almost closed my eyes as I tried to put it in the lock at the top. *Please don't fit, please don't fit*, I said to myself. What would I find if it did?

I couldn't even get it halfway in.

I let out a huge breath and was suddenly desperate to get out of there. 'Shona, maybe this is all a big mistake,' I said, backing out of the office. But then I knocked my tail against the stool and slipped backwards. A swarm of tiny black fish escaped from under the table, spinning out of the room and away from us.

'Emily!' Shona tugged my sleeve and pointed at something under the table.

I leaned forward to get a closer look. A wooden chest. Quite big, with brass edging and a chain looped all around it. It was like something out of *Treasure Island*. I swam under the table and Shona helped me drag it out. 'Flipping fins,' she said quietly, staring at something dangling at the front of the chain. A brass padlock.

As I slipped the key easily into the lock and the brass hook bounced open, I wasn't even surprised. A line of silver fish pecked at the chest as I opened it. It was full of files. I grabbed a handful of them. The colours changed from blue to green as I lifted them towards me. Rummaging through the pile, I pulled the rest of them out. Then I came to a folder that was different from the rest. For one thing, it was thicker than the others. For another thing, it looked newer.

And for another, it had my name on it.

Chapter Nine

I don't know how long I looked at the file. I realised at some point that my hand had almost gone numb from clutching it so tightly.

'What is it?' Shona came to look over my shoulder at the files. That's when I noticed another one at the bottom of the chest. I reached down to get it. It had my mum's name on it. Below that was another. I almost didn't dare to look at that one. I shut my eyes as I picked it up. When I opened them, I was looking at a name I'd been dreaming about for a week: Jake Windsnap.

I traced the words with my fingertips. Jake Windsnap. I said his name over and over, wondering if there was any way it could be a mistake or a practical joke or something. 'Jake *is* my father,' I said out loud.

Of *course* he was. I'd known it in my heart from the first time I'd heard his name. It just took seeing it in writing to convince my brain.

I opened the file, my hands shaking so much I almost dropped all its contents. The sheets inside it were plastic. And they all had the pitchfork image at the top: Neptune's trident.

'But what in sharks' name does Mr Beeston have to do with any of this?' Shona asked.

'Maybe he knows where my dad is, after all. I mean, if they were best friends, maybe he's trying to help him. Maybe they've been in touch all along.' My words came out in a rush, none of them convincing me – or Shona, by the look on her face.

'There's only one way to find out,' she said.

I held the files out in front of me. Once I'd looked inside, there would be no going back. I couldn't pretend I hadn't seen whatever was in there. Maybe I didn't want to know. I pulled at my hair, twiddling, twisting it round and round. I *had* to look. Whatever it said, I needed to know the truth.

I opened the file with my name on it. A scrappy bit of paper with a handwritten note scrawled across it fell on the floor. I picked it up, Shona looking over my shoulder as I read.

EW One: All clear.
Nothing to report. No mer-gene identified. Possibly nega-
tive. (50% chance.) Scale detection nil.

'What in the ocean is that meant to mean?'

I shook my head, pulling a bigger sheet out of the file.

EW Eight: Moment of truth?

Subject has requested swimming lessons again. (See MPW file for cross-ref.) CFB present to witness request. Denied by mother. Unlikely to be granted in near future. Needs careful attention. Almost certainly negative mer-gene but experiment MUST NOT be abandoned. Continued observation – priority.

'Subject!' I spluttered. 'Is that me?'

Shona winced.

Careful watch? Had he been stalking me? What if he was watching us now? I shuddered and swam over to close the office door. A lone blue fish skimmed into the room and over my head as I did.

We scanned the rest of the file. It was all the same: subjects and initials and weird stuff that didn't make sense.

I picked up my mum's file.

MPW Zero: Objectives.

MPW – greatest risk to mer-world detection. Constant supervision by CFB. M-Drug to be administered.

Shona gasped. 'M-Drug. I know what that is! They're wiping her memory!'

'*What*? Who is?'

'Mr Beeston. He must work for Neptune!'

'Work for Neptune? But how? I mean, he *can't* do. Can he?'

Shona rubbed her lip. 'They usually send them away afterwards, though.'

'Why?'

'It can wear off if you go near merfolk areas. We did all about it in science last term.'

'So you think they did it to my mum?'

'They probably still are. One dose is usually enough for a one-off incident – but not for a whole series of memories. They must be topping it up somehow.'

Topping it up? I thought about all Mr Beeston's visits. He wasn't lonely after all! He was drugging my mum!

We looked all the way through Mum's file. Page after page noting her movements. He'd been spying on us for *years*.

'I feel sick,' I said, closing the file.

Shona picked up Jake's file. There was a note stuck on the front with something scribbled on it. *East Wing: E 930.* We read in silence.

> *JW Three: Bad influence.*
> *JW continuing to complain about sentence. Sullen and difficult.*

> *JW Eight: Improvement*
> *Subject has settled into routine of prison life. Behaviour improved.*

JW Eleven: Isolation
Operation Desert Island discussed openly by prisoner.
Isolation – three days.

'Operation Desert Island!' Shona breathed. 'So it's true after all. There *is* a place! Somewhere merfolk and humans live together!'

'How d'you know that's what it is?' I asked. 'It could be anything.'

We read on.

'None of it makes any sense,' I said, swimming backwards and forwards across the room to help me think.

Shona carried on flicking through the file. 'It's all numbers and dates and weird initials.' She closed the file. 'I can't make fin or tail of it.' She grabbed another file from the chest. 'Listen to this,' she said. '"Project Lighthouse. CFB to take over Brightport Lighthouse until completion of Windsnap problem. Ground floor adapted for access. Occasional siren support available with 'unreliable' beam. Previous lighthouse keeper: M–drug and removal from scene."' Shona looked up.

'What are we going to do?' I whispered.

'What *can* we do? But hey – at least you've found your dad.'

My dad. The words sounded strange. Not right. Not yet. 'But I *haven't* found him,' I said. 'That's just it. All I've found is some stupid file that doesn't make any sense.'

Shona put the file down. 'I'm sorry.'

'Look, Shona, we know Jake's my – my father, don't we?'

'Without a doubt.'

'And we know where he is?'

'Well, yes.'

'And he can't come out. He's locked away. And he didn't *choose* to leave me . . .'

'I'm *sure* he never wanted to –'

'So we'll go to him!'

Shona looked at me blankly.

I shoved the files back in the chest, locked it firmly. 'Come on, let's go!'

'Go? Where?'

'The prison.' I turned round to face her. 'I've got to find him.'

Shona's tail flapped gently. 'Emily. It's *miles* away.'

'We're mermaids! We can swim for miles, no problem!'

'Maybe *I* can, but it's definitely too far for you. You're only half mermaid, remember.'

'So you're saying I'm not as good as you?' I folded my arms. 'I thought you were meant to be my friend. I even thought you might have been my best friend.'

Shona's tail flapped even more. 'Really?' she said. 'I want you to be my best friend, too.'

'Well, you've got a funny way of showing it. You won't even help me find my father.'

Shona winced. 'I just don't think we'd make it there. I'm not even sure exactly where it *is*.'

'But we'll never know if we don't try. Please, Shona. If you were *really* my best friend, you would.'

'OK,' she sighed. 'We'll try. But I don't want you collapsing on me miles out at sea. If you get tired, you have to tell me, and we come back, OK?'

I shoved the chest back under the table. 'OK.'

I don't know how long we'd been swimming. Maybe an hour. I started to feel as if I had heavy weights attached to each arm; my tail was practically dropping off. Flying fish raced along with us, bouncing past on both sides. An occasional gull darted into the sea, a white dart piercing the water.

'How much further is it?' I gasped.

'We're not even halfway yet.' Shona looked back. 'Are you all right?'

'Fine.' I tried not to pant while I spoke. 'Great. No problem.'

Shona slowed down to swim alongside me and we carried on in silence for a bit. 'You're not OK, are you?' she said after a while.

'I'm fine,' I repeated but my head slipped under the water while I spoke. I coughed as a mouthful of water went down the wrong way. Shona grabbed me.

'Thanks.' I wriggled away from her. 'I'm all right now.'

She looked at me doubtfully. 'Maybe we could

both do with a rest,' she said. 'There's a tiny island about five minutes' swim from here. It's out of our way, but it would give us a chance to get our breath back.'

'OK,' I said. 'If you really need to, I don't mind.'

'Great.' Shona swam off again. 'Follow me.'

Soon, we were sitting on an island barely larger than the flat rock that had become our meeting place. It was hard and gravelly but I lay down the second I dragged myself out of the sea, the water brushing against me as my tail turned back into legs.

It seemed only seconds later that Shona gently shook my shoulder. 'Emily,' she whispered. 'You'd better get up. It's starting to get light.'

I sat up. 'How long have I been asleep?'

Shona shrugged. 'Not long.'

'Why didn't you wake me? We'll never get there now. You did it on purpose!'

Shona squeezed her lips together and scrunched up her eyes. I thought about her pretending she needed a rest, and about taking me to her school and everything. 'I'm sorry,' I said. 'I know you didn't do it on purpose.'

'It's too far. It's probably even too far for me, never mind you.'

'I'm *never* going to see him. I bet he doesn't even remember he's got a daughter!' I felt a drop of salty water on my cheek and wiped it roughly away. 'What am I going to do?'

Shona put her arm round me. 'I'm sorry,' she said.

'I'm sorry, too. I shouldn't have been mean to you. You've been brilliant. Really helpful.'

Shona pulled a face at me, as if she was trying not to smile but couldn't stop a little grin from slipping out through her frown.

'And I know you're right,' I added. 'There's no way I could get there tonight, not if we're only half way.'

'Not even that. Look.' She pointed out to the horizon. 'See that big cloud that looks like a whale spurting water – with the little starfish-shaped one behind it?'

I looked up at the sky. 'Um, yeah,' I said uncertainly.

'Just below that, where the sea meets the sky, it's lighter than the rest of the horizon.'

I studied the horizon. It looked an awfully long way away!

'That's it. The Great Mermer Reef. It's like a huge wall, bigger than anything you've ever seen in your life, made of rocks and coral in every shape and colour you could imagine – and then about a hundred more. The prison's a mile beyond it. You have to go through the reef to get there.'

My heart felt like a rock itself – dropping down to the bottom of the sea. 'Shona, it's absolutely *miles* away.'

'We'll work something out,' Shona said. 'I promise.' Then she scrabbled around among the rocks and picked up a couple of stones. She handed one to me.

'What's this?' I looked at the stone.

'They're friendship pebbles. They mean that we're best friends – if you want to be.'

'Of course I want to be!'

'Look, they're almost exactly the same.' She showed me her pebble. 'We each keep them on us at all times. It means we'll always be there for each other.' Then she said, more quietly, 'And it's also a promise that we'll find your dad.'

I washed my pebble in the water; it went all shiny and smooth. 'It's the best present anyone's ever given me.'

Shona slipped hers into her tail and I put mine in my jacket pocket. I didn't want it to disappear when my legs returned! I looked at the patch of light spreading and growing across the horizon.

'Come on.' Shona slid back into the sea. 'We'd better get going.'

We slowly made our way back to Rainbow Rocks.

'See you Sunday?' I asked as we said goodbye.

Shona's cheeks reddened a touch. 'Can we make it Monday?'

'I thought you couldn't get out on Mondays.'

'I will. I'll make sure of it. Just that it's the Diving and Dance display Monday morning and I don't want to be too tired for the triple flips.'

'Monday then.' I smiled. 'And good luck.'

By the time I got home, I was so tired I could have fallen asleep standing up. But my head was spinning with thoughts and questions. And sadness. I'd found

106

out where my father was, but how would we ever get there? Would we really find him? It felt like I was losing him all over again. I'd virtually lost my mum as well. If only I could make her remember!

As I tried to get to sleep, something Shona had said swam into the corner of my mind. *Sometimes it doesn't work at all, especially if you go near merfolk areas.*

Of course!

I knew *exactly* what I was going to do.

Chapter Ten

*M*um always sleeps in on Sundays. She says even God had a day of rest and she doesn't see why she can't. I'm not allowed to disturb her until she says it's morning – which isn't usually till about midday.

I paced up and down the boat, willing her to wake up. What if she slept right through till the afternoon? Disaster! I couldn't take the risk of Mr Beeston turning up before I'd spoken to her. So I broke a Golden Rule. I crept into her room and sat on the bed.

'Mum,' I stage-whispered from the end of the bed. She didn't stir. I inched further up and leaned towards her ear. 'Mum,' I croaked a bit louder.

She opened one eye and then closed it again. 'Whadyouwan?' she grumbled.

'You have to get up.'

'Whassamatter?'

'I want to go out.'

Mum groaned and turned over.

'Mum, I want us to go out together.'

Silence.

'Please get up.'

She turned back to face me and opened her eyes a crack.

'We never do anything together,' I said.

'Why now? Why can't you leave me in peace? What time is it, anyway?'

I quickly turned her alarm clock round so she couldn't see it. 'It's late. Come on, Mum. *Please*.'

Mum rubbed her eyes and lay on her back. 'I don't suppose you're going to give me any peace until I do, are you?'

I smiled hopefully.

'Just leave me alone and I'll get up.'

I didn't move. 'How do I know you won't go back to sleep the minute I leave?'

'Emily! I said I'll get up and I will. Now leave me alone! And if you want to get back in my good books, you can make me a nice cup of tea. And then I might just forgive you.'

Mum took a bite of her toast. 'So, where do you fancy going, now you've ruined my Sunday morning for me?'

I knew *exactly* where we were going. Shiprock Bay. The nearest you could get to Rainbow Rocks by road. I'd been studying the bus routes and there was one that took us virtually all the way there. We could get off on the coast road and walk along the headland. It must be worth a go. I had to jog her memory somehow.

'I just thought we could have a day trip round the coast,' I said casually as I popped a piece of toast and marmalade in my mouth.

'What about Mr Beeston?'

'What about him?' I nearly choked on my marmalade.

'We'll have to be back for three. Can't let him down.'

'Oh, Mum! Can't you break your date with him for once?'

'Emily. Mr Beeston is a lonely man and a good friend. How many times do I have to tell you that? You know I don't like to let him down. He has not broken our arrangement once in all these years, and I'm not about to do the same. And it is *not* a date!'

'Whatever.' This wasn't the time to tell her what I knew about the 'lonely man'. What *did* I know, anyway? Nothing that made any sense. I swallowed hard to get my toast down. My throat was dry. We'd still have time to get there. Maybe we could accidentally-on-purpose miss the bus back. I'd think of something. I *had* to!

'This is quite nice, actually.' Mum looked out of the window as we bumped round the coast road. It had started to turn inland and I was trying to work out the best stop to get off. The sea looked *completely* different from this angle. Then I saw a familiar clump of rocks and decided to take a chance. I got up and rang the bell. 'This is our stop,' I said.

'You know, I think I'm almost glad you got me up,' Mum said as we got off the bus. 'Not that that's an excuse to do it every week!' She walked over to a green bench on the headland that looked out to sea and sat down. 'And you've picked such a nice spot, too.'

'What are you doing?' I asked as she reached into her bag and brought out the sandwiches.

'We're having a picnic, aren't we?'

'Not *here*!'

Mum looked round. 'I can't see anywhere better.'

'Mum, we're right by the road! Let's walk out towards the sea a bit.'

She frowned.

'Come on, just a little way. *Please*. You promised.'

'I did no such thing!' she snapped. But she put the sandwiches back anyway and we headed along a little headland path that led out towards the sea.

After we'd been walking for about fifteen minutes,

the path came to an abrupt end. In front of us was a gravelly climb down the cliff.

'Now what?' Mum looked round.

'Let's go down there.'

'You must be joking. Have you seen my shoes?'

I looked at her feet. Why hadn't I thought to tell her not to wear her platform sandals? 'They're OK,' I said.

'Emily. I am *not* going to break my ankles just so you can drag me off down some dangerous cliffs.' She turned round and started walking back.

'No, wait!' I looked around desperately. She mustn't leave – she had to see the rocks. A winding path lay almost hidden under brambles. Stony and rough but not as steep as the other one. 'Let's try here,' I said. 'And look – it goes flat again over there if we can just get down this bit.'

'I don't know.' Mum looked doubtfully down the cliff.

'Come on; let's try it. I'll go first and then I can cushion your fall if you go flying.' I tried a cheeky smile, and she gave in.

'If I break my legs, it's breakfast in bed every day until I'm better.'

'Deal.'

I picked my way through the brambles and stones, checking behind me every few seconds to make sure Mum was still there. We managed to get to the rocks in one piece.

Mum rubbed her elbow. 'Ouch. Nettles.' She

pulled at a dock leaf and rubbed it on her arm. I gazed in front of us. A few metres of sea separated us from Rainbow Rocks. I couldn't help smiling as I watched the sea washing over the flat rocks, rainbow water caressing them with every wave.

'Mum?'

'Hm?'

I took a deep breath. 'Do you believe in mermaids?' I asked, my throat tight and strained.

Mum laughed. 'Mermaids? Oh Emily, you don't half ask some silly –'

But then she stopped. She dropped the dock leaf on the ground. Looking out to sea, her face went all hard.

'What is it, Mum?' I asked gently.

'Where are we?' she whispered.

'Just by the coast. I just thought it'd be nice to go out for –'

'*What is this place?*'

I hadn't actually thought about what I'd say once we got here! What would she do if she knew – not just about Jake but about me, too? What if she only half remembered? She might think we were *both* freaks. Maybe she'd be ashamed of us. Why hadn't I thought this through?

I cleared my throat. 'Um. It's just some rocks,' I said carefully. 'Isn't it?'

Mum turned to me. 'I've been here before,' she said, her face scrunched up as if she was in pain.

'When?'

'I don't know. But I know this place.'

'Shall we go further down?'

'No!' She turned back the way we'd come. 'Emily. We have to go back. Mr Beeston will be expecting us.'

'But we've only just got here. Mr Beeston won't be round for ages yet.'

'I can't stay here,' Mum said. 'I've got a bad feeling about it. We're going home.' She started walking back so quickly I could hardly keep up.

We ate our sandwiches on that green bench on the headland, after all. A bus went whizzing past just as we were approaching the road so there was nothing for it but to wait. We ate in silence: me not knowing what to say, Mum gazing into space.

I kept wanting to ask her things, or tell her things, but where could I start?

Eventually another bus came and we rode home in silence as well. By the time we got back to Brightport pier, it was nearly four o' clock.

'Are you angry with me?' I asked as we let ourselves into the boat.

'Angry? Why? You haven't done anything wrong, have you?' Mum searched my face.

'I wanted to have a nice day out and now you've gone all sad.'

Mum shook her head. 'Just thoughtful, sweetheart. There was something about that place . . . ' Her voice trailed off.

'What? What was it?'

'It was such a strong memory, but I don't even know what it was.' She shook her head again and took her coat off. 'Listen to me, talking drivel as usual.'

'You're not talking drivel at all,' I said urgently. 'What was the memory?'

Mum hugged her coat. 'Do you know, it wasn't a memory of a *thing*. More a feeling of something. I felt an overwhelming feeling of . . . love.'

'Love?'

'And then something else. Sadness. Enormous sadness.' Mum took her coat down to the engine room to hang it up. 'I told you I was talking rubbish, didn't I?' she called. 'Now get that kettle on and I'll go and give Mr Beeston a shout. He'll be wondering where we got to.'

I glanced out of the window as I filled the kettle. Mr Beeston was on his way up the pier! My whole body shivered. He was pacing fast and didn't look happy.

POUND! POUND! POUND! He rapped on the roof as Mum came back in the kitchen.

'Oh good. He's here.' Mum went to let him in. 'Hello,' she smiled. 'I was just coming to – '

'Where have you been?' he demanded.

'We've been out for a day trip, haven't we Emily? Just along the –'

'Three o'clock I was here,' he snapped, stabbing a finger at his watch. 'An hour I waited. What's the meaning of this?' His head snapped across to face me. I swallowed hard.

Mum frowned at us both. 'Come on, no need to get upset,' she said. 'We'll have a nice cup of tea.' She went to get the cups and saucers. 'What have you got for us today, Mr B? Iced buns? Flapjacks?'

'Doughnuts,' he said without taking his eyes off me.

'I haven't done anything,' I said.

'Course you haven't, Emily. Now, are you joining us?' Mum held a cup out as Mr Beeston finally turned away. He took his jacket off and folded it over the back of a chair.

'No thanks.'

I lay on the sofa and eavesdropped, waiting for Mr Beeston to try to inject her with the memory drug. I had to catch him in the act, prove to Mum that he wasn't really her friend. But what if he got to me first? What if he injected *me* with the memory drug, too?

But he didn't do anything. As soon as he sat down with Mum, he acted as though nothing had happened. They just drank tea and munched doughnuts and chatted about B & B owners and the price of mini golf.

They'd hardly finished eating when Mr Beeston glanced at his watch. 'Well, that's me done,' he said.

'You're going?' But he hadn't drugged her yet!

Maybe he didn't do it every week. Well, I'd be waiting for him as soon as he tried!

'I have a 4.45 appointment,' he growled, the left side of his mouth twitching as he spoke. 'I don't like to keep people waiting.'

I didn't say anything.

'Goodbye, Mary P.' He let himself out.

Mum started clearing the cups away and I grabbed a tea towel.

'So, you were saying, earlier,' I began as Mum handed me a saucer.

'Saying?'

'About our outing.'

'Oh of course – the little trip to the headland,' Mum smiled. 'Lovely, wasn't it?'

'Not just the headland,' I said. 'The rocks.'

Mum looked at me blankly.

'Rainbow Rocks . . .' The words caught in my throat as I held my breath.

'Rainbow what?'

'Mum – don't tell me you've forgotten! The rocks, the rainbow colours when the sea washed over them, the way you felt when we were there. Love. And sadness and stuff?'

Mum laughed. 'You know, Mrs Partington told me you had a good imagination at the last parents' evening. Now I know what she means.'

I stared at her as she bustled about, straightening the tablecloth and brushing crumbs off the chairs with her hands.

'What?' She looked up.

'Mum, what do you think we were talking about before Mr Beeston came round?'

Mum shut one eye and rubbed her chin. 'Heck – give me a minute.' She looked worried for a moment, then laughed. 'You know – I can't remember. Gone! Never mind. Now fetch me the brush and pan. We're not leaving the carpet like this.'

I carried on staring at her. She'd forgotten! He *had* drugged her, after all! But how? And when?

'Come on, shape yourself. Brush and pan. Or do I have to get them myself?'

I fetched the brush and pan out of the cupboard and handed them to her.

'Mum . . . ' I tried again as she swept under the table. 'Do you *really* not remem–'

'*Emily.*' Mum sat up on her knees and spoke firmly. 'A joke is a joke, and it's usually not funny after a while. Now I don't want to hear any more rubbish about multicoloured rocks if you don't mind. I've got more important things to do than indulge your daydreams.'

'But it's not a –'

'EMILY.'

I knew that tone of voice. It meant it was time to shut up. I picked up the doughnut bags from the table and went to put them in the bin. Then I noticed some writing on one of the bags. *MPW.*

'Why has this one got your initials on?' I asked.

'I don't know. Probably so he knows which ones are mine.'

'What difference does it make?'

'Come on Emily, everyone knows I've got a sweet tooth. Mine had more sugar on.'

'But can't you tell which ones have more sugar just by looking at them?'

'*Emily*. Why are you being so *difficult* today? I *won't* have you talking about Mr Beeston like this. I'm not listening to another word.'

'But I don't understand! Why can't he just look in the bag?'

Mum ignored me. Then she started whistling and I gave up and went back to my cabin. I took the bags with me. They held some kind of answer, I was sure of it – if only I could work out what it was!

I stared so hard at her initials my eyes started to water.

And then, as the letters blurred under my gaze, it hit me so hard I nearly fell over. Of course! The memory drug!

It was in the doughnuts.

Chapter Eleven

*C*oming home from school on Monday, I slumped on the sofa and threw my bag on the floor. Mum was reading. 'Nice day?' she asked, folding over the corner of the page and putting her book down.

'Mm.' I got a glass of milk out of the fridge.

I could hardly bear to look at her. How was I ever going to get her to believe me? Somehow I had to make her see for herself what Mr Beeston was up to. *And* I still had to find Jake. What was I going to do?

A gentle rap on the roof startled me out of my thoughts. I clenched my fists. If that was Mr Beeston, I'd –

'Hello Emily,' Millie said in a mysterious kind of way as she unwrapped herself from her large black cloak.

'Are you going out?' I asked Mum.

'It's the Bay Residents' AGM. I told you last week.'

'Did you?'

'Nice to see I'm not the only one round here with the memory of a goldfish.' She tweaked my cheek as she passed me.

I checked my watch. 'But it's only six o'clock!'

'I need to get there early to open up. It's at the bookshop,' she called from down the corridor. 'Thanks for this, Millie,' she added as she came back in with her coat. 'Get the sofa bed out if I'm late.'

'I might just do that,' Millie replied. 'My energy is a little depleted today. I think it's the new Ginkgo Biloba tablets on top of my shiatsu.'

'Right,' Mum said, doing up her coat. Another knock on the roof made me jump again.

'Heck's becks Emily, you're a bit twitchy tonight, aren't you.' Mum ruffled my hair as Mr Beeston's face appeared at the door.

I froze.

'Only me,' he said, scanning the room without coming in.

'You didn't tell me *he* was going,' I whispered, grabbing at her coat as Mr Beeston waited outside.

'Of course he's going – he's the chairman!' she whispered back. 'And he's offered to help me set up,' she added. 'Which is nice of him, by the way.'

'Mum, I don't want you to go!'

'Don't want me to go? What on earth are you on about?'

What could I say? How could I get her to believe me? She wouldn't hear a word against Mr Beeston. The sweet, kind, lonely man. Well, I'd prove to her that he wasn't anything of the sort!

'I just –'

'Come on now. Don't be a baby.' She prised my fingers from her sleeve. 'Millie's here to look after you. I'm only up at the shop if you need me urgently. And I mean *urgently*.' She gave me a quick peck, rubbed my cheek with her thumb – and was gone.

'How come you don't go to the Bay Residents' meetings, Millie?'

'Oh I don't believe in all that democratic fuss and nonsense,' she said, shifting me up the sofa so she could sit down.

We sat silently in front of the telly. Once *Coronation Street* had finished, I waited for her to tell me it was bedtime. But she didn't. I looked across at the sofa; she lay on her side, her eyes closed, mouth slightly open.

'Millie?' I whispered. No reply. She was fast asleep!

Slinging my legs over the arm of my chair, I flicked channels. All boring. I settled on a programme about people doing mad stunts for no good reason. A woman who said she was scared of heights was about to do a bungee jump. *Why?*

I'd never seen anyone look so scared in my life. Her face was literally grey. As the camera zoomed out from her horrified eyes, she drew a breath – and then threw herself upside-down off the edge of the cliff!

After she'd done it, a little girl came running over to hug her. The woman was grinning like an idiot. 'I had to do it,' she said to the camera. 'Laura needs to go to America for an operation and I simply couldn't let her go alone, so I decided it was time to face my fears. Sometimes you just have to undo the ropes that bind you and go for it.' She hugged her daughter again; they were both crying. It was all a bit pukey, actually.

But later, as I brushed my teeth, the woman's words wouldn't leave me alone. There was something about them that seemed to be knocking on a door inside my mind. What was it? I ran them round and round in my head, until I was left with one phrase: 'Undo the ropes . . . and go for it.'

Oh crikey – that was it! That was what I had to do. The Great Mermer Reef might be too far to swim – but it wouldn't be too far by boat! And now was the perfect time. In fact, it might be my only chance.

Could I do it? *Really?* I looked at the bathroom clock. Half past eight. Mum wouldn't be back for ages yet and Millie was fast asleep in the other room. When would I get an opportunity like this again? I *had* to do it.

I grabbed the engine key and crept outside. There was probably another half an hour or so before it was dark. I could handle the darkness anyway; I'd got used to the sea at night.

But would I remember how to operate the boat? I'd only done it a few times. We have to go round to Southpool Harbour every couple of years to get the hull checked out and Mum usually lets me take it some of the way. We hardly ever use the sail. I don't know why we have it!

The promenade was quiet apart from the masts all clinking and chattering in the wind. I pulled at my hair, twisting it frantically round my fingers. I probably looked just like that woman before her bungee jump. But I knew how she felt, now. I simply *had* to do it, however dangerous or scary or mad it might be.

Pulling at the ropes, I had one last look down the pier. Deserted.

Almost.

Someone was coming out of the amusements. I ducked below the mast and waited. It was Mandy's mum! She was heading down the pier, probably to the meeting. A figure was standing in the doorway of the arcade. Mandy!

I ducked down again, waited for her to go back inside. Had she seen me?

The rope slackened in my hands – I was drifting away from the jetty. Close enough to jump back and pull the boat in again – but floating further away by the second. *What should I do?* There was still time to abandon the whole thing.

Then a breeze lifted the front of the boat off the

water and, without thinking, the decision was made. I glanced back at the amusements. She'd gone. I hurled the rope onto the jetty and turned the ignition key.

Nothing happened.

I tried again. It started this time, and I held my breath as its familiar 'dunka dunka' broke into the silence of the evening.

'OI!'

I turned to see who was shouting.

'Fish girl!'

Mandy! She stepped onto our jetty.

'What d'you think you're doing?' she called.

'Nothing!' *Nothing?* What kind of a stupid thing was that to say?

'Oh, I know. Are you running away, now Julie doesn't want to be your friend?'

'What?'

'She doesn't want to know you any more, after you dropped her last weekend. Good job she had me there to make her see *someone* cares about her feelings.' Mandy paused as she let an evil smile crawl across her face. 'Your mum knows you're taking the boat out, does she?'

'Course!' I said quickly. 'I'm just moving it round to Southpool.'

'Yeah, I'll bet. Shall we check, then?' She waved her mobile phone in front of her.

'You wouldn't!'

'No? Want to take the chance? You think I haven't

been *waiting* for an opportunity like this? Little miss goody-goody two shoes, making out you're soooo sweet and innocent.'

The boat bobbed further away from the jetty. 'Why do you hate me so much?' I called over the engine.

'Hmm. Let me think.' She put her finger dramatically to her mouth and looked away, as though talking to an audience. 'She gets me grounded, steals my best friend, turns the swimming teacher against me. She's a great big fat SHOW-OFF!' Mandy looked back at me. 'I really don't know.'

Then she turned and started walking back up the jetty, waving her phone in the air.

'Mandy, don't! Please!'

'Maybe I will, maybe I won't,' she called over her shoulder. 'See ya.'

What should I do? I couldn't go back. I *couldn't*. This was probably my one and only chance to find my father. And Mandy Rushton was NOT going to ruin it. I forced her words out of my mind. She wasn't going to stop me – she *wasn't*!

I turned my attention back to my plan.

Minutes later, I was edging away from the pier, holding the tiller and carefully navigating my way out of the harbour. I went over what I'd done when I drove the boat round to Southpool – and tried hard to convince myself that what I was doing now really wasn't very different.

As I sailed out to sea, I looked back at Brightport

Bay. The last rays of the sun winked and glinted on the water like tiny spotlights. Spray dusted my hair.

I closed my eyes for a second while I thought about what I was doing. I had to find the Great Mermer Reef. I knew more or less where it was, from the time we'd got halfway there, so I studied the horizon and aimed for the bit that was lighter than the rest. The bit that would shimmer a hundred colours when I got close.

It got dark quite suddenly as I sliced slowly through the water. *King* never does *anything* in a hurry. My hand was getting cold, holding onto the tiller. And I was getting wet. *King* bounced on the water, gliding along with the swell, then rising and bumping down over the waves. It had been quite calm when I set off. The further out I got, the more hill-like the sea became.

Above me, stars appeared, one by one. Soon, the night sky was packed. A fat half moon sat among them, its other half a silhouette, semi-visible as though impatient for the full moon to come.

King swayed from side to side, lumbering slowly through the peaks and troughs. Was I getting anywhere? I looked behind me. Brightport was *miles* away! If I closed one eye and held up my hand, I could hide the whole town behind my thumbnail.

Up and down we went, climbing the waves, bouncing on the swell, inching ever closer to the Great Mermer Reef.

My eyes watered as I strained to keep them on the patch of light on the horizon, shimmering and glowing and coming gradually closer. I let myself dream about seeing Jake.

I'd get into the prison and we'd escape. Hiding him in the boat, we'd cruise back to the pier before anyone even realised he'd gone. Then Mum would come home from the meeting. Jake would be waiting in the sea at the end of the pier and I'd ask Mum to come for a walk with me. Then I'd leave her there on her own for a minute and he would appear. They'd see each other and it would be like they'd never been apart. Mum would remember everything and we'd all live happily ever after. *Excellent* plan.

Excellent daydream, anyhow. A 'plan' was something I didn't exactly have.

'EMILY!' A voice shattered my thoughts. I spun round, searching the night sky. There was a shape behind me – a long way away but coming nearer. A boat. One of those little motor boats with outboard engines that they hire out in the summer. As it got closer, I could see an outline of two people, one leaning forwards at the front, one at the back at the tiller.

'Emily!' A woman's voice. And not just any woman. Mum!

Then I recognised the other voice.

'Come back here, young lady! Whatever you think you are doing, you had better stop it – and *now!*'

Mr Beeston!

I shoved the tiller across and quickly swapped sides as the boat changed direction, pushing the throttle as far forward as it would go. *Come on, come on,* I snapped. The boat sputtered and chugged in reply but didn't speed up.

'What are you doing here?' I shouted, over the engine and the waves.

'What am *I* doing here?' Mum called back. 'Emily, what are YOU doing?'

'But your meeting!'

The motor boat edged closer. 'The meeting got cancelled when Mrs Rushton's girl rang up in a right state. She thought you might be in danger.'

I should have known she'd do it! I don't know how I could have thought even for a moment that she wouldn't.

'I'm sorry, Mum,' I called. 'I've got to do this. You'll understand, honestly. Trust me.'

'Oh, please come back, darling.' Mum called. 'Whatever it is, we can sort it out.'

King's engine sputtered again and seemed to be slowing down. Seawater soaked my face as we bounced on the waves, rolling and peaking like a mountain range.

'Look what you're doing to your mother,' Mr Beeston shouted. 'I won't have it, do you hear me? I won't allow it.'

I ran my sleeve over my wet face. 'You can't tell me what to do,' I shouted back, anger pushing away my fear – and any desire to keep my stupid promise to Mr Beeston. 'It's not like you're my father or anything.'

Mr Beeston didn't reply. He was concentrating hard and had almost caught up with me. Meanwhile, the shimmering light was glowing and growing bigger all the time. I could almost see the different colours. *Come on, King*, I said under my breath. *Not much further now*. I looked back at the motor boat. Mum was covering her face with her hands. Mr Beeston held the tiller tight, his face all pinched and contorted.

'*Remember* my father, do you?' I called to him. 'You know, your "best friend". What kind of a person lies to their best friend's wife for years then? *Huh?*'

'I don't know what foolish ideas you've got into your head, child, but you had better put an end to them right now. Before I put an end to them for you.' Mr Beeston's eyes shone like a cat's as he caught mine. 'Can't you see how much you are upsetting your mother?'

'Upsetting my mother? Ha! Like *you* care!'

'Emily, *please*,' Mum called, her arms stretched out towards me. 'Whatever it is, we'll talk about it. Don't blame Mr Beeston. He's only trying to help.'

'Come *on, King*!' I said out loud as the engine crackled and popped. 'Mum.' I turned to face her.

130

They were only a couple of metres away from me now. 'Mr Beeston isn't who he says he is. And he's *not* trying to help you.'

Then the engine died.

'What's the *matter* with this thing?' I shouted.

'You know we never keep much diesel on board,' Mum called. 'It's a fire hazard.'

'Fire hazard? Who told you that?'

'I did,' Mr Beeston called. 'Don't want you injuring yourselves, do I?' He smiled his creepy smile at me. He'd been controlling our whole lives!

That was it. I stood up and lurched forward to grab the mast. I'd have to sail the rest of the way!

I undid a rope at the base of the mast and tried to hoist the mainsail up. I heaved and yanked at it, but nothing happened. I pulled at another rope to free the boom – that's the wooden pole that runs along the bottom of the sail.

As the rope at the far end of the boom swung free, I made a grab for it. Missed. The sail swayed out to the side and I watched helplessly as my last hope swung away with it.

'Oh Emily, please stop it.' Mum shouted as the boat lurched to the side. 'You don't need to upset yourself like this. I know what it's about.'

'*What*? If you know, what are you doing in there with him?'

'It's natural for you to feel like this, darling. Mr Beeston's told me about you being a little jealous, and how that might make you try to turn me against him.

But he's just a friend. There's no need for you to go fretting like this.'

The shimmering was really close now. I could see colours and lights dancing on the surface of the water. It was like a fireworks display. I groaned. 'Mum, it's not –'

I broke off when I saw Mum's face. It had turned white, like those buskers in the market square who pretend to be statues. In a soft voice I hardly recognised, she said, 'No one could ever take the place of your father.' She was gazing wide-eyed at the lights on the water.

'*My father?*'

For a moment, everything stood completely still, like a picture. The sea stopped moving; Mr Beeston let go of the tiller; my mum and I locked eyes as though seeing each other for the first time.

Then Mr Beeston leapt into action. 'Right, that's it,' he yelled. 'I'm coming aboard.'

'Wait!' I shouted, as a wave caught the side of the boat. *King* lurched sideways, the sail swinging across to the other side.

Mr Beeston had just pulled himself aboard when – thwack! – the boom swung back again and knocked him flying.

'Aaarrrgghh!' He clutched his head as he fell backwards. Crashing to the deck with a thump, he lay flat on his back without moving.

Mum screamed and stood up. The motor boat rocked wildly.

'Mum – careful!' I ran to the side and leaned over. 'Get on,' I shouted. She was alongside *King*.

Mum didn't move.

'You have to get on board. Come on, Mum.' I held an arm out. 'I'll help you.'

'I – I can't,' she said woodenly.

'You can, Mum. You've *got* to.' I scrabbled around in the bench seat and pulled out the lifebelt. *King* rocked like the rodeo horse on the prom. The sail was still waving about at the side, hopelessly out of reach. Holding tight to the railing, I threw the lifebelt to Mum. 'You'll be fine,' I called. 'Just get on board quick before you drift away.'

She stared at me.

'*Do it!*'

Mum stood up in her rocky boat, the lifebelt round her middle, and suddenly lunged for the steps. I grabbed her hand as she pulled herself onto the deck.

'Oh Emily,' she said. 'I'm so sorry.'

'What for?'

'It's all my fault,' Mum said, holding onto me with one hand and the railing with the other as we swayed from side to side.

'Course it's not your fault, Mum. If it's anyone's fault, it's Mr Beeston's. He's not what he seems, Mum; he's been –'

Mum put her finger over my lips. 'I know why we're here.'

'You – you –'

133

'I remember.' Mum pulled me towards her and held me tight. Over her shoulder, I could see the water shimmering and sparkling like an electric light show. The Great Mermer Reef.

I wriggled out of Mum's grasp. 'You remember — what?'

Mum hesitated. 'It's all a bit hazy,' she said.

All at once, the sky exploded with light. 'Look!' I pointed behind her. Pink lights danced below the water while a dozen colours jumped in the air above it.

'I know this,' Mum said, her voice shaking. 'He — he brought me here.'

'Who? Mr Beeston?' I glanced nervously across at him. He still hadn't moved. Mum clutched the railing as the boat tilted again and I made my way over to join her. Her face was covered in spray from the sea. Except when I looked more closely, I realised it wasn't seawater at all. It was tears. 'Our first anniversary,' she said.

She'd been here with Jake?

'He told me where they would take him.'

'*Who* would take him?'

'If they ever found us out. He knew they'd get him in the end. We both knew it, but we couldn't stop. Because we loved each other so much.'

Mum's body sagged; I put my arms round her middle.

'I'm going to find him,' I said, holding her tighter. 'That's why I took the boat. I did it for all of us.'

'I can't bear it,' she said. 'I can remember everything. How could I have forgotten him? He was taken away because he loved me and I forgot all about him. How can I ever forgive myself?'

'Mum, it's not your fault! You didn't just *forget* him.'

'I did,' she gulped. 'You know I did. You asked about him and I didn't even know. I couldn't remember anything.'

'But you weren't to blame.'

Mum wiped a curtain of wet hair off her face and looked at me. 'Who was, then?'

I nodded a thumb behind me. 'Mr Beeston,' I whispered.

'Oh, Emily. Don't start with that claptrap again!'

'It's NOT claptrap!' I tried to keep my voice down. I didn't want him to wake up and ruin everything. 'It's true,' I whispered. 'He's not what he seems.'

'Emily, please don't make this worse than it is.'

'Mum, *listen* to me,' I snapped.

She caught my eyes for a second. Then looked at Mr Beeston. 'We should see how he is.' Mum shook herself free from my grasp and stumbled along the deck to Mr Beeston.

'He'll be fine,' I said. 'Don't worry about him.'

Mum ignored me and crouched down next to Mr Beeston. I crouched down beside her as she leaned over his chest and listened. Then she looked up at me, her face whiter than the million stars shining above us.

'Oh my God,' she said. 'I think we've killed him.'

Chapter Twelve

'There's no heartbeat,' Mum said, rocking back on her heels.

I opened my mouth. What could I say? A second later, the side door suddenly swung open with a bang. Mum and I grabbed each other's arms.

Millie's face appeared in the doorway.

'Do you think there's anything you would like to share with me?' she asked as she hitched up her long skirt and clambered out onto the deck.

Mum and I looked at each other.

'I'm sensing some . . . disorientation.'

'No time now,' Mum said, beckoning Millie over. 'We have to do something. Mr Beeston has had an accident. I think he's dead.' She clapped a fist to her mouth.

Millie struggled over to join us, slipping and swaying on the wet deck. 'Let's have a look,' she said, kneeling down beside Mr Beeston. She undid his coat and lifted up his jumper. He was wearing a thick, padded jacket of some sort underneath. I flinched as I noticed a picture of Neptune's trident sewn onto a pocket.

'Armoured vest?' Millie murmured. 'Now why in the cosmos would he need something like that?'

I didn't say anything.

'That's your answer, Mary P.' Millie turned to Mum. 'You wouldn't hear a ten ton truck through that.'

Just then, the boat jolted to the side. I slid across the deck and bumped against the bench seat.

'Emily, get the tiller!' Millie ordered, suddenly in charge.

I did what she said, not that it made much difference. The boat dipped and swayed helplessly in the waves.

Millie reached under Mr Beeston's back and unbuckled the vest. Lifting it off, she bent over him, her ear to his chest. Mum came over and grabbed my hand while we waited.

'Absolutely fine,' Millie announced a few seconds later.

'Oh thank heavens.' Mum hugged me. 'I'd never have forgiven myself if anything had happ—'

'He just needs his chakras realigning,' Millie continued. 'A bit of reflexology should do it.'

She pulled off his shoes and socks and settled herself at Mr Beeston's feet. Placing her hands across her large chest, she closed her eyes and breathed in deeply. Then she lifted his right foot and started to massage it. A moment later, his foot twitched. She carried on massaging. He twitched again, this time his leg jerking about in the air. The twitching and jerking spread up his body until it reached his face and he started giggling. He was soon laughing loudly. Eventually, he leapt up, screaming, 'Stop, stop!'

Millie released his foot and stood up. 'Never fails,' she said, wiping her hands on her skirt and heading back inside. 'Right, give me a minute or two. Reflexology always drains my chi.'

Mum went over to Mr Beeston. 'Thank heavens you're all right.'

Mr Beeston straightened his coat as he glanced at me. 'Just a scratch,' he said. 'No harm done.' A red path was worming its way down the side of his head.

My hand tightened on the tiller. 'No harm done? You *reckon*?'

'Emily, this is no time to start your nonsense again. What on *earth* have you got against the poor man?'

'What have I got against the poor man? Where d'you want me to start?' I looked him in the eyes. 'Is it the fact that he's been wiping your memory since the day I was born, or the fact that he's been spying on us *forever*?'

Mum didn't speak for a second. Then she laughed. 'Oh Emily, I've never heard such –'

'It's true.' Mr Beeston spoke, his eyes still locked onto mine. 'She's right.'

'What?' Mum held tightly onto the mast with one hand; with the other, she clutched her chest.

'It's too late, Mary P. I can't pretend any more. And I won't. Why should I?'

'What are you *on* about?' Mum looked from Mr Beeston to me. Let *him* explain.

Mr Beeston sat down on the bench opposite me. 'It was for your own good,' he said. 'All of you.' His hands were still clutching his head, his hair all mangled and tangled up with blood and sweat and seawater.

'What was for my own good?' Mum's face hardened and grew thinner as she spoke.

'The two worlds – they don't belong together. It doesn't work.' He leant forward, his head almost between his knees. 'And I should know,' he added, his voice almost a whisper. 'You're not the only one to grow up without a father.' He spoke to the floor. 'Disappeared the minute I was born, he did. Just like all the others. Fishermen. All very nice having an unusual girlfriend isn't it? Taming a beautiful siren. Show off to your friends about that, can't you?'

A tear fell from his face onto the deck. He brushed his cheek roughly. 'But it's a bit different when your

139

own son sprouts a tail! Don't want to know, then, do you?'

'What are you saying?' Mum's voice was as tight as her face, her hand still gripping the mast. The sea lifted us up and down; the sail still flapped uselessly over the water.

'You can't put humans and merfolk together and expect it to work. It doesn't. All you get is pain.' Finally, Mr Beeston raised his head to look at us. 'I was trying to save you from that. From what I've been through, myself.'

The boat shook violently as another wave hit us. I clutched the tiller more tightly. 'I told you he wasn't really your friend,' I hissed to Mum, the wind biting my face.

'Friendship?' he spat. 'Loyalty is all that matters. To Neptune and the protection of the species. That is my life.' He held up a fist across his chest. Then he glanced at Mum. His fist fell open. 'That's to say,' he faltered, 'I mean – look, I never wanted to . . . ' His voice trailed away, his chin dropping to his chest.

Mum looked like she'd been hit over the head herself. Her face was as white as the sail and her body had gone rigid. 'I often wondered why they got a new lighthouse keeper so suddenly,' she said. 'No one ever did quite explain what happened to old Bernard. You just appeared one day. And something else I've never really thought about – you never invited me in. Not once in twelve years. Not like Bernard. We used to go up there all the time when I was younger, up on the top deck looking all round with binoculars and telescopes. But you – my *friend* – you always kept the door closed to me. And to think, I actually felt sorry for you.'

She put her hand on my arm. The boat was starting to career up and down, the sea getting wilder as we held the tiller together. 'He saw you once,' she said quietly into the darkness. 'At Rainbow Rocks. Held you against his chest at the water's edge. I wouldn't let him take you in the water. Maybe if he had. . .' Her words slipped away as she looked at me, her hair plastered across her face with sea water. 'Twelve years I've lost.'

I bit my lip, tasting salty water.

'Hidden from my own mind like everything else.' She stood up and inched over towards Mr Beeston. 'You stole my life from me,' she said, anger creeping into her voice. 'You're nothing but a thief! A nasty, rotten, scheming THIEF!'

'Hey now, hold on a minute!' Mr Beeston stood up. 'I've been *good* to you. I've looked *after* you. You should hear what some of them wanted to –'

'You had no right.' Mum shook his arm, tears rolling down her cheeks. 'He is my husband. Who do you think you are?'

'Who do I think I am? I know *exactly* who I am! I'm Charles –' He stopped. Glanced briefly at Mum and took a breath. Then he suddenly thrust out his chin, his eyes clear and focused for a brief moment. 'I am Charles Finright Beeston, adviser to Neptune, and I have conducted my duties with pride and loyalty for twelve years.'

'How dare you!' Mum snapped. 'All these years, pretending to be my friend.'

'Now wait a minute. I was – I mean, I *am* your friend. You think I didn't care about you? It's for your own good. We had to put a stop to it. It's wrong, unnatural – dangerous, even – don't you see?'

Mum paused for a moment, then flew at him, bashing her fists against his chest. 'All I can see is a beast. A despicable worm!' she screamed.

Mr Beeston backed away from her. As she went for him, Mum tripped on the lifebelt and nearly fell flat on her face. She stopped herself by clutching a rope tied onto the mast. The rope came loose in her hand, ripping the canvas that held the boom in place. All three of us watched as the wooden plank drifted away from us and the sail flapped over the sea even more uselessly than before.

We'd *never* get anywhere now.

I tried to hold the tiller steady as the boat lurched again. The waves were getting choppier, throwing us all over the deck. 'We need to do something,' I said, my voice quivering.

'I'll fix it,' Mr Beeston said, his words slow and deliberate, his eyes cold and determined. Then he turned and walked along the side of the boat to the door, holding the railing as the boat rocked.

'Mum, what are we going to do?' I asked as the waves rolled us from side to side again. Mum's steely eyes followed Mr Beeston down the boat.

'Forget him,' I said. 'We need to think of something or we'll never get home again – never mind see Jake.'

'Oh Emily, do you really think we're going to find –'

'I know where he is,' I said. 'We can do it. We're nearly there!'

Mum pulled her eyes away from Mr Beeston. 'Right. Come on,' she said, snapping into action. She lifted the lid up off the bench, rummaged through hose pipes and foot pumps. 'Put this on.' She passed me a lifejacket that was much too small for me and grabbed one for herself.

'Mum. I don't need one.'

'Just to be on the safe –' She stopped and looked at my legs. 'Oh golly,' she said. 'You mean you can . . . you're a –'

'Didn't you know?' I asked. 'Didn't you ever suspect?'

She shook her head sadly. 'How could I have done? Maybe somewhere in the back of my mind . . . ' A massive wave crashed over the side, washing away the rest of her sentence and drenching us both.

'Mum, I'm scared,' I yelped, wiping the spray off my face. 'It's too far even for me to swim back from here. We'll never make it.'

As I spoke, the boat gave one more enormous lurch to the side. I fell to the floor, slipped across the deck. As I clutched the railing and tried to pull myself up again, I noticed a shape in the sea in front of us. A fin! That was it, then. The boat was going to capsize; we'd be eaten by sharks!

Mum has never been religious and she's always said it's up to me to make my mind up. I never had done. Until then.

Without even wondering what to say, I put my hands together, closed my eyes and prayed.

Chapter Thirteen

*M*y lips moved soundlessly behind my hands, scanning all the words I could summon up: half-remembered prayers from half-listened–to assemblies. *Why didn't I take more notice?* I asked myself when I got to, 'Thy will be done on earth as it is in heaven,' and couldn't for the life of me think what came next.

'*Emily!*' Mum was tugging at my arm.

I shook her off. 'I'm busy.'

Mum tugged again. 'I think you should take a look.'

I opened my fingers wide enough to sneak a peek between them. It was hard to see anything, the boat was careering up and down so much. I felt even more giddy and reached out for the railing. That was when

I heard it – someone calling my name! I looked at Mum even though I knew it hadn't been her. Holding the railing beside me, she pointed out to the mountainous waves with her free hand.

'Emily!' a familiar voice called again. Then a familiar head poked out above the waves, bobbing up and down in the swell. Shona! She grinned and waved at me.

'What are you doing here?' I shouted.

'It's Monday. You didn't turn up at the rocks. I've been looking for you.'

'Oh Shona, I'm so sorry.'

'When you didn't come, I had a funny feeling you'd be doing something like this!'

'I've messed it all up,' I called, my throat clogged up. 'We're never going to get there now.'

'Don't be too sure!' she called back. 'Throw me a rope. I'll see if I can tow you.'

'But the boat must weigh a ton!'

'Not in water it doesn't. As long as I can get some momentum going with my tail. We do it in PE all the time.'

'Are you sure?'

'Let's just give it a try, OK?'

'OK,' I said uncertainly, and with a flick of her tail, she was gone. Her tail! Of course! Not a shark at all!

I made my way up to the front deck, untied the rope and threw it down. Mum came with me. I tried to avoid looking at her but I could feel her eyes boring into the side of my face. 'What?' I asked without turning to her.

'Is she a . . . friend of yours?' Mum asked carefully. 'Mm.'

Mum sighed. 'We've got a lot of catching up to do, love, haven't we?'

I carried on looking ahead. 'Do you think I'm a freak?'

'A freak?' Mum reached over to pick up one of my hands. 'Darling, I couldn't be more proud.'

Still holding my hand, she put her other arm round me. The boat had levelled out again and I snuggled into Mum's shoulder; wet, cold and frightened. Neither of us spoke for a few minutes while we watched Shona pull us ever nearcr to the prison – and Jake.

A few moments later, Mum and I caught each other's eyes, the same thought coming into our minds. *Where was Mr Beeston?*

'He might be hiding,' Mum said.

'I think we should check it out.'

Mum stood up. 'I'll go then.'

'I'm coming with you.'

She didn't argue as we stood up and edged our way down the side of the boat. The deck was still soaking and it was a slippy trip to the door.

I pushed my head inside. Mr Beeston was standing by a window in the saloon, his back to us, the window pushed open, a large shell in his hands.

'A conch? What on earth is he doing with that?' Mum whispered.

Mr Beeston put the shell to his mouth.

'Talking to it?' I whispered back.

He muttered quietly into the shell.

'What's he saying?' I looked at Mum.

She shook her head. 'Stay here,' she ordered. 'Crouch down behind the door. Don't let him see you. I'll be back in a second.'

'Where are you going?' But she'd slid back outside. I hunched low and waited for her to return.

Two minutes later, Mum was back with a huge fishing net in her arms. 'What are you doing with –'

Mum shushed me with a finger over her lips and crept inside. She beckoned me to follow.

Mr Beeston was still leaning out of the window, talking softly into his conch. Mum inched towards him and I tiptoed behind her. When we were right behind him, she passed me one end of the net and mouthed, 'Three . . . two . . . '

When she mouthed, 'One,' I threw my side of the net over Mr Beeston's head. Mum did the same on her side.

'What the – ' Mr Beeston dropped the conch and fell back into a chair.

'Quick, wrap it round him,' Mum urged.

I ran in a circle round him, dragging the net with me. Mr Beeston struggled and lashed out but we wrapped him up, like when someone's dog runs up to you in the park and knots your ankles together with its lead. Only better.

Mum pushed him back into his chair and lifted his

legs up. 'Get his feet,' she demanded, dodging his kicks. I slipped under his legs with the net. There was still loads of net left over so I ran round him again, fastening him to his chair. Mum grabbed my end of the net and tied it securely to hers and we stood back to admire our work.

'You won't get away with this, you know,' Mr Beeston said, struggling and trying to kick out. All he managed to do was make the chair wobble on its legs.

'I wouldn't do that if I were you,' a voice suddenly boomed from the other side of the saloon.

We all turned to see Millie clambering up off the sofa. She stood majestically in the centre of the room, arms raised as though waiting for a voice from heaven.

'Put my back out for weeks once, falling backwards off a chair. Had to see a chiropractor for six months. And they're not cheap, I can tell you.' She swept into the galley. 'Right, who's for an Earl Grey?' she asked. 'I'm gasping.'

The sea had calmed down and we drank our tea on the front deck. The sky sparkled with dancing colours. As we watched, the lights danced faster and faster. Pink, blue, green, gold – every colour you could imagine, in a million different shades, jumping around, stabbing at the water as though it was too hot for them to settle. It was as if the lights were speaking – in an alien language that I had no chance of understanding.

Millie looked at them intently for a while, then sniffed her cup of tea. 'I don't know what they put in this,' she said, draining the cup and heading back inside, 'but I'll have to get some in.'

Mum buttoned up her coat, her eyes fixed on the lights.

'All of this,' she whispered. 'I remember it all.'

'Do you remember Jake?' I asked nervously, remembering what happened last time I tried to find out about him.

'We never meant it to happen,' she said, her eyes misting over. 'He told me right from the start how dangerous it would be. It was after the regatta.'

'The regatta?'

'We used to hold it every year, but that was the last one. I don't know how we went so wrong, but we did. I went with Mrs Brighouse who used to run the Sea View B & B. She had a little two-man yacht. We got into trouble on the rocks. That was when I met Jake.' She looked at me for the first time. 'Your father,' she added, before looking away again. 'I don't know what happened to Mrs Brighouse. She moved away soon afterwards. But Jake and I – well, I couldn't help it. I went back to Rainbow Rocks every night.'

'*Rainbow Rocks?*'

'Well, near enough. I waited by those rocks you took me to. You know?'

'Yes. I know.'

She smiled sadly. 'You knew more than I did. But not any more. I remember it all.'

'So did he come?'

She shook her head. 'I waited every night. Then one night I told myself I'd give it one last try before giving up for good. I just wanted to thank him.' She turned to face me again. 'He saved my life, Emily.'

'And he came?'

She smiled. 'He'd been there every night.'

'Every night? But you said – '

'He hid. He saw me every time I went. Said he couldn't keep away either, but he couldn't bring himself to talk to me.'

'Why not?'

'You know, that first time, when he helped us . . . he never got out of the water.' Mum laughed. 'I thought at the time, what an amazing swimmer!'

'So you didn't know . . .'

'He thought I'd be shocked, or disgusted or something.'

I took a deep breath. 'And were you?'

Mum put her hand out to me, cupped my chin. 'Emily, when I saw his tail, when I knew what he was – I think that was the moment I fell in love with him.'

'Really?'

She smiled. 'Really.'

'So then what happened?'

'Well, that was when I left home.'

'Left home? You mean Nan and Grandad used to live here?'

Mum swallowed hard. 'I remember why we argued, now. They wouldn't believe me. They thought I was mad. Tried to make me see a psychiatrist.'

'And you wouldn't.'

She shook her head. 'So then they sold up and moved away from the sea. They gave me an ultimatum – either I came with them, or . . .'

'Or they didn't want to know.' I finished her sentence for her.

'The boat was your grandad's. He didn't want anything more to do with it – or me. Said he'd had enough of the sea to last him a lifetime.'

'He gave it to you?'

She nodded. 'I like to think the gesture meant that a part of him knew it was true. Knew I wasn't crazy.'

'And what about Jake?'

'I used to sail out to sea to meet him, or round to Rainbow Rocks.'

'Was that where they caught him?'

She dabbed the edge of her eye with the palm of her hand. 'I never believed it would happen,' she said. 'Somehow, I thought everything would be all right. Especially after you were born.'

'How come they didn't make you move away?'

'Maybe they wanted to keep an eye on us.'

'On me, you mean?'

She pulled me close, hugging me tight. 'Oh Emily,' she whispered into my hair. 'You only saw him once. You were so tiny.'

'I'm going to see him again, Mum,' I said, my voice coming out in a squeak. 'I'm going to find him.'

She smiled at me through misty eyes.

'I *am*.'

A moment later, I noticed Shona swimming round to the side of the boat. 'We're nearly there,' she called. 'Are you coming in?'

I looked at Mum. 'Is it OK?' I asked.

For an answer, she pulled me tighter – then let me go.

I ran inside and changed into my swimming costume. Millie came back out with me. I perched on the edge of the boat. 'See you,' I smiled.

Mum swallowed hard and held Millie's hand as I jumped into the water. Within seconds I felt my tail form. My legs melted and stretched, spreading warmth through my whole body. I waved to Mum and Millie, watching me from the front deck.

'Look!' I shouted, then ducked under the water. I flicked my tail as gracefully as I could, waving it from side to side while I stretched out in a downwards handstand. When I came back up, Mum was clapping. 'Beautiful,' she called, wiping something from her eye. She blew me a kiss as I grinned at her. Millie's eyes widened. She shook her head, then picked up Mum's cup of tea and finished that one off as well.

'Are you ready?' Shona asked.

'As I'll ever be,' I replied and we set off.

The Great Mermer Reef isn't like anything you are ever likely to see in your life. The highest, widest, longest wall in the world – in the universe, probably – made out of rainbow-coloured coral, miles and miles from anywhere. In the middle of the sea.

You don't realise what it is at first. It feels like the end of the world, stretching up and down and across, further than you can see in every direction. I shielded my eyes from the brightness. It reminded me of the school disco we had at the end of last term. They'd borrowed this machine that threw lights across the room, swirling around and changing colour in time to the music. The Great Mermer Reef was a bit like that, but about a million times bigger and brighter, and the colours swirled and flashed even more.

And somehow, we had to get past it! It was the only way to the prison.

As we got closer, the swirling lights became laser beam rays, shooting out at every angle from jagged layers of coral heaped upon coral.

Sharp, spiky rocks were piled all the way up to the surface – and higher – with soft, rubbery bushes buried in every crevice in the brightest purples and yellows and greens you've ever seen. A moving bush like a silver Christmas tree flapped towards us. Two spotted shrimps dragged a starfish along the seabed. All around us, fish and plants bustled and rustled about. But we were stuck – in a fortress of bubbles and bushes and rocks. We couldn't even climb over the top; it was far too high and rough. Above the water, the coral shot diamond rays from stones like cut glass. I was never, *ever* going to find Jake.

'It's hopeless,' I said, trying desperately not to cry. It was like that stupid game about going on a bear hunt. You keep coming across things that you've got to get past. 'We can't get over it, we can't get under it.'

Shona was by my side, her eyes bright like the coral. 'We'll have to go through it!' she exclaimed, her words gurgling away in multicoloured bubbles. 'There's bound to be a gap somewhere. Come on.' She pulled at my arm and dived deeper.

We weaved in and out of spaghetti-fringed tubes, swam into bushes with tentacles that opened wide enough to swim inside. But it was the same thing every time: a dead end.

I perched on a rock, ready to give up, while Shona scaled the coral, tapping it with her fingers like a builder testing the thickness of a wall. A huge shoal of fish that had been sheltering in a cave suddenly darted out as one, writhing and spinning like a kalei-doscope pattern. I stared, transfixed.

'I think I've found something.' Shona's voice jolted me out of my trance. She was scratching about at the coral and I swam closer to see what she'd found.

'Look!' She scrabbled some more. Bits of coral crumbled away like dust in her fingers. She pulled me round and made me look closer. 'What can you see?' she asked.

'I can't see anything.'

'Look harder.'

'What at?'

Shona pushed her face close to mine and pointed into the jagged hole she'd scraped away at. She pushed her fist into it and pulled out some more dust; it floated away, dancing round us as she scraped.

'It's a weak point,' she said. 'This stuff's millions of years old. I'm sure they have people who check the perimeter and maintain it and stuff, but there's always going to be a bit of it that they miss.'

I pushed my own hand into the hole, scrabbled at it with my fingertips as though I was digging a hole into sand. It felt different from the rest of the wall. Softer. I pushed further.

Scrabbling and scraping, we'd soon scooped all the way up to our shoulders, white dust clouds billowing around us.

'Now what?' I asked.

'Make it wider. Big enough to swim into.'

We worked silently at the hole. The coral didn't glint and glisten with colours once we got inside it. We scraped and scratched in darkness.

Eventually, as my arms were going numb and my whole body was aching and itching from the dust particles swirling all around us, Shona grabbed my arm. I looked up and saw it. The tiniest flicker of light ahead of us.

'We're through,' I gasped.

'Nearly. Come on.'

Filled with hope, I punched my fist deep into the hole, scratching my hand as I pulled at the wall. The hole grew bigger and rounder, eventually large enough to get through. I turned to Shona.

'Go on. You first,' she urged. 'You're smaller than me.'

I scrunched my arms tightly against my body and flicked my tail gently. Then, scratching my arms and tail on the sides, I slid through the hole.

Once on the other side, I turned and carried on scraping so Shona could get through as well. But nothing came away in my hands. No dust. I cut my fingers against jagged rock.

'I can't make it bigger,' I called through the hole.

'Me neither,' Shona replied, her voice echoing inside the dark cavern I'd left behind.

'Try to squeeze through.'

Shona's head came close to the hole. 'It's my shoulders. I'm too big,' she said. 'I'll never manage it.'

'Shall I pull you?'

'I can't do it.' Shona backed away from the gap. 'I'll get stuck – and then you won't be able to get back through.'

'I can't do it without you.' My voice shook as it rippled through the water to her.

'I'll wait here.'

'Promise?'

'I'll wait at the end of the tunnel.'

I took a deep breath. 'This is it then,' I said, poking my head into the opening.

'Good luck.'

'Yeah.' I backed away from the hole again. 'And thanks,' I added. 'For everything. You're the bestest best friend anyone could want.'

Shona's eyes shone brighter in the darkness. '*You* are, you mean.'

There was *no way* I'd been as good a friend as she had. I didn't tell her that, though – didn't want her to change her mind!

Then I turned away from the hole. Leaving the Great Mermer Reef behind me, I swam towards a dark maze of caves covered in sharp, jagged pieces of coral.

'I'm going to see my dad,' I whispered, trying out the unfamiliar thought, and desperately hoping it could be true.

Chapter Fourteen

 swam cautiously away from the reef, glancing nervously around me as I moved ever closer to the
prison. A solitary manta ray slid along the ground,
flapping its fins like a cape. Small packs of moody-
looking fish with open jaws threaded slowly through
the silent darkness, glancing at me as they passed.
Ahead of me, a barrel of thick blackness rotated slowly.
Then suddenly, it parted! Thousands of tiny fish scattered and reformed into two spinning balls. Beyond
them, a dark grey shadow, bigger than me and shaped
like a submarine, moved silently between them.

I held my breath as the shark passed by.

As I drew nearer to the prison, the water grew darker. Dodging between rocks and weeds, I finally reached the prison door. It looked like the wide-open mouth of a gigantic whale, with sharp white teeth filling the gap. In front of the door, two creatures silently glided from side to side. Slow and mean with a beady eye on each side of their mallet-shaped heads. Hammerhead sharks.

I'd *never* get past them. Maybe there was another entrance.

I remembered the note in Dad's file. 'East Wing,' it had said. Shame there wasn't one of those *You are here* signs, like you get in big shopping centres.

I figured I'd been heading west since I'd set off as I'd been chasing the setting sun all the way. We'd turned right to head towards the reef. Which meant I should now be facing north.

I turned right again. In front of me was a long tunnel attached to the main cave. It reminded me of those service stations on the motorway – the bit that joins the two sides together. Apart from the fact that this was made of rock, didn't appear to have any windows and was about fifty feet under the sea. The East Wing?

Swimming carefully from one lump of coral to another and hiding behind every rock I could find, I made it to the tunnel. But there was no entrance. I swam all the way along it, right to the end. Still no opening.

The front gate must be the only way in. I'd come all this way for nothing! There was *no way* I'd get past those sharks.

I started to swim back along the other side of the tunnel. Perhaps there'd be a doorway on this side.

But as I made my way along the slimy walls, I heard a swishing noise behind me. The sharks! Without stopping to think, I flicked my tail and zoomed straight down so I was underneath the tunnel itself. Pressing myself up against the wall, I wrapped a huge piece of seaweed round my body. Two hammerheads sliced past without stopping and I inched my way back up again, scaling the edge with my hands and looking around me all the way. A minute later, I noticed something I hadn't seen earlier. A gap. An oval shape about half my height and slightly wider than my shoulders with three thick, grey bars running down it. They looked like whale bones. The nearest thing I'd found to a way in − it had to be worth a try.

I tugged at the bars. Rock solid. I tried to swim between them. I could get my head through, but my shoulders were too big to follow. This wasn't going to work.

Unless I swam through on my side...

I tried again, coming at the bars sideways on. But it was no good. I couldn't squeeze my face through the gap. I never realised my nose stuck out that much!

I held onto the bars, flicking my tail as I thought. Then it hit me. How could I have been so stupid? I turned to face them. Just like before, I edged my head through the bars, as slowly and carefully as I could. All I needed to do now was flip onto my side and pull the rest of my body through.

But what if I got stuck – my head on one side, my body on the other, caught forever with my neck in these railings?

Before I had time to talk myself out of it, I swivelled my body onto its side. I banged my chin, and my neck rubbed on the bars – but I'd done it! I swished my tail as gently as possible and gradually eased my body through the gap.

I thought back to the time when we were changing to go swimming and how I hadn't wanted anyone to see my skinny body. Maybe being a little weed wasn't such a bad thing, after all.

I rubbed my eyes as I got used to the darkness. I'd landed in a tiny round bubble of a room full of seaweed mops hanging on fish hooks all around me.

I swam to the door and turned a yellow knob. The door creaked open. Which way? The corridor was a long, narrow cave. Closing the door behind me, I noticed a metal plate in the top corner. 'NW: N 874' North Wing? I must have got my calculations wrong!

I swam along the silent corridor, passing closed doors on either side. N 867, N 865. Each one the same. A big round plate of metal, like a submarine door, a brass knob below a tiny round window in the centre. No glass, just fishbone bars dividing each window into an empty game of noughts and crosses.

Should I look?

As I approached the next door, I swished up to the window and peeked in. A merman with a huge hairy stomach and long black hair in a pony tail swam over to the window. 'Can I help you?' he asked, an amused glint in his eye. He had a ship tattooed on his arm; a fat brown tail flickered behind him.

'Sorry!' I flipped myself over and darted away. This was impossible! I wasn't even in the right wing. And there were scary criminals behind those doors! Which was only to be expected, I suppose. This was a prison, after all.

Suddenly, I heard a swooshing noise. Hammer-heads! Coming nearer. I flicked my tail as hard as I could and swam to the end of the corridor. I had to get round the bend before they saw me!

With one last push of my tail, I zoomed round the corner – into an identical tunnel.

Identical except for one thing. The numbers all started with 'E'. The East Wing!

I swam carefully up to the first door. E 924. I tried to remember the number from that note in Mr Beeston's files. Why hadn't I written it down?

An old merman with a beard and a raggedy limp tail was inside the cell, facing away from me. I moved on. E 926, E 928. Would I ever find him?

Just then, two mallet-shaped heads appeared round the corner. I hurled myself up against the next door, frantically twisting the brass knob. To my amazement, it wasn't locked! The door swung open. Banking on the odds that whoever occupied it would be less scary than the sharks, I backed into the room and quietly shut the door. The whooshing noise came past the moment I'd closed it. I leaned my head against the door in relief.

'That was a lucky escape.'

Who said that? I swung round to see a merman sitting on the edge of a bed made of seaweed. He was leaning over a small table, his sparkly purple tail flickering gently.

'What are you doing?' I didn't move from the door.

He put the end of a piece of thread in his mouth and tied a knot in the other end. 'Got to keep myself busy somehow,' he said.

I slunk round the edges of the bubble-shaped room. The thread looked as if it was made of gold. Beads or something on it. Rainbow colours.

'You're making a necklace?'

'Bracelet, actually. Got a problem with that?' The merman looked up for the first time and I backed away instinctively. Don't make fun of criminals whose cells you've just barged into, I told myself. Never a good idea if you're planning to get out again in one piece.

Except he didn't look like a criminal. Not how you

imagine a criminal to look, anyhow. He didn't look mean and hard. And he *was* making jewellery. He had short black hair; kind of wavy, a tiny sleeper in one ear. A white vest with a blue prison jacket over it. His tail sparkled as much as the bracelet. As I looked at him, he ran his hand through his hair. There was something familiar about the way he did it, although I couldn't think what. I twiddled with my hair as I tried to –

I looked harder at him. As he squinted back at me, I noticed a tiny dimple appear. *Below his left eye.*

It couldn't be . . .

The merman put his bracelet down and slithered off his bed. I backed away again as he came towards me. 'I'll scream,' I said.

He stared at me. I stared back.

'How did you find me?' he said, in a different kind of voice from earlier. This one sounded like he had treacle blocking up his throat or something.

I looked into his face. Deep brown eyes. My eyes.

'Dad?' a tiny voice squeaked from over the other side of the cell somewhere.

The merman rubbed his eyes. Then he hit himself on the side of the head. 'Knew it would happen one day,' he said, to himself more than me. 'No one does a stretch in this place without going a little bit crazy.' He turned away from me. 'Dreaming, that's all.'

Then he turned back round. 'Pinch me,' he said, swimming closer. I recoiled a little.

'Pinch me,' he repeated.

I pinched him and he jumped back. 'Youch! Didn't say pull my skin off.' He rubbed his arm before looking up at me again. 'So you're real?' he said.

I nodded.

He swam in a circle around me. 'You're even more beautiful than I'd dreamed,' he said. 'And I've dreamed about you a lot, I can tell you.'

I still couldn't speak.

'Never wanted you to see me in this place.' He swam around his cell, tidying his jewellery things away. He picked some magazines up off the floor and shoved them into a crack in the wall; threw a vest under his bed. 'No place for a young girl.'

Then he swam back, came really close to me; held his hand up to my face and I forced myself not to move.

He cradled the side of my face in his palm, stroked my dimple with his thumb, wiped the tears away as they mingled with the seawater.

'Emily,' he whispered. It *was* him. My dad!

A second later, he was holding me in his strong arms and I clutched him as tightly as I could. 'A mermaid as well,' he murmured into my hair.

'Only some of the time,' I said.

'Figures.'

He loosened his arms and held me away from him. 'Where's your mother?' he asked suddenly. 'Is she here? Is she all right?' He dropped his arms to his sides. 'Has she met someone else?'

I inched closer to him. 'Of course she hasn't met anyone else!'

'My Penny,' he smiled.

'*Penny*?'

'My lucky penny. S'what I always called her. Guess it wasn't too accurate in the end.' Then he smiled. 'But she hasn't forgotten me?'

'Um.' How was I meant to answer that! 'She still loves you.' Well, she did, didn't she? She must do or she wouldn't have been so upset when she remembered everything. 'And she hasn't *really* forgotten you – at least, not any more.'

'Not any more?'

'Listen. I'll tell you everything.' And I did. I told him about the memory drugs and Mr Beeston and about what happened when I took Mum to Rainbow Rocks. And about our journey to the Great Mermer Reef.

'So she's here?' he broke in. 'She's that close?'

I nodded. He flattened his hair down, spun round in circles, swam away from me.

'Dad.' *Dad! I still couldn't get used to that.* 'She's waiting for me. She can't get into the prison.' I followed him over to his table. 'She can't swim,' I added softly.

He burst out laughing as he turned to face me. 'Can't swim? What are you on about? She's the smoothest, sleekest swimmer you could find – excluding mermaids, of course.'

My mum? A smooth, sleek swimmer? I laughed.

'I guess that disappeared along with the memory,' he said sadly. 'We swam all over. She even took sub

167

aqua lessons so she could join me underwater. Went to that old shipwreck. That's where I proposed, you know.'

'She still loves you,' I said again.

'Yeah.' He swam over to the table by his bed. I followed him.

'What's this?' I asked. There was something pinned onto the wall with a fish hook. A poem.

'That's me, that is,' he said miserably.

'"The Forsaken Merman"?' I read. I scanned the lines, not taking any of it in – until I came to one that made me gasp out loud. *A ceiling of amber, a pavement of pearl*.

'But that's, but that's – '

'Yeah, I know. Soppy old stuff, isn't it.'

'No! I know those lines.'

Jake looked up at me. 'You been to that shipwreck yourself, little 'un?'

I nodded. 'Shona took me. My friend. She's a mermaid.'

'And your mother?'

'No – she doesn't even know *I've* been there.'

Jake dropped his head.

'But she knows those lines!' I said.

I pulled the poem off the wall, reading on. 'She left lonely for ever the kings of the sea,' I said out loud.

'That's how it ends,' he said.

'But it's not!'

'Not what?'

'That's not how it ends!'

168

'It does; look here.' Jake swam over, took the poem from me. 'Those are the last lines.'

I snatched it back. 'But that's not how *your* story ends! She never left the king of the sea!'

Jake scratched his head. 'You've lost me now.'

'*The King of the Sea*. That's our boat! That's what it's called.'

His eyes went all misty like Mum's had earlier. 'So it is, love. I remember when we renamed it. I forget what her father had called it before that. But you see —'

'And she could never leave it! She told me that. And now I know why. Because it's you! She could never leave you! You're not the forsaken merman at all!'

Jake laughed. 'You really think so?' Then he pulled me close again. He smelt of salt. His chin was bristly against my forehead.

'Look — you'll need to go soon,' he said, holding me away from him.

'But I've only just found you!'

'Dinner bell rings soon. We need to get you out of here. I don't know how you got your way into this place, little gem, but you sure as sharks don't want to get caught here. Might never get out again.'

'Don't you want me?'

He held my hands and looked deep into my eyes, locking us into a world of our own. 'I want you alive,' he said. 'I want you free, and happy. I don't want you slammed up in some stupid place like this for the rest of your life.'

'I'll never see you again,' I said.

'We'll find a way, little gem.' I liked him calling me that. 'Come on,' he said, looking quickly from side to side. 'We need to get you out of here.' He opened his door and looked down into the corridor.

'How come you can do that?' I asked. 'Aren't you meant to be locked up in here?'

He pointed to a metal tag stapled to the end of his tail.

'Does that hurt?'

'Keeps me in my place. Take it across the threshold,' he pointed at the doorway, 'and I know about it. Like being slammed between two walls.'

'Have you tried it?'

He rubbed his head as though he'd just bashed it. 'Not to be advised, I tell you.'

I giggled. 'Why *have* doors then?'

He shrugged. 'Extra security – they lock 'em at night.' He swam back towards me. 'You understand, don't you?'

'I think so.' I suddenly remembered Mr Beeston's words, how he said my dad ran off because he didn't want to be saddled with a baby. But Mr Beeston had lied about *everything*. Hadn't he?

'What is it, little 'un?'

I looked down at my tail, flicking rapidly from side to side. ' It's not that you didn't want me?' I said.

'*What?*' He swam over to his bed. I'd totally scared him off. I wished I could I take the words back.

He reached under the bed. 'Look at this.' He

pulled a pile of plastic papers out. 'Take a look. Any of them.'

I approached him shyly. 'Go on,' he urged. 'Have a look.' He passed me one. It was a poem. I read it aloud.

'"I never thought I'd see the day,
They'd take my bonny bairn away.
I long-ed for her every day.
Alas, she is so far away.'

'Yeah, well, it was an early one,' he said, pulling at the sleeper in his ear. 'There's better than that in here.'

I couldn't take my eyes off the poem. 'You . . .'

'Yeah, I know. Jewellery, poetry. What next, eh?' He pulled a face.

Before I could say anything else, a bell started ringing. It sounded like the school fire alarm. I clapped my hands over my ears.

'That's it. Dinner. They'll be here soon.' He grabbed me. 'Emily. You have to go.'

'Can I keep it?' I asked.

He folded the poem up and handed it back to me. Then he held my arms tightly. 'I'll find you,' he said roughly. 'One day, I promise.'

He swirled round, picked up the bracelet from his bedside table and quickly tied a knot in it. 'Give this to your mother. Tell her –' he paused. 'Just tell her, no matter what happens, I never stopped loving her and I never will. Ever. You hear me?'

I nodded, my throat too clogged up to speak. He hugged me one last time before swirling round again. 'Hang on.' He pulled the poem off his wall and handed it to me. 'Give her this as well. Tell her – tell her to keep it till we're together again. Tell her never to forsake me.'

'She won't, Dad. Neither of us will. Ever.'

'I'll find you,' he said again, his voice croaky. 'Now go.' He pushed me through the door. 'Quickly. And be careful.'

I edged down into the corridor and held his eyes for a second. 'See you, Dad,' I whispered. Then he closed the door and was gone.

I wavered for a moment in the empty corridor. The bell was still shrieking – even louder outside the cell. I covered my ears, flicked my tail and got moving. Back along the corridors, into the cleaning cupboard, through the tiny hole, out across the murky darkness, until I found the tunnel again.

Shona was waiting at the end of it, just like she'd said she would be. We fell into each other's arms and laughed as we hugged each other. 'I was so worried,' she said. 'You were gone ages.'

'I found him,' I said, simply.

'Swishy!' she breathed.

'Tell you all about it on the way. Come on.' I was desperate to see Mum. I couldn't wait to see her face when I gave her Dad's presents.

'So tell me again,' Mum twirled her new bracelet round and round on her wrist, watching the colours blur and merge, then refocus and change again, while Millie looked on jealously. 'What did he say, exactly?'

'Mum, I've told you three times already.'

'Just once more, darling. Then that's it.'

I sighed. 'He says he's always loved you and he always will. And he had stacks of poems that he'd written.'

She clutched her poem more tightly. 'About me?'

I thought of the one in my pocket. 'Well, yeah. Mostly.'

Mum smiled in a way I'd never seen before. I laughed. She was acting just like the women in those horrible, gooey romantic films that she loves.

'Mum, we have to see him again,' I said.

'He's never stopped loving me and he never will,' she replied dreamily. Millie raised her eyebrows.

A second later, a huge splash took the smile off her face. We ran outside.

'Trying to get one over me?' Mr Beeston! In the water! How did he get past us? 'After everything I've done for you,' he called, swimming rapidly away from us as he spoke.

'What are you going to do?' I shouted.

'I warned you,' he shouted, paddling backwards. 'I won't let you get away with it.' Then in a quiet voice, his words almost washed away by the waves, he added, 'I'm sorry it had to end like this, Mary P. I'll always remember the good times.'

And then he turned and swam towards the Great Mermer Reef. Mum and I looked at each other. Good times?

Millie cleared her throat. 'It's all my fault,' she said quietly.

Mum turned to Millie. 'What?'

'I loosened the ropes.' Millie pulled her shawl around her. 'Only a tiny bit. He said they were hurting.'

Mum sighed and shook her head. 'All right, don't worry, Millie,' she said. 'Nothing we can do now, is there?'

As we watched Mr Beeston swim off into the distance, Shona appeared in the water below us. 'What's up?' she called. 'Thought I heard something going on.'

'It's Mr Beeston,' I said. 'He's gone!'

'Escaped?'

'He went over there.' I pointed towards the prison. 'I think he's up to something.'

'Should we go after him?'

'You're not going back there!' Mum said. 'Not now. It's too dangerous.'

'What, then?' I asked. 'How will we get back? We've no fuel, the sail's broken. Shona can't tow us all the way back to the harbour.'

'Radio the coastguard?' Mum said.

'Mum, the radio's been broken for *years*. You always said you'd get it fixed at some point – '

'. . . But I kept forgetting,' Mum finished my sentence with a sigh.

'We could always meditate on it,' Millie offered. 'See if the answer comes to us.'

Mum and I both glared silently at her. Ten seconds later, the decision was taken out of our hands. A loud voice wobbled up from below the surface of the sea. 'You are surrounded,' it gurgled. 'You must give yourselves up. Do not try to resist.'

'Who are you?' I shouted. 'I'm not afraid of –'

'Emily!' Mum gripped my arm.

The voice spoke again. 'You are outnumbered. Do not underestimate the power of Neptune.'

Before I could think about what to say next, four mermen in prison guard uniforms appeared on the surface of the water. Each one had an upside-down octopus on his back. In perfect formation, they leapt from the water, their tails spinning like whirlpools. They flipped on their sides, the octopus legs swirling above their backs like rotary blades, and headed towards us. Between them, they plucked Millie, Mum and me from the deck, spun themselves round and held us under their arms as they plopped back into the water.

'I can't swim,' Mum yelped.

For an answer, she was dragged silently under the water. Gulping and gasping, we were shoved roughly into a weird tube-thing. My legs starting turning into a tail straight away – but, for once, I hardly noticed.

We slid along the tube, landing on a bouncy floor. The entrance we'd slipped through instantly closed, leaving us staring at the inside of a white, rubbery bubble. Two masks hung from the ceiling. They looked like the things they show you when you go on a plane.

I grabbed hold of them and helped Mum and Millie put them on. Then we sat in silence as we bumped along through the water. Millie pulled some worry beads out of her pocket and twirled them furiously round her fingers.

Mum clutched my fingers, holding them so tight it hurt.

'We'll be fine,' I said, putting my arm round her. Then in an uncertain whisper, I added, 'I'm sure we will.'

Chapter Fifteen

*T*he good news – they didn't keep us in that tiny, wobbly cage forever. The bad news – they separated us and threw us each into an even tinier one. This time, it was more like a box. Five small tail spans from side to side and a bed of seaweed along one edge. It was all Mr Beeston's fault. How could he have done this to us?

I sat on my bed and counted the limpets on the rocky wall. Then I counted the weeds hanging down from the ceiling. I looked around for something else to count. Just my miserable thoughts. There were plenty of them.

A guard swam in with a bowl of something that looked nothing like food but which I suspected was my dinner.

'What are you going to do with –'

He shoved the bowl into my hands and disappeared without answering.

'It's not fair!' I shouted at the door. 'I haven't done anything!'

I examined the contents of the bowl. It looked like snail sick. Green, slimy trails of rubbery goo spread on top of something flaky and yellow that looked suspiciously like sawdust. Gross. I pushed the bowl away and started counting the seconds. How many of them would I spend in here?

The next thing I knew, I was lying on my side on my horrible bed. Someone was shaking me and I slipped about on the seaweed.

'Mum?' I jumped up. It wasn't Mum. A guard lifted me up by my elbows. 'Where are you taking me?' I asked as he clipped a handcuff onto my wrist and fastened the other one onto his own.

But of course he didn't answer. Just pulled me out of the cell and slammed the door behind us.

'Strong, silent type, are you?' I quipped nervously as we swam down long, tunnel-like corridors and round curvy corners and down more long corridors. We soon arrived at a mouth-like entrance with shark teeth across it like the prison door.

The guard knocked twice against one of the teeth and the jaw opened wider. He pushed me forward.

Once inside, another guard swam towards us. I was attached to a different-but-similar wrist and whisked along a different-but-similar set of corridors.

And then I was thrown into a different-but-similar cell.

Brilliant.

I'd only got as far as counting the limpets when they came back for me this time. And this journey took us somewhere different-but-different. *Very* different.

We reached the end of another long corridor. When the guard pushed me through the door, there were no more tunnels. I was looking out at the open sea again. For a moment, I thought he was setting me free. Except I was still attached to his wrist.

The sea grew lighter and warmer. Something was coming into view. Colour – and light. Not dancing and jumping about like the Great Mermer Reef, but shimmering and sparkling from the depths of the sea. As we drew closer, the lights emerged into a shape. Like a big house. A huge house! Two marble pillars so tall they seemed to reach from the seabed to the surface stood on either side of an arched gateway, a golden seahorse on a plinth in front of each pillar. Jewels and crystals glinted all the way across the arch.

'In there.' The guard gestured towards the closed doorway, nodding at two mermen stationed on either side. They both had a gold stripe down one side of their tails. As the mermen moved apart, the gates slowly opened.

We swam towards the arch. Long trails of shells dangled from silver threads above us, clinking with the movement of the water.

'What is this place?' I asked as we swam inside. We were in some sort of lobby; the sort they have in really posh hotels. Only even posher. And kind of dome-shaped.

Chandeliers made from glassy crystals hung from the ceiling, splashing mini rainbows around the walls. In the centre of the room, a tiny volcano shot out clouds of bright green light – an underwater fountain. The light flowed over the top of the rocky cauldron, bubbling and frothing and turning blue as it melted onto the floor.

'Don't you know anything?' the guard grunted. 'This is Neptune's palace.' He pushed me forward.

Neptune's palace! What were we doing *here*? I thought about all the things Shona had told me about him. What was he going to do to me? Would he turn me to stone?

We swam across the lobby. Two mermen with long black tails passed us, talking hurriedly as they swam. A mermaid looked up from behind a gold pillar as we came to the back of the lobby. Reaching into his tail, the guard pulled out a card. The mermaid nodded briskly and moved aside. There was a hole in the wall behind her.

'Up there.' The guard swam into the hole, pulling me along. Round and round, spiralling upwards through tubes, we climbed the upside down helter-skelter till we came to a trap door. The guard opened it with one push and nudged me through.

We came out into a rectangular room with glass walls. A giant fish tank – except the fish were on the outside! All brightly coloured yellows and blues, darting about, looking in as the guard led me to a line of rocks along one edge and told me to sit down. A notice in front of my row had a word written in capital letters: 'ACCUSED'.

Accused? Me? What had I *done?*

In front of me, there were rows of coral seats. Mer-people were dotted about, dressed in suits.

One wore a jacket made of gold reeds with a trident on his chest. I watched him flick through files, talking all the time to a mermaid by his side. A merman on the row behind them in a black suit was whispering frantically to a mermaid next to him as he, too, shuffled through files.

What was going on? *Why was I here?*

At the front, a mermaid facing the court sat at a coral desk examining her nails. Behind her was a low crystal table – and behind that, the most amazing throne: all in gold, the back of the seat tapered upwards into three prongs filled with pearls and coral, downwards into a solid gold block. The round seat was marble, with blue ripples carved outwards from the centre to the edges. A golden seahorse on either side of the throne: each arm a seahorse body, each leg its tail, stretching downwards and curling into a mass of diamonds at its base.

The throne towered over the court – powerful and scary, even when it was empty!

Every now and then, the mermaid in front of the throne rearranged the items on her desk. She had a row of reeds in a line across the top edge, with some plastic papers beside them. On top of these, a sign saying 'Clerk'. A huge pile of files was balanced in one corner. In the other, a grumpy-looking squid sat with its tentacles folded into a complicated knot.

She kept glancing backwards at a gateway behind the throne. Gold and arched and covered with jewels, like the palace entrance. The gates within it were closed.

A splashing noise opposite me drew my eyes away from the front of the court. Two guards were opening a door in the ceiling; they had someone in between them.

Mum! The guards unhooked a mask from the ceiling, like the ones she and Millie had when we were captured. Mum clumsily strapped it over her face, a tube leading from her mouth up through the top of the box.

She looked round the court with frightened eyes. Then she noticed me and her face brightened a tiny bit. She tried to smile through her mask and I tried to smile back.

What were we doing here?

Outside the fish tank, a row of assorted merpeople were taking their seats. A portly mermaid undid a velvety eel from round her neck as she sat down. She made the others all move up so she could have a seat for an enormous jewel-encrusted crab.

Another huddle of merpeople with notebooks and tape machines chatted to each other as they sat down. Reporters. Along the back of the court, a line of sea-horses stood in a silent row. They looked like soldiers.

Then a hush fell on the room as a sound of thunder rumbled towards us.

As the noise grew louder, the water started swishing about. The clerk grabbed her table, people reached out to grip the ledges in front of them. *What was happening?* I glanced round as I held onto the coral shelf. No one else looked worried.

The waves grew heavier, the thunder louder, until the gates at the front of the court suddenly opened. A fleet of dolphins washed into the room – a gold chariot behind them, filled with jewels and crystals. The chariot carried a merman into the room. At least seven feet tall, he had a white beard that stretched down to his chest and a tail that looked as if it was studded with diamonds. It shot silver rays across the room as the merman climbed out of the chariot. Sweeping his long tail under him, he slid into the throne. In his hand, a gold trident.

Neptune! Right in front of me! In real life!

A sharp rap of the trident on the floor and the dolphins swiftly left the courtroom, whisking Neptune's chariot away. Another rap and the gates closed behind them. A third, the water instantly stopped moving. I fell back on my seat, thrown by the sudden calm.

'U–U–P!' a voice bellowed from the front.

Neptune was pointing his trident at me! I leapt back up, praying silently that I hadn't just doubled whatever sentence I was about to get.

He leaned forward to talk to the clerk, gesturing towards me. The clerk looked up at me too, then picked up one of her reeds. Poking the squid with the reed, she wrote something down in black ink. The squid shuffled grumpily on the edge of the desk and refolded its tentacles.

Eventually, Neptune turned back to the court-room. He stared angrily around. Then, with another rap of his trident, he shouted, 'DOWN!'

Everyone took their seats again as the seahorses at the back split into two rows and swam to the front of the court. They formed a line on either side of Neptune.

The merman in the gold jacket stood up. He bowed low.

'APPROACH!' Neptune bellowed.

The merman swam towards him. Then he ducked down and kissed the base of Neptune's tail. 'If it please Your Majesty, I would like to outline the prosecuting case,' he began, straightening himself up. Neptune nodded sharply. 'On with it!'

'Your Majesty, you see before you a mermaid and a . . . *human*.' He screwed up his face as he said the word, as though it made him feel sick. Pulling at his collar, he continued. 'The pair of them have colluded and connived, they have planned and plotted –'

'How DARE you waste my time!' Neptune shouted. He lifted his trident. 'FACTS!'

'Directly, Your Majesty, directly.' The merman shuffled through a few more files and cleared his throat. 'The child before you today has forced an entry into our prison, damaged a section of the Great Mermer Reef in the process – and assaulted one of your own advisors.'

'AND? Is there more?' Neptune's face had turned red.

'It's all in here, Your Majesty.' The merman handed a file to Neptune, who snatched it and handed it to the clerk without looking at it.

The merman cleared his throat again. 'As for the *human*,' he forced the word out, 'the same charges apply.'

Neptune nodded curtly. 'Once again, Mr Slipreed, will that be ALL?'

'Absolutely, Your Majesty.' The merman bowed again as he spoke. 'If I could allude to one outstanding area of this case . . . ' Neptune clenched his fist around his trident. The merman spoke quickly. 'In apprehending the accused, a merchild, acting with the help of another *human* –' he cleared his throat and swallowed loudly – 'was discovered in the vicinity.'

Millie and Shona! I slapped my hand over my mouth to stop me gasping out loud.

'Both merchild and the other are being held awaiting instructions from the court.'

'From the COURT, Slipreed? ANY old court is that?'

'Your Majesty, they await your divine ruling.'

'THANK you Mr Slipreed!' Neptune boomed.

'If I may now call upon my first witness . . . Mr Charles Finright Beeston.'

As Mr Beeston entered the court, I folded my arms. I tried to cross my legs, but remembered they were a tail so I couldn't. He looked different, somehow. As he swam towards Neptune, I realised what it was. I'd never seen him as a merman before!

Mr Beeston bowed low and kissed Neptune's tail. He avoided looking at me or Mum. 'If I may refer to my notes . . . ' A line of bubbles escaped from his mouth and floated up through the water as he spoke.

To your lies, you mean, I said to myself.

'Your Majesty, I was last night tricked into a rescue operation involving a yacht and a small motor boat. I was beaten around the head with a mast and tied up while the accused' – he looked quickly at Mum, then at me. Suddenly breaking his flow for a moment, he looked away again and coughed quietly before continuing. 'Before they carried out their unlawful plans. Thankfully, the accused were amateurs and not equipped to deal with a high ranking professional such as myself.' He paused and turned towards Neptune.

'BEESTON – do not presume to look to me for compliments! CONTINUE!'

Mr Beeston's face reddened. 'Of course, Your Majesty. And so, I disembarked and sought the strong fin of the law.'

'You swam for the guards?'

'Indeed I did, Your Majesty.'

'Thank you.' Neptune banged his trident on the floor. 'DEFENCE!' he bellowed. 'Mr Thinscale? Your first witness?'

The merman in the black suit jumped up. 'Thank you, Your Majesty.'

I looked round the court, wondering who his first witness was going to be. 'Get up,' the guard next to me grunted. 'You're on.' Then he pulled me out of my seat and pointed towards the throne. I swam nervously towards Neptune. Taking my cue from the others, I bent to kiss his diamond-studded tail.

Neptune pulled on his beard and leaned down. 'You understand the charges?' he asked, in a slightly quieter voice.

'I think so.'

'Speak, then!' he snapped. 'Do you HAVE anything to say in your defence?'

'Well, I –' I stopped and looked round the courtroom, and at the merpeople watching on all sides. Some were staring at me. Others were talking quietly or laughing. At me, probably. My tail turned to jelly and I was about to say, 'No,' when I caught Mum's eyes. She removed her mask for a second and forced herself to smile.

'Do not make me wait,' Neptune growled.

That was when I realised what I had to do.

'Um sir, Mr –'

'Do I LOOK like a "*Sir*"? A "*Mr*"? Do I?'

I flicked my tail a little, propelling me higher than my one metre fifty, and looked nervously round at the courtroom. 'Your Majesty,' I corrected myself. 'I know this might sound weird, but, well, it's actually kind of nice to be here.'

A murmur flickered through the room and along the rows outside it. The reporters scribbled furiously on their pads.

'"Nice," did she say?' I heard someone ask.

'Is she being sarcastic?' another one replied.

'It's what I've always wanted,' I added quickly. 'Not being in court about to get locked up for the rest of my life, obviously. But being here. With all of you. It feels right.'

I glanced at Mum. 'I mean, I know I'm part human, and my mum's brilliant. She raised me all on her own and everything. But my dad's brilliant, too. Not just because he's a merman, so I get to be part mermaid.' I paused and looked Neptune in the eyes. 'That's absolutely wicked,' I said.

Neptune leaned forward. He scowled, narrowing his eyes at me.

'I mean, it's fantastic – it's swishy! But more than anything, I'm proud of him because of his belief in love.' I pulled the poem he'd written out of my pocket and held it out. 'My dad might have been locked away but his feelings weren't.'

I glanced at Neptune. A tic was beating in his cheek, a glare shone in his eyes, but his body had softened a little; the grasp on his trident had loosened. 'You can't make people stop loving each other just because a law says it's wrong,' I said.

The posh mermaid with the pet crab wiped her eel across her cheek. Another took a hanky out of her coat pocket. A few merpeople were nodding. I heard someone at the back say, 'She's got a point, you know.'

Neptune let out a thunderous sigh and a huge mock yawn.

'My dad fell in love. So what? What did *I* do to deserve to grow up without a father?'

Tutting noises were spreading through the spectators' seats. A couple of them shook their heads.

'I wanted to see my dad, that's all. Is that so wrong?' I paused and looked at Mum. 'If it really is so terrible, if love is such a horrible crime, then fine, lock me up. Lock my mum up, too.' I turned back to Neptune. 'Your Majesty. That merman' – I pointed to the first one who'd spoken – 'he wants us imprisoned because of laws that were written centuries ago. Things have changed. Humans aren't all bad, you know.'

As I looked round the courtroom, I paused on Mr Beeston's face. Neptune remained silent. 'Hey, even one of your top advisers had one for a father,' I said. Mr Beeston lowered his eyes as people turned to look at him. 'If it can produce such loyal, devoted merfolk as Mr Beeston, can it really be so wrong?'

I let my question hang in the air for a moment, before turning back to Neptune. I couldn't think of anything else to say. 'I only wanted to see my dad,' I said finally.

Neptune held my eyes for a few seconds. Then he banged his trident on the floor. 'I will NOT be told my laws are wrong! How DARE you presume!'

He got up from his throne, banging his trident again. Everyone instantly rose to their tails.

The gates behind him opened. His chariot was waiting outside. 'Court will adjourn,' he barked as the dolphins swam into the courtroom. Then he leapt into his chariot and swept out of the court.

I slumped back on my rock and waited to hear my fate.

Chapter Sixteen

*N*o one spoke for the first few minutes. Then, gradually, everyone started whispering quietly to each other, like at the doctor's when you have to act like it's a crime to talk. Maybe it was, here. Everything else was, it seemed.

I returned to my seat and looked up nervously to see if I could catch Mum's eye. She was sitting with her head in her hands. Was she cross with me?

We sat like that for ages, the court almost silent while we waited. Some people left; a few took out lunchboxes and munched on seaweed sandwiches.

Then the gates at the front of the court opened. Neptune was coming back in. Everyone leapt up.

Neptune waved us down impatiently with his trident.

He waited for the court to be absolutely silent before he spoke.

'Emily Windsnap.' He looked at me and indicated sharply for me to get up. I flicked my tail and stood as straight as possible. He looked at Mum and pointed upwards again. 'Mary Penelope Windsnap,' he read from the card in front of him and Mum stood up. 'You have both defied ME, and MY laws!'

I swallowed hard.

'My kingdom has held by these laws very well for many generations. *I* invent them; *you* abide by them. That's how it works!'

I tried to get used to the idea of living in a cell with a bed of seaweed and limpets on the wall.

'Do you DARE say I am wrong? ' he continued, his voice rising with every word. 'Do you think you know better than ME? You do NOT!'

He leaned forwards to stare at me. What would I get? Ten years? Twenty? Life?

He paused for ages. When he spoke again, a gentleness had fought its way into his voice. He spoke so quietly I had to hold my breath to hear him.

'However. . . ' he said, then stopped. He stroked his beard. 'However,' he repeated, 'you have touched on something today. Something beyond laws.' His voice softened even more. 'And therefore, beyond punishment.'

I held my breath as he paused, tapping the side of his trident.

'You will both be released!' he boomed eventually.

A gasp went through the court, followed by a stream of murmuring. Neptune lifted his trident and glared round the room. The chattering stopped instantly.

'You defied my laws,' he went on. 'But why? Shall I pretend I do not understand? Or that I have never felt that way? NO! I am no hypocrite! And I shall NOT punish you for love. I shall NOT! Mrs Windsnap.' He turned to Mum. A long deep sigh, his breath rumbling out from his throat. Then – 'Your husband is also to be released.'

Another gasp whizzed through the court.

'On one condition,' he continued. 'The three of you will join a community on an island with a secret location. This will be your home from now on. If you break this condition, you will be punished most severely. Do you understand?'

He stared at us both. I nodded vigorously. Had I heard right? Was I *really* going to see my dad again?

The gold-jacketed merman suddenly rose from his seat. 'Your Majesty, forgive me,' he said, bowing low. 'But the other merchild? You know, there could be trouble if –'

'Just get them all out from under my tail,' Neptune barked. 'She can join them, for all I care. Discuss it with her parents. Either that or a memory wipe.'

'Very well, Your Majesty.' He sat down again.

Neptune scanned the court. 'And perhaps you can all tell your kinfolk that your king is not only a firm ruler, but also a just and compassionate one.' His eyes landed on me. 'One who will no longer punish folk merely for loving.'

Then he got up from his throne, banged his trident on the floor. 'Case closed,' he bellowed and left the court.

It all happened so quickly after that. The room erupted in noise. People were clapping and cheering; others gossiped among themselves. A few came over to the dock to shake my hand.

'Can I go now?' I asked the guard. He nodded curtly and pointed to the exit as he undid my hand-cuffs.

Outside the court, a mermaid with her hair in a bun took my hand. 'Your mum will be escorted sep-arately; she'll meet you in a bit,' she said. 'Let's have you out of here.'

'Who are –' I began but she'd turned round and was pulling me towards a boat that looked like a cross between a limousine and a submarine. White and long, with gold handles on the doors.

A crowd was waiting by the boat. 'Emily, can you tell me how you feel?' one of them asked, a black reed poised above her notebook. I recognised her as one of the reporters from the court.

'Emily doesn't want to talk at the moment,' the mermaid said. 'She has to –'

'I feel great,' I said. 'I just can't wait to see my mum and dad together.'

'Thanks Emily.' The reporter scribbled furiously as I was bundled into the boat. There was someone else inside.

'Shona!'

'Emily!'

We hugged each other tight.

'We're going to an island!' I said. 'My dad's coming!'

'Seatbelts,' the mermaid instructed from the driver's seat. Then we shot forwards like a bullet. As we sped through the water, I told Shona everything that had happened. 'And they said you might be able to come, too!' I finished off. I didn't mention the other option. Surely her parents would agree?

'Swishy!' Shona laughed.

'Going up,' the mermaid called from the front as we tipped upwards, gradually climbing until we came to a standstill. Then she opened a door in the ceiling. 'Your stop,' she said to me, holding out her hand. I shook it, feeling rather stupid. 'Good luck, Emily,' she said. 'You're a brave girl.'

'See you soon,' Shona giggled and we hugged each other before I climbed out. I stood on the top of the boat.

Blinking in the daylight, I tried to adjust to the scene. *King* was moored just in front of me. A group of mermen waited in the water in front of it, holding on to two thick ropes. Mum was leaning right over the side, reaching down to someone in the sea. She was holding his hands.

I stood on tiptoe so I could see who it was. For a moment, I thought I must be imagining it. It couldn't have happened this quickly, surely! A mop of black hair, sticking up where it was wet, a pair of deep brown eyes. Then he noticed me and the dimple below his left eye deepened as he let go of Mum's hands and swam towards me.

'Dad!' Without thinking, I jumped into the sea – and into his arms.

'My little gem,' he whispered as he hugged me tight. Then he took my hand and we swam back to the side of the boat together. Mum reached down with both arms and we held each other's hands: a circle; a family.

A second later, a series of splashes and shouting exploded behind us. A bunch of reporters were heading our way.

'Mr Windsnap.' One of them shoved a microphone shaped like a huge mushroom in my dad's face. 'Simon Watermark, Radio Merwave. You've melted Neptune's heart. How does it feel to have made history?'

'Made history?' Dad laughed. 'At the moment, my only feelings about history are that I want to go back twelve years and catch up with my wife and daughter.'

The reporter turned to Mum. 'Mrs Windsnap, is it true that your babysitter helped with your plan?'

That was when I noticed Millie sitting on a plastic chair at the front of the boat. One of the mermen was perched on the deck opposite her, his tail dangling over the side, the pair of them frowning at a pack of tarot cards spread out between them.

'We couldn't have done it without her,' Mum said.

The reporter turned to me. 'Emily. You're a brave girl to do what you did. You must have had some help along the way. Is there anyone you'd like to say a special thank you to?'

'Well, I'd like to thank my mum for being so understanding. I'd like to thank my dad for waiting for us.' He kissed my cheek. 'And Millie for falling asleep at the right time.'

The reporter laughed.

'And I'd like to thank Shona. My best friend. I could never have done this without her.'

Out of the corner of my eye, I saw a familiar figure. Merpeople were talking and laughing in groups all around us, but he was on his own. He looked up and smiled a shaky, crooked smile at me, his head tilted in what looked like an apology.

And I forgave him.

Almost.

There was just one thing he could do for me first.

He jumped a little as I swam over to him. I whispered my favour in his ear.

'A mass memory wipe?' he blurted out. 'That's ridiculous – not to mention dangerous.'

'Please, Mr Beeston,' I begged. 'Think about all

the nice things I said in there. After everything that's happened, I should hate you forever. But I won't. Not if you do this one little thing for me.'

He looked at me hard. What did he see? A girl he'd known all her life? Someone he perhaps cared about, just a tiny little bit?

'Very well,' he said eventually. 'I'll do it.'

I kept my head down as we stood by the side of the pool. Everyone around me chatted in groups. Julie was with Mandy, giggling together in the corner. Fine. I didn't need Julie. I had Shona and no one could be a better best friend than her.

My heart thumped in my ears, blocking out everything else.

Bob arrived. I stepped forward, put my hand up. 'Please, sir – I'd like to show you something.'

Bob frowned.

'I've been practising.'

He waved a hand out. 'All right then,' he said with half a smile. 'Let's have it.'

I stepped towards the edge of the pool.

'Look at *fish girl*,' Mandy sneered from the corner. 'Showing off again.'

'That's right,' I said, looking her right in the eyes. 'Fish girl is showing off.'

I glanced up to the window. Too high. I couldn't see out, but I knew he'd be out there. He promised.

I had five minutes. Five minutes to be proud instead of scared. Five minutes to be free, to be myself. But mostly, I had five minutes to give Mandy Rushton the biggest shock of her life!

And so I dived in. Piercing the surface as gently as I could, I swam underwater all the way to the opposite end of the pool.

'Big deal!' Mandy snorted. 'So fish girl can do a length underwater. Whoopedee do!'

As she mocked me, something was happening under the water. My tail was starting to form. The familiar feeling filled me with confidence. This was it!

I dived straight down. And then, I flicked my tail up in the air. Spinning round and round under the water, I could feel my tail swirling and dancing, faster and faster. I couldn't wait to see Mandy's face!

I swam up to the surface, wiped my hair off my face and looked across. Thirty open mouths. Total silence. If they'd been playing musical statues, it would have been a dead heat.

Mandy was the first to step forward. 'But – but – ' she sputtered. 'But that's a – how did you –'

I laughed. 'Hey, guess what, Mandy? I'm not scared of you – and I don't care what you call me. You can't stop me being who I am. And you don't get to bully me any more, because I'm leaving. I'm off to a desert island, with a whole bunch of – '

A loud rap on the door stopped me saying any more.

Bob walked over to it in a daze. Mr Beeston. Right on time. He spoke quietly to Bob. 'Of course,' Bob said, his voice flat and mechanical. 'I'd forgotten. Come on in.'

He turned to the class. 'Right, folks, we have a visitor today. He's come to give us a special talk.'

Mr Beeston stood in front of the class, a large bag in his hand. 'Now then, children,' he said. 'Listen carefully. I'm going to teach you about lighthouses – and the dangers of the sea.'

He opened the bag. 'But before we start, let's all have an iced bun . . .'

I slipped quietly out of the pool as Mr Beeston held everyone's attention. It was almost as if I'd been forgotten. I would be soon!

'Thank you,' I mouthed as I passed behind the class. He nodded solemnly in reply.

I crept away from the pool, changed quickly and slipped outside. Looking back at the building, I smiled.

'Bye 7C,' I whispered. Then I turned and walked away.

We left that night. Mum, Dad and me, off to a whole new world where who knew what was waiting for us. All I knew for sure was that my life as a mermaid had only just begun.

But remember, it's just between you and me.

Emily Windsnap and the Monster from the Deep

Decorations by Sarah Gibb

For Hannah, Barney, Katie
. . . and Mum

Below the thunders of the upper deep;
Far far beneath in the abysmal sea,
His ancient, dreamless, uninvaded sleep
The Kraken sleepeth . . .

From 'The Kraken'
by Alfred, Lord Tennyson

Allpoints Island
Barracuda Point
Strong currents
North Bay
Double Arch Bay
Kraken's Cave
Grand Caves
Lagoon
Emerald Caves

Chapter One

*C*lose your eyes.

Think of the most beautiful place you can imagine.

Are you seeing golden beaches? Gorgeous clear blue sea? Perfect sky? Keep your eyes closed.

Now multiply it by about a hundred and you're halfway to picturing what my new home was like. The softest, whitest sand, palm trees that reached lazily out from the beaches, tall rocky arches cusping the bays, sea that sparkled like crystals in the sunlight. All thanks to Neptune.

He'd sent me here with my mum and dad to start a

new life. Somewhere we could live together. Somewhere my secret would be safe.

One of Neptune's guards, Archieval, accompanied
us here. He's a merman. He swam beside our little
sailing boat all the way, swishing his long black hair
behind him and occasionally ducking under, flicking
his tail in the air, silver and sharp, like a dagger.

We edged slowly into a horseshoe-shaped bay filled
with shiny turquoise water. Soft foamy waves gently
stroked the white sand. A few boats were dotted
about in the bay, half sunken, silently sloping. Some
were modern yachts, others great wooden craft that
looked like ancient pirate ships.

A tall rocky arch marked the end of the bay.
Through it, the sand and sea continued round a
corner. I caught my breath as I stood and stared.

'Shake a tail, someone,' Archieval called up. 'I could
use some help here.'

I leaned across to help him pull the boat up alongside a wooden jetty as Dad swam round to the back
and tied the ropes to a buoy. Mum was still inside
with Millie. That's her friend from Brightport. She
used to read fortunes on the pier. She did a tarot
reading for Archieval before we left and he liked it so
much he invited her to come with us.

She said she'd have to let the cards decide, so she set

the pack out in a star shape and sat looking at it in silence for about ten minutes, nodding slowly.

'Well, it's obvious what I have to do. You'll never catch me ignoring a call from the ten of cups,' she said enigmatically before throwing her black cape over her shoulder and going home to pack her things. She says everything enigmatically, Millie does. I've learned to just nod and look as though I know what she's on about.

Archieval swam round to the side of the boat. 'This is it then,' he said. 'North Bay, Allpoints Island.'

'Why's it called Allpoints Island?' I asked.

'It's right in the centre of the Triangle.' He stretched out an arm as he spun slowly round in a circle. 'Where the three points meet.'

The Bermuda Triangle. I shivered. He'd told us about it on the way here, about the boats and planes that had mysteriously disappeared inside it. An ocean liner had been found totally intact but utterly deserted. Twenty tables were set out for dinner. Another ship was found with skeletons on the decks, its sails ripped to shreds all around them. Others had vanished without trace, often after frantic mayday calls from pilots and fishermen who were never seen again.

I didn't know whether to believe the stories at first, but something had happened out at sea. We'd been sailing along normally, the swell rising and falling, the boat gently making its way though the peaks and troughs. Then it changed. The water went all glassy. The engine cut out, everything died. Even my watch stopped working. It felt as if the sea had frozen, almost as if time itself had frozen.

Then Archieval yanked his long hair into a pony-tail with some string and disappeared under the water. A few minutes later, we got moving again, gliding silently across the glassy sea.

'That was it,' he called up. 'Bermuda Triangle. That's what'll protect you from the outside world now. No one knows how to get through it except for a few chosen merfolk.' He threw a rope onto the deck. 'Well, a few chosen merfolk and . . . no, I'd better not tell you about that.'

'What? Tell me.'

Dad turned up then. 'I hope you're not filling my daughter's head with any more of your lurid tales, Archie,' he warned him. 'She has enough nightmares as it is.'

Archie lowered his voice. 'Just be careful,' he said. 'That glassy plane marks out the Triangle, but it's only like that on the surface. It's a raging torrent below: a huge well leading down to the deepest depths of the ocean. And you don't want to go disappearing down a hole like that.'

I rubbed at the goosepimples crawling up my arms.

We'd sailed on calmly after that, slipping through water that grew clearer and lighter every moment, melting from deep navy to a soft baby blue.

Gradually, the island came into view. It was quite

small, perhaps only a few miles across: a tall cliff at one end, a couple of lower peaks at the other and a low, flat stretch in between. As we drew closer, I could see the coastline was made up of long white bays fringed with tall palm trees and clusters of rocks and arches. It looked like a postcard. I'd always thought those pictures must be made up, somehow, and that when you got there, you'd just find a clump of high-rise apartments next to a building site.

But it was real. And it was my new home.

'Where's your dad?' Mum joined me on the deck, straightening her skirt and bending down to check her reflection in a metal railing.

I pointed ahead. 'Helping Archie.'

Mum looked slowly round the bay. 'I think I've died and gone to heaven,' she murmured as she grabbed the railing. 'Someone's going to have to pinch me.'

'I'll do it!' Dad's head poked out of the water, a glint in his eyes as he wiped floppy wet hair off his forehead. Mum smiled back at him.

A second later, the side doors crashed open and Millie clambered out. 'Tell you something,' she said, rubbing her large stomach. 'That Slippery Elm mixture works wonders on the seasickness.' She covered her mouth as she hiccupped. 'Especially washed down with a spot of brandy. Now, where are we?'

She squinted into the sunlight. 'That's it!' she said, pointing across at a wooden ship lying on a slant in the bay. It had three tall masts, polished pine railings and a name printed on the side: *Fortuna*.

'That's what?' I asked.

'Your new home. Archie told me.'

I looked at Mum. 'What's wrong with *King of the Sea*?' That's what our boat's called. I've lived on it with Mum all my life.

Millie pinched my cheek as she squeezed past me. 'Well, your dad can't live with you on a regular boat, can he now? Don't worry. I'll look after the place for you.'

Dad swam round to the side, staring across at *Fortuna*. 'Flipping fins! Bit different from where I've spent the last twelve years,' he said as he reached up to help Mum off the boat. Dad was in prison before we came here. He's not a criminal or anything. Well, he broke the law but it was a stupid law. He married a human. That's my mum. He's a merman. Makes it a bit difficult when she can't swim and he can't go on land, but they manage, somehow. She used to be a brilliant swimmer till she was hypnotised into being afraid of water. Neptune did that, to keep them apart. She's still nervous about it now, but Dad said he's going to teach her again.

Mum hitched up her skirt and stepped across onto the jetty. It led all the way out to the ship, bouncing and swaying on the water as we made our way along it.

I climbed aboard our new home. It was huge! At least twenty metres long with shiny brown wooden decks and maroon sails wrapped into three neat bundles. It lay perfectly still at a small tilt, lodged in the sand. It looked as if it had been waiting for us.

I stepped into the cabin in the middle of the boat and found myself in a kitchen with steps leading forward and behind. I tried the back way first. It led to a small cabin with a bed, a beanbag and a polished wooden cupboard. Circles of wavy light bounced onto the bed from portholes on either side. Definitely my bedroom!

I ran through to the other side. Mum was twirling round in a big open living room, a table on one side, a comfy-looking sofa tucked snugly into the other.

'What will we do with all this space?' she gasped. Sunny golden rays beamed into the room from skylights all along the ceiling. Ahead, a door led to another bedroom.

'What about Dad?' I asked. 'How's he going to live here?'

Before she had a chance to reply, a large trapdoor in the floor bounced open and he appeared below us. That was when I noticed there were trapdoors everywhere, leading down from each room into another one below. The ship was lodged in the seabed with a whole floor half submerged, so you could swim around in it underwater.

'You want to see the rest of your new home?' Dad's

eyes shone wide and happy.

I inched down through the trapdoor to join him. Almost as soon as I did, my legs started to tingle. Then they went numb. Finally, they disappeared altogether.

My tail had formed.

It does that when I go in water. Sometimes I'm a mermaid, sometimes I'm a girl. That's what happens when a woman and a merman have a baby.

I'd only found out recently, when I went swimming with school. Thinking about that first time made me tremble. In fact the thought of Brightport High made me feel sick, even now. I'd dreaded going there. School itself didn't bother me, only some of the people. One in particular: Mandy Rushton. Just thinking about her was enough to make my skin prickle. All those times she'd humiliated me, calling me names in front of the class, tripping me up, stealing my friends, turning them against me. I used to have nightmares about her staring at me inside a huge tank, calling me a freak. I'd wake up, cold and sweating, and then have to face her all over again in real life.

At least I'd got my own back in the end when I turned into a mermaid in the pool, right in front of her eyes. It was worth all the bullying just to see the look of stunned silence slapped across her face that day.

No it wasn't. The only thing that made the bullying worth it was knowing I would never, ever have to see her again.

Bullies like Mandy Rushton were a thing of the past.

'Bit bigger than *King of the Sea*, eh?' Dad said as I lowered myself down towards him. He took hold of my hand and we swam round the lower deck together. 'Look!' He pulled me through an archway in the centre and through purple sea fans that hung like drapes from the ceiling. Fern-like and feathery, they swayed delicately with the movement of the water. Dad squeezed my hand.

A couple of red and white fish swam in through an empty porthole, pausing to nibble gently at the side of the boat before gliding between the drapes. One of them swam up to slide along his tail. 'Glass-eyed snappers,' I said as he flicked it away. Dad smiled. He'd taught me the names of all sorts of fish on the way here.

I swam back to the trapdoor and hoisted myself up. 'Mum, it's amazing!' I said as I watched my tail form back into my legs. Mum stared. She obviously hadn't got used to it yet. She'd only seen it happen a few times.

Then Dad joined us and Mum turned to sit with her legs dangling over the trapdoor, gazing at him. He reached onto her lap to hold her hands. She didn't seem to notice the bottom of her skirt was soaking wet. Just grinned stupidly down at him while he grinned stupidly up at her.

I realised I was grinning stupidly at both of them.

Well, most people don't have to wait till they're twelve before they get to see their parents together. I never knew it would make me feel so warm, so complete.

I decided to leave them to it. They wouldn't notice if I went out to explore. They'd hardly noticed anything except each other since we set off to come here! Not that I minded. After all, I'd nearly got imprisoned myself, getting them back together. I guessed they wouldn't mind a little time on their own.

'I'm going out for a bit,' I called. 'Just for a look round.'

'OK, darling,' Mum replied dreamily.

'Be careful,' Dad added.

I nearly laughed as I climbed out of the boat. I looked out at the turquoise water and marshmallow sand. Careful? What of? What could possibly hurt me here?

I walked along the beach for a while, watching the sun glint and dance on the water in between the ships. The sand was so white! Back home, or what used to be home, in Brightport, the sand was usually a dirty beige colour. This sand was like flour. My feet melted into it as I walked. I could hardly feel the ground. A gentle breeze made the sun's warmth feel like a hairdryer on my body.

Wading into the sea, I couldn't help glancing around to check there was no one around. Just habit. I still hadn't got used to the idea that being a mermaid didn't make me a freak here, on this secret island where merfolk and humans lived together. The only place of its kind in the world, protected by the magic of the Bermuda Triangle.

There were some people up on the cliff behind me, standing in front of a cluster of white buildings. For a moment, I considered scrambling up the hill to join them. Then I looked out at the water and saw faces – and then tails. Merpeople! I had to meet them!

As my legs formed back into my tail, I wondered if there were any others on the island like me. Half human, half merperson. That would be *so* cool! Either way, at least I could live here with my mum and dad without us having to hide what we were.

Shoals of tiny fish escorted me out towards the group, gliding and weaving around me. Thin black bodies with see-through fins, they led me along through the warm water, slowing down every now and then, almost as though they were making sure I could keep up. Wavy lines rippled along the seabed like tyre tracks. A troupe of silver jacks swam past me in a line, each one silhouetted against the sand below, their shadows doubling their gang's numbers.

I flipped over onto my back, flicking my tail every now and then to propel myself lazily along, until I remembered I was meant to be looking for the merpeople.

I stopped and looked round. The island was a speck in the distance, miles away. How long had I been swimming?

The merpeople had moved on. A chill gripped my chest as I realised I was gliding over some dark rocks: hard, grey, jagged boulders with plants lining every crack. Fat grey fish with wide-open mouths and spiky backs glared at me through cold eyes. Long trails of seaweed stretched like giant snakes along the seabed, reaching upwards in a clutch of leaves and stems.

As I hovered in the water, I could feel myself being pulled along by a current. It felt like a magnet, drawing me towards it, slowly at first then getting stronger. I swam hard against it, but it was too strong. It was reeling me in like a fishing line. Blackness swirled ahead of me. Then I remembered. The Triangle.

Everything sped up, like a film on fast forward. Fish zoomed past, weeds and plants lay horizontal, stretched out towards the edge of the Triangle, the well that led to the deepest depths of the ocean.

My chest thumping, my throat closing up, I worked my arms like rotary blades, pounding through the water. My tail flicked rapidly as I fought to get away. I swam frantically. *Keep going, keep going!*

But every time I started to make progress, the current latched onto me again, dragging me back out to sea. We were locked in a battle, a tug of war between me and – and what? Fear surged through me like an electric current, powering my aching arms for one final push.

It was just enough. I was getting away. The current loosened its grip. The sea soon became shallow again, and calm, as though nothing had happened. I wasn't taking any risks, though. Catapulting myself through the water, I swam back to our bay and made it to the ship breathless. I pulled myself out and sat panting on the deck while my legs returned.

Mum poked her head out of the cabin. 'You OK, chuck?' she asked, passing me a towel.

I nodded, too out of breath to reply. I rubbed myself dry as I followed her back into the kitchen.

'Here y'are,' she said, passing me a couple of onions and a knife. 'Might as well make yourself useful.' Then she looked at me more carefully. 'Are you sure you're all right?'

Was I? That was a good question. I opened my mouth to answer her, but stopped when I heard voices coming from below deck.

'Who's that?'

'Oh, visitors, downstairs with your dad. They've been coming all afternoon.'

I gently shut the trapdoor. I couldn't face new people yet. I didn't even want Dad to hear what I had to say. I don't know why. Something to do with how happy he was, and the fact that he kept giving me all these smiley, loving looks. Well, he would do, wouldn't he? He hadn't seen me since I was a baby. And I didn't want him to know his baby wasn't quite so happy right now, or quite so sure about this new dream home of ours.

My hands shook as I started to peel the onions. 'Mum,' I said carefully.

'Mm?' she replied through a teaspoon lodged in her mouth. She says it stops your eyes watering.

'You know that stuff Archie told us on the way here, about the big well in the ocean?'

'Bu big well im be oshug?' she replied, the spoon waggling about as she spoke.

'What?'

She pulled the spoon out of her mouth. 'The big well in the ocean?' she repeated.

'The one that leads to the deepest depths of the ocean,' I added, as a shudder snaked through my body. 'I felt something just now. Pulling me out to sea.'

'Emily, you're not to go out there!' She said, grabbing my arms. 'You stay close to the island.'

The shudder jammed in my throat. 'It was really strong, Mum,' I said quietly.

'Of course it's really strong! It's protecting the whole area! You know what Archie said. Do you hear me, Emily?'

I nodded, swallowing hard. 'Yes, I hear you.'

She stared at me, holding my eyes with hers. 'I'm

not going to lose you, Emily. You promise me you'll keep away from there.'

'I promise.'

She pulled me towards her and hugged me tight. 'Good. Right,' she said. 'You silly thing, you're shaking.' She squeezed me tighter. 'Come on, it's OK. Let's get this veg done, and we'll try not to think about big wells and the deepest depths of the ocean, OK?'

'OK.' I forced a smile. 'I'll try.'

We worked in silence after that. I couldn't think of anything to say. All I could think was that it would take more than chopping a few onions to make me forget the fear I'd felt out there, clutching and snapping at me like a shark trying to drag me to the bottom of the sea.

Mermaids? Yeah, right!

You're as bad as my dad.

He reckons they're real, too. Reckons he's seen one. He says it was on his way back from The Fisherman. That's our local pub. Clear as day, he says.

'Well, that goes to show how reliable your vision is after ten pints of Guinness,' my mum says. 'You couldn't even tell it was the middle of the *night*!'

'Clear as day,' he says again. 'It's just an expression, love.'

Mum says he'll be seeing more than mermaids if he doesn't start pulling his weight. Then she has a go at me for leaving my *Girlchat* magazine lying around. Yell their heads off at each other and nag me. That's all they seem to do, nowadays.

They didn't always argue. Not this much, anyway. It's been like this ever since we heard that the council are planning to pull down our home. We live on a pier and they say it's not safe. Problem is, my parents work on the pier, too. So that's job and home gone in one swift swing of a crane. Or blast of dynamite. However they do it.

The place is a dump, anyway. I don't care what

happens. Well, maybe I do, a bit. But who cares what I think?

So today, right, Dad charges upstairs to the flat at lunchtime. He usually goes to the pub, but he says he's been somewhere else.

'Where?' Mum eyes him suspiciously.

'Look,' he says. He's got a magazine in his hand. A brochure.

Mum takes it off him. '*Mermaid Tours*?' she says. 'Oh, for Lord's sake, Jack, when will you grow up?'

'No it's not – it's not – ' he blusters. 'It's just the name of the company, Maureen. It caught my attention, that's all.' He grabs the brochure back off Mum, rifles through it as though he's looking for something in particular. 'I've been looking for something to take our minds off everything. I thought this might help.'

'There!' he says suddenly, opening it up and slamming it onto the table. Mum sits down to read it. I have a look, too. Not that I'm interested or anything. I just want to know what the fuss is about, that's all.

'A cruise, Jack?' Mum looks at him in this way she has, with her tongue in her cheek and her eyebrows raised so high they nearly disappear into her hair. 'We're on the verge of losing our livelihood and you want us to spend every last penny we haven't even GOT on some ridiculous holiday!'

Dad takes a deep breath. 'Maureen,' he says in a rumble. When he speaks again, he says each word on its own, like he's talking staccato. 'What. Kind. Of. Fool. Do. You. Take. Me. For. Exactly?'

Mum gets up from the table. 'You really don't want me to answer that, Jack.'

'Look!' Dad suddenly shouts. Dad never shouts. We both look. He's pointing at the page. 'I'll read it to you, shall I?' And before we have time to answer, he starts reading.

'Enter our EXCLUSIVE competition and you could win one of our superlative MERMAID TOURS holidays! Every month, one lucky reader will win this FANTASTIC PRIZE. Just complete the following phrase in 30 words or less: "Mermaid Tours are the best holidays around because . . . "

Remember to tell us which of our fabulous cruise holidays you'd like to go on, and post the coupon off to us. You could be our next lucky winner!'

Dad puts the magazine back on the table.

'Well,' Mum says, picking up the magazine. 'A competition. Why didn't you just say so?'

I roll my eyes at Dad. He clamps his jaw shut and doesn't say anything.

Mum and Dad are complete fanatics about competitions, especially Mum. She reckons she's got a system. It works, as well. Our home is littered with teddy bears and toasters and electronic dictionaries she's won from stupid competitions in magazines. We had three vacuum cleaners at one point. She even won a weekend break once. Not that I know much about that. She and Dad went without me. I had to stay at home with a babysitter while they went off to live it up in Paris. I still haven't properly forgiven them. Not that I should have been too surprised. I'm always bottom of the list round here.

But this. Well, I wouldn't mind a cruise holiday. Lying on a sun lounger on an enormous ship gliding through the ocean, hot sun, warm pool, all the food I can eat, non-stop sweets and no one to stop me drinking as much pop as I want. I've heard about these holidays. It's all included.

'You know how good you are at these things,' Dad says, edging closer to Mum.

'Don't try flattery, Jack,' Mum says. 'It doesn't suit you.'

But I know she'll do it; she can't resist. I catch Dad's eye. He winks and I half smile back. Well, he's still stupid believing in mermaids.

Later that day, I catch Mum leafing through the brochure. 'Look at this one,' she says. I glance over her shoulder. *Bermuda and the Caribbean. Experience the magic for yourself. Enjoy all the comfort and enchant-ment of our Mermaid Tours cruise. Swim with dolphins. Bask in year-round sunshine heaven.*

'That's the one, I'd say.' She nibbles the side of her mouth. 'Right, leave me alone, now. I need to think.'

She won't show either of us what she's written. Says it'll jinx it. But something changes around the place after she's sent it off. We all start talking about what we'll do on our cruise holiday and what it'll be like. Mum and Dad get on; they even smile at each other occasionally. Even more bizarrely, they lay off having a go at me. For a few days. The closing date's in a week.

But then the week's up and we don't hear anything. Another week passes, and another, and another. Nothing.

We haven't won. Mum's luck's run out, after all.

And gradually, the sniping starts again, and then the shouting at each other and getting at me every five minutes. Back to normal. And underneath it all is the looming truth that no one's saying out loud, that we're about to lose everything.

Well, why should I expect anything different? It is *my* life we're talking about here.

Oh, I haven't told you my name yet, have I?

It's Mandy. Mandy Rushton.

Chapter Two

J jumped out of bed. Shona was arriving today! Shona's my best friend. She's a mermaid. Full time. Not just when she goes in water, like me. Back home – I mean, back in Brightport – I used to sneak out at night to meet up with her. That was before anyone knew about me being a mermaid. Now we could see each other every day!

I couldn't believe it when she said they were coming too. It was Neptune's idea, but I'd never met her parents and didn't know if they'd agree to it. Mind you, looking around me, it was hard to imagine anyone *not* wanting to come and live here. As long as you didn't go anywhere near the edge of the Triangle. Well, I wasn't going to think about that today.

I'd stick close to the coast, like Mum said, and everything would be all right. It all looked different this morning anyway. Nothing this beautiful could be dangerous.

Maybe if I told myself that enough times, I'd believe it.

Dad swam up to the trapdoor in the living room as I was getting some breakfast. 'There's someone here for you, little 'un,' he said. 'And look, I got you something.'

He darted away as someone else appeared below me. Someone with long blonde hair and a big smile. Shona!

I shovelled a last spoonful into my mouth and jumped down through the trapdoor with a splash. My legs melted away, turning into a tail.

'I couldn't wait to see you,' Shona said, swimming towards me to hug me tight.

I hugged her back. 'When did you get here?'

'Late last night.' She nodded towards the porthole she'd swum through. 'Althea brought me over to North Bay. She lives next door to us at Rocksea Cove. Come and meet her.'

'Here you are.' Dad swam back over, smiling broadly as he held something out to me. A doll. It had bright red spots on its cheeks, golden hair and a frilly pink tail.

'Um. Thanks, Dad.'

'You like it?' he asked, anxiously tugging at his ear.

'Sure. I'll play with it later, perhaps.'

'I wanted to give you something like this years ago. I've been saving it,' he said, his eyes going all misty and dreamy. They seemed to do that a lot. I don't know if he realised I was nearly thirteen.

Once we were outside, I grimaced at Shona and she laughed. Then I had a pang of guilt. 'Hang on,' I said. I swam back in the boat and kissed Dad on the cheek. It wasn't his fault I'd grown up without him. It wasn't his fault we hadn't worked out how to communicate with each other yet, either. It would come. It had to.

'What's that for?' he asked, lifting his hand to his cheek.

I shrugged, smiling briefly. 'See you later,' I said.

Outside the boat, a mergirl with jet black hair tied back in a ribbon was waiting in the water with Shona. The ribbon looked as if it was made out of gold seaweed. Her tail was green, with silver stars painted on the end.

Shona turned to me. 'This is Althea. She's going to show us round the island.'

'Great,' I said with a tight smile as a pang of jealousy hit me. How could I compete with a full-time, proper mermaid with stars in her tail and gold seaweed in her hair? I was going to end up without a best friend again.

'We're picking up Marina first,' Althea said.

Shona linked my arm. 'That's Althea's best friend,' she added, laughing as she read my mind. She does that sometimes. That's why she's such a brilliant best friend.

'Stay close to the coast here,' Althea warned as we set off, doubling the fear that was already starting to gnaw at my insides. 'There's quite a current round the northern end of the island.'

As if I needed to be told that! I couldn't speak. My mouth was so dry it felt like it had sand in it.

Althea pointed to the hill behind us. 'That's where a couple of the human families live,' she said, pointing up at the white buildings I'd seen the day before. 'They look after allotments for the whole island.'

For a moment I wished I'd gone up to meet them yesterday, after all. If I had, maybe I'd be looking around at everything with wide innocent eyes like Shona was doing now, instead of waiting for something awful to happen. I had to shake the feeling away. I linked Shona's arm and smiled at her. Swimming on, I made sure we stayed as close to the shore as possible.

We followed a low line of rocks that jutted out into the ocean. 'That's Barracuda Point,' Althea said.

'Why's it called that?' Shona asked.

'You'll see,' she smiled. 'Wait till we're on the other side.'

We rounded the tip and swam on a bit further before Althea stopped. 'OK, look now.'

We turned and looked back.

'Sharks alive!' Shona gasped. I stared in silence. A low line of rocks twisted out from the shore, stretching out into a long thin body. At the tip, it narrowed into a sharp point, dinted and creased along the middle, like a jaw-line filled with sharp teeth. Jagged rocks stood along the top like fins. Dark and menacing, it looked as though it could easily come to life with a snarling twist of its body. A cold shiver darted up my spine, prickling into my neck.

'It's meant to protect the island,' Althea said.

'What from?'

'Everything. There's all sorts of bogey-mers lurking, you know.'

'Really?' I asked, shivering. 'Like what?'

Althea laughed. 'It's just kids' stories. Monsters and stuff.' Then she stopped smiling. 'But there's something to them, I reckon. I've never been able to quite put my fin on it but I've always had a sense of something…something below the surface.'

'Have you ever been pulled out to sea?' I blurted out before I could stop myself.

'What?'

'By – by the current,' I faltered.

'We avoid certain spots. We learn very quickly about that.'

'And what happens if you don't?' I asked, holding my breath while I waited for her to answer.

Althea lowered her voice. 'The bogey-mer will get you!' she said. Then she looked at my face and burst out laughing. 'Come on, I'm only joking. It's kids' tales, like I said.' Then she turned suddenly, shaking her hair so it splashed onto the water, spreading golden droplets in an arc around her. 'Come on. Let's go and get Marina.'

She moved on. As we swam, Shona gave me an occasional sideways look. I smiled at her and tried to act casual but my body felt stiff and clumsy as I pushed myself through the sea.

The water soon became warm and shallow and colourless as we skirted the edges of the island. No currents, nothing weird. Althea was right. We just had to avoid certain spots and everything would be fine. I began to relax. We came to a wide bay. Swimming into it, the water turned cool and deep. Twisted rock formations stood along the edges.

'Double Arch Bay,' Althea said.

Ahead of us, two giant arches were cut deep into the rocky shore. Althea ducked under to swim through one of them. Shona went next. Then I flicked myself down and slipped through.

We swam across a small reef. Neat clusters of plants and coral were dotted about like a well-tended park. An elderly merman with shiny blue eyes and a thin grey tail swam across them, snipping at weeds with a knife made from razor-shells.

'Hi Theo,' Althea said.

He nodded at us. 'Morning, girls.'

'Theo's the gardener,' Althea explained as he swam off to tie some wilting pink plants into a bundle with seaweed.

There were archways everywhere. Some were tiny gaps in the rocks that I'd have missed if Althea hadn't pointed them out, others wide jagged holes big enough for a whale to get through.

Eventually, we came to a shimmery purple rock with a neat round hole in the middle. 'This is where Marina lives,' Althea said. She tapped a pink fish hovering at the entrance, a gold bell dangling from its tail. Immediately, it wriggled its body and a delicate sound chimed out.

A mermaid swam towards us from inside. She had curly red hair and a long gold tail with a shiny crescent moon painted on the end. 'Shona and Emily!' she said, her freckled face creasing into a smile. 'Come in while I get my things.' She grabbed Althea's hand and they went on ahead, along a narrow pathway lined with rough walls. It soon widened out into a wide living space divided up by trails of fern and kelp. An older mermaid bustled past us. She had red hair like Marina's, only hers was longer and frizzy. Her tail was bright yellow, and tapered into soft white tassels at the end.

'Don't be out all day, Marina,' she said. 'It's jellied eel soufflé tonight and we're eating early. I've got my synchro-swim class at seven.' Then she smiled at Shona and me. 'Hello girls,' she added. 'Welcome to Allpoints Island.'

Shona and I smiled back before following the others into a small space with a soft seaweed bed and drapes all round it. A huge pink sponge was squashed into one corner, a crystal mirror in another.

'My room,' Marina said.

I sat on the sponge. It squelched and bubbled under me. Shona laughed. 'It's swishy!'

Swishy – that's Shona's word for *everything* she likes. 'Squishy, more like,' I said as I tried to get up.

Althea swam towards the entrance. 'Come on,' she said. 'There's loads to show you.'

Marina grabbed a patchwork bag made of leaves and reeds and we followed Althea through the arches and back out into the bay. We swam along stretches of rocky coastline, interspersed with coves of all shapes and sizes: some wide and sandy, others tiny winding channels you could almost miss.

Everywhere we looked, spots of sunlight bounced on the water, white foamy waves washed gently over rocks, palm trees reached gently out from marshmallow sand. High on the island, some people called down to us from a woody hill. In the sea, merfolk smiled and greeted us as we passed them. A couple of young mer-children playing piggyback rides on a dolphin waved and shouted to us. We waved back. A group of mermen diving for food nodded at us on their way out to sea. A mermaid with long flowing hair streaming down her back smiled as she was pulled along by a swordfish on a lead.

It was all so different – and yet so familiar. I belonged here. The fear that had gripped me yesterday floated further away with every new sight.

Swimming on, we approached a half-hidden cave in the rocky shoreline. 'There are loads of caves on the island but we only use a couple of them,' Marina said. 'School's in one of them. The other's only for really major events like when Neptune comes. That's the Grand Caves. We can show you the other one, though, Emerald Cave. You want to see your school?'

Did I? Just the thought of school washed the smile off my face. But surely this couldn't be anything like Brightport High. No one was going to make fun of me here, or delight in making my life a misery. And it *was* a mermaid school! A mix of emotions swirled around inside me as I followed Althea into the cave.

We inched along a narrow tunnel. As it twisted and turned, it grew darker and darker. Soon we were swimming in pitch blackness.

'Feel your way along the walls,' Marina called from somewhere ahead of me. I ran my fingers along the craggy layered sides as I edged down the tunnel.

Just as my eyes were getting used to the dark, the tunnel opened out and grew lighter. We came to a fork.

'Down here.' Marina pointed along a tunnel that shimmered with green light.

It led up into a deep pool inside the cave. Above us, the ceiling stretched high and jagged. Stalactites hung all around us: enormous pillars reaching almost to the water, tiny spindles spiking down like darts. Rocks glimmered and shone purple and blue and red. Next to the pool, smooth boulders were dotted about on the gravelly ground like an abandoned game of giants' marbles.

A long scroll hung from the ceiling, pictures of

underwater life drawn all over it, a pile of different coloured reeds underneath.

A young mermaid was cleaning some hairbrushes lined up on a rocky ledge that jutted out across the water. She smiled at us as we gazed around.

'Swishy!' Shona said, swimming over to the hairbrushes. 'You have Beauty and Deportment?'

Beauty and Deportment. Shona had told me all about that. I'd be studying it with her soon. And Diving and Dance, and all the other mermaid subjects. No more long division!

'Of course,' Marina smiled. 'It's my favourite subject.'

'Mine, too,' Shona breathed.

Althea looked at me. 'I prefer Shipwreck Studies.'

'Althea likes going out on Geography Reef Trips,' Marina laughed. 'Anything to skive her tides tables.'

'It's beautiful,' Shona whispered as we took it all in. 'Much better than my old school.'

'And about a million light years away from mine,' I added, trying not to think too hard about Brightport High.

'There are two classes,' Althea explained. 'This one's for the older kids. There's another one for the babies.'

'Two classes?' Shona asked. 'Is that all?'

'There's only about thirty families here altogether,' Marina said. 'Mostly mer-families and a few human ones.'

'Do they mix?' I asked. I realised I was holding my

breath while I waited for the reply.

'Yes, of course,' Althea said as she started swimming back out of the cave. 'But they're kind of separate, too.' She blushed. 'If you get what I mean.' She glanced quickly at my tail. I got what she meant. I was the only one. Still the odd one out.

The old fears resurfaced, hitting me like a punch in my stomach. I couldn't keep them away any longer. I'd *never* find a place where I could fit in.

'But everyone gets on brilliantly,' Marina said quickly, swimming across to touch my arm. 'And we're all really pleased you've joined us. The island's organising a party for you next week, once you've settled in.'

'We haven't had any new families here for ages,' Althea added. 'Come on, let's show you the rest of the island.'

They were organising a party, just for us? Maybe I was wrong. Maybe things would work out, after all.

We continued round the coast, Althea and Marina pointing out sights all along the way: a hole in the ground that spouted orange flames in the summer, little channels leading to a maze of caves and caverns where some of the merfolk ran craft stalls. I made a mental note to tell Dad about that. At least it could be something for us to talk about. He'd learned to make jewellery while he was in prison. Maybe he could have one of the stalls.

Swimming up the jagged east side of the island, we came to a channel leading into the rock.

'Now this is something you must see,' Althea said.

We set off in single file along the channel. The sides became steeper and higher as we swam; the water grew deeper and colder, and so dark it was almost black. A soft wind whistled through the chasm. Then nothing. No movement, no sound, the sun beating silently down. I'd never experienced such stillness.

As we wound our way along the channel, Althea and Marina kept pointing things out in our path: a fossil on the canyon wall, hairline cracks in the rocks making tiny channels that split off from the main one.

'Look.' Althea pointed ahead, to where the channel seemed to come to an end. I couldn't see anything at first, just a load of overgrown bushes and reeds lining the walls. Then I noticed what she was pointing at. A gap in the rock, through the reeds. There were pieces of driftwood attached to either side of the gap, virtually covered in plants and algae.

We parted the reeds as though they were curtains and peered through the gap in the rock. On the other side, a shimmering blue lagoon sparkled with diamond glints. The water lay virtually still; green fern hung down across gaping holes in the rock; a group of flamingos gathered at the edge, standing motionless on spindly legs, long pink necks stretched straight and high. Two pelicans flew past, their wings reaching wide as they skimmed the water's still surface.

It was like paradise. How you've always imagined paradise would look.

'Swishy!' breathed Shona.

I stared so hard my eyes watered.

Marina looked nervous. 'Come on. We need to get back.'

'But we've just got here,' I said.

'We shouldn't be here at all.'

'Why not? There's nothing to say keep out, is there?'

'It's n —'

'It's nice!' Althea burst in, nudging Marina. 'And it's naughty to go there because we're not really meant to.' She swam closer and lowered her voice. 'But *you* don't know that. You could go in and find out what it's like. I've always wanted to know.'

I stared at the lagoon.

'I'm not sure,' Shona said. 'I mean, if we're not allowed . . . '

'None of the kids are brave enough. We've been told not to go in there so many times,' Althea said. 'But you haven't. You've only been here five minutes! Who's going to tell you off?'

'She's right,' I said.

Althea smiled at me. 'Exactly,' she said.

This could be just what I needed! My chance to make sure Althea and Marina would definitely be our friends. I knew I had Shona, but I couldn't run the risk of her being my only friend. I had to make sure I was popular this time. I wasn't going to be whispered about and made fun of again. If they wanted us to do it, well, then, we would. Besides, it looked *so* tempting in there. I could almost feel it inviting me in.

Shona edged away from the reeds, her tail fluttering nervously. 'Let's think about it,' she said.

We dropped the reeds and drew back, but I couldn't get the image out of my mind. The stillness of the water, the ferns hanging down like delicate chains.

We set off in silence. All around us, nature bustled. Tiny brown lizards raced across rocks. Crabs scuttled under large stones, sneaking into the safety of their hidden homes. Above us, white birds with long sharp tails pecked at the cliff, disappearing into invisible holes in the rock. Eventually, the channel's walls widened once more and the sun warmed our necks as we arrived back at the open ocean.

When the others left us, Shona came to North Bay with me. I grabbed her before we went in the boat. 'We've *got* to go back,' I said.

'Oh Emily, I don't know,' Shona said. 'I mean, we've only just got here.'

'That's the whole point!' I said. 'Like Althea said, we're new, we don't know our way around, it would be *easy* for us to get lost. Think how impressed they'll be. Please!'

Shona half-smiled. 'It did look lovely,' she murmured. 'And I suppose we haven't really had long enough to properly understand the rules yet.'

'Not long enough at all,' I said, my tail flicking with excitement. 'We're just having a look round our new home. We're keen, we're a bit useless with directions and – whoops – we've gone wrong. *No one* will be cross with us.'

I'm the first one to the door when the postman arrives. I flick through the pile: just more bills for Mum and Dad to argue about.

But there's something else. A letter in a shimmery pink envelope. I turn it over. *Mermaid Tours*!

'Mum! Dad!'

They're at the door in seconds.

'Oh my God!' Mum says, snatching the letter from me. 'Who's going to open it?' Her hands are shaking.

'You do it, love,' Dad says. 'You wrote it.' He holds my hands. I'm shaking, too.

'It's probably just some junk mail or something,' Mum says, tearing at the envelope. 'Let's not get excited.'

She reads aloud. '"Thank you for entering our competition. We are delighted to inform you that you have won our—" Jack!' Mum drops the letter and stares at Dad.

I pick the letter up and read on. '"... delighted to inform you that you have won our *Bermuda and the Caribbean* cruise holiday. You and your family will spend a fortnight aboard one of our luxury ships and experience all the delights of a *Mermaid Tours* holiday. Many congratulations and have a good trip!"'

For a second, there's silence. Then Mum grabs me and screams. She pulls me into a tight squeeze. She's jumping up and down. 'We won! We won!' she yells. 'We're going on holiday! Oh my God, we won, we won!'

I jump up and down with her for a second, till I can hardly breathe. She's holding me too tight. I pull away. Mum grabs Dad round the neck and kisses him. Kisses him! I don't think she's done that for about five years.

It worked. She won us a holiday! Maybe they'll get on again and everything will be all right. For a couple of weeks, at least.

Two weeks away from this dump. Wonder if anyone will notice I'm gone. Julie might. She's kind of my best friend, not that she acts like it. She never really wanted to be my best friend. She always preferred that loser, Emily Windsnap. At least *she's* not around any more.

I wonder what happened to her and her mum? One day they were here, the next they'd gone. Took the boat and everything. Well, good riddance. All she ever did was ruin things for me and make me look stupid. She got me into trouble years ago when she told on me for cheating in the arcade. I wasn't even cheating; I was trying to help her. Trying to be nice. Taught me not to bother trying *that* again in a hurry. It never works. Best just to keep your mouth shut and not get your hopes up.

Anyway, we're out of here. We're going on a cruise!

Chapter Three

We swam side by side to begin with. Below us, occasional shoals of parrotfish and bright red snappers swept across the sandy bed. When the channel narrowed, I swam ahead, slinking along the silent passageway. The ground soon became uncluttered: clear golden sand beneath us, the sun shining down, almost directly above our heads. Two silhouetted mermaid figures gliding along below the surface, our shadows came and went, appearing briefly before suddenly growing distorted with the splash of a tail breaking the water's still surface.

We came to the curtain of reeds draped down the channel's walls and the algae-coated wooden plaques. Trying not to let Shona see my quivering hands, I parted the curtain and looked through the hole in the wall. The water sparkled and fanned out into a wide lagoon. Ferns hung down over cracks and gaps in the walls. A white tropic bird flew into a hole behind me, its long tail disappearing into the rock. Nothing else moved. Shona stared.

I turned to her. 'Ready?' My voice shook.

She broke her gaze to look at me. 'Let's just get this over with.'

I glanced around to check no one had followed us, then I squeezed through the gap and swam into the lagoon. The sun burned down, heating my neck and dancing on the water. Its light rippled below us in wavy lines across the ground.

As we slid across the stillness, the water grew colder and murkier. When the lagoon narrowed back into a channel, I couldn't see my reflection swimming along below me any more. The walls lining our trail had lost their hardness. They were like chalk. I stopped and scraped my finger down the sides; rock crumbled in my hand. The channel walls stretched upwards, cold and grey and deserted.

'Emily!' Shona was pointing at something ahead. An engraving on the wall: a perfect circle with a fountain spiralling out from the centre. It looked like a Catherine Wheel, full of energy, almost as tall as us.

'Look at *this*!' Shona had swum ahead while I stared at the engraving.

I joined her in front of some ferns loosely covering

a hole in the rock. The hole disappeared below the surface. We dived down. Under the water, it was just big enough to swim into.

'Cool!' I grinned at her. A secret tunnel reaching into the rock! 'Shona, we *have* to see what's in there.'

She frowned.

'Althea and Marina will be *so* impressed. No one else has dared do it.' And before she had a chance to argue, I'd slithered into the slimy, echoey darkness. Eventually I heard her follow behind.

The winding tunnel led us deeper and deeper into dead rock: tight, cold and claustrophobic, but gradually widening and growing brighter as we swam. Bit by bit, a growing circle of light opened up ahead of us.

We swam towards it, finally coming out into a dome-shaped space in the middle of the cave. A high ceiling rippled faintly with the water's reflection.

'I don't understand,' Shona said, looking around. 'What's that light?'

I shook my head as we swam all around the rocky edges. It seemed to be coming from under the water.

'Come on.' I dived down. 'That's our answer!' I gasped. The floor of the cave was absolutely littered with crystals and stones and gold, all shining so brightly I almost had to shield my eyes. I'd never seen jewels like these. Dazzling pink rocks with sharp white edges lay on the ground in a circle, joined together by a thin line of gold. In their centre, a bright blue stone shaped like a rocket pointed up to the surface of the water.

'What in the ocean . . . ' Shona swam round and round the display, her mouth open, her eyes huge, shining with the reflection of the blue stone.

I looked round. There was more. Once we started looking, it seemed that stones and crystals covered the entire floor of the cave, packed and tucked into gaps in the rock all around us.

'Emily, I think we need to get back.' A fat green angelfish hovered between us, startled eyes staring into ours before it spun round and disappeared into a rocky crevice. 'We've seen it now. We're not meant to be here.'

I stopped gazing around. Shona was right. 'OK,' I said. 'Let's go back.' We'd found the answer to Althea's and Marina's questions. The lagoon hid a cave filled with jewels. But why? It didn't make sense.

Shona turned immediately and started making her way back towards the tunnel. But then I noticed something on the cave's wall: a picture exactly like the engraving we'd seen earlier, only even bigger. It looked like a mosaic. As we got closer I could see it was made out of jewels: a huge golden one in the centre, oval shaped and about half as tall as me, with multicoloured strands spinning outwards from it. I put my hand out to touch it. It wobbled.

'Shona!'

'Come on.' She carried on swimming.

I pushed at the jewel. It was lodged in the rock, but only loosely. We could probably get it out. I *had* to try. There was a secret in here, I was sure of it.

'Shona!' I called again. 'Just look at this.'

She stopped swimming and turned.

'It's loose!' I pulled at it, edging my fingertips underneath to lever it up. 'Help me.'

She swam reluctantly back to me. 'I thought we were – sharks!'

'You thought we were sharks?'

Shona stared at the mosaic. 'What is it?'

'Help me get it out.'

'You're pulling my tail, aren't you? We can't go round vandalising the place!'

'We're not vandalising anything. We'll put it back. Let's just see what's behind it.' An image of Althea's and Marina's faces flickered across my mind, their eyes wide and impressed with my bravery. I might even end up being the girl everyone wanted to be friends with, instead of the weedy one who got picked on by the class bully. This cave was going to change my life, I just knew it.

Shona sighed heavily, then reluctantly dug her fingers under the jewel, and we gradually levered it bit by bit out of its hole. A moment later, we were holding it between us. We lowered it down to the ground and it plopped onto the seabed with a soft thunk, scattering a shower of sand in a swirl around us.

'Now what?' Shona stared down at it.

I swam up to the hole it had left behind and poked my head into it. Another tunnel. I grabbed Shona's arm, pointing into the blackness. 'We *have* to go down there.'

'We don't *have* to go anywhere!' Shona snapped.

'*Please*! Aren't you dying to know what's in there? Can't you feel it?' This wasn't even about Althea and Marina any more. It was more like a thirst, or a magnet pulling me.

A magnet? My throat closed up as I remembered . . . But it couldn't lead to the Triangle. We were in the middle of the island. There was no current here, no danger.

Shona peered into the tunnel. Her eyes sparkled against the reflection of the crystals. I could see the dilemma in them. 'We just have a quick look, see what's there, and then we go home,' she said eventually.

'Deal!'

We edged our way carefully into the hole, slithering along in the silent dark. Me first, Shona following closely behind. The tunnel grew colder as we edged deeper into the rock. The edges became craggy and sharp.

And then, without warning, it suddenly stopped. A dead end.

'Now what?' I called round to Shona.

'We go back. We've looked. There's nothing there. And I'm not exactly surprised, or disappointed. Come on.'

How could it suddenly end like that? I was *sure* it was leading somewhere. I felt around on the rock in front of me. It was different from the walls. Smoother. I inched my hands around it. Then I realised why it was different.

'Shona! It's a boulder!'

'What?'

'There's something blocking the tunnel. Look, it's different from the walls. Feel it.'

Shona squeezed forwards to touch the boulder.

I felt my way around its edges. 'There's a crack all around it.' It was almost the same shape as the crystal at the other end. 'Maybe it'll come loose.'

Shona looked at me.

'Let's just try.'

'How do I let you talk me into all these things?' she said with another sigh.

'Because you can feel it, too? Because there's something down here that's making you tingle with excitement? Because the last time we went exploring, we ended up finding my dad? Because being my friend meant you got to live on a beautiful desert island? Because –'

'OK, enough,' Shona half-frowned, half-smiled. 'Don't get your tail in a tizzy. Let's just get on with it.'

It didn't just slip out like the jewel at the other end. We pushed and pushed but nothing happened. Or nearly nothing. The boulder moved slightly, rocking backwards and forwards as though it was on a hinge, but we couldn't shift it.

'It's useless,' Shona gasped. 'We'll never get it out.'

'We need to use the rocking. Get a momentum going. Look, it's swaying. If we both push it from above, it might topple. Wait till I say. On the count of three. You ready?'

Shona nodded without looking at me.

'One.' I felt around for a good hold on the rock.

'Two.' I stretched out my tail, getting ready to flick it as hard as I could.

'Three!'

We swished and splashed and pushed, grunting and heaving.

'Now, let go!' The rock swayed away from us, and then back. 'And again.' Another shove against the rock, another slight movement. Again and again, we heaved and pushed until, finally, it started to loosen.

Then Shona stopped pushing. 'I've had enough. I'm exhausted.'

'But we're nearly there!'

'I want to go back,' she said. 'I don't want to do this.'

'What's the problem?'

'The *problem* is that we don't know what's on the other *side*!'

'Exactly! But there is something, isn't there? I can almost feel it vibrating in my body.'

'Me too. And I don't like it, Em. It doesn't feel good. I don't want to know what it is, and I want to go before this place collapses in on us.'

'It's just a boulder. It's not going to collapse!'

But Shona turned to go back.

'Just one more push.'

'You do it if you like. I'm going.'

'Fine!' I went back to the boulder. It was teetering on the edge of the hole now. I could probably push it on my own. I didn't even know why I was doing it any more. I just knew we couldn't come all this way without finding out what was down here. It might be our only chance. There was something here. I could feel it. Low vibrations hummed rhythmically through the cave. What *were* they?

Fuelled by frustration, I spun my tail as fast as I could, pushed all my weight against the rock, and heaved.

Very slowly, it teetered, swaying with the rhythm of the water before eventually toppling: a huge, smooth, oval rock slipping down and away from us, almost in slow motion. Water swirled all around. The boulder was still travelling, rolling, hurtling down through the water.

It felt like when you roll a snowball down a hill and it grows bigger and bigger. Something was building up on the other side of the tunnel, below us, below the island, deep inside the rock.

'I told you, I told you!' Shona screamed. 'It's caving in! We're going to be trapped!'

'It's OK. Look.' I tried to hold my nerve. Everything was still intact in the tunnel. It was just on the other side that the water was foaming and swirling everywhere. And there was something else: a presence. The vibrations had turned into a low rumbling, way down below. Something was down there. Something that didn't feel quite so exciting any more. What was it?

'What's *happening*?' Shona screamed.

'It's just – it's the rock falling to the bottom of the caves,' I said, much more confidently than I felt. 'It's all right. Just stay calm. It'll stop in a minute.'

The rock carried on plummeting and crashing, getting fainter and fainter. Sand and rock particles swirled around, a few of them spinning softly through the hole into the cave.

And then it stopped. No more crashing. No swirling rocks or sand, no hurtling anywhere. Complete silence.

Total silence. Kind of eerie silence.

I smiled nervously at Shona. 'See,' I said. 'Told you it'd all be OK.'

And then we heard it. The rumbling. Not a flutter of excitement in our stomachs, or a thrilling vibration that we might have imagined. This was very, very real. And it was growing. Soon, a roaring noise sliced through the caves, growling louder and louder, rumbling towards us. I couldn't move. I looked at Shona. Her lips were moving – but I couldn't hear a thing. The rumble turned into a high-pitched whine, shrieking and screaming through the hole into the tunnel. I slammed my hands over my ears.

The next thing I knew, Shona had grabbed one of my hands. She pulled it away from my head. 'We have to get OUT OF HERE!' she was yelling in my ear. 'QUICK!'

I'd forgotten how to move. My tail, my arms, everything had turned completely stiff.

'Come *on*!' Shona yanked my arm, pulling me with her. My body jack-knifed into action and we hammered through the tunnel as an explosion crashed into the water behind us.

I turned round to see the end of the tunnel crumble and dissolve. Rocks fell and bounced in the water, scattering sand and bubbles everywhere, clouds bunching and spilling across the seabed like lava.

Something was reaching out from the tunnel, feeling around. Oh God! What *was* it? A huge tube, almost as thick as the tunnel itself: slimy and dark green. One side was rubbery and shiny, then it flipped and twisted over and its underneath was grey and covered in black spots. They looked like giant warts. In between them, great thick suckers grabbed onto the wall like the suction cups on the soap holder Mum keeps in the shower, only about fifty times bigger – and a hundred times uglier.

The tube flapped and flicked about, manically batting and thwacking against the sides, reaching out further and further towards us. An icy stake of terror pinned me to the spot.

The siren noise shrieked into the cave again as the tube thing moved around in the tunnel, feeling its way along. Getting closer!

Someone was screaming and screaming.

Shona shook me. 'Emily, you have to pull yourself together!' she yelled. The screaming stopped. It had been me. She pulled me through the water. 'Just swim for your life!'

We threw ourselves along the tunnel, working our arms like windmills in a tornado. I tore brief glances behind us as we swam. The tube lashed out, extending towards us like a giant worm, ripping at the tunnel walls and doubling my panic.

Propelling myself faster than I had ever swum in my life, I flung my body through the passage until I finally made it to the open space. The rock was collapsing around us as we swam.

The thing was reaching out of the tunnel towards us! No! Its end was tapered and blood red, and covered with brown hairy strands swirling about as it felt its way around the tunnel. It slid further and further out as we dashed across the cave to the next tunnel, the one that would get us out of here.

CRASH! THWACK! Slamming against the roof of the cave, the walls, the ground, the monster worm was destroying the cave, bit by bit. We were almost within its reach. *Swim! Swim! Faster!*

As we heaved ourselves into the next tunnel, I glanced behind me again. The giant worm wasn't on its own. There were at least three others, maybe more, all searching and feeling around the cave walls, crashing through the water, reaching out towards us. Slimy, scaly tentacles. What *was* it? A giant octopus?

A scream burned silently in my throat. Shona had virtually disappeared. She was ahead of me but the water was murky with swirling pieces of rock and debris. *One more corner, one more corner,* I repeated to myself again and again as I ploughed down the long narrow tunnel.

I threw myself at the end of the tunnel. Nearly out! Panting and gasping, my energy was slipping away. And then a tentacle spun out, coiling itself down the tunnel. It touched me! *Arrggghhh!* Rubbery slime grazed my arm. My speed instantly tripled.

A moment later, I was out. Out of the tunnel! Back outside in the channel between the cliffs. Sunlight.

Shona was there, panting and heaving.

'It touched me! It touched me!' I screeched.

'Keep moving,' she said.

But I looked back. And this time I saw something I hadn't noticed before.

'Shona!'

'I told you, keep – '

'Look.' I pointed at the wall. How had I not seen it before? Carved into the wall. A trident. Neptune's trident!

'Keep moving,' Shona said again. But her face had turned white.

We swam on, scattering shoals of tiny yellow fish as we pounded through the creek. Back into the lagoon, and out through the hole on the other side. Turning to close the curtain of reeds, I noticed the wooden plaques again. They were covered in algae, but there was something underneath. I rubbed at the algae, brushed reeds away – and I could see it. Another trident. We'd been trespassing in Neptune's own territory! No wonder Althea and Marina didn't dare come down here. How could they set us up like this? Didn't they *know* what he was like? That his rage could create thunderstorms, or destroy islands? Destroy islands! Maybe that's what he'd do now!

What had we done?

Shona was ahead of me. I caught her up without speaking. Swimming in silence, I could hardly believe any of this had really happened. Everything was totally still and quiet. No movement at all. We stopped, listened.

'It didn't follow us,' I said lamely. 'We're safe. It's OK.'

Shona looked at me. There was something in her expression that I'd never seen before. A hardness in her eyes. 'You think, Emily?' she said. 'You really think so?'

Then she turned and swam on. She didn't say another word all the way back.

Well I don't know about you, but this is not MY idea of a luxury cruise!

Swimming pool? I don't *think* so. Non-stop food and drink? Erm, *hello*? Enormous ship? Yeah, right!

We've been conned. Our holiday of a lifetime, full of 'magic' and 'enchantment', turns out to be two weeks on an old wreck of a sailing boat with me, Mum, Dad and some old guy to drive us. Brilliant.

There's absolutely zilch to do. We've been out at sea for – well, I think it might be two days, but it's hard to tell as there is nothing to distinguish one deathly boring second from the next. I'll *never* forgive my parents for this. Especially Dad. Why did he have to see that stupid magazine?

He's the only one who's enjoying himself. Mum's spent all her time inside so far, cooking or sleeping and occasionally going green and rushing over to the side to be sick. Why I wasted my time thinking it would all be happy families I don't know. When will I learn that nothing nice *ever* happens to me?

I wish one day it would. Just once.

Even the captain has got a right gob on him most of

the time. Just stands at the wheel looking out at the sea. Not that there's anything else to look at. He hardly talks to any of us. He must be at least fifty so it's not as if I want to talk to him. But he could make a bit of effort.

Dad doesn't seem to realise that the rest of us are having the most awful holiday in the world. I wish he'd pay Mum some attention, but he's too busy running round with a fishing net, getting all excited over the stupidest things. Like now, for example. I'm lying on the deck reading a magazine – well, trying to read. It's not exactly easy while you're careering up and down and having to watch out for water splashing all over the place. Dad's on the deck next to me, leaning over the edge with a pair of binoculars. He's wearing bright yellow shorts and his back is bright red to match them.

Then he leaps up. 'Mandy, love. Come and see. Quickly!'

I put my magazine down. Maybe he's spotted the cruise that we're really meant to be on. Perhaps this was just a joke and we're on our way to start our proper holiday on a proper ship! I look out to sea. 'There's nothing there, Dad.'

'Wait. He'll do it again soon.'

Turns out he's seen a turtle. A turtle! Well, excuse, me but BIG DEAL!

I decide to go inside. It might be even more dull in there but at least Mum won't try to convince me that I'm having the time of my life.

Only, something stops me. I squeeze past the captain and I'm about to open the cabin door when I catch a glimpse of something. Not just a stupid turtle. A, well, a kind of nothingness. Just ahead of us, it's all dark. The sea looks black and shiny and the sky above it is suddenly filled with heavy clouds. Great. That's all we need now, a thunderstorm.

I look at the captain. He's taken off his cap. He rubs his eyes.

'What is it?' I join him at the wheel.

'Look!' He's pointing to a load of dials. They've got numbers on them but they're changing too fast to make any sense.

'What do they mean?'

He bends down to study the dials more closely. 'They should stay pretty much constant,' he says. 'Might just be a loose connection.'

'What about that?' I nod towards the compass. The pointer's spinning round like mad.

The captain wipes his cap across his forehead. Beads of sweat bubble down his face. 'I don't know what's going on,' he says, his voice quivering. 'It happened once before. It's – we need to get away from here!'

The boat's heading towards the darkness. And I don't know why I haven't thought of this before now, but I suddenly remember a comprehension test we did in English, about the Bermuda Triangle. It was called *The Ocean's Graveyard*, about all these ships that sailed into the Bermuda Triangle never to return.

The Bermuda Triangle. Is that where we are?

I glance across at Dad on the back deck. He's still staring through his binoculars.

'Dad.'

'Hang on, I think there might be another one in a sec.'

'Dad!'

He puts his binoculars down. 'What?'

I point ahead, at the darkness. We're getting closer and closer. It's as though we're being pulled along, towards where the water's lying motionless and black.

Dad turns round. 'Mother of . . . what's that?'

We gaze in paralysed silence as the boat slowly begins to pick up speed, gliding towards the glassy blackness.

I don't notice Mum coming out from below deck, but at some point I'm aware that she's there, too. We're slipping over to one side as we career through the water.

'We're going to drown,' Mum says suddenly. Almost calmly.

'Not if I can help it!' The captain grabs at the wheel, flinging it round as hard as he can. But it hardly makes any difference. His cheeks are purple. 'Hold on!' he yells.

We're edging closer towards the silent black water. It's pulling us sideways, drawing us in like a magnet. We're slipping further and further to the side. Bits of spray spatter the deck. The boat starts to rock.

Mum's fallen onto her knees. The captain's lurching at the wheel. I'm gripping the mast. I reach out to Mum. 'Get hold of my hand!' Spray lashes against my face as the boat leans further and further over to the side. Mum reaches out, our fingertips almost touching before she slips back across the deck.

'Maureen!' Dad lets go of his rail to reach out for Mum. He's holding her in one arm, gripping a rail with his other hand. He's got his arm round her – at last. I didn't want it to happen like this.

The captain is shouting something at us. He's spinning the wheel one way, then another. It's not making the blindest bit of difference. I can't hear what he's saying. I think I'm shouting, too. I don't even know what *I'm* saying. Seawater is everywhere. We're spinning sideways towards the strange glassiness, mast first, the bottom of the ship almost out of the water.

All is darkness, water, shouting, screaming. We're going to die! Out here in the middle of nowhere, on our own. A stupid, stupid death. I close my eyes and wait for the boat to veer into the blackness.

And it does.

Or it starts to.

We're teetering on our side when the boat suddenly jiggles and shakes. It's levelling out. What's happening? It slips and rocks a bit, there's water all over the deck and I'm soaking, but we're straightening out. We're not going to die! We're safe! Everything's going to be –

But then I see Dad's face, grey and heavy as though he's suddenly aged thirty years. He's staring at something behind me.

'Don't tell me you've seen another turtle,' I say shakily.

Then the boat lurches again and I fall to the floor. That's when I see it, rising out of the water. *What is it?*

First, huge tusks, curving upwards like giant bayonets. Below them, a long, long, olive green lumpy snout. It's taller than the ship's mast. It almost blocks out the sun. Horror seeps into my body. Huge white eyes bulging and popping out like great big fat full moons on either side, lumps all over the snout. Oh GOD!

Enormous tentacles slap the water, extending outwards and up, khaki green greasy things with suckers all the way down, waving around, splashing, making a whirlpool. We're spinning into it.

I'm trying to scream but all I can manage is a kind of dry clicking sound. We're being sucked into something, into the whirlpool, a mass of tentacles rising all around us.

And then Mum's screaming. I think maybe I am, too. One of the tentacles reaches right up into the air, then hurls itself down towards the boat, grips the mast.

I'm screaming for Mum, the boat's on its side. Where's Dad?

Water everywhere, a crashing sound, and then –

Chapter Four

*S*hona didn't talk to me all week. That first week in our new home. It was meant to be a fresh start, a dream come true. Instead it was the worst week of my life.

She started hanging round with Marina and Althea. I don't know how she could, after they'd tricked us like that. Maybe she thought anyone was better than me. Maybe she was right. After all, I was the idiot who had finally got to live with both of my parents and been given a new life on an island full of merpeople and glistening turquoise sea and white sandy beaches, and what did I do? It didn't bear thinking about.

And yet I couldn't think of anything else. I even forgot to be scared of starting school. I drifted through it, like everything else, in a daze. I couldn't even get excited when I learned to dive with the grace of a dolphin and brush my hair like a real mermaid and sing the wordless songs of the sirens. None of it mattered. Everything was ruined because of what I'd done, and marred by a constant fear of the consequences.

Millie and Archie came round one night. Millie stared at me all the way through dinner. 'Are you all right?' she asked as she helped herself to a huge scoop of ice cream.

Mum turned to look at me, cupping my chin in her hand. 'Are you, duck?' she asked softly. 'You have been quiet.'

'I'm fine!' I snapped. 'Why shouldn't I be?'

'Your aura's looking grey and patchy,' Millie said. 'Usually means you're fighting demons in your mind.'

Dad burst out laughing. 'Don't think my little 'un would stand a chance against demons,' he smiled. Millie glared at him.

I got up to clear some plates. Anything to get away. But just then, the boat rocked violently as a wave thrashed against the side, knocking half the dishes from the table and tripping me back into my seat.

Archie and Dad darted outside to see what had happened while I helped Mum and Millie pick up the broken crockery.

'Freak wave,' Archie said, pulling his hair behind his head as they swam back up to the trapdoor to join us again. 'Seem to have been a few of those lately. Wonder what that's about.' He seemed to look at me quizzically as he spoke. I must have imagined it. What could a freak wave have to do with me?

On Friday morning, Shona caught up with me on the way to school. For a brief second, I wondered if she wanted to make friends, but the look on her face said otherwise. Her expression was like mine when I'm faced with a plate of mushy peas, or a spider near my bed.

'Have you told anyone?' she asked, pulling me into a tiny cavern that led off from the main tunnel towards Emerald Cave.

'No! I don't know what to say. What are we going to do?'

'*WE*?' She stared at me. '*I* didn't even want to go up that stupid creek in the first place! *I* didn't want to go in the cave. *I* didn't want to knock the wall down. *I* am not going to do *anything*!'

A tear burned the corner of my eye. I'd never seen Shona like this. 'Well, what am *I* going to do, then?'

'I don't think we should say anything,' she said

more softly. 'We just forget it, OK?'

'Forget it?'

'Pretend it didn't happen. Whatever it was, it must have gone back where it came from. It didn't follow us. So we say nothing. Please?'

'But what if – '

'Em, think about it. We've only just got here. Do you want everyone to hate us before we've had the chance to make any friends?'

'Of course not. But – '

'But nothing. We leave it. Please, Emily.'

I nodded. 'OK.' A drop of water plopped down from the ceiling into the pool between us. 'You're still my best friend, aren't you?' I asked as we set off along the tunnel.

Shona didn't meet my eyes. 'Let's just act normal, OK?'

A couple of merboys were coming along the tunnel. Shona smiled at them as they caught us up, then swam ahead with them. I trailed behind, pretending to get something out of my bag.

We hadn't got much further when I noticed the water around me was swaying and swirling. It was building up, spinning round. I tried to move forward, but got thwacked against the side.

The caves were shaking. A thin stalactite fell and crashed down from the ceiling, missing me by inches. I jerked backwards through the water, scraping my back on the rock. Within seconds, merpeople were rushing from the caves.

269

'Quick – out!' a merboy shouted as he raced past me.

I didn't need telling twice. We pelted out through the tunnels, back to open water. Outside, others were already gathered. Someone was swimming in between them, talking to groups of people, telling them to move on. Then he turned and I saw his face. Archie!

What was going on?

I swam over to him. He hardly looked up. 'Just follow the others,' he said gravely. 'We'll meet in the Grand Caves.'

The Grand Caves? The ones Marina had told us about? But weren't they only for really special events?

I followed the others in a daze, my mind swirling and churning like the sea.

I gasped as I entered the Grand Caves. Impossible shapes hung all around us: upside-down forests, frozen bunches of arrows waiting to fall as one, long paper-thin flaps that looked like dinosaur wings. Drips from the ceiling bounced off majestic boulders and into the pool, ringing out like church bells.

Ahead of me, a stone platform jutted out over the water. On one side, thick marble-like columns reached down from the ceiling into the depths of the water, frilly edges folding around them like icing on a cake. On the other, the wall stretched up like a cliff side, stalagmites lining its surface, clumped together in chunky groups. Lanterns glowed among them, spreading shimmering lights across the pool as they shook. The walls were still trembling. Surely it wasn't safe to be inside if there was an earthquake?

I looked around for someone I knew. Shona had disappeared. Probably with Althea and Marina, I thought miserably.

In front of me, a long wooden walkway divided the clear azure pool. A few people were carefully picking their way along it. Then I spotted Mum. She was here, too, edging across the walkway with Millie.

'Mum!'

She looked up and waved briefly before grabbing the rails as the caves shook again. She pointed up to the stone benches that stretched high up on the cave's sides. I wondered if I should get out of the pool and join her, but then another mighty crash thundered through the caves, throwing me under.

Gasping, I gave myself up to the water. It wasn't as bad underwater: it was a bit like a jacuzzi. It might almost have been enjoyable if it wasn't for the fact that I didn't have a clue what was going on, my best friend wasn't speaking to me and the island seemed to be crumbling around us.

As I resurfaced, I spotted Shona with Althea and Marina. I knew it! A shot of anger speared through me. It wasn't fair! I hadn't exactly gone to that lagoon on my own. She'd done wrong just as much as I had. Nearly. I mean, it wasn't as if I'd forced her to go. And it was their suggestion in the first place! She looked up and caught my eye, just for a second. I nearly smiled. Then Althea said something to her and she turned away. She didn't look back. Traitor.

This was worse than Brightport High! At least then, I could sneak out at night to meet Shona. Now I'd lost her, and it seemed as if all three of them had turned against me. It was so unfair! I'd be better off going back to Brightport, I thought, my heart heavy, my eyes stinging with tears.

I didn't have long to dwell on it. All thoughts were catapulted out of my mind by an explosion of rocks as the caves shook even more violently. A column that looked like marble fell into the water with a mighty splash. Forests of stalagmites shuddered and trembled. I looked up to see Mum gripping the bench. Millie was holding her arm and looking serene. As serene as anyone can look when they're sitting on a bench that seems to be doubling as a seaside rodeo horse.

Where was Dad? I scanned the pools. And then I saw him. Terror on his face, he was hurtling across the pool.

'Emily!' he cried into my hair as he pulled me towards him.

I grabbed onto him while the caves crashed and crumbled all around us. It was growing louder. It sounded like thunder, cracking right over our heads, coming from everywhere.

And then something happened. Something almost familiar. I almost knew it was going to happen, almost remembered it from somewhere else.

The shaking stopped.

Just like that.

The sudden stillness was almost as much of a shock as the violent movement that had come before it, throwing people across the floor, dunking merfolk under the water. I gripped Dad so hard it must have hurt him. He held me close.

'Look!' Someone was calling out. I turned to see where everyone was looking. The caves were splitting! A crack opened up, starting from the base, shaking and creaking as it crumbled open. The whole thing would fall in on us. We'd be buried alive!

But I soon realised that nothing else was moving. Just one section of the caves was splitting open, almost like a hidden door. Almost as though it was being opened by someone. Or something.

Or Neptune.

The caves had split wide and high enough to let in a thick shaft of sunlight. I had to cover my eyes.

When I opened them, I saw him, riding into the caves, shrouded by dusty sunbeams. First the dolphins, then the chariot, gold and grand, carrying Neptune into the caves.

I should have known I'd be found out! Shona must have told, after all. She'd completely betrayed me. How could she?

The dolphins pulled Neptune into the centre of the caves before swimming back into the corners, surrounding us like bodyguards. Archie swam beside the chariot.

Pausing to wait for silence, Neptune rose in his seat, lifting his trident in the air. As he waved it above his head, the cave closed again, sealing us together to face his wrath. I knew what *that* was like. Knowing I was to face it again was almost enough to make me give up hope altogether.

Neptune looked around the caves. 'Do you KNOW why I am here?' he asked, his voice deep and grave. His question echoed over and over, *KNOW why I am here, KNOW why I, KNOW, know* . . .

No one dared answer. No one knew. Almost no one. He was here for me, I was sure of it. I tried to calm my thumping chest before Dad heard it.

'I shall ask another question,' he said, his voice ringing around the caves. 'Do you know why YOU are here?'

He looked round, narrowing his eyes. I willed myself to shrink into nothingness. Luckily his gaze passed me by.

More silence. Neptune clicked his fingers. At once, a line of seahorses appeared at the side of the caves. They gathered into a perfect formation and swam towards him. Then, hooking his golden gown in their tails, they raised it up behind him. Neptune sat down and nodded curtly, his diamond-studded tail fanning out in front of him. The seahorses instantly darted away.

'I will tell you,' Neptune said. 'You are here because of ME! Because of MY generosity. This island hasn't always been the happy little paradise you have here today. This was once a place of grave importance.'

He banged his trident on a rock. 'Archieval!'

Archie swam forwards. Then, bowing low, he kissed Neptune's tail. 'Your Majesty,' he said solemnly. I'd never seen Archie look like this. He had a gold sash running along his tail; his hair was tied back in a neat ponytail and seemed to shine with splashes of deep green against the pool's reflection.

'Tell these folk their history,' Neptune said coldly. 'It's about time they were reminded.' Then he sat back in his chariot, waving his trident at Archie to beckon him forward.

The caves went silent as we waited for Archie to speak.

He cleared his throat. 'Many years ago,' he began, 'life here was very different. The Bermuda Triangle was an important stronghold. Together with a most trusty servant of Neptune's, our bravest sirens worked well here, in the rich waters around Allpoints Island.' Archie paused. His tail flickered nervously. His cheeks had reddened a touch. 'This is where ships were brought down. They were relieved of their riches, which were returned to the rightful owner of all that passes on the oceans.'

Ships were brought down? What was he telling us?

That people had drowned here? I knew that was what sirens did, but to think of it happening right here! Was our new home one of those ships? Maybe someone had died in my bedroom!

My mind swirled with grim and gruesome images. But the images were real! All the stories Archie told us on the way here – they were all true. And what about the ones he *hadn't* told us? They were probably even worse. This place wasn't paradise at all. It was more like a setting for a horror film. I could hardly concentrate as Neptune started talking again. 'Thank you, Archieval. And then what happened?'

Archie glanced back at Neptune before clearing his throat again. 'The, er, the trusty servant I told you about. One day, he – '

'TELL THEM WHEN!' Neptune exploded.

'Almost a hundred years ago – '

'EXACTLY! NOT a hundred! Ninety-two years ago! Do you hear me? Ninety-two. That is my POINT!' As he shouted, a wave washed through the pool. I held onto Dad to steady myself.

Neptune sat back down in his chariot, his face purple with rage. He clicked his fingers and a dolphin rushed forward. Turning onto its back, it flapped its tail in front of Neptune's face like a fan. After a while, Neptune cooled down and he waved the dolphin away. He motioned to Archie once again. 'Continue.'

'Ninety-two years ago, this trusty servant went to sleep.'

Dad pulled away from me. 'You're talking in riddles, Archie.'

What was he doing? Had he forgotten how powerful Neptune was? Or that it was only thanks to him that we were here? Or how easy it would be to send him back to *prison*? He let go of me and swam towards Archie. 'Tell us what this is about. Who is the trusty servant that you keep mentioning? If you're telling us a story, tell us the whole thing.'

Archie glanced at Neptune, who shrugged disdainfully.

'All right,' Archie said. 'I'll tell you.' He took a deep breath. 'I'm talking about the kraken.'

The cave filled with sound: people whispering, talking, gasping. Merpeople turning to each other with questions on their faces and fear in their eyes.

A mergirl from my class was in front of me in the water. 'What's the kraken?' I asked in a whisper.

'It's a huge, fierce monster.' she whispered back. 'It's just a myth, though. It's not real.' She turned back to face Archie. 'Or at least that's what we've always thought.'

My body shook. My tail was spinning so vigorously the water was frothing around me.

A mermaid I didn't recognise held up her hand. She had deep wrinkles in her face and piercing blue eyes. 'Archieval, if this is true, why didn't our parents tell us about it? My great-grandparents would have been alive while it was around. Surely they would have passed this on?'

Archie glanced once more at Neptune for approval. A brief nod in reply.

'The merfolk who lived here at that time were the kraken's keepers. The kraken works for a hundred years, then sleeps for another hundred. The last time it went to sleep, one small ship somehow managed to find its way through the Triangle's border. With no kraken to bring it down, the ship ended up here.' Archie looked at the people sitting along the stone benches. 'Those folk were your ancestors,' he said.

'But we don't know anything about this,' one of the women called down. I recognised her from the ships in our bay. 'Surely someone would have told us!'

'Once the people had landed at the island, it turned out many of the merfolk were happy for them to stay. In a short time, friendships were formed. Apart from a very small number of the kraken keepers who were assigned to special duties elsewhere, most of the merfolk decided to stay here, as did most of the humans.'

'You haven't answered my question!' the woman shouted.

'Memory drug,' Archie said simply. 'They volunteered. That was their choice.'

'All of them?' the woman insisted. 'The merfolk, too?'

'We can use it on anyone,' Archie replied. 'And it will wipe out almost everything. What remains — well, you will all have heard half-tales, stories you never quite knew what to make of, myths passed on and distorted with every telling.'

Archie's words were slowly filtering into my brain. I didn't want to understand, didn't dare follow his thinking to its logical conclusion. But the memory drug, well, I knew all about that. It was what my mum had been given for twelve years, so she wouldn't remember that she was married to a merman. Fed to her in so-called treats from her so-called friend Mr Beeston. The so-called lighthouse keeper! He'd always given me the creeps. When it turned out he'd been spying on us my entire life, it all made sense. I'd half forgiven him in the end, when he helped me get my own back on Mandy Rushton. He used the memory drug on my class so no one would remember me turning into a mermaid. But he wasn't to be trusted – and nor was anyone else who went round doling out that drug!

'As you all know, Neptune is a just and kind ruler,' Archie continued, with a slight cough. 'He allowed them to live together here on the island. No one needed to know about the kraken. Not yet. And so, you are here today. Allpoints Island has existed in this way for ninety-two years.'

A mermaid with glitter in her hair and a pink tail that flickered and splashed on the water raised her hand. 'But why are you telling us this?' she asked in a timid voice. 'Why now? And who are you anyway? We hardly know you.'

Neptune rose from his chariot, motioning Archie

to move out of his way. 'Archieval works for me,' he said. 'And he has told you your history. Now let me tell you something about your present.'

He sucked in his cheeks, clenching his teeth. 'Someone,' he said, almost in a whisper, '*someone* has dared to challenge my power.' He took a breath, lifting his trident in the air. Then, in a voice that shook the caves as much as his arrival had done, he bellowed, 'Someone woke the kraken before its time!'

Darting backwards and forwards in the pool, agitated and angry, he spoke quickly. 'Eight more years. That's how long it had. That's how long it NEEDED. That's when I would have been here for it. But no! Someone couldn't wait that long. SOMEONE had to wake it early. Do you KNOW what happens when my kraken has not had the sleep it needs?'

The caves responded with silence. No one was going to attempt to answer Neptune in this kind of mood. Not that he was known for having any other kind of mood.

'I'll tell you. It wakes in a rage. Too much of a rage for even NEPTUNE to calm it. My truly loyal servant – someone has robbed me of it!'

'What will it do?' someone asked.

'The first signs are relatively small. It will lash around in its lair, creating freak waves. This is what it does while still in its cave. As far as we know, it still IS in there. But it will find its way to open seas sooner or later, and when it does, it will set out on the only path it knows.' Neptune paused as he slowly surveyed the caves. 'Destruction.'

My tail was shaking again. 'It's OK, little 'un,' Dad whispered, pulling me close. 'I'll look after you.' He knew nothing. Nothing.

'That is why I am the ONLY one who should wake the kraken. The one who wakes it is the ONLY one who – ' Neptune stopped abruptly. He smoothed back his hair, straightened his beard.

'Well. Let me just tell you this. Without my direction, it can destroy anything in its wake. Perhaps this whole island will crumble from its rage.'

The end of the island? All because of me? I tried to swallow and found I couldn't. I had to fix this!

'Oh yes,' Neptune continued. 'And you should know this: it can bring ships towards it. Apart from a few of my loyal aides, the kraken is the only creature who knows how to pierce the magic of the Bermuda Triangle. Once the kraken leaves its caves, you are no longer safe. Discovery cannot be far away. When this happens, the days of Allpoints Island are numbered.'

Neptune sucked in his breath again. 'I have not yet decided what I shall do about you all. In the meantime, I want to know WHO DID THIS! I WILL find out! It is IMPERATIVE that they come to me!'

He stared round the caves in the silence. An occasional drop of water plopped softly into the water. No! I couldn't. I *couldn't*! I *wasn't* going to get Mum and Dad thrown off the island. I wasn't going back to that awful jail. I had to think of something.

'WELL?' he bellowed.

Then someone coughed gently. There was a bustling sound up on the stone benches. Someone was getting up. Millie! What on earth was she doing?

She flung her black cape over her shoulder and stepped towards a barrier at the edge of the pool.

'Your Majesty,' she said firmly. 'I'm not one to interfere, but I may be able to help you.'

Neptune almost smiled. He looked as though he was smiling, anyway. It might just as easily have been anger twisting his face into a contorted frown. He pulled on his beard. '*Help* me?' he repeated.

'I can see things,' Millie explained. 'I don't like to boast but I *have* been told I have something of a gift. I just need your star sign.'

'My STAR SIGN?' Neptune yelled.

'Yes, you know, your horoscope, your – '

'I know what you meant! It's PISCES of course!'

'Thank you,' Millie said through tight lips. 'That anger won't do your karma any good at all,' she added in a stage whisper. Then she closed her eyes and folded her hands over her chest. 'I believe I can tell you exactly what has happened,' she said. 'I just need some quiet.'

Neptune looked as though he was about to burst, but he didn't speak. Nor did anyone else. Could she really see what had happened? Millie's cosmic ways didn't often come to much, but she did have the odd accurate moment. What if she had one now?

'I see riches of some sort,' Millie murmured. 'What is it? Gold? Let me focus.'

Gold! She was describing the cave! No! Trust Millie to have one of her flukes when I desperately needed her to come out with her usual barmy nonsense. I'd heard enough. I had to get out.

I glanced up and tried to catch Mum's eye. She was watching Millie with a look of admiration on her face. How would she look at me when she found out what I'd done? I couldn't bear to imagine it.

I edged quietly away from Dad towards the darkness at the back of the pool. I could hear Millie's voice warbling across the water. She sounded as if she was humming. Everyone was watching her. This was my only chance.

'I'm sorry,' I whispered into the darkness and slipped quietly away.

I swam frantically through the dark tunnels, not even thinking about where they were leading me. I pounded past underwater stalagmites faintly lit up with soft glowing crystals, round twists and turns and crevasses, almost gasping for the sight of the sky. I had to get out of the caves. Had to think.

Eventually, I came out into the open water. The light shocked me. Two little blueheads hovered at the cave's mouth, pecking at the rock as though giving it little kisses.

A noise behind me. Splashing. Someone was following me!

I dived down into a thin cave under the rocks, stumbling upon a group of fat hogfish who looked up at me with black eyes before scattering away to find another den.

I watched the cave's entrance. It was Dad!

I swam out from under the rock. 'What are you doing here?'

'Emily!' He swam over towards me. 'Why have you run away?'

I retreated further under the rocks. 'I've let you down. You, Mum, everyone. We'll get thrown off the island and it's all my fault. I'm so sorry.'

Dad squeezed into the crevasse with me, scattering clouds of sand as he slithered along the rock. 'No one's going to throw you off the island, little 'un. Why would they do that?'

'You don't know!' I wailed. 'You don't know what I've done.' A tear snaked down my cheek, mingling with the water. All this time! All those years without him, and now I'd found him I'd done something so stupid, so dreadful, he'd hate me forever. I'd ruined everything.

'What? What have you done?'

I bit hard on my lip, squeezing my eyes shut.

'Whatever it is, you can tell me. We'll sort it out together.'

My face was wet with tears. 'It was me!' I blurted out. '*I* woke the kraken!'

'You *what*? But how – '

'I went exploring! I knew I shouldn't have, but I did. It was in a cave. I'm so stupid! I found it. I woke it up, Dad. I've ruined everything. I'll never be able to show my face on the island again. You've only just got out of prison and now – oh Dad, I'm sorry.'

Dad stroked my face. 'Look. I don't quite understand, but it'll be OK. We'll sort it out. I'll look after you.'

I pushed his hand away. 'Dad, it *won't* be OK. Don't lie to me. I'm not a *baby*!'

He stared at me, his face red as though I'd hit him. As I held his gaze, he nodded slowly, as though he was watching me grow up in front of his eyes, catching up with who I really was, instead of who he remembered me being. 'You're right,' he said eventually. 'Of course you're not.' He turned to swim away.

'Wait.' I grabbed his arm. 'I'm sorry.'

'You know what you are?' he asked, his voice as tight as his mouth.

I shook my head, holding back fresh tears.

'You're my daughter, that's what you are. You're a Windsnap. And you know what that means?' Before I had a chance to answer, he added, 'It means we're going to sort this out.'

'I'm not going back to the meeting. I can't. Please.'

'Who said anything about going back there?'

'What, then?'

Dad stopped swimming and searched my face.

'We're going to the cave. Show me where it happened.'

'The *kraken's* cave?'

'Why not? You heard what Neptune said. It's probably still in there. Maybe we can sort this mess out, somehow. Seal it back up so it's safe again or something.'

'Dad, it was really frightening. It was the most terrifying thing ever!'

'Worse than going back to face Neptune? You stood up to him in his own court, remember.'

I dropped my head. 'I know. That was pretty frightening, too.'

'Exactly. And you did that, so you can handle this as well.'

'I suppose.'

'Come on.' He held out his hand. 'Let's see what we can do.'

'It's that way,' I said as we came to the lagoon. It looked different. The water was murky and muddier than I remembered. Sand-coloured flatfish skimmed over the seabed, moving beneath us like shifting ground.

My throat closed up. We'd reached the carving on the wall. The trident. How on earth could we have missed it last time? Maybe if we'd seen it, none of this would have happened.

It was pointless thinking like that.

We came to the Catherine Wheel, except this time when I looked at it, I realised I knew exactly what it was. The long shoots spiralling out from the round body in the centre ...

'That's it,' I said, my voice rippling like a breaking wave. 'I don't want to go any further.'

He stopped swimming. 'We need to do this, little 'un – I mean, Emily.'

'Dad, I don't mind you calling me – '

'No.' He put a finger over my lips. In charge. Strong. 'You're not a baby. You're a scale off the old tail and I couldn't be more proud of you. And we're going to sort this out, right?'

'But it's out of bounds. This was how the whole trouble started.'

'And this is how it'll end, too,' he said. 'You don't think we found ourselves at this place by the pair of us doing what we were told, do you?'

I didn't say anything.

He reached out for my hand. 'Come on. I'll go ahead, but you need to tell me where I'm going. I'll look after you.'

Eventually, I took his hand and we swam on in silence.

Everything looked familiar, until we came to an enormous gash in the rock. Maybe the size of a house.

'In there.' I held out a shaky arm. 'Except it was a tiny hole last time!'

Dad swallowed. 'Right, then. You ready?'

'I'll never be ready to go back in there.' A solitary fish flashed past me: soft green on one side, bright blue on the other, its see-through fins stretched back as it swam away from the cave. Sensible fish.

'Come on. You'll be OK. I'm right beside you.' He squeezed my hand and we edged inside, slipping back through the rock.

But it was completely different. So different that I started to wonder if we were in the wrong place. There were no thin winding channels, just huge gaping chasms all the way. We swam through them all.

And then we came to the gold. We *were* in the right place. Jewels and crystals lay scattered across the seabed. As we swam lower, the surroundings felt less familiar. Colder. And there was something else. Something very different. The deeper we got, the more we saw of them.

Bones.

Just the odd one at first, that could perhaps have passed for driftwood. Then more: clumps of them, piled up like the remains of a huge banquet. Long thin bones, twisty fat ones – and then a skull, lying on the sea floor. A dark fish slipped through an eye socket. I clapped a hand across my mouth.

'Dad!' I gripped his hand so hard I felt his knuckles crack.

'Don't look at them,' he said, his voice wobbling. 'Just stay close to me.'

We swam into every bit of the cave. Every centimetre.

'What do you see?' Dad asked as we paused in the centre of the biggest chasm.

I looked round. 'Nothing.'

'Exactly.' He turned to face me, suddenly not in charge any more. Not strong. Just scared. 'It's gone, Emily. The kraken – it's on the loose.'

How long have we been here? Couple of days? Who
knows? All I know is we're stranded on a deserted scrap
of an island, the boat's broken and I'm hungry.

Nuts! How long can a person live on nuts? And water
from a dodgy-looking stream. Dad reckons he'll catch us
some fish. And he reckons we could fix the boat if we all
'shaped up a bit'. He's acting as if he's on some kind of
Boy Scouts' trip, as if this is all part of the adventure.

Mum's hardly spoken. It's best that way. If we talked
more, we might end up talking about what happened.
About the –

Anyway.

It's hardly even an island. I can vaguely see something
that might be a proper island, out at sea. Far too far to
swim. Just our luck to get stranded on this tiny speck of
land instead. Two hundred paces from one side to the
other. I counted yesterday. Or the day before, I don't
remember. Some time when I was collecting twigs so
that Dad could build us a so-called shelter. Not that I'm
likely to get any sleep. It lends itself to a touch of insom-
nia, getting stranded on an island the size of a pair of
underpants with nothing to eat, no way of getting

home and no one to talk to except your parents.

Not even the captain.

That's another thing we don't talk about. I try not to think about that, either. What happened to him? Could he be . . .

Like I said, best not to think about that.

There's a splashing noise behind me.

'Mandy! Where's your mum?' It's Dad, coming out of the water with one of the nets from the boat. He's wearing purple shorts down to his knees and he's wad-dling onto the shore in his flippers. He's been off looking for fish. That's all he's done since we've been here. That and mess around banging and hammering on the boat. It's washed up on the tiny beach, half-filled with water and littered with shells and stones and broken bottles. Yeah, Dad. It's going to be so easy to fix.

The net's empty, as usual.

Dad pulls his mask and snorkel off. He's grinning. What on earth can he find to smile about? Doesn't he realise we're stranded and we're all going to die? Maybe he got knocked on the head when the boat went under.

He's shaking himself dry. 'Come with me. I've got something important to tell you both.'

I follow him back to the pathetic bundle of twigs that seems to have become our home. Mum's sitting on the ground leaning against a palm tree. She's not doing any-thing, just staring into space. Her hair's sticking out everywhere, as though she's had an electric shock. Her face is white, her eyes unfocused. She looks like a mad-woman.

'Maureen, Mandy - our problems are over!' Dad announces.

I can't help it; I burst out laughing. I mean, look around you Dad – wake up and smell the coffee. Oh, sorry, I forgot. THERE ISN'T ANY COFFEE BECAUSE WE'RE MAROONED ON A STRIP OF LAND YOU COULD MISS IF YOU BLINKED, WITH NOTHING BUT NUTS, INSECTS AND A SMASHED-UP BOAT FOR COMPANY!

'Just hear me out,' Dad says. 'You're not going to believe me, but I swear, every word is true.' There's a tic beating against his red cheek. 'I *swear*,' he repeats.

Mum sighs. 'Just tell us. What ridiculous idea have you come up with now?'

'It's not an idea, Mo. Well, not exactly. It's something I've seen.'

Mum raises her head a fraction. 'What have you seen, then?'

Dad puffs out his chest and looks from one of us to the other. 'Mermaids.' I watch the lump in his throat bob up and down. 'I've seen mermaids.'

'Oh for heaven's sake, Jack!' Mum pulls herself up and shakes out her skirt. 'When are you going to act like a proper man and sort out this mess, rather than indulging your stupid fantasies?'

She starts to walk off, wiping sand off the backs off her legs. Dad grabs her arm. 'It is not a fantasy, Maureen!' he says furiously. 'I swear on every breath I've ever taken, there are mermaids! Not here, further out. I've seen them swimming, under the water. They've got tails – long, glistening, shiny tails!'

Their eyes are locked. It's as if they're acting out some surreal sketch and the teacher has just said 'OK, freeze, everybody!'

But there's something about what he's said, something just out of reach . . .

'Don't you understand what this means?' Dad says. His neck's bright red and bulging. He's gripping Mum's arm.

Mum stares at him. 'No, Jack. I'm afraid I don't know what it means at all. That you're cracking up, perhaps? Well, don't worry, I'm sure I won't be far behind you.' She pulls out of his grip.

'Mo, I'm *not* cracking up!' he shouts. 'You've got to believe me! We could save our home, the amusement arcade - the whole pier!' He turns to me, his eyes wild and intense. 'Mandy, you believe me, don't you?'

'I – ' Of course I don't believe him. Of *course* I don't! But there's something. Something. What is it?

Mum's shaking her head. 'You'll forgive me if I don't quite follow your logic.'

Dad holds up his net. 'We capture one! Take it back to Brightport. We can have it on show, charge admission and everything. We'll look after it, of course. Give it a good life. People will travel from all over the country to see it! From all over the world, maybe! We'll be heroes in the town, we'll pay for the pier to be renovated. Don't you see? This could solve all our problems!'

Mum sucks in her cheeks. 'Jack,' she says, 'you haven't managed to catch so much as a *goldfish* since we got here! Even if I were to believe that you have seen a mermaid – which, frankly, I don't – how in heaven do you propose to catch the thing?'

Dad pulls at his net. 'I haven't got the whole plan figured out yet, have I? I've only just *seen* them. A group of them. Swimming in the deep water. One of them had gold stars shining in her tail. There was a merman too, with long black hair and a shiny silver tail. A merman! For God's sake, Maureen!' He grips her arm again. 'I'm telling the truth! You'll see I am.'

Mum pulls away and turns to me. 'Come on, Mandy. Help me fetch some dinner. I've had enough of your father and his daydreams for one afternoon.'

I follow Mum as we pick our way through under-growth, scavenging for crumbs like vagrants. As usual, we don't talk. But this time, it's because of the thoughts going round in my head, thoughts I'm not sure I dare share with Mum. There's definitely something familiar about what Dad said. Something niggling away in the back of my mind. I can't put my finger on it.

Maybe it's something I've seen on telly. A film about mermaids or something. I've got this picture in my mind. Someone swimming. She's got a tail and she's spinning round, smiling, grinning – at me! She's in a pool. It's not from telly. I'm sure it isn't. It feels real. It feels like a memory.

I grab a couple of nuts and shove them hard into my pocket. Mermaids! As if! I force myself to laugh.

We'd better get away from here before we *all* crack up.

Chapter Five

'Dad.'

He didn't reply. Just carried on staring out to sea. We'd spent half the day swimming round the coast, trying to keep out of sight, and trying to figure out what to do next. We stopped to rest at a large rocky bay on the east of the island, just a little further down from our bay.

I swam over to join him next to a huge boulder at the edge of the bay. 'Dad,' I said again.

'I'm thinking, love,' he said without turning round. 'Just give me a minute.'

I counted to ten. 'What are we going to do?'

He shook his head. 'I don't know, Em. I just don't know.'

I looked out to sea with him. The water lapped gently into the cove behind us. Daylight was starting to fade.

I stared out at the horizon. So much ocean, stretching out for miles and miles and miles, forever, it seemed. Nothing but water. And the monster. Somewhere. A cold shiver rattled through my body. The water lay still, but how long till it would seethe with the kraken's rage? The stillness was almost worse than that, knowing it was out there, waiting.

Something flickered on the horizon. A brief flash of light. I jerked upright and peered so hard my eyes watered. There it was again.

'*Dad*!'

'Emily, will you leave me alone! I've told you, give me five minutes. I need to think.'

I shook his arm. 'Look!' I pointed out to the horizon.

Dad followed the line of my finger. 'Mothering mussels,' he breathed, squinting into the distance. His words came out like a whistle. 'What's that doing there?'

'What is it?'

'Look, red, then green.' Dad turned to me. 'It's a ship, Emily.'

A ship had got in! The kraken had already pierced the Triangle's border.

'It's not coming any closer, is it?' I asked with a gulp.

'Doesn't look like it. Doesn't mean it won't,

though.' Dad pushed off from the rock and started to swim away. 'Come on.'

'Where are we going?'

'We'll have to say something.'

'Say something?' My words jammed up my throat. I swallowed hard. 'Who to?'

'I don't know. Archie, I guess.' Dad took hold of my hand. 'Emily, there's a ship coming towards the island. The others need to know that the kraken's got out.'

'No!'

'Em, love, the monster could attack that ship. Or the ship could discover us here. That'll be the end of us all. You heard what Neptune said. We can't stay here if the secret gets out. Can't you just see it? Hordes of tourists swarming the place? They'll turn us into a zoo or something.' He turned to swim away.

A zoo. My old fears of discovery resurfaced in a wave of anguish. What had I *done*?

'There must be something we can do,' I said, swimming hard to keep up.

'This is the only thing.' Dad's voice was firm.

He didn't speak again. The water soon grew warmer as we reached the shallow sand, rippling like tyre tracks across the sea floor.

Dad wouldn't look at me. 'You go along home. Mum'll be worried.'

'What about you?'

'I'm going to see if I can find Archie.'

I didn't move.

'It'll be all right,' he said with a tight smile. Then he turned and swam towards the end of the bay, taking my last shreds of hope with him.

Mum threw her arms round me the second I arrived back at *Fortuna*. 'Emily! I've been worried sick. Where've you been?'

'With Dad. I felt claustrophobic in the caves and we – we went exploring.' My cheeks burned. I hate lying to Mum.

'Mary P, you really should listen to me. I told you she was safe,' Millie said, pouring some herbal tea from a pot and settling down on the big sofa.

'Millie saw a ship,' Mum said.

'She *saw* it?' I burst out.

Mum looked at me quizzically. 'When she did Neptune's reading. She had a vision of a ship. What ship did you think I meant?'

'Oh. No. Nothing. Yes, that's what I thought you meant,' I blustered. Great move, Emily. Just give the game away to *everyone*. 'I thought you'd said something about gold.' I tried to keep my voice even.

'Yes, well, you can't be expected to get everything right, all the time,' Millie replied, sniffing as she picked up a magazine.

'So what did Neptune say about the vision?' I

asked, holding my breath.

Millie flicked the pages. 'Not everyone appreciates my gift.'

'He told her he'd throw her off the island if she wasted any more of his time with her hocus pocus,' said Mum, smiling.

How could she smile? I could hardly *speak*. I had to get away from here. 'I'm going to my room,' I said. Before they had a chance to argue, I'd gone through to the back of the ship and closed my door behind me. Shaking, I sat down on the bed and looked round. Like all the others, the room had a trapdoor that led to the floor below, to the sea. I'd hardly used it yet. The one in the living room was open all the time and it was bigger.

I crept over to the trapdoor next to my bed and opened it up. Maybe . . .

'Emily.' Mum was at my door.

I jumped away from the trapdoor. 'I was just looking at the fish,' I said quickly.

'Are you all right, love?' Mum stepped into the room and came over to me. She lifted a strand of hair off my face, stroking it behind my ear. 'If there's anything you want to talk about . . .'

'There isn't,' I said, trying to make myself smile. I expect I looked a bit like a scared rabbit with a twitch. 'I'm fine, honestly,' I said. 'Just a bit tired.' I stretched my mouth into a yawn. 'Look, see. I think I'll have a lie down.'

Mum stared at me quizzically for a moment before

shrugging. 'Well, we'll be next door if you need anything.' She kissed my forehead and left.

I waited five minutes. She didn't come back. Right, this was it. I knew what I was going to do.

I eased myself through the hole. Then, dangling over the side, I lowered myself down as gently as I could, and let go. I dropped down below with a splash. Had they heard? I held my breath and waited. Nothing.

I waited a bit longer, to make sure my tail had fully formed. When the tingling and numbness had completely gone, I ducked under, swam through the big open porthole, and headed towards the ship.

It was almost like the old days: swimming out to sea under a sky gradually filling up with stars. A stripy butterflyfish raced along beside me before slipping away into the darkness, disappearing under a rock. Shoals of silver bar jacks hovered nearby, shining like pins in the darkness. Purple fans waved with the current, caressing me as I sailed over them.

It was nothing like the old days.

In the old days, I was swimming out to meet my best friend; now I didn't even know if I still *had* one. My chest hurt as I pushed myself to swim harder, swim away from the painful thoughts. The water grew colder and darker. I picked my way out towards the ship, praying there was no current round this side of the island.

After a while, I stopped to scan the horizon. Two dim lights, facing me. It was a long way out, but definitely inside the Triangle. I couldn't even see the island any more. Just blackness, except — what was that? Something flashed through the water. A boat? I held my breath while I watched. Nothing. It must have just been the moon's reflection.

I swam on towards the ship. Maybe I could stop it from finding us, get it away from the island. I had to buy some time.

Eventually, I was close enough to study it: a cruise liner with three levels of portholes and balconies, all lit up with lamps. The sides rose steeply out of the water.

I swam all around it, looking for a way in. There was a rope ladder hanging down at the back. I tried to make a grab for it but missed by inches. I heaved and jumped up in the water. No good — it was just out of reach.

I swam round again, looking for something else. And right at the front, I found it. The anchor!

Gripping the chains, I pulled myself out of the water. My tail dangled and flapped in the sea. Panting and gritting my teeth, I managed to inch my way up. Eventually, I'd done it. I clung onto the chain like a koala, my body clear of the water. Within moments, I got that tingly sensation I knew so well. My legs had come back.

I hooked my feet into the loops, then slowly and carefully climbed up to the ship's deck.

Hauling myself over the metal rail, I landed heavily on the deck. A quick look around. No one. Just me and the darkness and a row of deck-chairs. I dried myself on a towel someone had left on one of them and pulled on the shorts I'd brought with me. Then I went to look for some signs of life.

It didn't take long.

Halfway down the side of the ship, I found some stairs and a door that led inside. There were sounds, somewhere near. I followed the noise, almost sniffing my way towards it. Music. Laughter.

Soon I came out of the narrow corridor into an open space with a few people dotted about. I tried to saunter in casually, as though I belonged there, even though I knew I'd be sussed out in a second.

But I wasn't. Some kids were playing in a tiny arcade on one side; on the other, a couple of men were drinking at a small bar. A man and woman behind the bar laughed together. No one even looked up.

A flight of stairs led up towards where the real noise was coming from. *OK, you can do it*. I took a deep breath, twirled my hair a few times, nibbled on my thumbnails – and went upstairs.

It wasn't till I saw all the food that I realised I was starving! I'd hardly eaten all day.

I grabbed a paper plate and joined the queue behind a girl who looked about my age. Maybe she'd know something.

'It's great, this holiday, isn't it?' I said as we shuffled along the food table, shoving tiny sausages and crackers and crisps onto our plates.

'Mm,' the girl replied through a pizza slice.

'Wonder how long before we move off,' I said casually.

She swallowed the pizza slice. 'My mum says we're not even meant to be here. She reckons we've gone off course. Doesn't matter though, if we see it.'

See it?

'Yeah, that's what I thought,' I said, trying to stay calm. I popped a mini sausage into my mouth. 'So has anyone seen it yet?'

The girl put her plate down. 'Don't you know?'

'Oh, I'd, um – I forgot. Remind me?'

'That's why we're here! Mum says more than half the passengers cancelled at the last minute. That's how we got our places. I bet Carefree Cruises are totally fed up with that captain!'

What was she on about?

'Yeah, I bet,' I said seriously. 'What did he do again?' I asked, quickly turning away to grab another handful of crisps.

'How can you not know? He saw Triggy of course! First sighting in absolutely YEARS!'

A crisp got stuck halfway down my throat. 'Triggy?' I asked, swallowing hard.

'Don't tell me you haven't heard of Triggy.'

I tried a lighthearted shrug and a frown.

'Triggy! The Triangle Monster! I've always believed in it. Mum said it was just a silly fairy tale, but now she's not so sure. I hope we see it, don't you?'

I couldn't reply. I couldn't do anything. I tried. I opened my mouth, even moved my lips a little, I think. But nothing came out. *Triggy*? It sounded like a cartoon character. She had no idea! I thought of the slimy tentacles racing down the tunnel towards me, the suckers all along it, grabbing at the walls, the way it extended out, the hairy tapered end touching me.

The bones.

Now these people were hunting it down. Which either meant it wouldn't be long before they found us – or they'd be its next victims.

'I – I've got to go now,' I said eventually. I staggered away from the food table.

'See you in the morning,' she called before going back to her friend.

'Yeah.' *Whatever.*

I stumbled back down the stairs. At the bottom, I took a turning which I thought led back to the corridor I'd come down earlier. But I emerged into another open space. I was about to turn back when I noticed a shop, just ahead of me. It was closed now, but there was a poster in the window. I went over to take a closer look.

It was the front page of a newspaper: *The Newlando Times.*

'BRAVE CAPTAIN TELLS OF HORROR AT SEA' the headline screamed across the top of the page. I read on.

The old myth of Triggy the Triangle Monster rose up again today when Captain Jimmy Olsthwaite was rescued from stormy seas by a local fisherman.

Captain Olsthwaite lost his boat when it was attacked by what he described as 'a monster beyond imagining. The size of a dinosaur! And a dozen tentacles that wrapped round the boat like a helter skelter!'

His story has horrified and delighted tourists in equal measure.

Katie Hartnett was among those setting sail today with Carefree Cruises. 'It's so exciting,' she told *The Newlando Times.* 'My parents used to tell me stories about The Triangle Monster when I was little – but we never thought it might exist for real!'

Others have cancelled in droves. Pensioner Harold Winters was among them. 'We wanted a peaceful trip, not the fright of our lives,' he said.

The captain's sighting has not been confirmed. Coastguards are warning that it could be a case of delirium brought on by his traumatic capsize and rescue.

Three others were believed to be on board the boat with the captain. Neither they nor the boat have yet been recovered.

The boat was owned by a company called *Mermaid Tours*.

I stumbled away from the shop. I was in one of those nightmares where you're stuck somewhere, trying every exit, but there's no way out and every step takes you deeper into the horror.

I found myself out on the deck again. Leaning over the railing, my stomach heaved. My mouth tasted like iron. I looked down at the sea, deep navy in the darkness. Little bright flecks sparkled white as the water lapped and splashed against the ship. There was another boat down there. I could just make out its shape. A small yacht. It looked as if it was coming towards us. Maybe they were checking their lifeboats were working or something. Well, they'd be needing them soon, unless I could come up with a miracle.

I had to do something! I couldn't just stand here staring at the sea.

Then it came to me.

I ran up steps, down ladders, along corridors, banged on doors, called through open windows: 'TRIGGY! THE MONSTER!'

People emerged from their rooms. Dressing gowns were pulled round bare bellies and boxer shorts, women came out of their cabins in silk nighties, kids in twisted-up pyjamas.

'*Triggy!*' I shouted at everyone I saw. 'The monster! I've seen it!'

'Where?' Open-mouthed gasps.

'Over there!' I pointed – away from the island. I pointed and pointed. 'Tell everyone. Tell the crew!' I ran on as everyone I spoke to gathered along one side of the boat: all gazing out to sea, desperate for a sighting of something I wished with all my heart I would never see again.

I had to find the captain.

I ran on, down more corridors – until I barged slap bang into someone.

'Hey, what's all this?' It was a woman with a uniform on. She grabbed hold of my elbows, holding me at arms' length.

'I need to find the captain,' I gasped. 'I've seen the monster!'

The woman frowned. 'Yes, dear. I'm sure you have. Now come on, why don't you – '

'I have!' I burst out. 'I can prove it. It's – it's – ' I gulped. The memory of it took my breath out of me for a second. I started again. 'It's enormous, and it's got tentacles.'

'We've all seen the papers, sweetheart,' the woman said, smiling. 'Now, if you want an excuse to visit the captain, you can just say so. He's always happy for you kids to have a quick look round the cabin.'

Bingo! 'OK!'

The woman gently shook her head as she pointed towards some stairs. 'It's up there. Turn right at the top, straight on to the end and it's through the door ahead of you. But knock first. He doesn't take kindly to being barged in on.'

'Thanks!' I took the stairs three at a time.

I bashed on the door. *Come on, come on!*

No one answered. Come *on!* No time for politeness. I tried the door. It swung open.

'I need to talk to the captain,' I said breathlessly as I burst into the room.

Two men were sitting in front of a load of dials drinking coffee. One of them swivelled round. 'Now hang on. What's the – '

'Are you the captain?'

'I certainly am,' he said, 'and you can't just – '

'I've seen the sea monster!'

The captain leaned forward in his seat. 'The sea monster?'

I nodded.

His face relaxed into a slight smile. 'Now listen, you want me to tell you something about this sea monster?' he asked. I swallowed, and nodded again.

He lowered his voice. 'It doesn't exist.'

I held his eyes. 'It does! I've seen it.'

The captain leaned back in his seat. 'Right, let's have it, then. Big thing with tentacles, was it?'

'Yes! That's exactly what it was!'

'Right.' He was smiling, laughing at me. I had to convince him.

'It's – it's enormous!'

'Mm hm. Anything else?' the captain asked in a bored voice.

'The tentacles – they're tapered at the end.'

He turned back to his tea. I racked my brain. *What else – what else?*

'And hairy! And they've got huge great suckers all along them!' I blurted.

The captain put his cup down. 'They what?' he asked, his face suddenly hard, and focused on mine.

'And they're – they're green, and grey underneath, and warty.' My voice trailed away as I remembered the sight of it. My teeth chattered.

The captain turned to the other man. 'That's exactly what my friend at the coastguard said.'

'Sir, the newspaper report – '

The captain shook his head. 'Those things weren't in there. Come on, man. Face the facts. You saw the dials. You know we've been stuck here, spinning on the spot like a Mini in a mudbath. There's something going on and it's time we faced up to it.'

He moved his chair closer to mine and leaned towards me. 'Right, then,' he said. 'You'd better tell me exactly where you saw the sea monster.'

I'd done it! The ship had changed direction and we were heading directly away from the island.

I sneaked along the empty deck. Every single person on the ship must have been crowded on the other side, peering into the darkness for a sight of something they thought would make their holiday. I thought of its flailing tentacles, the floor littered with bones, and I shivered. If only they knew. I hoped for their sake that they never would.

I had to get back to the island. Maybe I could confess, after all. If I told Neptune what I'd done here, how I'd stopped a whole cruise ship full of people from discovering us, he might even forgive me.

I checked round one final time to make sure no one could see me. Then I slipped back into the water.

Moments later, the familiar warm feeling spread through my legs as they turned back into my tail. It shone bright in the moonlight.

Fish around me seemed to be dancing. I could make out their shapes in the darkness. They must have been happy for me. Maybe it was a sign. It was all going to be all right. I swam along, lost in my hopes that I could somehow make up for everything that had happened over the last couple of weeks. Perhaps Shona and I would be best friends again and the island would be safe. The kraken might even go away and our lives in our new home could really start.

'EMILY!'

I started and looked back, twisting round in the

water. Two people were leaning out over a balcony, waving frantically. Why weren't they round the other side with everyone else? I edged back towards the boat.

That's when I saw who it was. Mum! Thin and wiry with wild hair, waving her arms about. Someone was with her. Larger than life in a black cape. Millie! What the heck were –

'Emily!' Mum screamed again.

I swam closer to the ship but it was picking up speed. I could hardly keep up.

'Watch the propellers!' Mum screeched. 'Don't come too close!'

Millie had sunk into a deckchair next to her, her head in her hands. A small yacht was moored on a buoy, near where the ship had been only moments ago. The one I'd seen coming towards us. I recognised it now: it was our old boat! They'd followed me!

'Mum! What are you doing there?'

'We came to find you but you'd just jumped off! It was Millie's idea. The vision, the boat. She'd seen you on it.'

'What? You never told me that.'

Millie got up and stumbled across to clutch onto the railing. 'I kept it to myself,' she wailed. 'I thought it would have sounded crazy. I've heard what people say about me.' She leaned out over the railing. 'I'm sorry, Emily. I was too busy worrying about my reputation.'

'We didn't think they'd get going again tonight.' Mum called.

Oh no. My fault again. I'd made things worse *again*. The ship was only on the move because of me. And now it was moving faster and faster away – and taking my mum with it!

'Mum!' I tried to keep up. She was shouting something but I couldn't hear her any more. I could hardly even see her as the ship picked up speed.

'MUM!' I yelled again, uselessly, into the darkness.

As the ship slipped away, I let the current carry me along. No energy left. I drifted away from the ship, from the island, from everything that mattered. Tears streamed down my face as I howled in the darkness.

And then –

Noise.

Clattering – shuffling. What was happening? I mopped my cheeks with my palms.

I'd got caught in – what? Seaweed? I flapped and scratched at it. *Please not the monster*. I looked around me.

A net! I was trapped in a net! A man was holding it, pulling at a piece of rope, dragging me through the water, propelling himself along with flippers.

Flapping my tail, I tried to push myself away, but he was too strong. I struggled and fought, biting at the net, pulling at it with my fingers, cutting my hands, scraping myself all over. It was like wire. There was no way I could get through it. I scratched and screamed as he drew me through the sea.

Soon the water grew warmer and shallower. We were at a tiny island: a little sandy bay with a few palm trees, a small boat moored to a pole and a makeshift lantern propped on the beach. The man tied my net to the pole.

He pushed his mask and snorkel onto the top of his head. I couldn't make out his face properly in the shadowy light. 'I'm not going to hurt you,' he said, panting from swimming so hard. 'Trust me.'

I didn't say anything.

'Do – you – speak – English?' he asked in a very loud voice. I ignored him.

'Stay here,' he said, as though I had a choice. He disappeared up the beach as I scraped and scratched at the net, trying to get out. Moments later, he was back with someone.

'Dad, you are completely obsessed,' a girl's voice was saying. 'It's the middle of the night!' The voice sounded familiar. But it couldn't be.

'I said, didn't I?' the man replied as they came closer. 'I told you – I TOLD you! *Now* do you believe me?' He pointed in my direction. The other person waded towards me and peered at me in the darkness. As she came closer, I could just make out her face from the lantern's light.

It was –

It was –

I gasped and jerked backwards against the net, my mouth stupidly open. It couldn't be! How – ?

It was someone I knew. Someone I knew well. Someone I'd thought I would never *ever* have to see again.

Dad's caught a fish at last.

Hallelujah.

He's screaming and yelling at me to come and see it. You'd think no one had ever caught a fish in the sea before.

But it's not a fish. He's got someone with him.

'I told you! I told you!' he's yelling. 'I said I'd catch a mermaid, didn't I? Do you believe me now?'

I get closer, and I notice a tail. No! It can't be!

He has! He's actually caught a mermaid!

It turns round. I see its face, its mousy hair, skinny runty little arms. It *can't* be! It's impossible! But it is. It is. I grab the lamp and bring it closer as I stare at her.

It's Emily Windsnap!

And then I remember. I remember everything! The pool, the swimming lessons. She came to us once before she left, showing off as usual. She had a tail! She swam in front of us all, swirling it round. Grinning at me as if to say she'd won. It wasn't enough for her that everyone thought she was *so* wonderful. Julie, the swimming instructor – they all liked her more than they liked me, all thought she was better than me. She had to rub it in, didn't she? Had to prove they were right.

How could I have forgotten?

There was something afterwards – they gave us cakes. That was when it all faded. The cakes! Had they drugged them or something? And what the heck is she doing *here*?

Our eyes meet. She's as shocked as I am.

'Mandy!' she says.

I pull myself together quickly. 'Oh, hi Emily,' I say, nice and calm. I sniff and turn to Dad. 'Why are you collecting garbage, Dad?'

Dad pulls off his mask and snorkel. 'What are you on about, Mandy? It's a mermaid!'

'Dad, have you actually looked at her face?'

He gawps at me for a second before turning to Emily, and then back to me. I can almost see the realisation crawling into his mind. He points at Emily. 'But that's, that looks like – '

'Yeah, Dad,' I say, trying to sound bored, or at least as if I've got a *clue* what's going on here, 'it's Emily Windsnap.'

'But how . . . but she's a . . . ' His voice trails away. He looks at her again, then at me. 'Don't be stupid, Mandy,' he says suddenly. 'Of course it's not Emily Windsnap. It just looks a bit like her. This is a mermaid!'

Mum's on the beach. 'What's the fuss, Jack?'

Dad runs towards her, ignoring me, and ignoring reality it seems. 'No time now, Maureen,' he says. 'We need to get ready. Where's all our stuff?'

'What stuff?'

'Everything. Everything we need. Get it in the boat. We're off as soon as it's light.'

'Off?' I follow Dad out of the water. 'What d'you mean "off"? Where are we going?'

Dad stops and turns back to me. 'We're going home, Mandy. With our mermaid. We're going to save the pier. Just like I said.'

He runs over towards the boat.

'But it's broken!' I say, following after him. 'We capsized, remember.'

'I've been working day and night on this boat,' he calls back. 'I think she's ready to sail again. Pack your things, and then get some more sleep. First light of dawn and we're away.'

'Mum?'

Her eyes are vacant. She looks as if she's already given up hope. 'I haven't got a clue what's going on,' she says. 'What's that he's got in the net?'

I leave her to find out for herself as I follow Dad to the boat. Maybe we can sort everything out. Maybe he's right. It's worth a try I suppose. Anything's better than rotting on this stupid island for the rest of our lives. Even if it does mean sailing home with *fish girl*.

The boat seems to be just about holding up. It would be better if Dad had the slightest idea how to drive it. We're buffeting about all over the place. He keeps yelling things at Mum, like 'Get over onto starboard!' and 'We need to tack! Watch the boom! Lee oh!"

She yells things back but her words are washed away

by the wind and the sea water spraying us on the back deck. Just as well. Judging by her expression, it's probably best if neither of us can hear what she's actually saying.

Anyway, I'm busy with Emily. I've got to keep an eye on the net, make sure it doesn't come loose. Can't have her escaping.

'Comfy down there, are you?' I call down to her. She's being pulled along like a water-skier. She should be grateful for the free ride. 'Enjoying your little trip?'

'What are you going to do with me?' she whimpers. She's scared. Good.

'Oh, didn't Dad tell you? We're taking you back to Brightport.'

The boat swerves and surges so I don't hear her reply. Just a kind of yelp from inside the net. It could almost make me feel sorry for her.

As if!

'Yeah, we're going to put you on display,' I continue when she bobs up above the surface again, her hair plastered across her face with sea water. I smile down at her. 'Hey, maybe all your old school friends will come and visit. That'd be nice for you, wouldn't it? We were thinking maybe five pounds a visit. What d'you think?'

'What about my mum? She's stranded on a ship! I've got to find her! And my dad? Let me at least get a message to him!'

'Yeah, right!'

'Mandy, I need you!' Dad's calling.

'Back soon,' I call down to her. 'Don't go anywhere

now. Oh, sorry, I forgot. You can't!'

I stand up to see what Dad wants. But I don't need to ask. The boat has levelled out; all is calm. But just ahead of us is something I'd almost forgotten about.

The darkness, spreading like an oil slick in the pale morning light, pulling us in.

'Dad, what are we going to do?'

He shakes his head. 'I haven't got a clue, love. We've got to get across it, somehow.'

Mum's inching along the side deck to join us. 'Jack, are you mad? Have you forgotten what happened last time? The last fortnight foraging for food like beggars after near enough drowning? And that *poor* captain. *Have* you?'

'What choice do we have, Maureen?'

'We can think about our choices as soon as you've got us away from here. But I, for one, am not going to gamble with my life when the odds look like that!' She points to the sheet of water, glistening like glass ahead of us.

'Well, *I*, for one, am not going to live on nuts and berries for the rest of my life!' Dad yells. 'And I'm not going to go back and watch my home and my livelihood demolished either.'

'So you'll kill us all then, will you?' Mum screams.

'Mum! Dad!' I try to get between them, but the boat suddenly lurches and I slip across the deck. We're starting to tilt. We're being drawn towards it again.

Neither of them is listening anyway. They'd rather scream at each other than try and work out what to do.

318

'DAD!' I yell, clutching the railings as the boat dips further. I nearly fall over the side. Emily is down below in her stupid net. We're going to capsize again. I'm going to drown out here, all because of *her*. I can't believe it!

The boat lurches again.

'I can help.' A voice from down below.

'What?'

'I'll help you.'

I grab the railing as the boat leans over. Spray hits us on all sides as we skid through the water, soaking me. She looks up at me pitifully, her big brown eyes round and shiny. I turn away. I bet she's only putting it on anyway. 'And why would you do that?' I ask.

'I don't want you to die,' she says.

'I'm meant to believe that, am I?'

'I've got enough on my conscience,' she calls up. 'I don't need that as well. You can keep me in the net. Just let the rope out. I'll pull you away.'

I glance over at Mum and Dad. They're not screaming at each other any more. Mum's trying to make her way over to me. She's not even holding onto anything.

'Mum! Stay where you are!'

'Let the rope out!' Emily yells. 'Do you want to be killed?'

I glance at the rope. It's looped round and round over a hook. 'Don't try and do anything clever, right?'

'Just do it!' she shouts. 'It'll be too late in a second.'

I lurch over to the back of the boat. One last glance at the water ahead of us, then I unhook the rope. 'I'm warning you,' I shout as I throw it into the water.

The coil lands with a splash. Then nothing. Where's she gone? She's disappeared! I scan the surface of the water. Where is she? She must be in there somewhere.

I'm staring so hard at the water it looks like it's changing colour, getting darker. It *is* changing colour! There's a shape in there! A huge grey outline of something – something very, very big.

Without warning, it bursts through the surface. A piercing, screaming siren sound screeches into the sky as an olive green tentacle rises up, way up above us, then sears downwards to wrap itself over the top of the boat like an arch.

No!

'Mandy!' Emily's yelling. Where is she? Did she know it was here? Did she make this happen?

The monster lifts the boat right out of the water, high up into the air. I can see the underside of its tentacle. It looks like a giant worm, extending and retracting, slithery and lumpy. Gasping and retching, I fall against the railing, clutching on for my life.

With an almighty crash, it drops us back down onto the water, exploding against the surface.

We're such fools! How could we let it happen *again*? *She's* done this to us. She's made it happen. She tricked us, somehow.

The thing has tentacles all over us, sliming over the boat, roaming, searching for things to grab and lurch onto. I'm slipping across the deck, water everywhere. It sucks the boat down, throws it around, tosses us one way and then another.

Any second now, we'll all be in the water. Should I pray?

As if praying would help.

The only thing giving me courage as the boat is thrown over, as I clutch the railings, hold my breath, grab the lifebelt, is one single thought:

I'll get you for this, fish girl. I will SO get you for this.

Chapter Six

*T*otal stillness. Utter darkness.
  What had happened? Where was I?
 I rubbed my eyes, tried to move. I was still inside the net, trapped under a rock. Out of the darkness, a shape was coming towards me. It looked like a submarine, gliding along the very bottom of the sea, black on top, white underneath, large fins flapping below. As it came closer, it opened its jaw. Serrated lines of teeth, above and below: the sharpest bread knives.

A killer whale!

I grabbed the net, rubbing it hard on the edge of the rock, sawing and scraping frantically. My fingers bleeding and raw, I yanked and tugged at the net. *Come on, come on! Break!*

The string started to fray and tear. I was nearly out.

But then the water was swirling all around me, whisking up and round, faster and faster like a whirlpool.

It was back.

The sea filled with giant tentacles, writhing and grasping and sucking. I crouched tight under the rock and prayed it wouldn't see me.

THWACK! They crashed against a rock, only metres away from me. It split and crumbled instantly. My tail flapped wildly; my teeth rattled so hard my jaw hurt.

CRASH! The tentacles came down again, scattering a spiralling shoal of barracuda before searching around for their next target.

And then they found it. The whale! Jaws wide open, the whale thrashed around, snapping its teeth at the monster. I crouched under my rock as the kraken moved closer, and for the first time, I saw its face. I clapped a hand over my mouth, swallowing back a scream.

Horned and full of snarling lumps, with huge white eyes on either side of its head, it opened its mouth to reveal teeth like shining daggers. Briefly opened wide, the teeth came crashing together, snapping shut, again and again, pulling and tearing at the whale. On and on it went, the whale flung from one side to the other as tentacles and horns and teeth grabbed and tore at its skin.

Eventually, the thrashing slowed. The whirlpool stopped. The sea began to change colour, blood seeping into the cracks around me. *Go away, go away*, I said silently, over and over, until, miraculously, the water became calm again, almost as though it had heard me.

In the darkness, I cried.

Mum.

I kept seeing her, reaching out to me from the ship, wild and screaming as she was taken further and further away. The image bit into me like wire. I curled into a ball and tried to push it away.

I had to find Mandy and her parents. They were my only hope now. I tore at the net till I'd made a hole big enough to squeeze through. Edging out of my hiding place, I forced myself not to think about what I'd just witnessed, although my twitching body made it hard for me to forget. I scanned the water. Nothing. It had gone.

Swimming away from the rocks, I searched desperately for something familiar. I soon came to a deep sandy stretch, rocks on either side. Around them, weeds floated and swayed, surrounding me like a thick curtain. I swam along the sandy channel until it came to a rocky reef, full of holes and ridges and grey peaks like castles and hills.

I fought the rising panic in my chest. This wasn't familiar at all. I was completely lost. A large, sullen grey fish drifted silently ahead of me, hovering like a hawk. Bright blue eyes bore down on me as I passed it.

'Who's that?'

A voice! A male voice.

'Come no further!' The voice called out again. I stopped swimming.

'Who are you?' My words bubbled away from me.

Silence. Then, 'You'll do as I say. I am armed. Do you understand?'

Armed?

'I – yes, I understand.' Understand? Of course I didn't! I didn't understand any of this.

Out of the shadows, a thin, lanky figure swam towards me. A young merman, maybe in his twenties. He pulled some fishing line out from a packet on his back. 'Hold your arms out.'

'Who are you? Why should I – '

'Do as I say!' he bellowed, reaching for something that looked like a knife by his side. I thrust my arms out in front of me and watched while he tied my wrists together. 'This way.'

With that, he turned and swam, pulling me along behind him. All thoughts of my mum and the kraken and Mandy were dragged away by this – my second capture in one day. I let myself be pulled along. What choice did I have? No strength left to fight, this time.

The reef stretched and curved, a lunar landscape dotted with ornamental gardens. Deep brown plants lined rocky chasms. Round boulder-like chunks of coral clung to every surface; thick green spongy tubes waved and pointed threateningly as we passed over them. I glanced at the merman as we swam. He had a thin grey tail with silver rings pierced all along one side. Wild blond hair waved over his shoulders, a chain made of bones hung around his neck.

We came to a cave with green and blue weeds hanging down from the top of its mouth in a curtain. Crystals were embedded in the rock all around the entrance.

'In here.' He pushed me forward.

'Where are we?'

'You'll see.'

Inside, the cave ballooned out into an enormous dome. Crystals, jewels and gold lined the route. Mosaics filled with gems of every colour swirled along the seabed; a round body, swirling arms . . .

'Where are we?' I gasped. 'Who are you?'

'You'll find out soon enough,' he replied. We'd reached a building. It looked like a castle, or a ruin of a castle. Half-collapsed turrets were filled with dia-monds; crumbling walls held pale jewels in clusters around their base. A giant archway for a door, a marble pillar on either side. As we came closer, I could see something embossed onto each pillar. A golden seahorse.

I knew this archway! I'd seen it before, or another one very much like it. 'This is one of Neptune's palaces, isn't it?' I asked, shuddering as I realised we were swimming over a mosaic shaped like a mass of tentacles.

The merman didn't reply.

Through the arch, a chandelier hung from a high ceiling, jangling with the water's rocking. That confirmed my fear. Neptune had found me.

We ducked low to swim through a smaller arch, adorned, like the others, with elaborate jewels. A wooden door lay ahead. The merman paused to neaten his hair. Then he turned a shiny brass handle and nudged me inside.

We were in a small room. A stone desk embedded with shells took up half the space. Conches and oyster shells lay scattered on its surface. Next to it, an old merman turned as we came into the room. He had a straggly beard and dark eyes that stared at me, holding me still.

'What's this you've found, Kyle?' the merman asked in a deep grumble. As he spoke, he stroked something lying very, very still by his side. It looked like a giant snake. Greeny yellow with purple teddy bear eyes, its gills slowly opening and closing as its mouth did the same, it swayed its head gently round to face me. A moray eel!

I opened and closed my mouth too, rigid with fear. Nothing came out.

'She was trespassing, sir,' Kyle answered briskly.

'Untie her. She won't try leaving here in a hurry, if she has any sense.' The old merman smiled at his pet. It leered back, stretching up almost as tall as him.

Kyle clenched his sharp jaw into a scowl as he pulled at the fishing line. I rubbed my wrists. 'Tell us how you got here,' he demanded.

'I don't know!' I said, tearing my eyes away from the eel. 'I don't even know where I am. I had an accident, got lost and you found me.' Then, trying to control the quiver in my voice, I added, 'Can I go home?'

'Home?' The old merman leaned towards me. The eel rolled its neck down into a spiral and closed its eyes. 'And where would that be?'

I looked away from him. 'Allpoints Island.'

The two of them exchanged a look. What was it? Shock?

'Allpoints Island?' Kyle blurted out. 'So you know about – '

'Kyle!' the old merman snapped. 'I'll handle this.'

'Of course. Sorry.' Kyle drew back, bowing slightly.

Pausing briefly to pat the moray, the old merman

swam towards me. 'Now then,' he said, in a voice as slimy as the eel. 'I don't believe we've been introduced. 'I'm Nathiel. And you are ...?'

'Why should I tell you who I am?' I said, my heart bashing against my chest. 'Why won't you let me go? What are you going to do with me?'

Nathiel laughed and turned away. 'Questions, questions. Where shall we start, Kyle?'

Kyle shuffled his tail, pulling on his necklace. 'Um ...'

Nathiel waved him away. 'Very well, little girl. I'll tell you who we are. Seeing as you've been kind enough to drop in. We are your biggest fear ... or your greatest protectors. Depending on how you view your situation at this moment.'

'You're not my biggest fear,' I said, my heart thumping. 'My biggest fear is much worse than you!'

'Oh yes?' Nathiel swam back towards me, no trace of kindness or favour on his face. He twitched his head and the eel rose up, uncoiling itself to slither along behind him. I flinched as it stretched almost up to my face.

'Do you know how powerful we are?' Nathiel asked in a quiet, biting voice. I shook my head quickly, without taking my eyes off the eel. 'We are Neptune's chosen ones, his elite force, the only ones he trusts with his most prized possession.' Nathiel edged a centimetre closer to me, his cold eyes shining into mine. 'We, little visitor, are the kraken keepers.'

A million questions jammed into my mind. 'The kraken keepers? But if you're, but it's – '

Nathiel laughed, a throaty sound that echoed around the room. The eel slowly stretched up. It was about three times taller than me. *Please don't open your mouth, please don't open your mouth,* I prayed silently as its jaw twitched.

With another click of Nathiel's fingers, the eel slithered to the back of the room, folding itself once more into a perfect coil.

'Now,' Nathiel said, 'that's my side of the introductions. I think it's time we heard a little more about you. You see, we know quite a bit about Allpoints Island, don't we, Kyle?'

Kyle swam forwards. Copying Nathiel's sneer, he replied, 'Neptune tells us everything.'

'That's right. So, for example, he tells us about merfolk who break his laws.' Nathiel swam further forwards. 'Merfolk who go meddling in places they shouldn't,' he added, edging closer still, his nostrils flaring. 'Merfolk who WAKE his beloved KRAKEN!' he shouted.

'But, I – how did you know?' I cried. My body was shaking. Water frothed around my tail. I tried to make it lie still.

Kyle stared at Nathiel. 'Yes. How did you?'

'I *didn't* know!' Nathiel replied. 'Swam right into

it, didn't she? Come on, Kyle. What do you get if you add the kraken on the loose, an island full of merfolk who know nothing about it and a scared merchild clearly running away from trouble? It's a simple case of mathematics.'

'So we've found her?' Kyle said.

'We've done good work.' Nathiel patted Kyle's arm. 'Neptune will be very pleased with us. Very pleased indeed.'

'Neptune? You're going to tell him?' My voice quivered.

'Of course! That is the whole point. Don't you realise the danger we are all in, you foolish girl?'

'But Neptune! He'll be furious with me.'

'You think we give a fin about that?' Kyle snapped. 'We need you. All of us. There's more than just your-self to consider.'

'What do you mean? What use am I to you?'

Nathiel shook his head. 'Kyle, I've had enough of this whingeing. I think it's time we got the boss in.'

'The boss? Neptune? He's coming here?' I squeaked.

'Not Neptune, no. One of his most trusted aides.' Nathiel picked up a conch. Turning away from me, he spoke softly into it. I couldn't hear what he said. I quickly scanned the room, looking for an escape. My eyes met the eel's. *Try it*, they seemed to say. I shivered back against the wall.

'He'll be along very shortly.' Nathiel put the conch down and tidied some shells on his desk.

A moment later, the door opened. I squeezed my eyes shut in terror. Someone was swimming towards me. I bit my lip as hard as I could, forcing tears away.

'Well, what have we here, then?' a voice said. A creepy voice.

A very familiar voice.

My eyes snapped open, to see a crooked smile, an odd pair of eyes: one green, one blue.

It couldn't be!

'Hello Emily,' said Mr Beeston.

He turned to the others. 'Good work, both of you,' he said, snapping something around my wrists. Handcuffs made from lobster's legs! They bit and scratched at me.

Then he pushed me towards the door. 'I'll take over now,' he said before turning back to give me another of his lopsided smiles. 'It's time we were reacquainted.'

How could they let this happen? Twice! I can't *believe* my parents! I can't believe I agreed to this stupid holiday in the first place.

We're hanging onto our useless, broken boat, lying across it, gripping onto ropes. Only problem is, it's upside down! How long before it sinks and we *totally* end our holiday in style? I grab the rope tighter as the swell carries us up and down. My stomach seesaws with it.

Are we through that, that whatever it was, that great big sheet of glass in the middle of the ocean?

And the other thing.

I refuse to think about it. It didn't happen. Mum and Dad haven't mentioned it. I must have imagined it. Delirious, that's what I am. It was probably just the waves. Or a vision, because I'd seen it before. A memory. Yes. That's it. Definitely. A mirage.

There's nothing to worry about. I'm just cracking up.

'Maureen, Mandy – look!' Dad lets go of the rope with one hand and points out to sea.

It's a ship. Coming towards us!

'Wave! Both of you! Splash your feet!' Dad yells. For

the first time in our lives, Mum and I do what he says without arguing.

The ship's coming closer and closer. Have they seen us? They *must* have! There's nothing except us moving for miles all around us. We're kicking and yelling, every atom of hope screaming out of us.

'I can't splash any more, Dad. My legs are killing me.' I stop kicking for a moment while I catch my breath. The ship's stopped moving. They haven't seen us, after all. That's it. There's nothing we can do now. The realisation slams into my mind like a block of ice: we're going to die.

But then I notice something attached to the ship.

'Look!'

They're lowering a lifeboat into the water! It's coming to get us.

We've been saved!

Chapter Seven

Mr Beeston unhooked the lobster claws from my wrists and pulled out a couple of jelly-like cushions. He motioned me to sit down on one of them while settling himself on the other. I'd hardly ever seen him as a merman. He was half human and half merperson like me, the only other one I'd met. He looked just as creepy either way, with his crooked teeth and his crooked smile and the odd-coloured eyes that stared at you from the corners.

We were in a bubble-shaped room. It felt like the inside of a huge round shell. No windows, just one small hole divided by thick metal bars.

Tiny chinks of light threw pencil-thin beams across the darkness. A black damselfish with fluorescent purple spots and a bright yellow tail wove between the rays.

I tried to stay calm. My mind wouldn't stop racing, though. What were they going to do with me? Would anyone find me? Dad? Shona? Were they looking for me? And what about Mum and Millie? My heart ached at the thought of them on that ship. They'd be miles away by now.

'What are you doing here?' I asked in a daze. Among the millions of questions racing round in my head, it was the only one I could seem to form into words.

'Surprised to see me?' he asked, his voice slipping across the room like slime.

'Of course I'm surprised to see you! Who's looking after the lighthouse in Brightport?'

'The lighthouse?' Mr Beeston laughed. 'Emily, why would I be looking after a lighthouse?'

'It's what you do!'

'The lighthouse was a cover. You know that.'

'Oh, yes. Of course,' I said numbly. I'd found out before we left Brightport that Mr Beeston was one of Neptune's agents and that he'd been spying on us to make sure we never found out about Dad. Well, it didn't work, did it? I found my dad. I'd beaten Mr Beeston once. Maybe I could do it again. 'But that still doesn't explain – '

'I was promoted,' Mr Beeston said, a crooked grin

twitching at the side of his mouth. 'For my bravery and good work.'

'*Good work*?' I spluttered. 'Is that what you call turning me and Mum over to Neptune? You were meant to be our friend. We could have been thrown in prison, like my dad.' I squeezed my eyes shut and pressed my fingernails tightly into my palms. I wasn't going to cry. He wasn't having that satisfaction.

Mr Beeston flicked his tail nervously. 'I – well, Emily, I did my duty. And look, I was needed here. They're working on rebuilding this palace, and there's a lot to do, monitoring activity in the area and keeping a gill open for any kraken-related incidents.' He narrowed his eyes at me accusingly.

'So what are you going to do with me?'

'Do with you? It's not about what I want to do with you. It's about what you need to do for us.'

'What d'you mean?'

Mr Beeston shuffled forward in his cushion. I shuffled backwards in mine. He tightened his lips. 'I am still an agent of Neptune's, you know,' he said sharply. 'One of the highest ranking of all, now. And if I tell you that you are going to do something, you will do it. You don't question my authority.'

I folded my arms, anxiously flicking my tail while I waited for him to continue.

'We are all in grave danger. The kraken is on the loose. It has to be calmed and brought back to Neptune.'

'But what's that got to do with me?'

337

He held my eyes for a long time before replying.
'You, Emily, are the only one who can do it.'

Someone was banging on the outside of the shell. Mr Beeston opened the porthole-shaped door we'd come through. Kyle surged into the room on a sudden wave. It flung me against the wall.

'Sir,' he said breathlessly. 'I've had a sighting. It's coming closer. The sea – it's getting rough.'

'Thank you, Kyle. Good work,' Mr Beeston said.

'It's heading towards the palace!' Kyle panted. 'I think it's going to get us all. We might have to make our escape.'

'Make our escape? Are you off your fins, boy?' Mr Beeston barked. 'Have you been given the wrong job? You have one purpose and one purpose only. Do you hear me?'

'Yes sir.' Kyle reddened. 'I'm sorry.'

'Now, don't let it out of your sight. I'm dealing with it. Have some faith.'

Kyle retreated, leaving a swirling cloud of silt behind him.

'Are you going to explain any of this to me?' I asked as Mr Beeston swam back into the room. A tiny silver fish swam towards him, slithering across his stomach. He batted it away.

'The kraken is Neptune's pet,' Mr Beeston began.

'I know that.'

'And it sleeps for a hundred years. Without its full sleep, it wakes in a murderous rage.'

'I know that too.'

'Stop interrupting me, child! I shall tell you the story my way or not at all.'

I slammed my mouth shut.

'All but Neptune are forbidden to approach the kraken during its sleep. Neptune is the only one who should wake it. And only at the allotted time. You see, when it wakes, the only person it will listen to it is the one who wakes it, the one it sees first on opening its eyes. This should only ever be Neptune. But this time, it was you.'

'You mean . . . ?'

'Yes, Emily. The kraken will obey you and only you.'

I realised I wasn't saying anything. My mouth moved. Opened. Closed. Nothing. The kraken would obey me and only me? I slumped back against the wall, my mind empty, my limbs numb. A thin ray of sunlight threw a diagonal line across the room like a dusty laser beam, lighting up barnacles that lined the walls. The beam shimmered and broke, rocked by the water's constant movement.

'What do you want me to do?' I asked eventually.

'We need to move quickly. Neptune's power over the kraken is fiercely protected. It's not expected that anyone else would ever wake it. *Most* merfolk obey his rules.' He paused to scowl briefly at me. 'First, you have to go to the edge of the Triangle, where its magic is strongest.'

'The edge of the Triangle?' I gasped. 'You mean the torrent that leads to the deepest depths of the ocean?'

'Nonsense!' Mr Beeston snapped. 'It doesn't do that. That's what we tell folk to keep them out of the way.'

'So where does it go, then?'

'It leads into the realm of the kraken.'

'The realm of the kraken?' My voice cracked. Somehow, that didn't sound much more inviting than the deepest depths of the ocean.

'The place where you can communicate with it. You must go to the edge of the Triangle and come face to face with it.'

'Face to face?' I burst out. 'With the kraken?' I couldn't face the monster again. Please no! An image squirmed into my mind: those horrific tentacles, searching, batting and thrashing, smashing into the tunnel. My eyes began to sting with tears. I didn't care any more if Mr Beeston saw me cry. I couldn't hold it back.

He spoke softly. 'It's the only way.'

'What happens then?' I asked, swallowing hard. 'When we're at the Triangle's edge?'

'It will come to you. It will listen to you.'

'And I can save the day?'

'What? Yes, yes, of course you can save the day.'

'And it'll do what I tell it?'

'As I told you, it will listen only to you. Its power lies in your hands.'

I suddenly realised what Mr Beeston was telling me. I could end all of this. I could bring the kraken into my power. It would listen to me. I could calm it down and everything would be all right. I just had to face it one more time.

'OK,' I said. 'I'll do it.'

Mr Beeston smiled his crooked smile. 'I knew you would.'

He turned to leave. 'There's just one last thing,' he said, pausing at the door. 'You *were* on your own when you woke the kraken, weren't you?'

'I – why do you want to know that?' I blustered.

Mr Beeston darted back towards me. Coming so close that I could see the jagged points of his crooked yellow teeth, he leaned into my face. 'If someone else was with you when the kraken woke, we need them too.'

'Why?' I asked in a tiny voice.

'Emily, if there was someone else there, it means the kraken will not obey you on your own. Whoever it saw on waking, that is who it will obey – whether that is one person or twenty. We need them all or the plan will fail.'

'I . . .'

I couldn't do it. I couldn't! Not after everything. I wasn't going to drag Shona into this. They'd have to think of something else. 'There was no one,' I said eventually, my cheeks on fire.

Mr Beeston grabbed my arm, jerking my body like an electric shock. 'You're lying! You *have* to tell me. There was someone with you, I know it. Who was it?'

'I can't tell you!' I cried. Tears slipped down my cheeks. 'I can't do it! You can't make me.'

'Oh, I think you'll find we can,' he hissed.

I gulped. 'What if I refuse?'

Mr Beeston twitched slightly. 'Then the kraken won't stop until it has destroyed everything in its sight. These waves we're seeing – you know they're just the start of it.'

I thought back to what I'd seen: the kraken smashing up Mandy's boat, what it did to the reef, the rocks . . . the whale. But could I really make Shona face it again? Could I betray her like that? It would finish off our friendship forever.

'I – I'll think about it,' I stammered.

He swam over to the door. 'Don't think for too long, Emily,' he said quietly. 'Time is an option we don't have.'

Now, this is more like it! This is what our holiday was meant to be like all along. Luxury cruise liner, sunbeds, swimming pool, free drinks. We're even getting special attention from the crew because of our trauma.

Yeah, it's all great.

Except. Well, except Mum and Dad haven't spoken a word to each other since we were saved. The atmosphere's so cold when they're around, you'd think we were on a cruise to Antarctica. And neither of them even cares about me. They've hardly noticed me since we got here.

So it's not only that my home's about to be pulled down; my family's falling to pieces too. That's just great. We're back where we started, only worse.

And then there's Emily. Apart from wondering what she's doing here anyway, and not to mention the fact that she happens to be a *mermaid,* I just can't believe I let her get one over me, yet again.

We set sail again soon. They've been trying to get away from here, but there's something wrong with the ship. It keeps going off course for some reason. They're trying to sort it out, and once they have done and we're away from here, I'll *never* get a chance to repay her. She'll always have won.

For once, Dad had actually come up with a brilliant plan, and we let it slip away. If only I could find her. Kill two birds with one stone. Get fish girl back AND save our home. Now *that* would be satisfying!

Maybe I could. Who says it's too late?

I'm wandering round the back of the ship trying to think of something when I hear voices. Three people are standing near the lifeboats. One of them's waving her arms in the air, shouting at someone in a Carefree Cruises uniform.

'But why on earth can't you just let it down?' she's yelling. 'I know you used one of them to let a family come aboard. We have to get off the ship! I have to find my daughter!'

'Madam, they were in trouble. We couldn't leave them to drown,' the Carefree Cruises person replies. 'And you won't tell me anything about your daughter's whereabouts. You won't even give me your name. You can hardly expect me to break ship's regulations just because you and your friend here fancy a trip in a lifeboat.'

The other one looks up. That's when I see who it is. A big woman in a black cape. It's Mystic Millie, the crazy lady who used to read palms on the pier in Brightport! What the –

'A child is in trouble,' she says. 'That's all you need to know. We've seen things. *I* have seen things. And if you don't mind my saying so, I am rather known for the

344

accuracy of my visions. Isn't that right, Mary Penelope?'

The other woman turns her head as she nods. I duck down behind a plastic box full of diving equipment before she spots me. But I've seen her face. It's Mrs Windsnap! What are they doing here?

They're moving away. I can't hear the rest of the conversation. But then a thought occurs to me. They want to get off the ship to find Emily. That means she must be near here somewhere.

I could get her! She's probably really near us. I could find her and then get one of those lifeboats to rescue me again. Someone's got to do something – and it doesn't look as though Mum and Dad are going to bother. Too busy ignoring each other. I'm absolutely *sick* of them.

It's not as if they'll even miss me. And if I get lost out at sea, well, they'll be sorry then, won't they!

I yank open the plastic box and rifle through the contents. There's all sorts here: lifejackets, rubber rings, inflatable beds, snorkels, masks, flippers.

Before I can talk myself out of it, I'm grabbing everything I'll need and clambering down a ladder that reaches almost down to the water. I'll do it. I'll get her back, save our home. I'll be a heroine. Mandy Rushton, the girl who single-handedly put Brightport on the map. Yes!

I drop into the water. For a second, the cold jams my brain. What am I doing? The ship's speeding away. Too late to change my mind. Oh God, what am I *doing*?

Then Emily's face comes into my mind and I remem-

345

ber. I pull the mask on and start swimming.

I can see all the way to the bottom of the sea. It's incredible: so clear, so blue. Tiny speckled fish, spongy purple and green plants, trees almost. It's a whole other world down here.

There's something else kind of nagging at me. A tiny voice is telling me not to do this. There's a threat down here.

But I'm not thinking about that. I refuse. It didn't happen. Mum and Dad would definitely have said something by now if they'd seen it. It's not exactly the kind of thing you miss. It was just a wave. A mirage. I was delirious. But I'm not now! I've never felt so clear-headed in my life!

I'm swimming away from the ship. She must be around here somewhere. She can't have got far – she was in a net. I swim on.

And on.

And on.

The rocky coral is just below me, all furry as though it's covered in dust and fluff. Pink, gooey, jelly-like clumps clutch at the rocks. A dull grey fish glides towards me. Then suddenly it flaps bright purple fins. It looks like an aeroplane with fancy painted wings.

Where am I?

I'm exhausted. There's no sign of her anywhere. I tread water for a bit while I adjust my mask and look round. That's when I realise how far away from the ship I've come. It's *miles* away. What am I doing? I've gone mad! I need to get back to the ship.

346

There's a plank of wood floating nearby. I've just got enough energy to reach it. It looks like a piece of our boat! My teeth chatter as I cling to it and try to work out what the heck I'm going to do next.

The water's really dark here, and murky. I dip under to look round but I can hardly see anything. The jelly stuff seems to be reaching higher, trying to grab me. And there are too many sea urchins.

And then I see something stringy, floating up towards the surface. I paddle over to examine it. It's a piece of net; I'm sure it's hers.

She got away then.

There's something else. Something very big. Black on top, white underneath, a giant fin on its back. It's coming towards me!

I want to scream. I know I want to scream – but I can't. I can't get anything out of my throat. I couldn't even if I wasn't underwater, in the middle of the sea, miles from anywhere. It's the monster! I knew it! I should have trusted my instincts. I'm an idiot. And now I'm a dead idiot.

Maybe I can get away before it eats me.

But it's not moving.

Yes it is. But not towards me. It's floating, gliding slowly upwards. And it's not the monster.

It's a killer whale. And it's dead.

As it floats past me, I watch with a morbid fascination. There's a chunk missing from its side. My body starts to shake.

Fear finally kicks in, and so do my legs. I am *so* out of

here! OK, fish girl, I surrender. You win. I don't care; I just want away from this place.

My legs don't seem to be working any more. Please just get me back to the ship! Please get me away from here. I'll do anything. I'll be nice to Mum and Dad; I'll even forgive Emily for tricking me. Just get me back to the ship alive! *Please!*

Something grabs my legs. That's it. I'm dead.

I don't even struggle. I can't. My body feels as useless as the half-eaten whale. I close my eyes and wait for –

'Who are you?'

What? I open my eyes. A man's face has appeared in front of me in the water. Young, almost a boy. He's gripping my arms. Where did he come from?

I open my mouth and swallow about a gallon of water. He waits while I splutter half to death and put my snorkel back on.

'Come with me,' he says.

Still holding my elbow with one hand, he pulls me along in the water. I catch a glance under the water as we swim – and that's when I see. He's not a man. He's a merman! He's got a long tail with silver rings all the way down.

We're heading towards something that looks like an island. As we get closer, I realise it's just a collection of rocks and caves. We swim among the rocks.

'Nathiel,' the merman calls. Still holding onto me, he yanks me downwards. I quickly adjust my snorkel so I can still breathe.

Below us, a rabbit warren of rocks and tunnels and

caves spreads out as far as I can see. It's like a city, packed with too many buildings crammed together as closely as possible.

An old guy with a straggly beard appears from inside a large crevice. Another merman! We come back up to the surface together.

'Another one?' he says.

'Another what?' I burst out. 'Have you got Emily?'

The young merman looks at the older one. 'Emily?' he says. 'Sharks alive, Nathiel – d'you think this is the one?'

The older merman turns to me. 'You're Emily's friend?' he asks.

'I – ' What has Emily got to do with this?

'You were looking for her!' he demands, shaking me.

'Yes!' I burst out. 'Yes, I'm looking for Emily. Is she here?'

'Kyle, tell the boss straight away,' the old merman orders. 'Take her to the Lantern Cave first. It's the only safe place above water.'

Kyle turns to swim away with me.

'No!'

They both swivel their heads to stare at me.

'Please,' I say. A tear streaks down my cheek. I don't care. Anyone would cry in these circumstances. Anyway, I'm not crying. It's the sun. It's shining right into my eyes. 'Please let me go home.'

'Where's home?' Kyle asks.

Good question. Home. You know, the place that's about to get pulled down, where I live with two people who can't stand the sight of each other.

'I need to get back to my parents. Please,' I blub like a baby. Have I really been reduced to this? Begging to be with my parents!

Nathiel says, 'And where are they?'

'I don't know.'

He turns to Kyle. 'Just get her to the Lantern Cave for now. We can always – '

'They're on a ship,' I say.

Nathiel snaps back to face me. 'What?'

'They're on a ship, over there somewhere.' I point back in the direction I think I came from. I sob. I can't help it. 'Please let me get back to it.'

The pair of them look at each other.

'A ship.' Kyle's eyes are shining. 'This is it! We need to move fast.'

What's he on about? 'Are you going to let me go?' I ask.

Nathiel turns to me, grips my shoulders. 'You want to go back to your ship?' he asks.

I nod.

'And you can show us where it is?'

'I – I think so.'

Nathiel lets me go. 'Handed to us on a plaice,' he says, smiling at Kyle. 'Good work.'

Kyle's cheeks flush. He doesn't speak again, just takes me towards a cave. I squeeze through the tiny entrance. It opens out when we get inside. It's dark, and creepy. I can just about make out strange shapes hanging down from the roof. Tiny chinks of light coming through holes way above me, huge boulders with brown gooey stuff that looks like toffee icing dribbled over them.

He closes a metal barred door and locks it from the outside. I grab the bars. 'Wait!'

'We'll look after you,' he says, his face cold and expressionless. 'Don't worry.'

Don't worry, I think to myself as he swims away from me. I climb out of the water onto a rocky ledge, my body shaking and cold. Sure. Absolutely. Why would I worry? I mean, I've only been locked in a dark cave on my own, with nothing but weird clumps of rocks hanging from the ceiling like enormous crooked fingers pointing at me.

I turn away from the pointing fingers. I've got to get out of here. I just need a plan. I'll think of something.

I shiver as the darkness closes around me.

Chapter Eight

I swam round my cell for the hundredth time.

'Let me out!' I yelled, scratching my hands down the rocky walls. My voice echoed around me. Finally, I slumped in the corner.

The next thing I knew, the door was rattling. I leapt up as Mr Beeston came in carrying a net basket filled with shellfish and seaweed. He placed it on a rocky ledge beside me. Water crashed around me as I reached for it, throwing me against the sides.

'See that?' he snarled as I grabbed the ledge to stop myself being thrown back against the wall. 'That's virtually constant now. And it'll keep getting worse, until you've done what you need to do.'

I didn't reply.

'Eat your breakfast,' he said, nudging a finger at the basket. 'You need to be strong.'

'I haven't said I'll do it.'

'No,' he said, his face breaking into an uneven smile. 'But *I* have.'

'I don't have to do what you say.' The edges of my eyes stung.

'Really? Well you won't be interested in our new visitor, then. Kyle tells me he's found someone who might make you feel differently.'

'A visitor?'

'A friend.'

I quickly rubbed my eyes. 'You've got her here? But how did you know – '

'Eat up quickly,' he growled in a voice that made my skin itch. 'It's time for a reunion.'

We swam up towards the surface, Mr Beeston's hand gripping my wrist so tightly it burned. The water grew lighter and warmer as we made our way along tunnels and out into clear water. He pulled me down under a clump of rocks, scattering a group of stripy triggerfish. A metal gate filled a gap between the rocks.

'Up there,' he said.

My heart thudded. I was really going to see Shona! But what if she wouldn't speak to me after everything that had happened? She'd probably hate me even more now, for being dragged into it again. I had to explain. 'Can I see her on my own?' I asked.

'What for?'

'It's personal.'

'Ah, friendship, so sweet,' Mr Beeston snarled, his throat gurgling into a laugh. He gripped my arm, his broken nails scratching my skin. 'You can have five minutes,' he said. Then he fiddled with a lock, and the gate bounced open. I swam through it, along a narrow crack. 'And don't try anything clever,' he called through the bars.

'I won't.'

I swam all the way up to the surface. I was inside a cave, in a tiny pool. Grey pillars lined the edges, their reflections sombre in the greeny blue water. A tiny shaft of sun lit up the stalactites hanging from the ceiling like frozen strands of spaghetti. Where was she?

I swam between the pillars, where the pool opened out. Slimy brown rocks lay all around. Thick clusters like bunches of candles protruded upwards from the water, black as though they'd been singed.

'Shona?' I called.

And then I saw her. Sitting on one of the rocks, her back to me.

But it wasn't Shona.

Her hair was short, and black. She turned round. For a moment, she looked shocked. Then she forced her angular face into a twisted smile.

'Hi there, fish girl,' she said. There was a smarmy look on her face, but I was pretty sure her voice wobbled a little. 'Long time no see.'

'Mandy!'

'Having fun?'

'Having *fun*? You think being captured and locked in an underwater tunnel is *likely* to be my idea of fun?'

'Oh, sorry. I didn't realise.'

'Didn't realise what?'

'That they didn't like you as much as me. Should have guessed though. I mean, people never do, do they?'

'What are you on about?'

'Oh, aren't they looking after you nicely? Haven't they promised to take you home?' She glanced at my face. 'Oops. Obviously not. Sorry. I always seem to say really hurtful things, *totally* by accident! Don't worry. You can't help it if people don't like you, can you?'

'Yeah, right, Mandy. I don't think so,' I said, clenching my hands into tight fists.

Mandy shrugged. 'Thing is, some of us understand how to get what we want; some of us don't. It's just the luck of the draw. Not your fault, I suppose.'

'You're lying.'

'Whatever.' Mandy picked up a stone and threw it

into the water. I watched the ripples grow wider and more faint. Then she stepped back up the rock and twirled round the pillars, prancing around the place as though she owned it.

'Why would they like you?'

She stopped prancing and glared at me, eyes wide open and innocent. 'What's not to like?'

'Where do you want me to start?' I spluttered.

Mandy frowned. 'Anyway, they're stupid,' she said quickly. Then she turned to look at me. 'Hey, that's a point. *They're* stupid and so are you. Funny that, isn't it? You'd think you'd get on a bit better, having something in common like that. Anyway, I don't care. They're taking me back to the boat soon.'

'Your boat? You didn't sink?'

'Not that old washed-out lump of tin,' she laughed. 'No, our new boat. Oh, did I forget to mention that we got saved by a luxury cruise liner? Funnily enough, they want to treat us like royalty, too! Shame, isn't it?'

'A cruise liner?' My voice suddenly shook. 'What cruise liner?'

'The one that we should have been on in the first place. The holiday we were *destined* to have. But not to worry. It's all OK now. They're taking me back later today.'

'Taking you back? But why?'

Mandy bit her lip before turning away. 'Told you. They like me.'

'Mandy, you can't trust these — '

A sound of metal on metal clanked below me. Mr Beeston appeared. 'Five minutes is up.'

'Why are you taking her to the ship?' I demanded.

'We're going together,' he replied.

'*Why*?'

'It's at the edge of the Triangle,' he answered quickly.

'How do you know? How do you know where it is?' I could feel the panic rising in my throat, edging into my voice. 'There's something you're not telling me! Why won't you *tell* me?'

'You know all you need to know,' he said. 'Let's go.'

'It's not Shona!' I yelled, pointing at Mandy. '*She's* not my friend! *Look* at her!'

Mr Beeston glanced across at Mandy as she turned round, and suddenly faltered. 'But that's, but you're — '

'*You*!' Mandy spluttered, looking up at him for the first time. 'Does someone want to tell me what's going — '

Just then, a huge wave rushed into the cave, filling it almost to the ceiling. Mandy lost her footing, slipping into the water beside me. I grabbed her.

'Get your hands off me, fish girl,' she spat. 'I can look after myself!'

'No you can't. You don't know what you're involved in!' I shouted.

Mr Beeston had disappeared under the water. A moment later, he resurfaced, fighting his way back up against the tide. I turned to face him. 'I'm not doing anything for you till you tell me exactly what's going on.'

'Want to bet?' he replied. Mandy opened her mouth to speak but a wave washed her words away. She spluttered and swam for the edge of the pool. Mr Beeston lunged towards me, grabbing my arm. I tried to struggle but he tightened his grip, his fingers scorching into my flesh as he pulled me back towards the grille at the bottom of the cave.

Mandy was shouting something as Mr Beeston pushed me out, fighting against the raging water. I couldn't hear her words any more.

'What are you doing with me?' I cried as a wall of white water rushed towards us, flinging me against a wall. 'What's going on? Tell me!'

'Don't you understand?' he shouted. 'We're *all* in danger here. Look at this. We can't live like this. You're the only one who can fix it.' We'd reached my cell. He yanked on my arm, pushing me inside. 'And you *will* do!'

Without another word, he turned and left. I heard the bolt slam across the door.

I slumped back against the wall and closed my eyes. How had it come to this? All I'd wanted to do was explore the island and make some new friends. How had I managed to cause such devastation? I looked round my dark cell. Shadows came and went on the walls as the hours passed and daylight faded, along with my hopes.

'Emily?'

Who was that? It sounded like ...

'Emily!'

Dad? I swam to the door. '*Dad*!' I screamed.

The door burst open. It was! It was him. He wrapped me in his arms.

'How did you find me?' I asked, pressing into his chest.

'I –'

'Wait!' I pulled away from the door as I heard a noise outside. 'There's someone out there,' I whispered. 'How did you get past them?'

Dad took hold of my hands. 'Emily,' he said in a tight voice. He wouldn't meet my eyes.

'What? What is it?'

'They know I'm here.'

'They know? But how – '

'Archie,' Dad said simply. He looked briefly at my face and turned away again. Letting go of my hands, he swam round the cell. 'They came to see him,' he continued. 'Told him what had happened.' He ran a hand through his hair, pulling at it as he struggled to speak. Eventually, he looked up at me. 'He told me you hadn't been on your own.'

Suddenly it clicked. I felt as though he'd punched me. 'So that's why you're here,' I said. 'You just want me to tell you who I was with.'

Dad looked down. 'We've no choice, Em.'

My throat ached. He hadn't tracked me down, after all. He only came because he had to. Well, I didn't blame him. Why would he want me back after what I'd done?

Dad swam back towards me. 'Emily, I *begged* Archie to let me come. He wanted to do it himself.'

I didn't say anything. I couldn't. Lifting my chin, Dad spoke almost roughly. 'Remember when you found me, at the prison?'

I nodded, gulping a tear away.

'That was the happiest day of my whole life,' he said. 'Did you know that? And you know what was the worst?'

I shook my head.

'Last week, when I thought I'd lost you again.'

I held his eyes for a moment before falling back against him. 'Oh, Dad. It's been so awful!' I cried. 'They want me to face it again.'

'I know, little 'un, I know.' He held me tight while I sobbed.

'It was Shona,' I said eventually. I squeezed him tighter. 'What will you do?'

'We have to tell them, Emily. You don't know what it's been like at the island. Typhoons, giant waves. One side's totally devastated. All the trees knocked flat. Ships have come off their moorings, and it's only going to get worse.' Dad swallowed hard. 'There's something else I've got to tell you.' He held me away from him and picked up both of my hands. 'It's your mum and Millie. They went out looking for you, and we can't find them. There's folk out searching and I'm sure it won't be – '

'Dad! I know where they are.'

He jerked backwards. 'What?'

'I've seen them.' I told him about everything: the ship, Mandy, Mr Beeston.

Dad listened with wild eyes. 'Emily, there's no time to waste,' he gasped when I'd finished. 'We've got to do this. I'll send a message to Archie.'

'Don't leave me!' I gripped his arm.

'I'm not going anywhere,' he said firmly. 'I'll be by your side the whole time.'

'Do I really have to do this?' I asked, my voice quivering.

Dad held me close as he spoke into my hair. 'I'm sorry, Emily. It's the only way.'

That creepy Mr Beeston's pulling me along through the water on a kind of raft. I *never* liked him, back at Bright-port. He's even worse now. He keeps shouting things to me. 'Where's the ship?' he bellows.

'I – I think it's – '

'WHERE'S THE SHIP!' he repeats, about ten times louder.

'It must have moved,' I call back to him. 'It was some-where over there.' I point vaguely ahead of us.

'You know nothing, child,' he says. 'I don't know why we even brought you. No matter, we'll find it soon. It's probably already there.'

'Already where?' Emily calls. She's here too, with another merman. I think it's her dad. He keeps giving her these gooey sickly smiles.

'The edge of the Triangle. Same place we're heading.'

'You have to *tell* me!' Emily's screaming. '*Why* do you need the ship?'

'We're just getting our bearings,' Mr Beeston says.

Emily turns to the other merman. 'He's not telling us everything,' she whimpers. 'I *know* he's not. Why would they be taking Mandy home? It doesn't make sense.'

'Shh, let's just get there. We want your mum back. This is our best chance,' he replies in a quiet voice, glancing nervously at Mr Beeston. What are they up to? 'It'll be OK,' he says, holding Emily's hand. 'I'm here to look after you.'

Puke.

We swim on. I keep having visions of seeing Mum and Dad again. *Please get me to the boat. I promise I'll change. I won't be horrible any more.*

The water breaks in sharp waves all around us. It's getting really rough as we plough through enormous peaks and crash down into huge troughs. I'm grabbing the side of my raft, totally soaked.

And then I see it.

In the distance. On the horizon. I think it might be portholes, glinting in the sunlight. Yes, it is! A whole row of them! It's the ship!

'That's it!' I shout. 'Over there!' I point to the right.

We speed towards the cruise ship. I'm going to see Mum and Dad again! I'm going to be safe!

As we get closer, I can see its shape more clearly. And then it goes out of sight. There's something in the water, in front of the ship. It's like an island; a sickly khaki green island with hills and bumps. And it's moving. Long arms reaching up, propelling it forwards, blotting out the sun. I grip hard onto the raft as my stomach turns over.

The monster's going to get the ship.

I realise I'm screaming.

'Mandy, we can stop this!' Emily yells to me. 'They've told me I can calm it.'

'Why should I believe you?' I shout back. 'You think you're so special, don't you. Think you can do everything better than anyone else!' Tears are streaming down my face. Mum, Dad. They're so near and I'll never see them again.

'Listen to me!'

'No! I *won't* listen to you. If I hadn't been trying to find you, none of this would have happened! It's all your fault! Every single thing that's gone wrong here is YOUR FAULT!'

Emily doesn't speak again. Her face looks like it's been slammed between two walls. I don't care.

Why should I care? No one cares about *me*.

I'm going to die out here, and absolutely no one cares.

Chapter Nine

I gulped as we swam, trying to swallow, trying to breathe. Trying not to think about what I had to do.

Could I really calm the kraken's rage? Did I have any choice?

We were getting nearer to the ship – and so was

the kraken. The thought of Mum on the ship was all I needed to spur me on. I *had* to do it.

'Look!' Dad pointed at two shapes in the water. Archie and Shona!

Archie swam up to Mr Beeston, pulling Shona along with him. 'We've got her,' he said simply.

Mr Beeston nodded curtly. 'Just in time.'

Shona wouldn't meet my eyes. I didn't blame her. After everything I'd put her through, now she had to come face to face with the kraken again, and it was thanks to me – again.

Archie looked across at me. 'I'm glad you're safe,' he said, trying to smile.

'Safe? What makes you think I'm safe?'

'Come on. We've no time to lose.' He started swimming again, Shona joining me and Mandy as we trailed along behind the others. Dad swam up ahead with Archie.

'I'm not surprised you're not speaking to me,' I said as we sliced through the water.

Shona looked at me through heavy eyes. 'What d'you mean?' she asked. 'I thought you wouldn't be talking to me! I was so horrible to you. I've been a coward and a terrible friend. I wouldn't be surprised if you never want to speak to me again.'

I grabbed her hand as we swam. 'Shona, you weren't a terrible friend! If anyone was a terrible friend, it was *me*. I dragged you to somewhere you didn't want to go.'

Shona squeezed my hand. 'I should never have let

you take the blame. I'm so sorry,' she said. Then more quietly, she added, 'And so are Althea and Marina.'

'Althea and Marina?'

'They didn't think we'd really do it. They were scared of getting into trouble – that's why they kept out of your way. They feel dreadful. They wanted me to tell you they're going to make it up to you at the welcome party, when we get back.'

The welcome party. Were they still really going to hold a welcome party for us? Would I really ever be truly welcome there?

'We are friends again, aren't we?' Shona asked.

'*Best* friends! If you still want to be.'

She grinned.

'Well, excuse me for not joining in the happy moment,' Mandy burst in, 'but does either of you realise we're all about to *die* out here? Shouldn't we be trying to get *out* of this mess?'

'Mandy's right,' I said, suddenly realising Mandy and Shona had never met. Somehow, this didn't feel like the best time for introductions. 'We need to think about what we're doing.'

Ahead of us, the kraken had dipped underwater, an occasional tentacle lashing out across the surface. The sea bubbled with expectation.

Shona turned to me. 'What *are* we doing?'

That was a very good question.

We were there. The edge of the Triangle; the realm of the kraken. It was no longer a glassy plane over the ocean. An endless chasm stretched across the sea, giant waterfalls tearing down into the blackness below.

The ocean raged as the kraken surfaced in front of the chasm. Huge tentacles surged out of the sea, thick and lumpy, spraying water all around as they crashed onto the surface again and again.

I froze.

I couldn't do it.

Someone was shouting at me. I think it was Archie. It could have been Mr Beeston, or even my dad. It didn't matter. I couldn't change this, I couldn't face the kraken. I closed my eyes.

'The ship.' Mandy was pulling at my arm. 'The ship,' she said over and over again. 'It's going to sink the ship! *Do* something!'

The monster was looming over the ship as it edged towards the chasm. Tentacles reached high into the air. One swipe and it would all be over. 'MUM!' I screamed into the wildness, my eyes blind and blurred from tears and sea water.

Archie grabbed my arm. 'Face it!' he screamed. 'Both of you!'

'*Then* what?' Shona cried.

'Just do it! Face it together and be silent. Wait till it turns this way. I'll tell you what to do then. Quick!'

Shona turned to me.

'Come on,' I said. 'It'll be OK.'

I grabbed her hand and we turned to face the kraken together, waiting in silence for the awful moment when it would turn that long, hard, horrible face towards us.

And then it did.

Nothing else moved. The sea and swell stopped. The crashing waves leading down into blackness, the chasm – everything was still, held on a freeze frame. The kraken stood like a terrifying statue, motionless like iron, a giant tentacle poised over the ship, its bulging, weeping eyes locked with ours.

'It's working,' Dad whispered into the stillness. 'It's working!'

In the distance, a chariot was gliding over the water, pulled by dolphins. Neptune was on his way.

Archie glanced across at the chariot. 'You have to do it now!' he urged. 'Bring the kraken here, calm it down. Now!'

'What do we do?'

'Think.'

'Think?'

'In your minds, try to communicate with it.'

'*Communicate* with it?'

'Try to hold it in your power, bring it out of its rage so it can return to Neptune. You have to move fast.'

'OK.' I pulled at my hair, twirling it round as I flicked my tail. I glanced at Shona. She nodded quickly. OK. I just have to calm the kraken's rage. Think thoughts.

OK.

Calm down, nice kraken. I forced the words into my mind, my face squirming up with disgust and horror. A tentacle twitched, lashing out into thin air.

'You have to really feel it,' Archie said. 'It's no use pretending. It'll know.'

Neptune was coming closer. I had to do something before he got here, prove I wasn't completely and utterly useless, that I hadn't ruined absolutely everything. Shona's eyes were closed, her face calm and focused. OK, I could do this.

Please, I thought. *Please don't destroy anything. There's no need. Take it calmly, listen to us, trust us, it's all OK. No one's going to hurt you.*

Random thoughts raced through my head, anything I could think of that might have some effect.

And it did – it started to. The kraken's tentacles were softening, flopping back down onto the water, one by one. The swell of the sea had started shifting slowly, rising and falling steadily, the huge choppy waves with their sharp crests smoothing into deep swells. The chasm closed over, lying shiny and smooth like an oil slick.

'Good!' Mr Beeston called. 'Keep doing it!'

Don't be angry. Everything will be all right. Just be calm, calm, calm.

Beside me, I could almost feel Shona's thoughts, the same as mine, weaving in between my own words. The kraken was calming down. Its tentacles lay still and quiet, spread out across the ocean's surface.

The chariot was coming closer. I could see Neptune, rising out of his seat, holding his trident in the air.

'We've done it,' he cried as the dolphins brought him to my side. 'Bring it here. Bring it to me now. Only when it is right in front of you can you bring it fully back into my power.'

I swallowed. Here? Right in front of us?

'Now!' Neptune repeated.

I cleared my throat as I glanced at Shona again. Her face was white, her eyes wide and terrified.

I closed my eyes. *Come to us,* I thought, half of me praying it wouldn't work, the other half knowing that if it didn't we were all lost.

Nothing happened.

'You have to *mean* it!' Archie said. 'I've *told* you that.'

I took a deep breath and closed my eyes. Then, forcing myself to concentrate totally on my thoughts, I let the words come into my mind. *Come to us, now. We can end this. No more rage, just calm . . . come to us now.*

Something was happening in the water. Movement. I could sense it. I kept my eyes closed. *It's all right,* I said in my mind. *No one's going to hurt you. Just come to us now and we can work it out. Calm. Stay calm.*

'You're doing well,' Neptune said. His voice sounded as though he was talking right into my ear. 'Now, open your eyes. You have to come face to face with it, both of you. You need to hold it with your minds until the rage has completely gone.'

'How will we know when the rage has gone?' I asked.

'It will come back to me.'

I counted slowly to three, and then opened my eyes. It was all I could do not to scream from the top of my voice. It was there! In front of me! A face as tall as a tower block; lumpy and dark and pocked with holes and warts, tapering towards huge white eyes streaked with blood red veins. Enormous craggy tusks pointed up, disappearing into the clouds it seemed. Tentacles lay still all around it, like a deflated parachute.

I could hear cheering coming from the ship! The danger had passed. We'd done it. We'd really done it! I grabbed Shona's arm. She was laughing.

'We're not finished!' Neptune barked. 'Beeston, get ready. Archie, ready?'

'Yes, Your Majesty,' Archie replied, swimming away from me.

'Ready for what?' I asked. No one answered. Mr Beeston and Archie were swimming towards the ship. I grabbed Dad. 'Ready for what?' I asked again. 'What's going on?'

Dad shook his head. 'I don't – '

'What do you think?' Neptune growled. 'It's time to put it back to work.'

A queasy feeling stirred inside me. Something wasn't right.

'You don't think this is all merely to save your lives,

do you?' Neptune asked. 'Don't you think there is more to my kingdom than that?'

'I – I don't know. I don't under – '

'The kraken is getting back to work, as I've told you. It's been nearly a hundred years, and now it will return to what it knows best: relieving humans of what they do not need. It will bring me riches in quantities I haven't known for many years.'

What did he mean? He couldn't possibly –

'And that,' he pointed to the ship.' . . . that is where we start.'

'But you can't!' I yelled. The kraken stirred as I shouted, a tentacle hitting the water with a splash that covered us all. 'You tricked us! You made us do all this, just so you can destroy everything!'

Mr Beeston turned in the water. 'We're not going to destroy everything. That's what the kraken would have done without you. We want to regain the control that is rightfully ours.'

'And the riches,' Neptune added, stroking a gold sash around his chest.

'Exactly, Your Majesty,' Mr Beeston added with a smarmy smile.

'Why didn't you just let it sink the ship then?' Shona asked.

'It will sink it for me! When I am ready. Otherwise, it is wanton destruction.'

'Wanton destruction?' I spluttered. 'And this isn't?'

Neptune's face bulged red. 'Without me, the kraken will destroy everything in its sight, losing it

forever into the chasm. I will *not* suffer that waste!'
He waved his trident in the air. 'Now go to it! I want
every jewel from that ship!'

'But you'll kill them all!' I screamed, tears lashing
down my face. 'My mum's on that ship!'

'Did we ASK her to be there?' Neptune boomed.
'Did we ASK you to start this?'

'But you can't just *kill* her! And Millie – all of
them!'

Mr Beeston looked at Neptune, then me. 'Your
mother's on the ship? What the –'

'I want my mum!' Mandy was crying next to me. 'I
want to go home.'

'You can't!' I screamed at Neptune. 'Make it not
happen – it can't be happening.'

The kraken twitched in the water, lifting a tentacle, tipping its head to the side.

'DO NOT lose it!' Neptune bellowed at Mr
Beeston. 'We're too close. It's getting confused. We
mustn't lose it now. Beeston, we need to sort this.'

'Please don't do it!' I cried uselessly.

Mr Beeston wouldn't look at me as he set off
towards the ship. 'I'm sorry, Emily,' he said.

Dad lunged after him, grabbing his arm. 'My WIFE
is on that boat!' he screamed.

Mr Beeston's left eye twitched. 'That – it's not our
concern,' he stammered.

'Not your concern? Don't you care that people are
going to die when you sink their boat?'

'Tough tails!' Mr Beeston suddenly exploded.

'They shouldn't stray into Neptune's kingdom. He is the ruler; everything in the ocean is his. He is only regaining what he's owed. Humans have stolen from him for centuries, poaching his seas for their own needs. We're just redressing the balance.'

He was mad. They all were.

Something was happening in the water. The kraken's tentacles were twitching, batting the water, spraying us all.

'OBEY ME!' Neptune screamed. 'It's caught between your control and mine. We have to combine them or it will go insane.'

'We won't!' I yelled back. 'We WON'T obey you!'

I grabbed Shona and Mandy. 'Come on!'

Mandy pulled away from me. 'Look what you're doing!' she shouted. 'You're making it *worse*!'

She was right; the kraken was coming back to life, tentacles rising to smash against the water.

'It's going to kill *everyone*!' Mandy yelled. 'You have to stop it!'

'Then what? If we obey Neptune, it'll go back into his power again, and he'll make it sink the ship anyway!' I cried. 'What can we do?'

It was ahead of us. Mr Beeston was calling it to the ship. No!

The kraken lashed forwards, tearing a hole through the sea as it spun towards the ship. The Triangle's surface was opening up again!

And then. And then.

I saw it in slow motion.

A tentacle, rising into the air, water spiralling off around it in an arc of colour and light. It came crashing down onto the water, hitting out, thwacking at the surface, swiping at the ship. The ship! It was so close. I could see people lined up along the decks, running madly, but there was nowhere to run. The tentacles rained down. It had the ship! It knocked at it, mad and hungry for destruction. The ship was tilting, people tossed from the deck – hundreds of people in the water, screaming for their lives.

'MUM!'

I whirled towards the kraken, edging towards the chasm; I could feel it pulling me – something holding us together; I couldn't fight it.

For a split second, everything stopped. The calm came back. The kraken had disappeared under the water. In silence, I watched the chasm close up, covered over again with the glassy surface of the sea.

Just one brief moment of calm, before a screeching wail split the air around us. Lights flared. The glassy surface splintered and cracked. The torrent raged below. And the kraken rose. It burst through the water, screaming up from deep below the surface, its long face stretched wide by angry, gaping jaws, dagger-like teeth, tentacles scrambling madly like a mass of giant maggots, smashing the still surface of the sea. As we watched, the water fell away, pouring like a waterfall, leaving just the kraken, surrounded in its fury by utter, black emptiness.

'We've lost our power,' I said feebly, to no one. 'It's not listening.'

I was being dragged towards the kraken. I could feel its mind pulling me towards it. Nothing I could do.

I couldn't save anyone. This force pulling me was too strong. No energy, no power to do anything.

I let myself slip towards the chasm.

And it closed behind me.

Down, down, into complete darkness. Nothing to see. No water, no land. Nothing. Falling through nothingness. Spiralling down, whisked round in a vacuum of whirling blackness, twisting me, throwing me round and round.

It grabbed me.

Lashing at me, scorching my face, my hands, my body, the kraken's tentacles screamed across me, again and again. I writhed and struggled, but it was imposs-ible. I couldn't keep out of its clutches.

I touched something that felt like jelly. With shud-dering, horrified disgust, I realised it was the edge of a sucker the size of a dinner plate. I gripped my body, trying to curl into a tight ball of nothingness.

'Why are you doing this?' I shouted uselessly as sticky, slippery tentacles slithered across my body, creeping around my tail, round and round, pulling me into a locked coil. I couldn't move a single thing. Brown hairs brushed across my face, writhing like a nest of worms. Terror sucked my breath away.

What could I do to stop it? Beg? What could I say? Why wasn't it *listening*? I'd woken it up! It should be in my power!

My thoughts rambled uselessly as tears lashed down my cheeks.

The tentacles reached higher and tighter, wrapping me up, trapping my arms, climbing up my body, finally closing over my neck.

This was it. This was where it ended. No one to save me.

The darkness slowly grew darker.

The ship's safe! It's all stopped. The monster's gone. But the people are still in the water. Loads of them. Someone's got to save them.

'What have you done with her?' Emily's dad is screaming at the really tall merman in the throne. 'What have you done with her? Give me my *daughter*!'

The big merman waves this great big fork thing around. 'Do you DARE question me in this manner?' he yells at the top of his voice. What is his *problem*? Can't he see people are in *trouble* here?

'Give her back to me!' Emily's dad howls, his voice cracking. 'Give her *back*!'

'We can't,' the big merman answers. 'The kraken has her.'

There's uproar after this. The merman's yelling. Some of the people from the ship have broken away. They're swimming towards us, shouting, calling things. They're coming closer.

'MANDY!'

It's Mum! My mum's in the water! I try to paddle my raft towards her. I can't get away. Mr Beeston's tied it up to that stupid chariot thing.

'Mum!'

What if that massive hole opens up again? What if it sucks us *all* in?

Someone's calling Mum from one of the lifeboats. She hovers in between us.

'Get in the boat!' I yell.

'Stay there, Mandy!' she shouts to me, swimming back to help the others. 'I'll get them to come for you.'

I nod, swallowing hard as I cling to my raft.

I can't stop thinking about Emily, in there with that thing. I can't let it happen. Was she honestly that bad? What did she ever really do to me?

Maybe I was wrong. Maybe she never had it in for me. It was always me who had it in for her. It was me who tripped her up in swimming, and called her names and stole her best friend. What did she do wrong, exactly? So, a few people liked her more than they liked me. Could I really blame them? *I* like her more than I like me at times.

I edge towards the big merman in the chariot.

'Please,' I beg. 'You have to do something. She's going to die in there.'

He turns slowly round towards me, looking down on me as though I'm an ugly beetle that's just crawled out of the sea. 'What am I expected to do about that?' he says, his eyes flickering towards the chasm. He looks away from me. 'I didn't cause it. She brought it on herself.'

'But can't you end it? Make the monster stop?'

'I cannot and I WILL not. Now leave me al—'

'HOW DARE YOU!' Someone suddenly shouts from the other side of the chariot. 'Give me a leg up will you, Jake,' she says in a quieter voice to Emily's dad. Then she hauls herself up onto the chariot. Millie! It's Mystic Millie!

The merman glares at her. 'Don't you know who I am?' he asks, his voice rumbling like an approaching typhoon.

'Yes of course. You're Neptune,' she says. 'But that – '

'KING Neptune!' he booms.

Millie presses her lips together, sucking on her teeth. 'Look, you could be King Kong for all I care,' she says, squeezing out her long black skirt over the sea. 'That still doesn't give you the right to let a poor innocent child get eaten by your precious monster.' She stares into his eyes and pulls something out from under her cloak. It looks like a gold pendant. 'Now are you going to do something about it?' she asks in a low drawl.

He stares back, his eyes flickering to the pendant. No one says anything. As he glares at her, something changes in his eyes. It's as though a flame starts to flicker behind them.

'Well, I . . . ' he says.

Millie moves closer to him. 'You know, even the greatest among us are allowed to change our ways if we want to,' she says quietly.

Then there's splashing in the water behind me.

'Mandy!'

It's Dad!

He's panting hard. He grabs me, clutching onto the

raft. 'Thank God,' he says. 'Thank God.' He's crying. I've *never* seen my dad cry. 'We've got to do something,' he says, his words coming out in rasps. 'Too many people in the water – not enough boats – someone's got to help.'

'Where's my *wife*?' Emily's dad gasps. He reaches up to grab Millie's hand. 'Make him do it,' he croaks. 'Get my daughter back. Promise me!'

Millie folds a hand over his. 'We'll get her back, Jake,' she says. 'I promise.'

He dives under the water and heads towards the ship.

I pull away from Dad. 'PLEASE!' I scream at Neptune. 'There has to be something we can do.'

He lifts his fork thing in the air again. 'Leave me alone, all of you,' he says. 'I do not need this. I will make MY decisions. I will NOT be influenced by ANY of you. If I choose to change my mind, it's not because of anything that you have said to me. Do you hear me?'

'Yes, yes, anything!' I scream.

Millie rolls her eyes, slipping her pendant back inside her cloak. 'Whatever you say,' she says with a frown.

'Well, then,' says Neptune, 'there is one last thing that may calm its rage and release the child. It comes from an ancient rhyme. It has never been used.'

'Why not?' I ask.

'Once its magic is invoked, I lose my power over the kraken forever. It will never return to its old ways. It will be a passive, weak shell of its former self.' He frowns in disgust.

'But the old days are gone. Surely you can see that! We can't cause death just to bring you jewels,' I say, adding more quietly, 'not that you're likely to even find a whole lot of jewels on that ship anyway.'

'So your ways are *better*, are they?' he snaps. 'Only the guilty die in your world, do they? Only for "good" reasons?'

'No, but . . . ' My voice trails away.

He waves me away. 'But I will not stand by and see this happen. You may be right. Perhaps we will find a different way. Let's get that girl out of there.'

'What's the rhyme?' Millie demands.

Neptune lifts his eyes to the sky.
'When old hatred's rift is mended
Thus the kraken's power is ended.'

'That's it?' My dad yells. 'A *nursery* rhyme? That's ridiculous! You said you were going to sort it.'

They're all shouting again. But I move away. Can I do something? *When old hatred's rift is ended.* I've hated Emily Windsnap for years. Maybe I don't have to any more. I could change this, do something good. Can I?

She communicated with the kraken just with her mind, didn't she? Maybe I can do the same, somehow. I'm going to do it!

I close my eyes and think of Emily, then I force a thought into my mind:
I'm sorry.

I say it over and over again in my thoughts. And then I wait.

Nothing.

What was I expecting? More flashing lights? I should have known nothing would happen. Nothing ever does when I try to do something good.

She's dead. The kraken's killed her. And I never had the chance to say I'm sorry.

I can see her in my mind. A picture from years ago. We used to play on the pier together. We were almost best friends. Why did I let her slip away?

Years of sorrow well into a tight ball, pressing against my throat.

But then –

I forgive you.

What was that? Who said it? I look around. No one's near me. They're all too busy shouting at each other, arguing over where to find the old hatred that they have to mend. I swipe a hand across my cheek, wiping away tears and sea water as I listen hard.

I forgive you.

It's Emily. It's her voice. I can hear her, again and again.

And then the chasm opens. It's starting again. It's whirling, throwing water around everywhere, splashing us all. A giant wave heaves towards us, knocking me off the raft.

'MANDY!' Dad yells, lunging for me. He swims away from the current, grabbing the raft and dragging us both back onto it.

'Please, no!' he sobs. 'Don't let me lose you.' He holds me tight, clutching my face to his chest as we kneel together on the raft.

When did my dad last hold me like this?

Over his shoulder, I can see the ship – but it's on the other side of the chasm. How will we ever get back to it?

As I stare into the raging water, all thoughts are suddenly swept from my mind. The monster's coming out of the sea again. Its head bursts out through the surface, scratched and veined with black lines, pus oozing out of crater-like holes in its skin. Piercing sounds of agony fill the sky.

Tentacles lash everywhere – it's out of control, screaming, on and on, the screeching siren sound. Roaring with anger, the monster lashes out again and again. And then I notice something in one of its tentacles. Emily! It's got her, holding her tight, throwing her into the air, crashing back down to the surface. She looks so tiny, like a little doll.

Please don't kill her . . . She's my friend.

Instantly, one final piercing scream shoots out from the water, exploding like a bomb, sending colour and water everywhere.

And it gradually quietens, slows. Stops. The giant waterfall stops raging. It's just a giant hole, spreading and cracking in a line through the ocean.

The monster crashes down onto the water and lies still, tentacles like bumpy highways, bridging the long well, jerking slightly, its head half sunk in the water. The sea fills with colour, purple lights flowing out of the kraken, seeping into the water all around us.

No one speaks. We hover in the sea, in silence, focused on the sight in front of us: the monster lying still, no one moving an inch.

We've done it. We've really done it.

Chapter Ten

J was having the cruellest dream. It started off as a nightmare. The kraken had me. Trapped and half strangled, I was in its clutches under the water. Then I heard a voice: Mandy, apologising. I thought, yes, let's make friends, I'm going to die any second now anyway.

And then it changed. I was above the water, in the air, thrown high by the kraken. But it let go of me and I came crashing back down onto the water, sinking, then rising back up to the surface.

The worst part was what happened next.

It was the best part really, but so cruel.

I dreamed my mum and dad were there. They'd come to save me. Shona was with them. We were best friends again. Even Mandy Rushton was there, and they were all asking if I was OK. No one was angry with me. All those eyes, looking at me with concern, helping me, carrying me somewhere, forgiving me for all the awful things I'd done. I wanted to call out to them, touch them, but I couldn't move; I couldn't speak.

I can't remember what happened next.

'Emily?'

'She can't hear you.'

'She's opening her eyes!'

Mum? I blinked in the sunlight. 'Mum? Is that really you?' I asked shakily.

She leaned over me, rocking as she held me tight. 'Oh, Emily,' she whispered into my neck, her voice choked and raw.

As she pulled away, I rubbed my eyes to see Dad's face next to hers. He was leaning out of the water, reaching up to hold my hand.

Shona was in the water next to him, smiling at me. 'You're OK!' she said.

I looked round: gold and jewels beside me, dolphins at the front. I was in Neptune's chariot! And I wasn't on my own. Millie stood at the front, talking in a low, deep voice. I knew that tone. She was hypnotising someone! But who?

'Now, moving your tentacle very, very slowly, lift another person out of the water,' she said softly, 'And carry them across the chasm, placing them gently on the deck of the cruise ship. Good, good ... '

The kraken was doing what she said.

I shuddered as I remembered being in its clutches, the horror of its tentacles around my neck ...

'We did it, then?' I asked numbly.

Shona beamed at me. 'You're a heroine, Emily. How could I ever have been angry with you? I'm such a jellyfish at times. Do you realise what you've done?'

'I — no. I don't know.'

I knew one thing, though. Whatever I'd done, I hadn't done it on my own. I pulled myself up. 'Where's Mandy?'

Shona pointed out to sea. 'She's on her way back to the ship,' she said. 'I think they'll be setting off soon.'

I got up, shakily. I had to see her. My legs wobbled.

Mum grabbed my arm. 'Emily, you need to rest.'

'Later,' I said. 'I've just got to do something.' Before she could stop me, I dived into the sea. I waited for my tail to form. It wobbled and shook just like my legs had done, but I could move it. I could get there. I had to see Mandy.

'I'm coming with you then.' Shona swam over to my side.

We made our way towards the edge of the Triangle. I gasped as I saw what lay ahead: a gulf of utter black emptiness. My body shuddered violently as I looked down. Across the chasm, the kraken reached a tentacle from one side to the other and out towards the ship, carrying people carefully across.

'I can't!' Mandy was screaming. 'It's HORRIBLE!'

'Quick! Come on. It's the only way across.' Her dad held his hand out to her. Mandy climbed up onto her awful slimy bridge. My body shuddered. I couldn't go near it!

She tiptoed along the tentacle. It was so huge it almost looked like a road, bridging the emptiness below. By the time I got there, she was nearly across.

'Mandy!'

She turned. The tentacle was starting to slip. Two more steps and she'd be there.

'Emily,' she said.

I swallowed. 'Thank you.'

Two steps away. She paused, stared at me. And then she smiled. I'd never seen her smile before. Not like that anyway. The only smile I'd ever seen from her was a sarcastic sneer. This one suited her better. It looked nice. Made her look like someone I might want to be friends with.

'Yeah, well,' she said. 'I didn't really do anything.'

'No, you're wrong.' I smiled back at her. 'You did a lot.'

Then she lurched across the tentacle, making her way back to the ship.

They'd gone. All of them back on the ship.

As the kraken lay still, I noticed someone in the water beside it. Tall, proud and silent, Neptune bent forward to stroke a tentacle, holding it sadly. Then he turned and looked around him.

'Beeston!' he called. Mr Beeston swam towards us from the ship.

'Have you completed the memory wipes?'

'Every last person, Your Majesty.'

Neptune nodded. 'Good work.' Then he clicked his fingers. Instantly, his dolphins squirted water in the air and dived down to pull the chariot through the water. Neptune clambered aboard.

'It's over,' he said. 'The kraken is falling back into its sleep. Who knows when it will wake now, or if it will even wake at all.' He beckoned Mr Beeston. 'We need someone to take on the responsibility of watching over it.'

Mr Beeston's mouth twitched into a crooked smile. 'Do you mean ...?'

'Who else could I trust with such an important task?'

Neptune looked round at us all. 'The rest of you will return to your lives. The kraken keepers will join you at Allpoints Island and you'll live together. The Triangle shall be sealed when I have left. Now, back to your island, everybody, and try to keep out of trouble this time.'

The ship was almost out of sight, a silhouette slowly gliding along the horizon.

Dad put an arm round me. 'Come on then, little 'un.' He nodded towards Allpoints Island as he pulled me close. 'Ready to go home?'

Shona caught up with us, linking an arm in mine. Mum and Millie smiled at me from inside the lifeboat.

Home. I thought about our bay, about *Fortuna*, Barracuda Point, the Grand Caves, mermaid school, the million things I hadn't yet discovered about All-points Island – and everyone waiting for us. Althea and Marina, and all my other new friends.

'Yes, I'm ready,' I said eventually. Then I turned to Shona and smiled. 'We've got a party to go to.'

The Brightport Times – 25 March
LOCAL HEROES SAVE BRIGHTPORT PIER
Brightport Town Council today voted unanimously to retain and modernise the town's historic pier. The decision came after local residents Jack and Maureen Rushton made a substantial donation from their recent windfall.

The Rushtons came into the money with their stunning photographs of a raging sea monster on the open ocean. The photographs have been sold to newspapers across the world.

The photographs were taken whilst on holiday with Mermaid Tours. Bizarrely, the couple have no recollection of their holiday.

'We were as surprised as anyone when we got the pictures developed,' Mrs Rushton said.

The Rushtons plan to expand their amusement arcade on the pier and are currently in negotiations with planners about a theme park which they will open later this year. The star ride will be a massive rollercoaster with a multitude of twists and turns along tentacle-like tracks.

The ride is to be called The Kraken.

Emily Windsnap and the Castle in the Mist

Decorations by Natacha Ledwidge

This book is dedicated to 'the other SAS',
especially Celia Rees and Lee Weatherly,
without whom Emily might still be lost at sea

Also to my sister, Caroline Kessler,
without whom I would have been pretty lost myself

And if our hands should meet
in another dream, we shall build
another tower in the sky.

From 'The Prophet'
by Khalil Gibran

Prologue

*I*t's midnight, and as light as day.

A full moon shines down on the ocean, making the waves dance as they skirt the edges of the tiny island, lapping on to jagged rocks and stony beaches.

A chariot glides through the sea, tracing a circle around the island. Solid gold and adorned with jewels on every side, the chariot is pulled by dolphins, each decorated with a row of diamonds and pearls along its back and head.

Inside the chariot sits the king of all the oceans: Neptune. Grander than ever, a chain of sparkling jewels around his neck, his gold crown glinting above his white hair, his trident by his side, his green eyes shine in the moonlight as he looks across at the island. He is waiting for his bride to appear from the castle that stands above the rocks, half hidden by mist, its dark windows gleaming in the bright night sky.

'Go around again!' he demands, his voice booming like thunder. His words send ripples bouncing away from the chariot. The dolphins draw another circle around the island.

And then she is there, smiling as she steps towards the water's edge, her eyes meeting his, their gaze so fierce it almost brings the space between them to life. A bridge between their two worlds.

A small flock of starlings approach the water as she does, circling the air above her head like a feathered crown. Twisting her head to smile up at them, she holds out a hand. Instantly, one of the birds breaks off from the circle and flies down towards her open palm. Hovering almost motion-less in the air, it drops something from its claw into her palm. A diamond ring. As the woman closes her hand around the ring, the starling rejoins the other birds and they fly away into the night, slinking across the sky like a giant writhing snake.

'I give you this diamond to represent my love, as great as the earth itself, as firm as the ground on which I stand.' The woman flicks back shiny black hair as she reaches out towards the chariot to place a ring on Neptune's finger.

A twist of the trident and a dolphin swims forwards. As it bows down to Neptune, it reveals a pearl ring, perfectly balanced on its brow. Neptune takes the ring. Holding it out in his palm, he speaks softly. 'And with this pearl, I offer you the sea, my world, as boundless and everlasting as my love for you.' He slides the ring on to her finger. 'This is a most enchanted moment. A full moon at midnight, on the spring equinox. This will not happen for another five hundred years. It is almost as rare as our love.'

She smiles up at him, her white dress wet at the bottom where she stands in the sea by his chariot.

Holding his trident in the air, Neptune continues. 'These rings may only ever be worn by two folk in love – one from the sea, one from land – or by a child of such a pair. As long as they are so worn, no one can remove them.'

'No one can even touch them,' the woman says, smiling.

Neptune laughs. 'No one may even touch them,' he says. Then he holds his other hand up, palm facing the woman. She does the same and their arms form an arch, the rings touching as they clasp hands. A hundred stars crackle in the sky above them, bursting into colour like fireworks. 'When the rings touch like this,' Neptune continues, 'they will undo any act born of hatred or anger. Only love shall reign.'

'Only love,' she repeats.

Then he spreads his arms out in front of him. 'At this moment, night and day are equal, and now, so too are earth and sea. For as long as we wear these rings, the symbols of our marriage, there will always be peace and harmony between the two worlds.'

With a final wave of his trident, Neptune holds out a hand to help the woman into the chariot. Hand in hand, they sit close together, her long dress flowing from one side of the chariot, his jewel-encrusted tail lying over the other side.

The dolphins lift the reins and the chariot glides silently off, taking its royal owners away to begin their married life together.

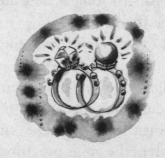

Chapter One

'Emily! I won't tell you again.' I opened an eye to see Mum pulling back the curtain across the porthole in my bedroom. Outside, an oval moon hung low in a navy sky. Fourth quarter, I thought automatically. We'd been learning about the moon's cycle at school. 'It's still night,' I complained as I pulled the quilt over my face and snuggled back into my pillow.

'It's half past seven,' Mum replied, perching on the edge of my bed. She folded the quilt back and kissed my forehead. 'Come on, sweet pea,' she said.

'You'll be late for school.' As she got up, she added under her breath, 'Not that you'd miss much if you were. They haven't exactly taught you anything useful at that place so far.'

She'd left the room before I had a chance to reply.

I let out a heavy sigh as I lay in bed, looking up at the ceiling. Mum seemed to be really down lately. That was the third time she'd grumbled about something in the last week. Personally, I couldn't see what there was to complain about. We were living on a beautiful secret island: Mum, Dad and me, all together on an elegant old wooden ship, half sunk in the golden sand and sparkling water that surrounded the whole island. Merfolk and humans together in peace.

I realise that last bit isn't necessarily a requirement in everyone's ideal living situation, but it comes in handy when your mum's a human, your dad's a merman and you're half and half.

I pulled on my swimming costume and joined Mum at the breakfast table. As with everything else in our home, the table lay on a slant, so I held on to my cereal bowl as I ate.

Dad swam up to the trapdoor next to my seat

and pulled himself up to kiss me on the cheek. 'Morning, my little starfish,' he said with a smile. 'Ready for your Ocean Studies test?'

'Test me!' I said.

Dad scratched his head. 'How big can a Giant Japanese Spider Crab grow?'

'Three metres,' I said instantly.

'Very good. Hm. What colour is a banded butterfly fish?'

'Black and silver. Too easy!'

'Too pointless, more like,' Mum said under her breath. What was *wrong* with her?

Dad turned to her with a frown. 'Not again!' he sighed. 'What is the matter with you? Don't you want our daughter to do well at school?'

'I'm sorry,' she said, reaching down for Dad's hand. 'It's just . . . '

'What? What is it? She's learning lots, she's enjoying herself, getting good grades. I couldn't be more proud.' Dad winked at me as he talked. I smiled back.

Dad and I hadn't got on all that well when we first came to Allpoints Island. I mean, we didn't get on badly; it just wasn't easy. I'd spent most of my life without him and we didn't really know what to talk about, or where to start.

I didn't know he existed at all till recently. It was only a few months ago I'd even found out about myself – that I became a mermaid when I went in water. It terrified me to begin with. The first time it happened, I didn't know what was going on. It was in a school swimming lesson, of all places. But then I got used to it, and I'd sneak out to swim in the sea at night. That's how I met my best friend, Shona. She's a mermaid too. A proper full-time one. She helped me find my dad. Best day of my life, that was, when I sneaked into Neptune's prison and saw him for the first time.

I guess it all took a bit of getting used to. But the last few weeks had been brilliant, once all the trouble with the kraken was sorted. That's the most horrific, fearsome sea monster in the world, and I accidentally woke it up! Since then, Dad and I had been out swimming together every day, exploring the golden seabed around Allpoints Island; racing against the multi-coloured fish that filled every stretch of sea round here; playing tag in among the coral. Dad was officially the BEST dad in the world.

'That's just it,' Mum was saying. '*You* couldn't be more proud. And you've every right to feel proud. Yes, Emily's coming on leaps and bounds in . . . ' She paused to reach over to the pile of textbooks I'd brought home the previous day. I *loved* all my schoolbooks. They weren't like any schoolbooks I'd ever had before, that's for sure! For one thing, they were all made from the coolest shiny materials, or woven with seaweed and decorated with shells and pearls. And for another, they were in the swishiest subjects! School had never been such fun.

'. . . in *Seas and Sirens*,' Mum read from the top one. She picked out a couple more books from the pile. 'Or *Sailing and Stargazing*, or *Hair Braiding for Modern Mermaids*. I mean!'

'You mean what?' Dad asked, his voice coming out pinched and tight. 'Why shouldn't she learn about these things? It's her heritage. What exactly don't you like about it, Mary?'

That's when I knew something was really wrong. No one *ever* calls my mum Mary, least of all Dad. Most people call her Mary P. Her middle name's Penelope and Dad's always called her Penny, or his lucky Penny when they're being particularly gooey. Which they hadn't been for a while, now I thought about it. And while I was thinking about it, I guess Mum had a point. I mean, don't get me wrong. I loved all my school subjects. But maybe I did sometimes miss my old school subjects, just a tiny bit. Or just English, perhaps. I used to love writing stories. I even liked spelling tests! That's just because I was good at them.

'What's wrong,' said Mum, 'is that while *you* may be happy for *your* daughter to learn nothing more than how to brush her hair nicely and tell the time by looking at the clouds, *I'd* like *my* daughter to get a proper education.'

'My daughter, your daughter? You make it sound

as if she's two different people,' Dad said. Below the floor I could see the water swishing round as he swirled his tail angrily. It splashed up on to the kitchen floor.

'Yes, well, maybe she is,' Mum snapped, picking up a tea towel and bending down to wipe the floor. Then she glanced up at me and her face softened. 'I mean, of course she's not. She's not two different people at all. It's not Emily's fault.' Mum smiled at me, reaching up to take hold of my hands. I snatched them away, turning my face at the same time so I couldn't see the hurt look in her eyes. That's one thing I absolutely can't stand.

But it wasn't fair. She wasn't being fair. I'd never enjoyed school this much in my life! And OK, so maybe it would be nice to write stories sometimes, but so what if I wasn't learning languages and logarithms or fractions and French? Who said there was any point in those either? Was I ever really going to need to know how much John earns in a week if he gets 4% commission and 3% interest? Surely learning about my surroundings was more important? Knowing which fish were the most dangerous and which were almost friendly. Learning how to look and act like other mermaids, like *proper* mermaids. Even if I did feel a bit silly perching on a rock combing my hair sometimes, at least I was learning how to fit in. Didn't Mum care about those things? Didn't she want me to be happy?

I carried on eating my breakfast.

Mum drew a breath. 'It's just that it's two different worlds,' she said in a quiet voice. 'And I sometimes wonder if they're simply *too* different. I mean, look at my life here. What do I do all day? Sunbathe, comb my hair, maybe go to Synchro Swim a couple of times a week. This isn't a life for me, Jake. I want more than this.'

No one spoke for ages. Mum and Dad stared at each other. I'd just taken a spoonful of cereal and didn't want to chew in case it crunched really loudly, so I sat there with my mouth full of cornflakes and milk, waiting for one of them to say something.

'We'll talk about this later. I need to go out,' Dad said eventually and I swallowed my mouthful. It was too soggy to chew anyway.

Dad left so quickly he didn't even give me a kiss. Not that I was bothered. I mean, I am twelve. I'll be thirteen in a couple of months. It's not as if I need my dad to kiss me goodbye when he goes out!

But. Well, it showed something. Maybe this was all my fault. It was only because of me that they had to try to bring the two worlds together at all.

That and the fact that they loved each other, of course. But maybe they didn't any more. Maybe they'd grown away from each other so much in the twelve years they'd been apart that they didn't love each other at all now, and just had to stay together because of me. And they both hated it, and hated each other, and in the end they'd both end up hating me, too. And now, Mum didn't even like her life any more!

A strange cold feeling started to spread inside me, creeping around my body, seeping into my bones. Only weeks ago, we'd been given a new start on this island. A dream come true. Everything we'd ever wanted. But maybe it wasn't a dream come true at all. Maybe it was going to turn into a nightmare, like so many of my dreams did. Or used to.

Perhaps it was only a matter of time before Mum and Dad decided to abandon ship and not bother being together at all. Then what? Would I have to choose between them? Would either of them even want me if it was all because of me that their marriage had gone wrong? They'd probably fight each other *not* to have me.

I tried to shake the thoughts from my mind as I got ready for school. The Ocean Studies test was this afternoon and I was determined to do well. I'd show Dad that I really could follow in his footsteps, or wash in his wake, as he liked to say.

The thought cheered me up and I even allowed myself to smile as I packed my books. Till another thought chased the smile off my face like a shark chasing off a shoal of unsuspecting barjacks.

The more I did well in my mermaid lessons, the less time I was spending on land with Mum, doing what she liked. The closer I got to Dad, the further away I moved from her. Now I thought about it, I wasn't surprised she was unhappy. I'd been so busy getting to know Dad, I'd hardly done anything with Mum.

Perhaps she was right after all. Perhaps the two worlds were simply too different to coexist. Perhaps my parents weren't meant to be together at all.

I slunk away from the boat, dropping into the water without even saying goodbye, too miserable to speak, too scared to think.

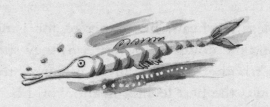

Chapter Two

*A*s I dived down, my thoughts melted away, falling off me as though I was shedding a skin.

My legs felt heavy like concrete, for a moment weighing me down in the water as they stiffened. It didn't bother me, though. I was used to it. In fact, it was the best feeling in the world because I knew what was going to happen next.

My legs joined together, sticking to each other so tightly it was as though someone was taping them together and winding bandages round and round them.

And then my tail formed.

I stretched out like a cat and watched as the bottom half of my costume faded into shiny silver scales, glinting and sparkling and spreading further and further as my tail flickered and swished into life. I would never get bored with that feeling. It was like having been shut up in a box and then taking the lid off and throwing the sides open, and being told you could move wherever you wanted, however you wanted. It was like having the whole world opened up to you.

I hovered in the water, flicking my tail to make sure it had fully formed. It glinted purple and green as I batted away a pair of tiny silver fish swimming along its side. Every toss sent little bubbles dancing up to the surface.

I let myself sigh happily. Nothing could go wrong while I was a mermaid.

I swam along the tops of the coral, glancing down at the underwater forests as I made my way to school.

Bright green bushes waved at me as I sailed over them; rubbery red tubes nodded and bobbed from side to side. A pair of golden seahorses wove their way around long trails of reeds that swayed and dipped in the current, their tails entwined. Gangs of paper-thin fish with bright yellow tails and round-bellied blue fish with black eyes darted purposefully around me. I tried to remember what they were called, just in case it came up in the Ocean Studies test, but they weren't familiar. There was something new to see here every day. I could never tire of Allpoints Island, even if Mum had had enough of the place.

I came to a cluster of rocks at the edge of a tunnel and waited. School was at the other end of the tunnel, in the Emerald Caves. Shona and I had started meeting up here so we could go in together.

A few of the others from my class smiled as they came past me. Most of the class were mermaids. There were a few merboys and two human boys and two girls. I hadn't got to know that many of the others yet, although Shona and I hung around quite a lot with two other mermaids, Althea and Marina. I was the only one who was half and half. The only semi-mer. There was a name for us, even if there were hardly any of us in existence!

I'd got used to being the only one, I suppose, even though I sometimes wished I wasn't. It would just be so cool to have someone else who knew what it felt like to transform like I did.

Well, there was *one* person. The only other one like me I'd ever met, but he hardly counted. For one thing, he was an adult; for another, he was the most untrustworthy, sly person you could ever meet. Mr Beeston. My mum's so-called friend. Who'd turned out to be so much of a friend that he'd spent my whole life spying on us and reporting back to Neptune!

Anyway, that was all history now. At least he wasn't trying to drug us or lie to us any more.

'Emily!' A familiar voice tinkled across to me, sending Mr Beeston far from my mind. Shona!

She swam towards me, clutching her satchel against her side. It was silver and gold and covered in tiny pink shells. Shona always had the prettiest things. She was the kind of mermaid you imagine mermaids to be, all girly and sparkly with shiny long blonde hair. Not like me. I was trying to grow my hair, and it was past my shoulders now, but it still never looked anything like Shona's: sleek and beautiful and, well, mermaid-like, I guess.

'Have you revised?' she asked excitedly as we followed behind a group of younger mermaids with their mums. Holding hands as they swam, they raced ahead to their class, leaving their mums chatting as they glided along behind them.

'Dad tested me this morning,' I replied. 'Think I got them all right but I don't know if I've learned the proper fish.'

'We've got till this afternoon anyway,' Shona said. 'And you know what this morning is, don't you?'

I smiled as I answered her. 'Beauty and Deportment. What else?'

B & D was Shona's favourite lesson. Nothing made her happier than learning a new way to style her hair or get the best shine out of her tail, or swim with perfect elegance. I was more interested in Shipwreck Studies and Siren Stories, but the whole idea of mermaid school was still so new to me that I didn't really mind what we did or what we learned as long as it wasn't long division!

We swam on down the channel. You had to feel your way along the walls as you swam along the first bit. My heart rate always sped up here. The walls, slimy and wet and cold, set off too many memories of what had happened when I'd discovered the kraken in a slimy dark tunnel.

We soon rounded a corner and the tunnel opened up again, growing lighter and filling with colour. I smiled away the memories. I never told Shona how I felt going along that channel. I always wondered if she felt the same way, but it was something we didn't talk about. She'd been with me when I woke the kraken, and was probably as keen as I was to forget about it.

We bumped into Althea and Marina as we reached the fork that led down to our class. Marina swam hurriedly over to us, her long gold tail flicking rapidly from side to side. 'Hey, I overheard Miss Finwave talking to one of the mums on the way in,' she said with a grin. 'And guess what?'

Shona's eyes opened wide, glistening even more than they usually did. 'What?' she replied in the same excited tone as Marina's.

'We're going on a B & D outing!'

'Swishy!'

Althea turned to me. I must have looked puzzled. 'It means we get to go out exploring the reef and the rocks,' she explained.

'What, you mean like when we studied the creeks through the island?'

She shook her head. 'That was a Geography Reef Trip. More scientific. This one will probably have something to do with looking for material to make new hairbrushes, or finding the perfect rocks to sit on the edge of.' Althea pretended to yawn as she spoke.

Marina punched her arm and laughed. 'Come on, you know you love it,' she said.

Althea grinned back at her friend. 'Yeah, I suppose it beats this afternoon's OS test.'

We carried on chatting as we followed the fork that led up to our class. It still took my breath away every time I arrived here. A cave filled with smooth greeny-blue water. Above, shimmering stalactites drooped down from the high ceiling in thin folds like a pterodactyl's wings, or pointed down to the pool like sharp bundles of arrows frozen in mid-flight. All around us, blue and green and purple lights glimmered and winked, dancing on the surface of the deep pool. We swam into the cave, taking our places among the rest of the class.

At the front of the pool, a long scroll hung from the ceiling. In swirly, loopy writing, it always had a message for us when we arrived. Today it read:

Emerald Class: Please remember we have a test this afternoon. This morning, you will not need reeds and scrolls so don't unpack your bags. Leave them somewhere safe for now and please wait for me to arrive.

Underneath, it was signed,
Miss R Finwave

'Told you!' said Marina. 'We must be going out first thing.'

A moment later, Miss Finwave arrived and the class hushed instantly. Her blonde hair shone as she swam into the class. It trailed all the way down her back, glistening and perfectly combed. Her tail was sleek, thin and pale pink with tiny gold stars all along it. It hardly twitched when she moved. She always seemed to glide rather than swim.

She was one of the prettiest of the adult mermaids on the island, and one of the youngest. We always took notice of her and tried to do what she said – and tried to stay in her good books. She knew exactly when to praise and when to tell someone off. And she did the praise thing so nicely and the telling off so sharply that we all knew which one we wanted to get more of.

I patted down my hair and tried to sit up straight. We all perched on rocks just under the surface. Shona always looked exactly like the mermaids in textbooks. I tried to copy her, but usually slipped off the edge, or got pins and needles in my tail from sitting awkwardly.

'Excellent, Shona,' Miss Finwave said as she looked round the class. 'Lovely posture as always.' She glanced at me. 'Nice try, Emily. Coming on quite well there.'

I couldn't help the edges of my mouth twitching into a smile. I know that 'nice try' isn't exactly a gold medal, but it was better than a telling off for slouching, which was what one of the boys behind me got.

'Let's have straight backs please, Adam,' she said as she glanced round. A moment later, she nodded. 'Much better.'

Once she was happy that we all looked our best and were paying attention, Miss Finwave folded her arms and surveyed the class. 'Now then, children,' she said. 'This is a very important day. Can anyone guess what is important about today?'

One of the mermaids in my row put her hand up. 'Is it the Ocean Studies test?' she asked.

Miss Finwave smiled gently. 'Good girl, Morag, I'm glad you've remembered the test,' she said. 'But that's not what I'm thinking of. Anyone else?'

Shona raised her hand. 'Is it the Beauty and Deportment outing?' she asked shyly.

Miss Finwave pursed her lips. 'Well, who told you we were doing anything like that?'

Shona blushed, but before she had a chance to say anything, Miss Finwave continued. 'In a roundabout way, it is something to do with that. I shall explain. In fact, I have a very important announcement to make.'

Then she lowered her voice so that she sounded even more authoritative than usual. 'We are extremely privileged at Allpoints Island to receive a visit from our king this week.'

She paused as the class erupted in gasps and whispers. 'All right, that's enough, thank you,' she said firmly. The classroom hushed instantly.

'Now then, I am not at liberty to tell you too many details of this visit. Normally a visit from our king would be preceded by many weeks of preparation. This visit is different. It has been kept secret under Neptune's strict orders. What I can tell you, though, is that a few of the adults in positions of responsibility here at Allpoints have been asked to conduct some extremely important work.' She smiled proudly. 'I am one of those adults,' she said, 'and I have decided to enlist your help. That is why he is visiting us. I just heard the news this morning. Aren't we lucky, children?'

She beamed round at us all. Most of the class stared back at her with wide eyes, excitement shining on their faces. All I could think was, *Not Neptune. Not here. Please no.* I'd only met Neptune twice, and both times it had led to trouble. BIG trouble.

'I thought it would be nice to combine this project with a Beauty and Deportment lesson,' Miss Finwave continued. 'You will, I'm sure, be as delighted and honoured as I am to hear the news of this visit.'

I gulped.

'And I am confident that you will make me proud,' Miss Finwave went on. 'I know you will be as polite and well-behaved as you can be for our most distinguished guest.'

She looked round the class, as though assessing her opinion of us, just to make sure that she was right and could trust us to behave, or daring us to prove her wrong.

Her eyes fell on me. 'I know you won't let me down,' she said sternly. I didn't know if she was talking to the whole class or just me. There was no way I would let anyone down, though. I'd nearly got myself imprisoned the first time I met Neptune, and was nearly crushed to death by a sea monster the second time! I'd melt into the background and keep my mouth shut this time, for sure. He wouldn't even know I was there.

Miss Finwave nodded. 'Listen carefully, all of you, so you understand what to do. For now, all you need to know is that we are looking for jewels.'

'Might have known,' Althea whispered to me. 'Why else would Neptune come here if it wasn't for gold or treasure? What else does he care about?'

'Thank you, girls,' Miss Finwave said with a sharp glance in our direction.

'Sorry, Miss Finwave,' we replied mechanically as half the class turned to stare at us.

'We will split up into small groups and each group will choose a small area of the island and its surroundings, particularly the bays and beaches,' she said. 'You are searching primarily for crystals, gold, that kind of thing. But you will also search for anything you can find with which to adorn yourself in some way. That is where B & D comes in. Remember, children, you are dressing to meet your king!'

I glanced at Shona. She was smiling as though someone had just told her she'd won the lottery. If mermaids have a lottery, which I don't think they do.

'You will use all you have been studying this term in B & D, and combine this with a bit of initiative and a touch of local knowledge. Then you will come back to class and share your findings. There will be a gold starfish for whoever finds the finest jewel, and another for the best decorated child when we return. Remember, use anything you can to enhance your appearance just that little bit, for our guest, for me, for each other and, most importantly, for yourselves. Now, any questions?'

Shona and I decided to go out on our own. We picked North Bay. That's where I lived with Mum and Dad on *Fortuna*. There was something about our bay that seemed to sparkle more than all the others. I was pretty sure anything glittery would wash up there eventually. Also, it had more boats than the other bays. Shona reckoned that made it a good place to find things as there were so many nooks and crannies round the underside of the boats where lost jewels could easily get lodged and stuck. Some of the oldest boats were lived in; most were abandoned and unused.

Millie lived in North Bay too, on our old boat, *King*. Millie is Mum's best friend who came with us to live at Allpoints Island. She used to have a kiosk in Brightport called *Palms on the Pier*. Recently, she'd started doing tarot readings and hypnotism for some of the mer-families because they were so impressed with the way she helped deal with the kraken by hypnotising him. She's a funny one, Millie. Most of the time, she's obviously the world's biggest phoney, but just occasionally she gets something right, and you have to take back everything you've said about her.

I thought it might be an idea to search near her as she always had crystal balls and fancy jewellery herself. Perhaps she'd dropped something over the side that we could use.

Shona swam ahead. She was determined to win the gold starfish for best decorated mermaid. I went along with her, too distracted to concentrate properly. Neptune. In our classroom. Today!

'Fancy Neptune coming to our class!' Shona said, reading my thoughts, as she so often did.

'Yeah, fancy,' I said, without any of her enthusiasm. I thought back to the times I'd met him so far, and how I'd managed to get on his wrong side both times. Not that he was especially known for having much of a right side.

We had an hour before we had to get back to class with our findings. Gliding silently into the bay, I scoured the seabed for anything that could be used as a mermaid accessory. It wasn't the kind of thing I normally bothered with, but I wanted to try to look the part at least, for Miss Finwave, and for Neptune. And Shona was so excited by the whole idea, I didn't want to dampen her enthusiasm.

Mostly the seabed was just pure white sand, soft and powdery. Every now and then, we swam over a rock. We'd dive down and scrabble around it, coming back up with lengths of golden seaweed to wrap round our tails, or shells that had holes worn right through the middle. Great for necklaces if we could just find a thick chain somewhere.

'Come on, let's try this one.' Shona swam ahead towards an old fishing boat that lay wrecked on the seabed.

We swam over the top of it. The front end had been smashed against a huge rocky layer of coral and lay exposed and ruined. Moss and weeds had grown around it over the years. Groups of fish swam in and out of the wreckage that had become part of their habitat. Two black and white harlequins pecked at the rotting wood, covered as it must be by now with the tiniest forms of sea life, perhaps a small breakfast for this pair. A lone parrotfish swam into the hull of the boat. We followed it in.

'Nothing much here,' I said as we looked under the frayed benches and all round the edges of the boat.

'Hey, look at this.' Shona swam into the wheelhouse. Spongy coral had somehow made its way in, filling the little room as though it was a greenhouse. She was pulling at some delicate purple sea fans. 'I could wear them in my hair,' she said, holding one up against her head. It looked like a feathery hat.

'Nice,' I said, tugging at a blue and pink vase sponge. 'Hey, maybe we could use this in class. Miss Finwave could put flowers in it.'

'Swishy idea!' Shona grinned.

Pink jellyfish lined the bottom of the boat. 'Shame they're poisonous,' Shona said as we swam back out into the bay with our findings. 'They would have made nice cushions.'

I laughed. 'Where to next?'

'How about your boat?'

'*Fortuna*?'

Shona nodded happily. 'It's so old I bet all sorts of things have got lodged underneath it over the years.'

'OK. And then *King*,' I insisted. 'I want to see if we can find any of Millie's discarded lucky pebbles!'

'Come on,' Shona said. 'Let's go.'

We swam all round the edges of *Fortuna*. Portholes lined the lower level. Some had glass in them. The biggest one near the front, the one Dad and I used for getting in and out of the boat, didn't. The whole lower floor was half submerged. That was how Mum and Dad managed to live there together.

Green ferns reached up all around the front end

426

of the boat. It was like an underwater garden, except that we never had to water it!

'Let's take some of these,' Shona said, grabbing at the ferns. She held them against her tail. 'We can wear them as skirts.'

Under the ferns I spotted some silver seaweed, thin and wispy. It was just the thing to help turn our shells into necklaces. I carefully ripped out some strands.

Swimming round the boat, we scavenged under the rocks, trailed along the hull with our fingers, batted fat red fish out of our way, and created sandstorms as we burrowed for treasure, picking up anything colourful that we could carry.

'Come on,' Shona said. 'We've got enough of the B & D stuff. I really want to find some of the jewels. Think how pleased Neptune would be!'

'Hm,' I said. It was hard to imagine Neptune being pleased about *anything*, let alone something I'd done.

'Let's try *King*.' Shona said. Then she stretched out her long tail and swam off. I started to follow her – but something was drawing me away. It was as if I was being pulled in another direction by something attached to me, tugging at me. What was it?

'Shona, let's try over there,' I said without even knowing why. I pointed towards a bunch of rocks nestled among a tiny forest of bushes and reeds.

Spiky black anemones sat along the rocks' edges, lining them like guards. The bushes were grey and dull.

'There won't be anything down there.'

'Please,' I said, my chest aching with the need to look in the rocks. 'Let's just try it.'

Shona sighed. 'Come on, then.'

She scavenged away under the rock with me, dodging the anemones and burrowing into the sand, without knowing why we were looking here any more than I did. A small sandstorm built up around us as we scratched and scrabbled at the seabed, digging out broken shells and pebbles. But nothing more than that.

'How about this?' Shona said, holding up a razorshell. 'It would do for a comb, perhaps, if we just cut away a few ridges.' She turned the shell over in her hands, held it to her hair.

I nodded. 'Yeah,' I said absent-mindedly. But I knew there was something else there. I could feel it shining into me, almost calling me. It reminded me of a game we used to play where someone hides an object and the others have to look for it. Move nearer, you get warmer. Move away and you're cold again. *Warmer, warmer.* I could feel it, close to me. What was it?

'Come on, let's try one more boat,' Shona said. 'We need to be back in class soon.' She started to swim away.

'Wait,' I called.

Shona turned. 'What is it?'

Could I really say what I felt? That I had a burning in my chest that told me I had to stay here, had to find whatever it was that was down here? Look what had happened last time I made Shona help me follow my instincts. We'd ended up disturbing the kraken and threatening the safety of the whole island. No, I couldn't do it.

But I couldn't leave it alone either.

'You go on,' I said. 'I'll just have a bit more of a look here.'

'But there's nothing to see. It's just a bunch of rocks, Em.'

'I know. I just – I just fancy one more scout round.'

Shona flicked her hair back. 'OK, if you're sure. I'll meet you by *King*. Don't be long.'

'Great. See you there,' I said, trying to return her smile. I hurried back to my task as soon as she'd turned away. What was down here? Why was it drawing me in? One way or another, I was determined to find out.

I worked like a dog burrowing down a hole on the trail of a rabbit. I scratched my tail on the coral, my hair was matted and tangled and my nails were filled with sand and broken from tearing at the rocks. But I couldn't stop. Whatever was down here, I needed to find it. I could almost hear it calling me, as though it *wanted* me to find it.

'What are you doing?'

I jerked my head up. Shona!

'I – '

'I've been waiting ages. I thought you were going to meet me at *King*?'

'I was,' I stammered. 'I just – I wanted to – '

'Your nails!' Shona screeched. I instantly curled my hands into fists, but it was too late. Shona swam over to me and uncurled them. 'Miss Finwave's going to hit the waves!'

'Yeah, I know,' I mumbled. I didn't want to talk about my nails! I wanted to get back to my search.

'Come on,' Shona said. 'We're going to be late.' She had some fine wispy pink seaweed draped round her neck. She must have found it by *King*.

'Right,' I said. I didn't make any effort to move.

Shona pursed her lips and pulled her hair to the side. 'Emily, what's going on? You're acting all weird.'

'No, I'm fine,' I said with a lame smile. 'Really. Sorry, come on, let's go.'

I dragged myself away from the hole, pretending I was going back to class with Shona. There was no way I was leaving this, though.

'Hang on a sec,' I said as we passed *Fortuna*. 'I'll just nip in and clean my nails.'

'What?' Shona flicked her tail impatiently.

'Because of Miss Finwave,' I faltered. 'I won't be long. I'll just nip in. I'll be right behind you.'

'I'll wait,' Shona sighed.

'No. You go ahead. I'll catch up. I don't want you to be late.'

She shrugged. 'OK,' she said, and swam away.

As soon as she was out of sight, I went straight back to the rocks. Whatever was down here was pulling me hard, like a fish caught on a piece of bait. As I burrowed deeper and searched, I almost had to hold my hand over my heart to stop it hurting.

And then I saw it.

Turning over one final stone, there it was, glinting at me, throwing light in a multi-coloured arc all around. I gasped out loud.

A ring. A thick gold band with the biggest, brightest diamond I had ever seen in my life. It must have been in an accident, as the band had been dented and bent out of shape. I squeezed it on to my middle finger and examined it. I could tell that it used to be much bigger, but with all the dents, it fit my finger perfectly. Looking down at it, I had the strangest sensation. It was like a tight knot inside me that made me want to scream or cry or laugh, I didn't know which. All of them.

I could have stared at it all day. But I had to get back. Glancing down at my hand every few seconds just to check the ring was still there, I smiled to myself as I swam back to class.

Chapter Three

I joined the rest of the class huddled round a huge
flat rock in the centre of the pool where we
examined our multi-coloured findings. I'd managed
to sneak in while Miss Finwave was looking away, so
she didn't notice I'd got back after everyone else.

The rock was covered with a stash that lit up the
classroom, splashing a hundred colours all around
us. I stared at the collection. Seaweed in bright
pinks and greens, shells with the prettiest swirling
patterns, sea flowers of every colour, ancient jars
filled with sand so bright it was more like glitter.

Bright blue and green and orange crystals, shining white rocks. Neptune was going to be very pleased.

When Miss Finwave noticed me milling at the edge of the pool, she did a double take. Her face turned pale. 'Shooting sharks, Emily!' she said, clasping a hand over her mouth.

'What?'

'Your hair!' she gasped, looking around frantically. 'Quickly, someone get me a comb! Hurry!'

'Here, she can use mine,' Marina said, pulling a razorshell comb out of her rope bag.

'Thank you, Marina,' Miss Finwave said tightly as she proceeded to pull at the tangles in my hair, yanking my head again and again till the comb ran smoothly through.

'That's better,' she said, examining me. 'Now, let's see your contribution.'

My hand was in my pocket. I was about to bring it out to show her the ring, but the strangest thing happened. The ring seemed to be weighing my hand down. I could almost hear it, begging me not to show it to Miss Finwave.

'Shona's already put our things out,' I said, pointing to the sea fans and shells she'd collected while she was with me. I held my breath while I waited for the reply. My hand still firmly in my pocket, I twisted the ring round on my finger so I could feel the diamond against my palm. Then I curled my fingers around it. Safe.

Miss Finwave simply nodded. 'Very good. Nice work, you two,' she said quickly before moving on to someone else.

I let my breath out with a sigh. Then I glanced over to see Shona staring at me. 'What's going on?' she whispered.

'Tell you later,' I whispered back. 'I found something!' Now that I'd managed to find out what it was without getting Shona into trouble, I couldn't wait to share it with her!

Shona's eyes went all round and big, but before she had the chance to reply, Miss Finwave had snapped her tail to get everyone's attention.

'Now then, children,' she said. 'Well done. You have created quite a treasure trove in here! Neptune *will* be pleased with you. He'll be with us very shortly and I want each one of you to adorn yourselves with your findings, making yourself as beautiful or as smart and handsome as you can. And the politest class I have ever had, please. Is that understood?'

We replied with a synchronised 'Yes, Miss Finwave,' and then erupted into a scuffle of noise as we shared and compared our findings, bartering and bargaining with each other to get the best combinations of colours, textures and patterns.

I looked around the pool at what we'd managed to do with our appearance. It was incredible how a few bits and pieces from the ocean floor had transformed every one of us. Althea had created extensions from some bright blue seaweed. Next to her jet black hair, they made her look gothic and glamorous. Marina had made a starfish brooch for her bikini top and a belt from oyster shells. Adam had attached a shiny silver crab's husk to some black ship's rope to make a belt that could have been worn by a rock star. Shona and I made bangles and necklaces from the shells we'd picked up, wove the fans into hats, stuck shiny stones in patterns on our tails and surrounded them with swirling patterns made from glittery pink sand. We laid all the jewels we'd found on the rock in the centre of the classroom.

'Not bad, not bad at all,' Miss Finwave said with a satisfied smile as she examined us. 'Very good work. You should all feel as proud as piranhas.'

Just then, a strange thing happened. Strange – but familiar. Horribly familiar. The classroom started to shake. The water in the pool bubbled and frothed. Stalactites shivered and wobbled above us, threatening to crash down and spear any one of us. The last time it had happened, I'd thought it was an earthquake. But it wasn't. At least I knew what it was this time.

'That will be Neptune,' Miss Finwave called

above the noise of water swirling round and round, creating a whirlpool. 'Get to the sides, children. It'll stop in a moment.'

Don't panic. Relax. I tried to breathe smoothly. But my breath came out in sharp spiky puffs.

He wasn't coming to see me. I hadn't done anything wrong, I told myself again and again. I'd make sure I didn't put a scale out of place this time. He wouldn't even know I was there.

We swam to the side of the pool, falling over ourselves and each other, and only just managing to keep our new accessories in place.

And then the water calmed, just as suddenly as it had started. The pool shone brighter than ever, the walls glistened and beamed, the cave was silent as we waited.

The dolphins came first, swimming into the pool in a row as straight as an army's front line. Behind them, Neptune's chariot slid smoothly into view. Gold, grand and adorned with a thousand jewels, it snatched my breath away every time I saw it. I had to shield my eyes from the dazzling light it shone around the cave.

The class fell even more silent. And then there he was. Neptune. In our classroom! Sitting back in his chariot, his golden crown on his head, his trident held high, beard reaching down to his chest, and the deepest frown on his face, Neptune arrived in the cave.

As the chariot came to a halt, the dolphins immediately swam round the back and lined up along the opposite side of the pool from us.

Without speaking, Neptune raised both hands in the air. Holding the trident aloft in one hand, he clicked his fingers twice with the other. A second later, someone else swam into the pool. We couldn't see who it was at first. He had his head down, reverently bowing to Neptune. But as soon as he raised it, I gasped. I'd know that face anywhere: the broken teeth, the odd eyes, the creepy sideways looks.

Mr Beeston.

Neptune nodded to him and he swam to the edge of the chariot. 'Your Majesty,' he said in a deep voice, 'please allow me to attend to your wishes. Whatever it is you need, you know you only have to – '

Neptune banged his trident impatiently on the floor of the chariot. 'Enough!' he bellowed.

Miss Finwave swam forward and bowed her head. 'Your Majesty, it is an honour,' she said simply. 'I have taken your orders very seriously and have set about my work, enlisting the help of the children, as I told you – '

Neptune raised an eyebrow into a wide, white arch.

Miss Finwave went on quickly. 'I have told them nothing of the purpose of your visit. We have merely begun some collections in your honour.'

Neptune sniffed. 'Very well,' he said. Then he clicked a finger and motioned for Mr Beeston to come towards him. Mr Beeston swam forwards again, simpering and drooling like the creep that he was.

'Explain to the children why I am here,' Neptune said to him.

'I – certainly, your Majesty,' Mr Beeston stammered. 'Right away.' Then he pulled on his crooked tie and cleared his throat before swimming towards us. Flicking his tail to propel him higher in the water, he glanced back at the chariot. A brief glower from Neptune was all the encouragement he needed to get started.

'Children,' he began, smiling round at us with his horrible creepy smile. 'As you know, Allpoints Island is a very special and important place. For many reasons. And one of those reasons is the kraken.'

A sound like thunder boomed into the cave. I looked round to see what it was. No one else seemed to have noticed it. They were all looking at Mr Beeston.

There it was again.

That was when I realised it was my heart, beating so loud I could feel it thud in my ears. The kraken. Neptune's sea monster. Had something happened to it? Had it woken again? That was the absolute worst thing he could possibly have come to tell us. Not only would it mean we were all in danger again, but Neptune would remember whose fault it was, who had released it in the first place. I slunk low in the water, trying to hide, trying to make myself invisible. I could feel my face heating up. As it did, the ring seemed to burn in my pocket, almost singeing my fingers which were still folded tightly around the diamond.

'As you all know, the kraken was disturbed recently.' Mr Beeston paused and looked me directly in the eye. Why couldn't I make myself invisible? *Why*?

Then he looked away again, surveying the whole class. 'Well, then. Since that time, I am pleased to say that as the chief kraken keeper, I have ensured no further disturbances have taken place. I have regarded my duties with the utmost vigilance, loyalty and – '

'Beeston!' Neptune growled.

'I'm sorry, your Majesty,' Mr Beeston said, twisting to bow low again. Turning back to the class, he continued. 'However, there are one or two unresolved matters from that sorry period. Not everything is exactly as it should be.'

'GET TO THE POINT!' Neptune exploded, shaking the cave so much that a rock fell from its perch and splashed into the water, spraying us all.

Reddening, Mr Beeston spoke quickly. 'The

kraken held many jewels in its lair. The spoils of many a warship, the cargo of many a cruiser were safely buried and out of danger while it slept. But since the recent troubles, some of these treasures have become dislodged. Items which were buried deep, deep down in the caves under Allpoints Island have emerged or been dispersed.'

At this point, Mr Beeston stopped and closed his eyes. Continuing more quietly, he said, 'Most have been recovered. I have made sure of that. Entrusted with such an important task, I would not have dared fail. However, I – '

'Beeston, that is ENOUGH!' Neptune rose in his chariot. His head towering high above us all, it seemed he was almost as tall as the ceiling. 'I shall continue. Then maybe the children will understand what has happened here. And WHY.'

Pointing at Mr Beeston with his trident, he said, 'Yes, children. What you hear is true. Certain folk have let me down. Those entrusted with the highest of honours have allowed the privilege of my trust to slip through their fins. And as a result, I have lost some of the treasure that is rightly mine. This is not a situation I am prepared to endure.'

He paused, looking round the silent classroom. 'I want it back,' he said eventually, in a voice as quiet and threatening as a rumble of thunder from miles away. 'Every last jewel, every last coin. All of it.'

I felt my hand burning up as though it was on

fire. The ring! It was scorching a hole through my palm.

I tried to lift it out of my pocket, but I couldn't! My hand was jammed fast and wouldn't budge. I bit hard into my cheek to take my mind off the sensation.

Just then, Miss Finwave swam forward. 'Your Majesty,' she said, 'please allow me to show you what we have collected for you.' She motioned to us to clear a path towards the rock in the centre of the pool and waved a hand out towards it. Treasure winked and sparkled from every centimetre of the rock.

'The children have done well, wouldn't you agree?' Miss Finwave said, turning to Neptune.

But he wasn't listening. His eyes feasted greedily on the jewels as he swam all the way round the rock. 'Perfect,' he said, his mouth dribbling slightly, his eyes glinting as much as the jewels. Reaching out with both arms, he swept the multi-coloured gems towards him, clutching them to his chest.

As he glided back to his chariot, his hands crammed with jewels, he turned back to us. 'Well done, children,' he said. 'You've done the island proud. Miss Finwave, excellent thinking. I wonder if anyone else who was set this task has fared so well. I shall visit them all, and reward the most conscientious. Now that I am here to oversee this operation and ensure no one attempts to trick me out of my treasure, I will no longer keep it confidential. You may speak freely of your task. And you may be proud of your work.'

His eyes only leaving the jewels for seconds at a time, Neptune looked round at us all. I'm sure he stared directly at me when he spoke again. 'It will all be returned. Every last item. Do you hear me?'

With one final, terrible stare at all of us, Neptune banged his trident loudly on the floor of his chariot. The row of dolphins returned in a flash, picking up the reins in their mouths. Now he had a chariot full of jewels, he wasn't interested in us.

'Beeston, wrap it up,' he called over his shoulder. 'Return to me if you have any more news on my lost treasure. And not before.'

With that, the dolphins swam into action, whisking Neptune out of the cave.

Once Neptune had left, Mr Beeston seemed to swim higher in the water. When he spoke to us again, his voice contained the old creepy snarl I knew so well, rather than the simpering drool that he adopted whenever Neptune was around.

'You have heard your king,' he said, looking slowly round at us all. 'I do not need to tell you how powerful he is. When he says he wants something to happen, it will happen. It will indeed. And I, my friends,' he raised a hand to smooth down his hair, 'I shall make sure of that. Now that this mission is no longer secret, every single inhabitant of this island will take part in this project, until our king is satisfied. Do you hear me?'

We all nodded. Most of the others looked too nervous to speak. I wasn't nervous, just annoyed. Who did he think he was, telling us what to do like that? He didn't frighten *me*!

Just then, Mr Beeston's eyes fell on me. He looked into my eyes, then glanced towards the pocket at the side of my tail. Did he know? Should I tell him now? I tried to pull my hand out. Again, it felt chained down. I couldn't even move it! What if I could never move my hand again? The panic must have shown in my eyes as Mr Beeston swam closer to me. 'Got something to share, Emily?' he asked, his voice as slimy and ugly as a conger eel.

'No!' I said quickly. What else could I say? *Well, yes, possibly, but it appears to be a magic ring which is digging into my palm holding my hand down so I can't actually show it to you just at this moment?* I don't think so.

He swam closer. 'Are you sure? I hope you know how seriously Neptune would view it if anyone tried to trick him out of anything, even the smallest jewel.'

That was when I lost my nerve.

'I – I found something,' I said.

He moved closer. 'Found something?'

'A – a ring.'

'What kind of ring?' he asked.

I would have shown it to him. I *would* have. I'd have handed it over on the spot if I could. But I couldn't. The ring felt like a claw, gripping my palm, pinning my hand to my pocket. 'A diamond,' I said, feeling warmth flood through me as I thought about the ring. 'A huge diamond. All shiny and sparkly – the most beautiful diamond ring you've ever seen.'

Mr Beeston sniffed. 'There was no such ring in the collection,' he said, starting to swim away from me.

'And it had a thick gold band that was battered and twisted out of shape,' I called to his retreating back.

Mr Beeston stopped and turned. 'Wait a minute!' His face had turned grey. 'Diamond, you say?' he sputtered.

I nodded.

'A huge diamond, a battered gold band?'

I nodded again.

'Battered as though it had been thrown away, discarded?'

'As though it had been through a war!' I said.

Mr Beeston swallowed and wiped a strand of hair from his face. 'I don't believe it,' he said. 'That must be the − 'Then he stopped. 'Where is it?' he hissed quietly, close to my ear.

One last time, I tried to lift my hand. I couldn't do it. What was I going to do? I couldn't say the ring wouldn't let me take my hand out of my pocket! How utterly ridiculous would that sound? No one would believe me, let alone Mr Beeston.

'I lost it,' I said eventually.

'Lost it?' Mr Beeston spluttered. '*Lost* it? You can't have lost it!'

'I dropped it in the sand. Sorry,' I said, turning my face away and praying he wouldn't notice my reddening cheeks. They felt almost as hot as the ring, still burning a hole in my hand.

At that moment, Miss Finwave swam in between us. 'Mr Beeston, in case you hadn't noticed, the children gathered plenty of jewels for Neptune. And he seemed perfectly happy with our work. So I would be very grateful if you could please acknowledge our efforts just a little bit, and leave us to get on with our school day. We have a lot to do.'

'Very well,' Mr Beeston said. With a curt bow to the teacher, he swam to the edge of the pool, towards the tunnel that led out of the cave. Turning back to us once he reached the tunnel's entrance, he added, 'Thank you children,' and smiled.

Then Miss Finwave flicked the end of her tail in a loud snap to get our attention and everyone turned back to face her. Everyone except me. I was still looking at Mr Beeston. He was still looking at me. 'We're not done yet,' he mouthed.

And with that, he flicked his tail and disappeared into the darkness of the tunnel.

I pretended to listen like the rest of the class as Miss Finwave started to talk about the afternoon's test. I pretended I didn't care about Mr Beeston's silly threats, or Neptune's anger, or any of it. Neptune had been here to see us all, not just me. And Mr Beeston hadn't really whispered a threat to me as he left. Not really. I must have misread his lips, or he was talking to someone else. It was just me imagining things again.

I gripped the ring for comfort. At least I had that.

And if it felt as though it glowed and burned on my finger, reaching out for me with a sharpness that almost cut through me – well, surely I was imagining that, too.

Chapter Four

*I*t was hours before I got the chance to speak to Shona. We didn't manage to catch a moment on our own, with everyone crowding round in groups to talk about Neptune's visit all the way through lunch and then having to sit in silence for the Ocean Studies test.

At the end of the day, we swam out through the tunnels with Althea and Marina.

'That was easy!' Marina said as soon as we were out of earshot of the classroom.

'What did you put for number four?' Althea asked.

'Angelfish,' Marina replied quickly.

'Yeah, me too.'

Shona was busy stroking the glittery gold starfish she'd won for best outfit.

'So swish, Neptune coming to *our* school,' Althea murmured.

'I know,' Shona replied dreamily.

'I wonder if he'll get all his treasure back,' Marina added, and the three of them talked about his visit all the way to the end of the tunnel where Shona and I said goodbye to the others.

As soon as they were out of sight, Shona turned to me, her eyes almost popping out with excitement. 'So? What were you trying to tell me this morning?' she asked. 'Was it about the ring? Did you really lose it?'

I glanced around before replying. Some younger mer-children were laughing and playing in the sea on their way home from school. A couple of them had caught a ride home on a dolphin. Others were chasing each other or jumping over waves. The sun beat down on us.

I pulled Shona into a rocky crevice. We swam between the rocks, taking a long route home. Once I was sure there was no one around, I pulled my hand out of my pocket. It slid out easily this time. Twisting the ring round so she could see the diamond, I held my hand out.

'Swirling seahorses!' Shona said, swimming up to

look more closely. 'You had it all along! But why did you say you'd lost it?'

I wondered whether to tell her the truth about the weird feeling I'd been getting from it all day. How crazy would it sound, though?

'You promise not to tell anyone about this?' I said.

Shona looked at me blankly. 'Why? Why the big secret? How come you didn't give it in, Emily?'

I shook my head. 'I couldn't.'

'Didn't want to, you mean?' Shona said. 'Emily, you heard what Mr Beeston said. Neptune will go mad if anyone – '

'I *couldn't*, Shona,' I said more firmly.

She stopped and stared at me. 'Why not? What do you mean?'

I looked up at her from under my eyelids. I could feel my tail quiver as I blushed. 'You'll think I'm mad,' I said.

'Course I won't,' Shona said, laughing. 'I *know* you're mad. Come on, it's me, your best friend. Tell me!'

I smiled, despite my weird feelings about it all. 'OK.' And before I could talk myself out of it, I found myself telling Shona all the things I'd been feeling since I'd been wearing it, and about my hand getting stuck in my pocket while Neptune was at school.

'It was weird when I was looking for it. I had

such a strong feeling, as if it *wanted* me to find it,' I said.

I stopped talking and waited for Shona to speak. This was where she would tell me I'd completely lost it and she didn't want to be my friend any more. Why had I risked her friendship again? Was it too late to take it all back, say I was joking?

I stared down at a skinny seahorse bobbing along the seabed, its bright orange colour standing out against the white sand. A shoal of butter hamlets drifted by, taking no notice of the seahorse or of us.

Finally I looked up at Shona. She was staring into my face. 'You promise you're not making this up?' she asked.

'Course I'm not making it up! Why would I want you to think I'm even barmier than you already do?'

'It must be magic, then,' she said, her eyes shining with delight. 'It's so beautiful,' she added with a touch of envy. 'Can I try it on?'

I laughed. I might have known Shona would want to try it for herself.

I tried to pull it off my finger, but it was stuck. I pulled harder – and a rushing noise flooded into my head. Thundering and rolling. What was it? There was a storm raging out at sea. I could feel it. Waves crashing everywhere, thunder booming into every corner of the sky, lightning cracking the world open. And grief. I wanted to cry. Wanted to break down in floods of tears and cry till I'd filled an ocean. I squeezed my eyes shut, stopped trying to pull the ring off and clasped my hands over my ears.

Instantly, the storm stopped.

'What was *that*?' I asked.

'What?' Shona looked bemused.

'The storms, the sea crashing.'

'I don't know what you mean,' Shona said. 'I didn't feel anything.' She looked at me sideways for a second, then shook her head and examined the ring again. I flicked my tail to stay upright and still as she stared at it. Was she joking with me? How could she not have noticed the storms? 'It's really the swishiest thing I've ever seen,' Shona breathed, still acting as though nothing had happened.

Well, I could do that too! 'I can't get it off,' I said.

'Here, let me try.' Shona reached out and I held my hand open for her. But the second she touched the ring, she catapulted away from me as though she'd been shot out of a cannon, landing in a bunch of mossy seaweed.

I swam over to her and pulled her out. 'You all right?' I asked.

'It burned me!' she shrieked, pointing at the ring. 'Or bit me, or something!'

I yanked at the ring again. 'Don't be silly, it's just – '

'I don't want to try it! You keep it. It's fine.' Shona dusted her tail down, wiping sand and moss from her scales.

I twisted the ring back round on my finger so the diamond could stay hidden against my palm. I felt safer with it that way.

'Come on,' Shona said. 'Let's go back to yours and do our homework.'

She swam off without another word.

I knew as soon as we reached *Fortuna* that something was wrong. The first person I saw was Millie. Not that that was so unusual. She often came round to see Mum.

But she was on her own, sunning herself on the front deck. If sunning herself was the right expression. Millie must be the only person in the world who managed to sunbathe in a long black gown. She never wore anything else. She'd pulled it up to her knees and was stretched out on a blanket, a packet of cards spread out in a star shape next to her.

'Where's Mum?' I called as we approached the boat.

Millie looked over and squinted into the sunlight. Sitting up and pulling her gown back down to her feet, she shuffled the cards into a pile. Shona and I swam up to the side of the boat. 'She had to go out,' Millie said, in the mysterious way that she says everything.

'*Had* to? Why? Where?'

'She just – look, it's not really for me to explain.'

'Fine, I'll ask Dad.'

I swam to the front of the boat and was about to dive down to the porthole when Millie said, 'He's gone out, too.'

I stopped, treading water with my tail. 'They've gone out together?' I asked hopefully, knowing even before she spoke what the answer was going to be.

'No.' She refused to meet my eyes. 'No, they've gone out separately. Your mum asked me to babysit for you. I thought perhaps we could play canasta, or I'll do your tarot cards for you if you like.'

'They've had an argument, haven't they?' I said.

Millie still wouldn't look at me. She started dealing out the cards for a game of patience. 'I really think you need to talk to your parents about it,' she said awkwardly. 'I just don't think it's my place to – '

'It doesn't matter,' I said, cutting her off. 'Come on, Shona, let's go inside.'

We swam silently through the porthole into the downstairs floor of the boat, the part that was filled with water, where Dad lived. I knew exactly what Millie was telling me or, rather, what she wasn't telling me. It was obvious they'd had an argument. They'd been heading in that direction for days.

I'd managed to push the morning's row out of my mind for most of the day, what with everything else that had been going on. But now. Well, that was it. They'd walked out. On each other, or on me, too? Would either of them ever come back? Was it because of me? If they didn't have to argue about how to bring up their daughter, everything would probably be fine between them.

Shona tried to jolly me out of my mood by making silly faces behind the fern curtains and offering to share the bottle of glitter she'd brought home from school. But it was no good. Nothing could lift the heaviness of my mood, or the dark cloud of my thoughts.

Mum and Dad were going to split up, and it was all my fault.

'Emily, are you down there?' Millie called down from the kitchen.

I raced up to the little trapdoor. Maybe she wanted to tell me Mum and Dad had come home! 'Are they back?' I asked.

'I — I'm sorry love,' Millie said. 'I was just thinking I'd make us some tea. I thought you might be hungry.'

I suddenly felt empty, but not with hunger.

'No thanks,' I said sullenly, and slipped back down without waiting for her to reply.

Shona was busy painting swirly patterns on her tail with scale polish. She looked up as I swam back towards her.

And then it happened. The shaking, the rocking, waves rolling over each other; even the boat seemed to be moving. Water sploshed in from the trapdoor above us.

'What's going on?' Shona shouted, smearing the swirly patterns into a smudge down her tail.

'I don't know!' I called back, half of me relieved that at least I wasn't imagining it this time. 'Hold on to the porthole!'

We swam as hard as we could to get to the front end where the large open porthole seemed like the steadiest thing to hold. Gripping its sides, our tails flailing out all over the place, we waited for the shaking to stop.

'Are you all right down there, girls?' Millie's voice warbled from upstairs.

'We're fine!' I yelled back. 'Hold on to the rails, Millie!'

'I am doing!' she replied. 'I'm fine. It'll be all right, don't worry,' she added, her voice wobbling with fear. 'I'll look after you!'

Gripping the sides tightly, our bodies were flung from side to side, our tails hitting the wall as the boat rocked and shook. It was like an underwater rollercoaster ride! Up, down, thwacking us all around, our bodies slapped backwards and forwards in the water so violently I was nearly sick.

And then it stopped. Just like that. The boat stopped rocking. Shona and I looked at each other for a moment as we caught our breath. Just for a second.

In that second, a sharp pain stabbed my hand. The ring! It was gripping into my finger! *Aargh!* I curled my hand into a ball, the diamond tight inside my fist. Catching my breath, I looked up to see a dark shadow fall over the porthole.

Something was outside. Something big. And it was heading towards the boat.

Chapter Five

'I might have KNOWN!' The voice boomed into the boat like an explosion.

Surely this couldn't be real. Neptune! He was outside the boat, his chariot gleaming in the sunlight, dolphins surrounding him as he raised his trident. The sea around him bubbled like burning lava.

'Come HERE!' he bellowed.

I looked around, desperately hoping I'd spot who it was that he was addressing. I mean, it couldn't be me. It *couldn't* be. What had I done *this* time?

'Yes,' he growled in a quieter voice that was even

more threatening than a shout. 'You.' He pointed directly at me.

I swam through the porthole that we used as the underwater door, my tail shaking so much I thought it would fall off.

'Alone!' Neptune barked as Shona approached the porthole behind me.

'I'll wait here. You'll be OK,' Shona whispered, sounding as if she believed it about as much as I did.

I wobbled towards Neptune like a jellyfish and waited for him to speak.

But he didn't. He just stared. Stared and stared at me until I wondered if he was going to turn me to stone with his eyes. But he wasn't even looking into my eyes. He was looking at my hand, at the diamond.

'For once, Beeston did well,' he said in a quiet voice. Quiet for Neptune anyway. It still vibrated through the air, splashing water across the sides of his chariot with each word. 'All those years and it was right here,' he murmured, even more quietly, his eyes still fixed on the ring.

My hand burned under his gaze. It felt as though it was on fire, flames scorching through my fingers, screaming along my arm into my body, all through me. I clenched my teeth and waited.

Eventually, Neptune raised his head to look me in the eyes. 'Remove it,' he said simply, holding out his hand.

'I – '

'The ring. Give it to me. NOW!'

As he waited for me to hand over the ring, the sea rocked and ebbed around us. I bobbed about, bouncing up and down on the water while I fumbled and pulled at my finger. My hands shook with terror. I couldn't do it. The ring was completely stuck. My finger swelled and throbbed.

'I – I can't,' I stammered, my words jamming through the thudding in my mouth.

At this, Neptune rose higher in his chariot. As he did, the waves grew sharper, splashing against me, slapping my face, pulling me under. 'Come here,' he said. Swirling my tail round as hard as I could, I propelled myself back up, and swam towards the chariot.

Neptune held his trident in front of me. 'Put your hand out,' he said. I did what he said. Then he reached towards me with the trident and touched the ring.

The result was electric. Literally. I felt as if I'd been struck by lightning. My body zipped into life as though a thousand volts were buzzing through every nerve. Neptune looked as if he felt it too. His beard seemed to have flames flying from it. His tail was shooting sparks out in every direction. A jagged orange light danced and crackled between us, alive and on fire.

Neptune finally pulled the trident away.

Breathless, he paused to gather himself. Then he reached out with his hand. Grabbing my wrist, he pulled at the ring.

'AAARRRGGH!' he screamed, leaping backwards. He shook his hand, blew on it, plunged it into the water. As he did so, the sea raged around us, building into the worst storm I'd ever seen. Clouds darkened, blackening the sky, closing down on us. I was being tossed around everywhere. Even *Fortuna* shook so violently it was starting to break free from the spot in the seabed where it had been deeply stuck for over two hundred years! The boat heeled madly from side to side.

'Damn those vows!' Neptune bellowed. 'They were not meant to prevent *me* from touching the rings! I am the king of all the oceans!'

What did he mean? What vows? Why couldn't he touch the ring?

As if he'd heard me, Neptune snapped his head round to face me. 'That ring has been out of my sight for hundreds of years,' he said. 'And that is exactly where it should have stayed. Never have I thought of it in all those years. Never. Not once did I question its whereabouts.' He laughed sardonically. He wasn't smiling, though. 'Although I should have known the kraken would have found it and protected it. The kraken understands loyalty.'

Neptune looked up to the sky. 'It should have remained hidden, out of sight, buried in the seabed,' he called to the clouds that split apart and cracked in claps of thunder. 'I need it to be buried, along with everything it represents.'

Then he turned to me. 'You have brought back to life what should have remained forever out of mind, forever forgotten,' he said. 'Get out of my sight.'

I didn't need telling twice. I swam as hard as I could towards *Fortuna*.

I could see Millie, gripping the rails with both hands, her legs thrown from side to side on the deck, her black gown whirling out around her. Shona must have still been inside. Ploughing through the water as hard as I could, sinking with every stroke, plummeting down and swirling around before being thrown back above the water and landing again with a splash, eventually I made it to the boat. I gripped a lower railing and tried to steady myself.

'Wait!' Neptune called to me. 'I will not allow this to happen!' A streak of lightning zigzagged across the sky, ripping it in two. The boat swayed again, dragging me under the water and hurling me back up. Gasping for breath, I clung to the porthole as thunder exploded across the sky. It sounded as though someone was beating a bass drum with speakers the size of a planet.

Neptune's face had turned purple. 'You cannot defy me!' he barked. 'I am Neptune, king of all the oceans, and you will NOT take advantage of my laws. Do you hear me?'

I nodded frantically. 'Yes, your Majesty,' I said, my voice shaking. 'I hear you. I – I'm sorry. I didn't mean to steal your possessions. Please, I'll give it back, I'll put it back exactly where I took it from.' I struggled with the ring. Again, it wouldn't budge. My finger felt bruised.

But there was part of me that was glad it wouldn't come off. The ring made me feel – what was it? Comforted. Safe. Important.

'Enough!' Neptune boomed. 'I WILL have it back. And I know how to get it – even if it means invoking a curse that has not been used for many generations.'

'What do you mean?' I asked, gripping the side of the boat as it swayed in the waves that were still crashing all around us. 'I don't understand what I've *done*!'

'It's what your parents did in creating you!' Neptune bellowed. 'And now I shall *un*-create that.'

Neptune paused for a moment and looked away. When his eyes returned to bear down on me, I thought there was a tear in them. Neptune, crying? If I wasn't so terrified, I might almost have laughed. The thought was ridiculous. Neptune didn't cry!

He slowly raised his trident. As he held it above his head, the waves increased, the sky darkened even more, *Fortuna* rocked over on one side. 'YOU!' he boomed over the cacophony of the raging storm. 'You shall no longer be semi-mer. You shall NOT share my world with any other.'

'What do you mean?' I cried. 'I don't understand!'

'THIS is what I mean!' And then he waved his trident above his head, swirling it round and round. As he bellowed his curse at me, the sky began to swirl, too. A dark cone of clouds spun across the horizon, skating towards us, whipping up the sea in its wake, gathering pace, growing in size, and darkening in colour with every second.

'No longer may you be a semi-mer. You will be one or you will be the other.'

'No!' I shrieked. 'Which will I be? Do I have to decide?'

'You do not CHOOSE! You do not have a say. It is *my* choice, your fate. And here is where the curse begins.'

Another wave of the trident; another black cone spinning towards us. I clung more tightly to *Fortuna*, trying as hard as I could to pull myself into the boat.

'You will know the curse is on you as soon as I finish speaking,' said Neptune. 'You will feel its effects begin. In a matter of days, when the moon is full, the curse will be complete. And you shall take your new form.'

My new form?

'In the meantime, while the curse unfolds, you will be neither one nor the other.'

In that moment, I lost the ability to fight back, to argue, even to believe there was anything I could do. There was a tiny split second when everything became calm. The sea, the sky, even the air around me – it just stopped. Stopped dead. Like my thoughts.

'Emily!'

Someone was calling me from the boat. Millie! I'd forgotten about her! She was still on the deck, soaked and bedraggled. Her hair was plastered all over her face, her gown stuck to her like an extra skin. 'Emily! Get inside – quick!' she yelled.

Without thinking, I darted through the porthole – just in time. A second later, Neptune howled, 'I will NOT be cheated. I WILL NOT forgive. I am Neptune, the ruler of all the ocean, and my rule is the law!'

And then it struck us. All I saw was blackness, spinning blackness surrounding us. Then the tornado wrapped itself around the boat, drilling into the sea and sending us spinning.

I couldn't hear Neptune's words any more, but I could still sense his rage, still feel him shouting to the sky as *Fortuna* was raised and hurled in a million directions.

It seemed to last forever. It was like the scariest ride you could ever imagine at a fairground; the fastest, most dangerous waltzer in the world, multiplied by a thousand. I clung to one of the benches that stretched across the lower level of the boat. I tried to scream for Shona but I couldn't even use my voice. My words were whipped away from me as soon as I tried. Was she still there? All I could see was water whirling round and round, a cyclone even within the boat. Side to side, back and forth like a rodeo horse we tipped and spun and clattered around. I tried to scream, but again and again the water snatched away my words, my gasps, even my thoughts.

In the end I just hung on, praying that it would soon stop – and that I would still be alive when it did.

Eventually, the cyclone slowed. It felt as though we'd been in the storm for hours and hours. It was stopping. The boat still rocked and dipped, still turned uncontrollably, but there were calm moments in between. It was in one of these calm moments I finally managed to call for Shona.

'Emily?' Her voice, from somewhere at the opposite end of the boat, was the most welcome sound in the world.

'Shona!' I called again. 'Where are you?'

She emerged from under the table that used to have all Dad's things on it. I shook away the pain that stabbed at my chest when I thought of him.

Shona looked as I've never seen her look in my life, and as I don't think she'd ever want anyone to see her again. The blonde hair that she spent an hour each day brushing was matted and splayed across her face; the glittery patterns she'd been painting on her scales all day had run and splattered into dark smudgy splodges all over her tail. Her face was so white it was almost transparent. She looked like a ghost. A mermaid ghost.

As she swam towards me, I could tell by the expression in her eyes that I probably looked about as bad. At any other time, we would have laughed. I'm sure we would. But laughter seemed as out of reach as every other normal thing in my life. We fell into a hug.

'What happened?' Shona asked in a numb voice.

I shook my head. 'I have no idea. Neptune – he was angry. So angry.'

'I told you what his anger could do, didn't I?' Shona said. 'I told you it could create storms!'

'I thought that was just stories, things you learned in your history lessons. I didn't think we could actually be caught up in one!'

'No,' she said, 'nor did I.' She looked out through the porthole. 'At least it seems to be stopping,' she said hopefully.

Just then, Millie shouted down through a trapdoor. 'Emily, are you all right?' she called, her voice coming out in gulps. 'Oh Emily, please answer me. Are you there?'

I swam over to the trapdoor. 'Millie, I'm fine! And so's Shona.'

'Oh thank the goddess, thank the lord, thank you, thank you!' Millie sobbed. 'Oh if anything had happened to you, I just don't know what I – oh Emily, I'm so sorry.'

'It's not *your* fault!' I said, reaching up to pull myself through the trapdoor. Millie was sitting on the floor shaking, surrounded by the contents of our home, which were scattered around her. Clothes were strewn all over the floor. Drawers were hanging open, glasses and crockery smashed to pieces everywhere. I could hardly bear to look.

I hitched myself up and sat on the floor with her. My tail flapped and wriggled as it started to fade away. Starting from the tip and working all the way up, I felt it turn numb then gradually disappear as my legs re-emerged, tickling like a nerve recovering from a local anaesthetic.

'Come on Millie, it'll be OK,' I said, reaching out to put an arm round her. I've no idea what made me say that. Perhaps I hoped Millie would believe me, and then she could convince me it was true.

Her big shoulders heaved and shook, her head bowed as I tried to comfort her.

As I sat awkwardly patting Millie's shoulders, I waited for my tail to finish transforming. But something wasn't right. It seemed to be taking longer than usual. My legs were fine. A bit numb, a bit tingly, but they looked normal enough. It was my feet. They weren't forming properly. *Come on, what's the matter?* It didn't usually take this long. My toes still seemed to be joined together, kind of webbed.

Webbed? A cold dart of terror stabbed at my ribs. Neptune's words.

The curse had begun.

'Emily, Millie, I think you need to look outside.' I didn't have any time to dwell on my thoughts any longer. Shona had swum over to the trapdoor and was pointing urgently out through a porthole. 'Go up on deck,' she said. 'I'll swim round and meet you.'

I stood up and helped Millie to her feet and we stumbled together out on to the deck, picking our way through the debris that lay everywhere. I tried not to focus on the strange rubbery feeling in my feet as I walked across the deck.

I don't know what I expected to see outside the boat. Don't know if I thought somehow it would all look the same as before, now that the storm had passed, or if there was a part of my brain clinging to the crazy hope that we were somehow still at Allpoints Island.

But if I had thought anything of the sort, I was

in for the biggest disappointment of my life.

I didn't recognise anything. I could hardly *see* anything, for that matter. Just sea. And sky. No island. No other boats, no bay. And not another soul in sight.

There was a stillness in the air as though the world was holding its breath, waiting till it was sure that the storm had really passed.

At first, all I could see was the ocean, deep navy blue, lying still all around us, still as a hundred miles of glass. Just above it, a low mist hovered in a perfect line.

The sun was beginning to set, the sky bruised with clouds, like bunches of deep mauve cotton wool, stealing whatever bits of blue they could find. Wispy grey mists floated higher up, racing the slow heavy gangs below them.

Then the edges of the clouds began to change and brighten, as though someone had taken out a peach-coloured felt-tip pen and was drawing an outline round each one. As though they wanted to make up for the heavy blackness of the storm. Soon, pink and orange seeped into the spaces in between the clouds. The sun forked out through every gap it could find, in bright orange fans. It was like a painting.

A lone seagull sailed across the sky, as though signing off the picture with its own signature.

And then we saw it.

'Look,' Shona whispered. She pointed into the thickest part of the mist. Millie and I peered to follow the line of her finger. Gradually it came into view as we stared, standing out above the mist as though balancing on it.

A castle.

Chapter Six

'Where are we?' I whispered.

No one replied. How could they?

We carried on staring, each thinking our own thoughts, and silently asking our own questions. I didn't ask any more of them out loud. What was the point?

Standing at the very front end of the boat, I slowly turned in a circle, taking in the whole view. Absolutely the same, all around us. Totally, totally still sea. Stiller than I had ever known it, bluer than I had ever seen it, quieter than I had ever heard it.

The boat lay on the slightest tilt, lodged on something. But what? There was no land to be seen, nothing to be seen at all in fact, except the ocean, and the castle, and the mist.

Shona ducked under and swam out of sight. A moment later, she emerged, wiping the hair from her face. 'We're lodged on a sandbank,' she said flatly.

A sandbank. In the middle of the ocean?

Shona shrugged and shook her head in answer to my unasked question.

I squinted at the castle to examine it more closely. It stood, proud and majestic, above the sea: a gothic silhouette against the sunset like a cardboard cut-out. It was a child's picture of a castle, perfectly symmetrical, a turret balanced squarely on each side, a tower in the centre. Two thin arched windows were just visible in each top corner. As I looked, something tugged at me. It felt as though there was a wire between the castle and my chest, pulling at me. I knew in that moment I would have to go there.

The sky was turning red behind it, blacking out everything except its outline and the line of mist wafting around it like cigar smoke. As the mist ebbed and flowed, I noticed the castle seemed to be standing on an island of rocks. Jagged and threatening, they held it high as though carrying it on a platform, a grand stage in the middle of the ocean.

Millie was the first to shake herself out of the

trance we all seemed to be in.

'Right, girls,' she said, dusting herself down and shaking out her gown. 'I'm going to find out where we are.' As soon as she spoke, the feeling about getting to the castle left me, as rapidly as it had come.

Shona looked blankly up at her from the sea, as though Millie had spoken in a foreign language.

'How?' I asked.

Millie gave me a big false smile. Just like the ones Mum gives me when she hasn't got a clue how to sort something out either. 'I'll find a way,' she said. 'We'll have you back with your mum and dad in no time. Just you see.' Then she looked down at Shona and gave her one of the not-real smiles too. 'You too, love. I'll work something out. Don't worry.'

She stepped carefully across the deck and patted the big long sail that lay rolled up along the side. 'Come on, let's see if we can get this up,' she said. 'We could sail back, no problem.'

I stared at her in disbelief. Surely she didn't really believe we could sail *Fortuna*?

But then I thought again. Why not? Perhaps we could! If only we could figure out where we were, maybe we could get it started and sail back to Allpoints Island. I'd managed to sail *King* out to sea when we were back in Brightport. Who said I couldn't do the same with *Fortuna*? I mean, sure, it was an ancient pirate ship that had been wrecked on the reef two hundred years ago and hadn't been sailed ever since. But we weren't exactly overwhelmed with other options. What harm could it do to try?

Together we pulled and tugged at the ropes and poles, Millie heaving the boom high enough for me to dodge underneath, the sail in my hands. Round and round I went, unwrapping the maroon fabric until it lay across the whole deck.

'Oh,' Millie said, looking down at the torn, fraying, useless sail at our feet.

I looked down at it with her. 'Maybe we could sew it?' I said eventually.

Millie sighed and smiled tightly. 'We'll give it a go, dear,' she said, patting my arm. Neither of us mentioned the fact that the boat was lodged on a sandbank and that the lower half of it was submerged in water. Or the fact that we didn't happen to have the tiniest idea where we were. We needed something to cling to, even if it was an illusion.

'We'll work something out,' Millie said as she turned to go back inside the boat. 'Now I'll just have a cup of Earl Grey and then what say we get started on the clearing up?'

We managed to put everything back where it belonged. Everything that wasn't smashed to smithereens, that is.

The worst bit was when I came across a glass that Dad had given Mum only a couple of weeks ago. He'd painted two hearts on the side with their initials. It was broken right across the middle of the heart, their initials on separate shards of glass at opposite ends of the boat. It wasn't significant, I told myself again and again. It didn't mean anything. I wasn't superstitious.

But I couldn't convince myself at all. It was all I could do to hold back the tears lining up behind my eyes, desperately trying to squeeze out.

It wouldn't have been so bad if I hadn't seen Millie suck in her breath between her teeth and shake her head when she saw it. As soon as she spotted me, she did the smiling thing again. 'It's only a glass, love,' she said. 'We'll get your mum a new one, soon as we get back, eh?'

Then she ruffled my hair and sent me off to the saloon with a brush and pan.

It was pitch black outside by the time we'd finished. I went downstairs to see Shona while Millie made us all some tea. She'd figured out that if we rationed ourselves tightly enough, we could survive for a week on the food we had on the boat. 'Not that we'll be here anything like that long,' she'd said brightly. 'But just so's we know.'

Shona and I talked about what had happened, going over it again and again, trying to make sense of it.

'So he tried to get the ring from you, but he couldn't even touch it?' she asked for the fifth time. 'But Neptune can do anything! Why couldn't he get it back if he wanted it so much?'

'I don't know,' I said, as I'd said each time we came round to this point. 'He said something about his own law stopping him.'

Then I paused. I hadn't mentioned the curse yet. I didn't know how to. If I wasn't going to be a mermaid any longer, that would mean I'd lose Shona as well as everything else that was going to happen. I'd never be able to go out swimming in the sea with her again. I might have a memory drug put on me and never even remember her! My best friend, the best friend I'd ever had.

And there was something else, too. Something so awful I didn't even want to let myself think the words. But they were there, in the centre of everything. My parents. Was I ever going to see them again? If I lost half of what I was, did that mean I would lose one of them as well? The thought was like a kick to my stomach.

'Shona, there's another thing,' I said nervously. 'A really bad thing.'

So I told her about the curse, about how it would take a few days to work, and I wouldn't know which way it would go, but whichever it was, that was where I would stick. I stopped short of telling her it had already started, about how my feet hadn't completely formed when I was on the deck. And how even now, swimming down here as a mermaid, I could feel something was different. Just here and there, a scale missing. Bits of flesh showing through my tail. She didn't need to see that yet, the proof that the curse had already started.

'Fighting fins!' Shona exclaimed when I'd finished. 'That's awful! What are we going to do?'

'That's what I thought you'd help me work out.'

Shona reached out and grabbed my hands. 'I will, Emily,' she promised. 'We'll stop this from happening, OK? As sure as sharks have teeth, I'm not going to lose you. And you're not going to lose your parents either.'

I winced at her words as though she'd lashed me with a piece of wire. Just the thought of it hurt.

'We're going to solve this, all right? You and me, we can do anything, can't we?' Shona looked at me desperately, her eyes begging me to say yes.

I looked at her and squeezed her hands. 'Of course we'll solve it,' I said, lying as much as she was lying to me with her words, and as much as Millie had lied with her smile. 'Course we will.'

I stood on the front deck with Millie. Shona was in the water next to the boat. I rubbed my stomach, trying to ignore the fact that it was rumbling from my rationed dinner of a third of a tin of beans and a piece of toast. A feeling of warmth spread into me from the ring against my body. Everything was going to be OK. I could feel it. The ring was telling me so.

'That's the Plough, and that's Orion's Belt,' Millie said, pointing up at the stars clustered together in tight clumps. I craned my neck to follow the outline she was pointing out. I don't know how she could tell what was what. The longer I stared, the more it just looked like a completely black sky filled with a million billion tiny white dots.

'What's that?' I asked, pointing to a dark shape in the distance. It was coming closer, changing its shape as it slid across the sky. Another cyclone? Please no!

A dark shadow slinking across the skyline, it looked like a giant snake, gathering and bunching up into an arc, then stretching out to form a long black line cutting through the stars. It was heading for the castle. The shape disappeared into the mist, re-emerging above it to swirl around the top of the castle, encircling it, spinning into a spiral, round and round, tighter and tighter, faster and faster, until it faded into nothing.

We stared into the black night. The shape didn't come back.

'I have no idea,' Millie said eventually. 'And I'm not one for superstition, as you know, but I'll bet it's portentous. Let me have a think.'

'What about the stars though?' Shona said. 'There are constellations that can help us work out where we are, I'm sure of it. I just can't remember what they're called. Or what they look like.'

Which was a big help.

'I've got it!' Millie said, her eyes brightening. 'I've had a great idea.' She headed back inside the boat and beckoned me to follow.

For a moment, for one silly, ridiculous, heart-stopping moment, I actually thought she'd come up with a plan to get us out of this. I let myself hope. Until she said, 'I'll do our tarot cards.'

I followed Millie into the kitchen. 'You clear a spot for us in the saloon and I'll lay out the cards,' she said.

Shona swam up to the trapdoor as I pushed a couple of chairs to the side. She poked her head through and I sat on the floor by the trapdoor to join her. Then Millie came in with the cards and we watched intently as she shuffled, spread the cards in a six-pointed star and slowly turned them over, one by one. She didn't speak, didn't explain anything. When they were all face up, she sat looking at them for ages, nodding slowly.

'What do they say?' Shona asked.

'Do they say anything about my mum and dad?' I asked.

'Or mine,' Shona added quietly. That was the first time I had really thought about her parents. She'd been taken away from them, too. They wouldn't have a clue what had happened to her. They hadn't seen her since she went to school that morning. I'd been so selfishly wrapped up in my own problems, I hadn't thought about Shona's.

Would anyone tell them anything back at Allpoints Island? What would happen when Mum and Dad came home – assuming they ever did – and found that *Fortuna* wasn't even there? Would they come after us? Would they know where to look? They'd find out, wouldn't they? But what if they didn't? Suppose they didn't come home at all! Suppose they'd had such a row they'd split up and both forgotten all about me!

No! I couldn't let myself think like that. I couldn't! Surely they'd do something. They'd get together with Shona's parents and send out a search party or something.

They'll find us. They'll find us. They'll find us. I repeated the phrase over and over and over like a mantra. *Please let me believe it*, I added.

The cards didn't tell us anything. Anything beyond what they normally said when Millie read anyone's tarot cards. We had a long journey ahead and the outcome was uncertain. A tall skinny stranger with jet black hair would help guide us, the truth would elude us and all would be well in the end. Blah. Why I ever put faith in Millie's card reading I don't know. It was about as useful as trying to tell the time from examining your freckles.

'Look, let's all try and get a bit of sleep,' she said, shuffling the cards away when it was clear they hadn't impressed any of us, or helped us find an answer to any of the questions we weren't asking out loud. 'Things are bound to look better in the morning, once we've had a few hours' nap – and perhaps a cup or two of Earl Grey.'

I stifled a laugh. Admittedly, a slightly hysterical one. It was really rather hard to see how things were going to look better. But she had a point about the sleep thing. I was exhausted.

'Shona, you take Jake's room,' Millie said. 'You'll be all right down there, won't you?'

Shona bit her lip and nodded.

'I'll join you if you like,' I said softly.

'No, you're OK. I'll be fine.'

'I'll be just above you. Knock if you need me.'

Shona smiled, although her eyes stayed misty and sad.

'It'll look better in the morning,' I said, repeating Millie's lie. It kind of helped to keep saying these things out loud. If we did it often enough, perhaps they'd come true.

'Night night, you two,' Millie said. 'I'm going to get some shut-eye myself now. Although goddess only knows how I'll sleep without my agnus castus tablets.'

We each withdrew to our own rooms, our own thoughts and our own fears.

The moon rose as I lay on my bed. I watched it climb past the porthole. A fat wonky shape like a slightly deflated ball, it shone down on me, right at me as though it was personal. Just me and the moon, staring each other out.

The black sky, endless behind it, filled slowly with clouds, some huge and unmoving like snow-clad hills, others grey and broken up like crazy paving. Lighter wispy clouds sailed slowly in front of them all. And the moon stood firm, almost whole, like a circle drawn freehand by a child. Not quite perfect but not far off.

Please let this be a dream, I whispered, twisting the ring round and round on my finger, talking to it as though it could hear my thoughts and turn them into reality. Was it a friend or enemy? What was its hold over Neptune – and over me? I couldn't tell. All I had was the knowledge that it was caught up in this whole nightmare with us — and the tiny feeling that it might help us find our way out of it, too.

Please let me be back at Allpoints Island in the morning, I prayed. Please let me hear Mum and Dad arguing in the kitchen as soon as I wake up. Please.

Next time I looked, the clouds had all moved on. The stars were no longer visible either. Just the moon remained, bright and proud. *See?* it seemed to snigger at me. *I win.*

There was a split second when I woke up when everything felt normal. Any second now, Mum would call me to get up and I'd have to drag myself out of bed. She hadn't called yet, though. Still half asleep, I stretched and turned over in my warm bed. I was about to go back to my dreams — and then I remembered.

I sat bolt upright, then jumped out of bed and ran to the porthole. Let me see Allpoints Island. Let us be back there.

I was greeted by the sight of mauve sea stretching out forever, everywhere I looked. Baby blue sky. And the white line of mist hovering in the middle, dividing the two worlds.

'Emily, are you up?' Shona's voice called quietly from below.

I ran to the trapdoor and dropped myself down to join her. As soon as my legs touched the water, I felt them change. *Please work properly this time,* I said silently to myself, and I held my breath as I felt my tail form. Closing my eyes, I focused for a moment on the feeling, willing it to work completely. But it didn't. In fact, it was even worse. Patches of scales were missing, the shine of my sparkling tail seemed duller, my tail moved more stiffly.

I swallowed my feelings down and hoped Shona wouldn't notice. I still didn't want to admit it out loud. I wasn't a mermaid half the time any more. Now I wasn't even a proper mermaid at all.

'Look.' Shona pulled me over to the large porthole door. We swam out through it, round the huge sandbank under the boat, and up to the surface where we trod water by the side of the boat. Directly ahead of us, hovering on the line of mist as though it was floating, the castle stood bold and gleaming in the sunlight. 'I think we should go to it,' Shona said, echoing my thoughts from yesterday.

'On the boat? How? You saw the sails.'

Shona was shaking her head. 'No, I meant just

you and me. We could swim there. It doesn't look far.'

It was still early. I could tell by how low the sun was in the sky. In fact, now I looked, I could still see the moon, hanging on like the last guest at a party, reluctant to leave but fading and tired. Millie would still be in bed. She always slept late. We could get there. As soon as the thought came into my mind, my hand grew hot. The ring – it was telling me something, I was sure of it!

It was telling us to go.

'Come on,' I said, feeling hopeful for the first time since we'd landed here. 'Let's do it.'

Chapter Seven

'*H*ow long have we been swimming?' I asked, panting to catch up with Shona. Surely she was swimming faster than usual! I could hardly keep alongside her.

'Not sure. Maybe twenty minutes, half an hour tops.'

I stopped where we were and flicked my tail round in fast circles to tread water. 'Look,' I said, pointing to the castle. It seemed to be looking back at me, willing me to approach it. Pulling me along. But there was a problem. A big problem.

Shona looked across at the castle. 'What?'

'It's no nearer. It looks just as far away as it was from the boat.'

'Don't be daft,' Shona said with a laugh. 'It's just . . . ' Then she glanced back to see where we'd come from. *Fortuna* was a dot in the distance. She turned back towards the castle. 'But that's . . . but it's not possible.'

'It's like a rainbow,' I said. 'The nearer you get to it, the further away it seems.'

'But how?' Shona's voice broke into a whine. Her eyes moistened as her bottom lip began to tremble. I almost expected her to howl, 'I want my mummy!' And why shouldn't she? That was certainly what I wanted to do. I felt like a burst balloon.

'Come on,' I said flatly. 'Let's go back to the boat. Maybe Millie will have some idea what's going on. You know she thinks more clearly in the mornings once she's had a cup of tea.'

'Or ten,' Shona added with a hint of a smile.

I smiled back. 'We'll figure it out,' I said. 'Don't worry.'

As we swam back, I didn't tell her how stiff my tail was getting, how it was starting to feel as if I was dragging a lead weight behind me. I pretended I wanted to go more slowly to take in the view: the sea, calm and smooth as we cut through it, the mist lying low and still on its surface.

Eventually, we got back to the boat and swam in through the porthole. Almost as soon as we did, Millie's voice warbled down to us. 'Emily? Shona? Is that you?' she called, an edge of panic in her voice.

'Hi! We're here!' I called back.

'Oh, thank heavens,' Millie breathed, her face appearing at the trapdoor as she leaned over it to look down at us. 'Where have you been?'

'We just went out for a quick swim,' I said.

'Emily.' Millie's tone had turned serious. Her voice a low rumble, she said sternly, 'You must never, ever go out without telling me again. I am responsible for you. I will never forgive myself if anything happened to you. Do you hear me?'

'I'm sorry,' I said. 'We were just – '

'It doesn't matter now.' Millie waved the rest of my sentence away. Just then, I heard a cough from somewhere behind her.

'Who's that?' I blurted out. My heart lifted. Millie had been kidding me! Mum and Dad were here! They were waiting for the right moment and were going to appear any second, big smiles, and tell me this had all been a joke, or a mistake or –

'There's someone to see you,' Millie said in a voice as flat and lifeless as a dead eel. And then, cutting my hopes like the sharpest knife, a face appeared next to hers.

Mr Beeston.

'Hello girls,' he said, squinting down at me and Shona.

'What are you doing here?' I asked through a tight throat. 'How did you find us? Where are my parents?'

'Now, now,' Mr Beeston said with a crooked half-smile. How could he smile? Didn't he understand anything that was going on? Or was I mistaking him for someone who cared? 'One thing at a time. You calm yourself down and then meet me on the front deck.' He nodded at Shona. 'And you, child,' he said. 'You'll all need to hear what I have to say.' He pulled back a sleeve of his old nylon suit to glance at his watch. 'Let's say ten minutes.' And then he'd gone.

'I'll be with you,' Millie said softly. 'I'm not going to leave your side till we've got this sorted, right?'

I nodded. My throat felt too thick and too dry to speak.

Mr Beeston was waiting on the front deck, sitting on a bench looking round at the horizon.

'Now then,' he said as Millie and I sat on the opposite bench. Shona perched on the edge of the deck, her tail draped loosely over the side, flicking the water with tiny splashes. *How much longer will I*

490

be able to do that, too? I glanced at my hands. The skin reached up along my fingers, joining them together, lodging the ring even more tightly in place. What was happening to my body? It was just as Neptune had said. Until the curse was complete, I wouldn't be one thing or another. What did that make me? A nothing?

I couldn't bear to see the evidence, so I stuffed my hands in my jeans pockets and waited for Mr Beeston to explain what was going on.

He cleared his throat. 'Now then,' he said again. 'You are probably wondering why I'm here.'

D'you THINK?

I bit my lip. It was never a good idea to interrupt Mr Beeston. It only took another half an hour for him to get going again. He wasn't a big fan of sarcasm either – or of cheek. Or of me. So I kept my mouth shut and counted to ten.

'As you know, I was entrusted by Neptune with a most important job. And as you also know, there had been a certain amount of disturbance which I was in the process of endeavouring to correct. In fact, even as I speak, some of the folk at Allpoints Island are gathering the final few items of lost treasure. The project has been very successful, largely thanks to your resourceful teacher. All of which helps make Neptune happy. However, as we *all* know . . . ' At this point, he looked round at the three of us with one of his crooked smiles, trying to include us as though we were all in this together. How could we be when he was the only one who had any idea what was going on?

Again, I stopped myself from saying anything. I counted to twenty this time.

'As we all know,' he repeated, 'the situation has changed somewhat. Since events took the turn they did, Neptune's attention has wandered from his initial intentions. And so we have found ourselves in this situation.'

He folded his hands in his lap.

'What situation?' Millie asked. 'I haven't got the slightest idea what you are talking about. Now are you going to explain what in the cosmos is going on here or am I going to have to – '

'Calm down, calm down.' Mr Beeston waved a hand at her. 'I am coming to it.'

Then he fixed his eyes on the ring. 'Emily here has found something we never even realised was there, something that Neptune wants back, and perhaps if I tell you a little bit about it, you will understand why. Then maybe we can work together to solve the problem and all will be well.'

'All will be well?' I exploded. I couldn't stop myself this time. There weren't enough numbers to count to that would halt my rage. 'All well? We're lost out in the middle of the ocean, with nothing but sea and mist and a spooky castle that doesn't even seem to exist. Shona's parents haven't seen her since yesterday morning. *My* parents have fallen out and probably never want to see each other or me again – '

'Come on Emily, you know that's not true,' Millie interrupted me.

I ignored her. 'And to top it all, Neptune's done *this*!' I pulled my hands from my pockets and held them out in front of me. The skin had reached even further up my fingers. They were joined at least a third of the way up, lodging the ring so tightly on my finger it hurt.

'Emily!' Shona gasped, edging forward to look more closely at my hands. 'What's that?' She looked disgusted. I knew she would.

'I didn't want to tell you,' I said. 'I didn't know if you'd still want to be my friend if you knew.'

'Knew what?'

'The curse. It's already started,' I said. 'I'm not a proper mermaid any more, or a proper girl. I'm nothing.'

I felt a couple of tears roll down my cheeks, salty drips running into my mouth. Millie was gazing at the ring. 'What in the name of the goddess is that?' she breathed. 'And where did you get it?'

Mr Beeston pulled at his tie. 'Millicent, if you will allow me to explain.'

Millie waved a hand at him. 'Go on. Whatever you've got to say can't make things any worse, I suppose. Just say what you've come to say and get on with it. And then maybe you can go away again and leave us to work out what to do next.'

'I shall indeed say what I have come to say,' he said, in that annoying I'm-so-much-more-important-than-you voice of his. 'If you will let me.'

Mr Beeston pulled on his tie and flattened down his hair again, and eventually said, 'You need to understand the importance of what you have here, Emily.'

'What I have where?' I asked. As if I didn't know.

Mr Beeston pointed at my hand. 'There,' he said simply. 'You see, this ring has lain out of sight, hidden and protected by the kraken, for many years. For generations.'

'Why is it so important if it's been buried all that time?' Shona asked. 'Why was it buried at all if it's that important?'

'It wasn't. It was discarded.'

'Discarded?' Millie burst out. 'Who by?'

'By Neptune.'

For a moment, we all fell silent. Then in an even voice, Millie quietly said, 'Charles, we would appreciate it if you could stop talking in riddles and please explain what is going *on* here.'

'I shall tell you everything!' Mr Beeston blustered. Then he paused for ages, clasping his hands together and looking out to the still sea that lay waiting silently like the rest of us. 'Many many years ago, Neptune was in love,' he began. 'As you know, he loves easily, and has many wives, but none like this one. None like Aurora.'

'Aurora!' Shona interrupted. 'But I've heard of her! She's the human. The one who broke his heart. The one who turned him against intermarriage and everything. We did it last year in history!'

Mr Beeston nodded. 'Exactly.'

I couldn't help holding my breath while I waited for him to continue.

'Aurora was the only wife Neptune truly loved with all his heart. When they married, they had rings made to symbolise their love. One contained a diamond, to represent land. The other held a pearl, to represent the sea. On the day of their marriage, they exchanged these rings. Aurora gave the diamond ring to Neptune. He gave her the pearl.'

I touched the diamond as he spoke. I was wearing a ring that was given to Neptune on his wedding day? Given to him by a wife who left him and broke his heart? No wonder he had gone into such a rage! But how was I to know? It wasn't my fault!

No. It wasn't your fault, a voice seemed to echo. Not even in words; it was just a feeling. A feeling of comfort and reassurance – and it was coming from the ring. Twisting it round to hold the diamond against my palm, I curled my fingers around it, my heartbeat settling as I did so.

'On the day she broke his heart, Neptune took her ring from her and buried it.'

'Where?' I asked.

'That I cannot tell you,' Mr Beeston said. 'That information is not something you need to have.'

He spoke so haughtily I knew it wasn't worth asking again. It would only give him the chance to refuse me again, and make himself feel even more self-important than he already did.

But I couldn't help wondering about it. There was another ring similar to mine, buried out in the sea somewhere. A ring Mr Beeston didn't want me to ask about – which in itself meant it was probably important!

'What about his own ring, the diamond one?' Millie asked.

'In his rage, Neptune hurled it with all his might across the oceans. This is the first time it has been seen since that day. No one knows when the kraken found it. All we know is that it did, and it kept it safe and hidden with the many other jewels at Allpoints Island.'

'And when the kraken woke, the ring was disturbed with the rest of the jewels?' Shona asked.

'Exactly.'

'And now he wants it back.' I swallowed. 'But it

won't come off me.'

'Why not?' Millie asked.

Mr Beeston looked down, flattening his jacket and picking off an imaginary speck of dust. His suit was wonky as usual, a button missing on one side, a hole overlooked on the other. 'The rings can only be worn by certain folk. Either by a couple where one is from the land and the other is from the sea, or a child of such a couple. It was in the wedding vows between Neptune and Aurora, and the rings were infused with this power. Worn by a semi-mer, this ring cannot be removed.'

'Sharks!' Shona breathed.

'So how did he remove their rings in the first place?' Millie asked.

Mr Beeston sniffed. 'The love was dead. The connection was broken.'

'That's why he cursed me,' I said quietly. 'So he can remove the ring.'

'Correct. When the moon is full, the spell will be complete. You will no longer be a semi-mer. You will not be able to touch the ring – and it will not be able to touch you. It will fall from you as you would jump from a fire.'

'And Neptune can have it back,' Shona said.

'He wants it hidden again, along with his memories and his long-buried grief. He cannot exist like this, and if Neptune can't live, none of us can. You yourselves have felt the effect of his current state. It will only get worse. That is what we would all have to look forward to if the ring is not buried again. Just more of that and nothing else, for the whole mer-world.' He turned to me. 'Is that what you want, Emily? Is it not an honour to make a sacrifice like this for your king?'

I couldn't speak.

'So why are you here?' Millie asked coldly. 'Has he sent you to do his dirty work?'

'Dirty work?' Mr Beeston spat. 'Dirty work? I consider it the highest of honours to be called to duty by my king, to be graciously offered the opportunity to make amends for my earlier failure.' He pulled himself up straighter in his seat.

'Like I said, do his dirty work,' Millie said under her breath.

'I am responsible for this ring, and I will ensure it is returned to Neptune. Make no mistake, that is what I will do,' Mr Beeston concluded.

'How did you find us?' I asked numbly.

'The ways of our king are immeasurable. He made it possible for me to be here. That is all I need to know. It is not for you – or me – to question his methods beyond this.'

'That means he's got no idea,' Millie said. I smiled, despite everything.

'I have to go soon,' Mr Beeston said, ignoring her as he glanced around at the endless ocean, as though waiting for his signal to leave. The ocean responded in the same way as it did to everything else – with silence and stillness. Then he turned to me. 'But Emily, I shall not be far away. I shall be back very soon.'

'How will you get back? Can't you let us go with you?' I asked, knowing it was pointless as soon as I'd uttered the words.

'I'm sorry. I have to do as bidden by my king. You will stay here for now.'

'How far are we from Allpoints Island?' I asked, edging closer to the questions I really wanted to ask.

'Many hundreds of miles.'

I nodded. Another kick, this time in my chest. Finally I said, 'And what about Mum and Dad? Where are they? Do they know what's happened? Are they going to come after us? Will they find us, too?' The questions ran out in a rush. My heart banged in my ears like thunder while I waited for his reply.

Mr Beeston puffed out his chest. 'Your parents do not know your whereabouts,' he said, in that oh-I'm-*so*-important voice again.

'Where are they?' I asked, holding back my anger.

'Your mother is staying on the old boat.'

'On *King*?' Millie asked.

He nodded.

'Does she know what's happened?' I asked.

'She knows only that you have been called upon to assist Neptune in a grave matter.'

'Has she looked for me?' My throat was full of knives.

Mr Beeston lowered his head. 'She has, yes. We've told her you're not at the island. The other islanders will look after her, and I am close at hand to support both your mother and Shona's parents.'

'And Dad?' I asked. 'Where's he staying?'

Mr Beeston at least had the decency to look slightly uncomfortable this time as he looked at me. What did he see in my face? A reminder that every word he uttered was crashing into my world like a sledgehammer? 'I'm afraid they have been separated,' he mumbled. 'He is staying with Archieval for now.'

Archie was another of Neptune's helpers, and my dad's friend. At least they both had people around them who cared, not just slimeballs like Mr Beeston, I told myself, desperately grasping at anything that might provide a grain of comfort.

'Why have they been separated?' I asked.

'Neptune has decided to go back to the old ways.'

'What old ways?' Shona asked.

'He's banned intermarriage again. For good, this time. He says he has had enough of the trouble it causes.' Mr Beeston looked me in the eyes.

'Your parents will not be together again,' he said drily.

And that was it. The end of my world. With those simple words. Game over. My insides turned cold and hardened. At that moment, I believe I could have broken into a thousand pieces.

In a matter of days, I would no longer be a mermaid. Or I'd be a mermaid and would never again be able to live on land. And my parents would never see each other again. With a feeling of utter horror, I realised what this meant: I couldn't have both parents. I would have to say goodbye to one of them forever.

'No!' I begged. I pulled on Mr Beeston's arm. 'Please, no!' Tears hurtled down my face. '*Please*,' I begged. 'You have to make Neptune change his mind. You have to do something. Please!'

'There is nothing that will change his mind,' Mr Beeston said, his voice steady and cold. 'Neptune's word is law. Your parents will come together one last time when Neptune brings them to you. Under the full moon, when the curse is complete, you will have a chance to say goodbye to one parent. You will go home with the other.'

'No!' I fell to my knees in front of him. I hated myself for begging Mr Beeston, of all people. But it couldn't happen. It *couldn't* happen. It couldn't.

But as Mr Beeston shook me away and dived off the side of the boat, disappearing deep down into the sea, I knew the truth. It was going to happen. It really, really was. And there wasn't a single thing I could do to stop it.

Chapter Eight

'Right, that settles it,' Millie said, blowing on a cup of tea. 'I'm not letting you out of my sight. If Neptune can send Mr Beeston here from nowhere, who knows what might happen if you went out there?' She cocked her head to point out at the endless ocean. 'You could be kidnapped and taken away forever.' She shuddered. Then she reached out to pat my knee. 'You're my responsibility now, lovey,' she said gently. 'And I'm going to look after you.'

True to her word, she didn't leave us alone after

that. Which meant Shona and I didn't get another chance to try to swim to the castle, or even talk about it.

The day passed in a blur of Earl Grey, beans on toast and several games of canasta. I moved along in it as though I was walking through fog. And in a way, I was. The mist all around us seemed to have totally clouded my thoughts. Or perhaps it was more to do with the fact that my world as I knew it was collapsing around me. The sadness Mr Beeston had left me with felt like a physical weight dragging me down.

The night wasn't much better. It was filled with dreams about my parents, and about the castle. In one, I was swimming towards it as hard as I could. Mum and Dad were waiting for me there, but it kept getting further and further away. With every stroke, it became more distant, but it was calling me, willing me to find a way to get there. All around me, voices were urging me on. Then the ring on my finger turned into a knife and cut through the sea so I could walk there – but I had no feet. My tail flapped lifelessly on the ground for a moment, till the ring shone a beam that lifted me and carried me towards the castle. I had almost reached it – it was centimetres away. And then I woke up.

Panting and sweating, I got up and looked out through my porthole. Directly ahead of me, the castle loomed just as it had done in my dream, the mist flowing around its middle like a skirt. Its windows were black and closed like sleeping eyes. But as I stared, they seemed to brighten, shining at me, just at me. Blinking and glinting, it was as though they were spelling something out in a code I had yet to crack. I knew one thing for certain, though. I had to get to the castle.

It was early; too early for anyone else to be up. Even the sun hadn't risen yet. The sky was a deep purple. I crept out on to the deck and looked around. In the distance, the castle was almost hidden by the mist. Just the turrets were visible, reaching upwards, tall and dark and forbidding.

As I looked across, my chest burned. I felt the ring tight on my finger, the diamond smooth and bright. 'What is it?' I asked silently. 'What do you want?'

The ring didn't reply. Well, no, it was a ring. But as I closed my fingers around it and breathed in the salty air, I knew I had to try again. My dream had been telling me there was something waiting for me at the castle. I just knew it. The thought was too strong for me to ignore. I had to get there, and I had to go now. If I waited any longer, Millie would be up and there was no way she was going to let me out of her sight again. And it wasn't fair to keep dragging Shona off on my crazy stunts. I'd already got her into enough trouble. No, let her sleep.

I slipped into the water as quietly as I could. The sea rippled around me as my legs jerked and twitched, stiffening, sticking together, and finally stretching out to form my tail. What there was of it. Again, patches were missing all over. Fleshy white bits of my legs poked through the scales. As I moved, my tail felt taut and tight. It didn't bend properly. It was getting worse.

Never mind. Just get there. Determination drove me on, and I ducked my head under the water and swam.

But it was just like last time, and just like my dream. The more I swam, the further away the castle seemed to be.

I ploughed through the water as hard as I could, thrashing my tail with every bit of energy I had, stretching my arms as wide as they would reach, pushing myself further and faster with every stroke. But it was useless. I was getting nowhere.

Below me, the sea looked dark and unwelcoming.

Jagged rocks were piled on top of each other as though they had been dumped there and forgotten long ago. Small pockets of sandy seabed were dotted about in between. Tiny black fish darted away as I swam across them. A round yellow fish slid slowly in and out of the crevices like a submarine.

I came to the surface to catch my breath. I didn't seem to be able to stay underwater as long as usual. That must be the curse too. Where would this end?

No, I couldn't think about that. I couldn't think about anything. I just had to get to the castle. But it was as far away as ever.

As I flicked my tail to tread water, I looked at the ring. 'What do I do?' I said out loud. And this time, it did reply. Not with words, but with a feeling, like it had before. A feeling that seeped through me like heat filling my bones. A feeling of trust. I had to trust the ring. Just as it had done in my dream, if I gave in and let it guide me, it would get me to the castle.

So I did. I stopped trying. I stopped swimming, stopped pushing myself to get there faster or sooner – and instead, I listened to the ring. It felt as though I was tuning a radio: finding the right station and getting it clear and sharp enough to hear it properly.

I held my hand out in front of me, letting the ring guide me. Immediately, the water became smoother; a gentle current started to glide me along. With the slightest, tiniest flicks of my tail, I zoomed forwards. Heading towards the castle.

At last, it was coming closer! Soon the current slowed. The water seemed to grow thicker, and colder, and much darker.

Below me, a shoal of silver fish swirled down like a light beam, flashing briefly through the black sea. In their wake, a group of manta rays slowly flapped their long capes as they slithered by. I kept well out of the way, watching from behind a rock till they'd passed.

Ahead of me, the sea looked even blacker. As I got closer, I could see a big dark hole, a tunnel. Sharp rocks formed a ring around its entrance.

The strangest fish seemed to pace across the tunnel's entrance, gliding heavily and slowly. Five or six of them. I knew what these were. I'd never seen one in real life, but we'd studied them in Aquatics & Animals. Humphead parrotfish. Almost twice as big as me, they looked like big burly bouncers wearing silly masks and gum shields. Their bodies were grey, with a purple splodge of paint in a line up their heads, like mohicans, or war paint. These fish had jaws you didn't want to get in the way of. Each time one of them passed the tunnel's entrance, it opened its enormous mouth and took a bite at the rock, dissolving it into soft sand. A tiny beach lay around the entrance.

My tail shook. The castle lay beyond this tunnel. I knew it.

I waited for ages, counting the seconds in between each sweep of the tunnel's entrance until I'd worked out the best time to go. One more parrotfish passed the entrance – and then it was bare. This was it. They were all facing away, swimming to opposite sides. Any second now, one of them would turn and swim back. It was now or never. And never wasn't an option.

So I darted into the tunnel.

It was so cold in there, and so dark. And I felt so alone. Every now and then, I passed something. Thin black fish swam in single file along the sides of the tunnel, coming from behind and overtaking me. Thick chunky silvery-blue fish flopped by in pairs, swimming towards me and sailing over my head. Trails of seaweed hung from the walls, waving with the current and making me jump when they brushed against me.

I swam on.

The tunnel twisted and writhed about like a giant snake. *Round the next corner, round the next corner,* I said to myself again and again. It had to end some time.

And then it did.

The tunnel led upwards, growing lighter and

warmer with every stroke until I emerged, panting and breathless, into a round pool. I took a few seconds to catch my breath as I glanced around. Where was I?

I swam all round the edges of the pool. The walls were grey rock and covered in green algae, chunks of bubbly seaweed hanging down into the water like bunches of grapes on a vine.

Above water, the pool was enclosed by walls. Grey, lumpy, dark and cold, dripping with damp, it was like a long-forgotten cellar, with a metal door in one corner.

I'd done it. I was in the castle. In a cellar. On my own.

What was I *doing*?

I shivered as I pulled myself out of the water and waited on the side, watching my tail flicker half-heartedly, flapping on the surface of the water as it faded away. My legs slowly emerged, numb and tingling. This time the numbness in my feet didn't go away. I looked down. Webbed. Even more so, like my hands.

I didn't have time to think about that, or about any of the fears I could so easily think about if I gave myself half a chance. Just one question remained: Why was I so sure the castle offered me something? I tried to bat that question away with the rest of my dark thoughts. Whatever the castle wanted with me, I had to find out and get back to the boat. The others would be up soon.

Edging round to the doorway, I felt for a handle. A brass knob turned slowly, creaking like an ancient floorboard as I twisted it both ways. Despite the creaking, it turned easily enough, and I opened the door.

I inched my way up a spiral staircase, gripping a rope handrail for support. Round and round, the stairs climbed steeply and tightly. I felt as though I was climbing into the clouds, floating upwards. By the time I reached the top, I was dizzy and disorientated. Another door. This time I held my breath and turned the knob as slowly and gently as I could.

I was in a corridor, wide and long, with pictures all the way along the walls. Battle scenes, shipwrecks, storms at sea; the kind of thing you always see in castles like this.

I almost laughed at myself. Castles like this? How could I even think for a moment that this was like anywhere I'd ever been?

I mean, yes, from the inside it looked a bit like the kind of place your grandparents might visit on a Sunday afternoon. But there was something different about it, too. Apart from the fact that it seemed to float on a mist in the middle of the ocean, something about it felt unreal – like a film set or a cartoon. I couldn't put my finger on it exactly, but it was just a tiny step removed from reality. As I stepped along the corridor, I felt a bit like an actor in a film where everything except them is computer-generated animation. Unreal.

I kept glancing at the pictures to see if anything had changed while I looked away – whether the boats had moved, or the storms had raged while I wasn't looking. They didn't. Of course they didn't. I was imagining it. I must be.

I crept on down the corridor. Ahead of me, another door lay open. I went in.

It was a smallish, box-shaped room, jam-packed from floor to ceiling with dusty books in fancy bindings, all bronze and gold. The titles were full of words I could hardly read. Most were foreign, a few were English. All looked hundreds of years old. Not exactly your light-hearted bedtime reading.

Then I noticed the window. A large rectangle that covered half of one side of the room, it was set into a recess with a small bench. I sat on the bench and looked out. The sea stretched out for miles and miles, all the way to the horizon, just like it did from *Fortuna*. But down below, waves lapped on rocks that were gradually surfacing like bared teeth as the tide edged out. It was as though the castle stood on a podium above the rest of the world; separate from the world, floating above it as though in a dream. *What was this place?*

Another door took me out of the library into a smaller room. One side of the room was filled with weapons. Opposite, the wall was covered in silk banners painted with flags from all over the world. I recognised some of the shapes and colours from geography lessons back in Brightport. Others were completely unfamiliar. There was even a skull and crossbones on one flag.

I moved on quickly. The room led out to another corridor. More paintings on the walls, this time portraits. Men in naval uniforms, beautiful women smiling up at them, young men standing proud on the decks of warships, girls perched on rocks. I moved closer to examine the pictures in more detail. Hold on. Were they girls, or were they –

What was that?

A bell clanged loudly, echoing down the corridor.

I glanced furtively around. Was it me? Had I tripped an alarm? Was someone going to come out and catch me? *No! Please don't let me be captured again!* Memories rushed through me with a horrible judder, of being caught and imprisoned in an underwater cell after I'd woken the kraken. I couldn't get caught here!

There was a recess behind me, a heavy wooden

door at the back of it. I jammed myself up into it, my heart almost bursting out of my mouth. Pinning my body to the door, I held my breath, shut my eyes tight and prayed for the alarm to stop.

And then it did. Stopped dead. Silence, all along the long corridor. Nothing moved.

My body sagged in relief as I leaned against the door, letting out a long breath and trying to decide what to do next.

The relief didn't last long. A moment later, I heard footsteps. They were coming from behind the door, getting closer! There was no time to hide. My body froze as I stood in the recess.

And then the door opened.

Chapter Nine

I was looking into a pair of very green and very surprised eyes.

'Who are you?' asked the boy, staring back at me. He was tall, taller than me anyway, and skinny like me, too. He was probably about the same age, maybe a little older, and dressed in black flared trousers and a black T-shirt. He had long jet-black hair, parted perfectly in the middle, and the most piercing green eyes I'd ever seen, which he continued to fix seriously on me.

For a brief second, I remembered Millie's prediction about tall dark strangers. Was this him? What had she said about him? I couldn't remember. I tended not to listen carefully to Millie's fortune-telling. For once, I wished I had done.

'I – I – ' was all I managed to say.

The boy glanced quickly down the corridor before beckoning me into the room. 'You'd better come in,' he said. His voice was silky and smooth, like his hair, and serious like his face.

As I followed him into the room, I forced myself to speak. 'I'm Emily,' I said. I couldn't think of anything else to say. I looked awkwardly around me. Three of the walls were covered with maps and scrolls. There wasn't a blank centimetre. Every country and every ocean in the world must have been on these walls. The fourth wall had a long rectangular window that looked out to sea. Beneath it, a thick wooden bookcase held rows and rows of books, brown and bound in gold like the ones in the library. The room felt almost unreal, as though the books and maps were part of a stage set, and underneath them lay a thousand years of history and mystery.

The boy noticed me looking. 'They're from my ancestors,' he explained.

'Your ancestors?'

'Pirates, captains, travellers of all sorts,' he said. 'Many ships have been wrecked on the rocks of Halflight Castle.'

I nodded, as though I understood.

'Look, sit down,' he said, gesturing to a huge armchair. With its thick dark wooden arms and green velvet seat, it reminded me of the furniture in the stately homes I used to visit with Mum sometimes. Mum. Just the thought of her made me ache. Where was she now? Was she trying to find me? Would I ever see her again? Each question was like a knife twisting round and round in my chest.

The boy carried on staring at me as I sat down. He pulled up an identical chair and sat opposite me. 'I'm Aaron,' he said. He held out a skinny arm to shake my hand, but almost instantly changed his mind and pulled it away.

We fell silent. I didn't have the first idea what to say. Well, come on. How many times do you think about what you'll do if you swim to a spooky castle floating on a mist in the middle of the ocean and accidentally land yourself in some strange boy's room?

Exactly.

He was the first to pull himself out of the shocked silence. 'How did you get here?' he asked.

'Um, I swam,' I said uncertainly.

His eyes opened even wider. 'You swam?'

I nodded. 'Through tunnels. But where am I? What kind of a place is this?'

'Halflight Castle. It's my home,' said Aaron. 'I

don't know any other.'

'You've lived here all your life?'

He nodded. 'All my life. Here and nowhere else, like every generation before me, all the way back to . . . ' He looked up at me through his thick black eyelashes. 'No, I can't tell you that.'

'Can't tell me what?'

'My family history,' he replied with a grimace. 'It's not exactly straightforward. You'll never believe me.'

I laughed. 'You think *your* family history is hard to believe. Wait till you hear mine!'

He didn't smile. 'Trust me. It's complicated. Or it was. Nothing too complicated now though, as it's just Mother and me.'

'Just the two of you in this whole place?'

'And a few si – ' He stopped himself, covering whatever he was about to say with a cough.

'A few what?' I asked.

'Servants,' he said quickly.

'You weren't going to say that. What were you going to say?' I insisted.

Aaron shook his head and stood up. 'I don't think I can tell you,' he said. 'I'm not sure. Look, why don't you tell me about you instead? How *did* you get here? It's meant to be impossible.'

'It nearly was,' I said. 'I tried again and again.' Could I tell him about the ring? It was tight on my finger, the diamond warm against my closed palm.

I could feel it almost scorching my hand, getting hotter. What was it saying? Tell him? Or keep it to myself?

Why should I keep it secret anyway? I had nothing to hide. 'Look, if I tell you, you promise you'll believe me?'

'Why would I do otherwise? Why would you lie?'

'OK,' I said. 'Well, it was this. It kind of led me here.' I held my hand out and opened my palm. 'Now, I know you'll think I'm making it up or you'll think I'm mad or something but I promise I'm telling you the – '

'Where did you get that?' Aaron reached out and grabbed my hand, pulling it towards him to look more closely. His voice shook so much I could barely understand what he'd said. He swallowed hard, catching his breath. His face had turned even paler. 'Where did you get it?' he repeated.

'I – I found it,' I said uncertainly.

'Do you know what it is?' he asked.

'Well, I, yes, I think I do.' Did *he* know what the ring was? Had he heard of Neptune, heard the story?

'I've never seen it,' he said in a whisper. 'Not the real one!'

He fell silent, squeezing his mouth into a tight line and his eyes tightly closed while he thought. 'Right,' he said, making up his mind about something.

'We've got time. Come with me.'

With that, he motioned to me to follow him to the door. Glancing down the corridor again, he nodded back to me. 'Come on,' he said. 'I want to show you something.'

Aaron led me down a maze of corridors, scurrying quickly along till we came to a thick wooden door with bars and bolts across it. I followed him outside. Below us, the sea washed against rocks in the semi-darkness. We ran round the front of the castle and back inside through a small arched door. Following Aaron inside, I felt as though I was stepping further and further into a dream. Was any of this real? I mean, it *felt* real. The bricks of the castle were thick and hard, the rocks below were jagged and cold. But still, something in the atmosphere made me feel as though I was floating, suspended just above reality, as if the castle were floating on the mist.

I closed the door behind me.

We were in what looked like a small church, a tiny chapel in a remote wing of the castle. A few rows of seats all faced a raised platform at the front. Stained glass windows were filled with pictures of Biblical scenes.

I followed Aaron to the raised platform. Right at the back of it, there was a chest. He opened it. 'Look,' he said, pointing inside.

I peered into it. It contained a glass cabinet and, inside that, two rings. I looked more closely at the one on the left, comparing it with the ring on my finger. It was identical!

'But that's – but they're – '

'Imitations,' he said. 'My great-grandfather made them. From the descriptions, from the stories passed down through generation after generation.'

'What stories? What descriptions?' I asked, my head spinning. 'Do you mean about Neptune and Aurora?'

'You know?' he gasped. 'You know the story?'

'That's all I know,' I said. 'Please, tell me.'

Aaron moved away from the cabinet. 'When Neptune and Aurora married, they cast a spell on their rings. While they were held by a human and merperson who were in love – '

He glanced at me to check I understood what he meant, to check we were talking about the same thing. Maybe to check I didn't think he was ridiculous for believing in mermaids. *I don't only believe in them*, I thought. *I am one!* But I wasn't going to say that. Not yet. Not if it was just a story. Surely boys like him didn't really believe in mermaids!

I nodded for him to continue.

'As long as the rings were worn by one from the land and one from the sea who loved each other, there would always be harmony between the two worlds,' he went on. 'And there was. For the brief time the marriage lasted, there really was peace between land and sea. No ships were wrecked on rocks, no cargo was stolen, no sirens lured fishermen to their watery graves. Just peace. The two worlds thrived together. It was a magical time.'

'And then she left him,' I said, remembering what Shona had said about her history lesson.

Aaron's green eyes bore down on me. 'She *what*?' he asked angrily.

'She – she left him?' I said more uncertainly. 'Didn't she?'

'You know nothing!' he snapped. 'Believing in such rubbish. How dare you?'

I pulled at my hair, twisting it round my fingers. 'I'm sorry,' I said. 'I thought she did. I thought she broke his heart. I'm sorry.'

'She did not leave him,' Aaron said firmly. 'She loved him more than anything in the world. I'll tell you what her love for him drove her to do.'

I clamped my mouth shut. No more interruptions.

'She loved him so much, and believed so strongly in the magic they had created, that she attempted the impossible. One night, she decided to show him what she could do out of love for him. You know what she did?'

I shook my head.

'She thought she could swim underwater to his palace. She believed their love was so great it surpassed the normal laws of her human world. She believed she could become a mermaid. She drowned.'

Neither of us spoke for a long time. As we stood in the silence, it felt as though the chapel was the whole world. That the sea outside the window was only there for us. We were somehow at the centre of everything, the centre of something so important that – that what? I couldn't tell.

'It was her birthday. She'd wanted to surprise him as her present to him,' Aaron went on. 'Her own birthday, and she wanted to surprise *him*. They'd only been married a year and a week.'

'Go on,' I said softly.

'When Neptune found her body, he took the ring from her and – '

'I know this bit,' I said quickly – even if it wasn't exactly how Mr Beeston had told it! I had to get it right this time; show him he could trust me. 'He tore the pearl ring from her finger and threw away his own ring, the diamond one.'

'That's right,' Aaron said. 'And no one has ever seen the rings – till now.' He fell silent.

'The kraken had Neptune's ring,' I said. 'I found it.'

Aaron stepped towards me. 'Emily, these rings can only be worn by certain folk.'

'I know,' I said, swallowing.

'A human and merperson in love, or a child of theirs . . . ' His voice trailed off into a question mark.

I didn't reply. Finally, I nodded.

'I thought as much,' Aaron said, suddenly smiling. 'You're a semi-mer! You are, aren't you?'

'How did you know?'

'You said you swam here through the tunnels. No human can swim underwater that far. It's impossible.' He grinned wider. His whole face changed with his smile; it was like watching a two-dimensional picture come to life. 'You found the diamond ring!' he said. 'You really found it!'

'Why is that so great?' I asked.

Aaron led me back to the glass cabinet. 'Look,' he said, pointing to an inscription written in black swirly writing beneath the rings. I read aloud. 'When the rings touch, they will overrule any act born of hatred or anger. Only love shall reign.'

I looked up at Aaron. 'I don't understand,' I said.

'There's a curse,' he answered me, his face darkening. 'It must be undone. And soon.'

'What curse?'

Aaron brushed my question away with a flick of his hand. 'We still need to find the pearl ring, though,' he said. 'And that's impossible.'

'Who says it's impossible? I found this one!' I said, my breath tripping over my words as it raced into my throat.

'The second ring will be much harder to find. The one Neptune ripped from Aurora's finger. He swore it could only be found when it was seen under the light of a full moon. But there was a catch.'

'A catch?'

'The ring was buried so deep it has never seen the moon's light. And so it has never been found. Neptune and Aurora married under a full moon on the spring equinox, at midnight. At that moment, the sea's tide is the lowest it will ever be – and only then is it low enough for the ring to be visible. But those conditions only occur every five hundred years. It's virtually impossible to find it. We'll never stop the curse.'

'What curse?' I asked again.

Aaron walked to a small recess. His breath misted the window pane as he looked out. 'After Aurora died, Neptune turned to hatred and anger. There were storms for years. Ships were wrecked at sea. Many fishermen died, many humans perished in the seas over the years that followed. But even that wasn't enough for Neptune. Even that couldn't take away his rage.'

'So what did he do?'

'First, he banned any more marriages between humans and merfolk. He swore the two worlds would never again live in harmony.'

Well, yes, I knew all about *that*. 'And second?' I asked.

'Neptune and Aurora had three children,' said Aaron. 'Two sons and a daughter.'

'What happened to them?'

'In his grief and sorrow, Neptune cursed them,' he went on. 'His own children. Each of his own children, and their children and every generation that followed, every single one of them would die young, and always on Aurora's birthday, as she did. He couldn't forgive her – and because of this, her family would forever be punished.'

'His family too,' I said.

Aaron nodded. 'Their family. And there was another curse placed on them. They would never fit in, never be of one world or the other. They would be not quite human, not quite merperson. Whichever form they took, it would always be held back by remnants of their other form. Every single generation forever would be the same. Do you understand?'

Did I understand? If only he knew how well I understood! 'Aaron. Look!' I thrust my hands in front of his face, opening my fingers so he could see how they were webbed.

'You too?' he said simply. 'You're the same.'

I nodded.

'The only way to undo these curses would be to bring the rings together again,' said Aaron.

'Because the curse came from hatred and anger,' I said, finally understanding the significance of what I had found. We just had to find the other ring and we could end the curse on his family! And end the curse on me, too! I could carry on being a semi-mer! I'd never have to lose my parents! The thought sent my hopes soaring. Till Aaron spoke again.

'But that will almost certainly never happen,' he said. 'The chance will only come once every five hundred years.'

'When was the marriage?'

'No one knows for sure. It must be about five hundred years ago, though. It could be more. The moment has probably already passed. So the curses will remain forever, and nothing will ever bring back harmony between land and sea.'

Aaron fell silent. His words spun round and round in my head. I'd found one ring. Why couldn't we find the other?

'Where was it buried?' I asked suddenly. 'The second ring. Where was it buried?'

'Right where she died. Just beyond her home.'

Aaron ran a hand through his sleek hair.

'Her home?' I asked. I was pretty sure what he was going to say. Pretty sure he wasn't just telling me any old story. Someone else's story. I was pretty sure it was his story. That her home was his home, her family was his.

'Yes,' he said. 'She lived here at Halflight Castle. In fact, Neptune had the castle built especially for her, for them. A place of magic and beauty and love where their two worlds came together. And ever since, it's been a symbol of the exact opposite, keeping every generation separate from the rest of the world.'

'Completely separate? Don't you ever see anyone else?'

'There has been more life here, at different points in the castle's history. But it's never been a happy place since that time. And with the curses, the family's dwindled more and more over the years. It's just me and Mother now. We have a few visitors who bring us our supplies but they hardly talk to us.'

'Why not?'

'Mostly they're sirens, employed by Neptune. They daren't go against Neptune's rule. They're all instructed not to talk to us, although there are a few who I'm secretly friends with,' Aaron said. 'It's a pretty lonely life,' he added.

Sirens! That's what he was going to say earlier,

when he changed it to servants. I knew it! And I was right about Aaron being descended from Neptune and Aurora too! Before I had a chance to say anything, the alarm sounded again, crashing into every bit of space around us, filling my head with noise.

Aaron jumped as though he'd been stung. 'Mother,' he said. 'I forgot!'

'What is it?' I called over the din.

'It's my mother. She's confined to bed. She rings it when she needs me. I didn't go to her earlier. Emily, I have to leave.' Aaron hurried to the door. Outside the chapel, waves crashed against the rocks. The sky was starting to grow light; above the mist, clouds were turning pink, anticipating the day ahead. Cobwebs shone brightly in the doorframe. Elaborate spiralling mazes in one corner, half-finished scraps and threads dangling loosely in another, gaping and half-empty like derelict houses.

'Quick. Go back to the tunnels. It's the only way. It's too dangerous on the rocks.' Aaron led me back to the door that would take me back down to the cellar. 'Down there,' he said, opening it and virtually shoving me inside. 'You'll find your way back?'

'Yes, of course.'

'Come back soon!' he said urgently. '*Promise* me!'

'I promise,' I said.

'Good.' He allowed himself a brief smile. 'I have to go now.' And with that, he closed the door and left me in the darkness.

Chapter Ten

*L*owering myself down, I made my way smoothly back to the cellar and set off towards *Fortuna*. Heading back didn't feel half so difficult. The current drew me along. The ring vibrated in my hand, buzzing warmly. It seemed as excited as I was! It was willing me to get back to Shona and tell her everything.

As I swam, I watched the sky changing, moment by moment, the clouds growing orange and bright. The sun rose in front of me, shining hard into my eyes as though it was a weapon sent to blind me.

Beneath it, the mist rolled along the top of the sea like a thin layer of snow. *Don't let Millie be up yet*, I said to myself, swimming as hard as I could to get back, despite my tail feeling as though it was made from iron, and despite my breath coming out in rasps, shorter and shorter with every stroke.

The second I swam through the porthole, Shona was there.

'Where have you *been*?' she whispered fiercely.

'Is Millie up?'

'No.' She shook her head. 'I couldn't sleep and I was calling you. I figured you must have still been asleep.'

'Shona. I got there,' I said. 'I got to the castle!'

Shona whistled. 'Flipping fins! How? What's it like? Did you go inside? Does anyone live there?'

I laughed, holding up my hands to ward off any more questions. 'I'll tell you everything,' I said. 'Just let me get my breath back.'

Shona listened in silence to the whole story. When I'd finished, she simply stared at me.

'What?' I asked.

'Emily, you have to find the other ring. It's your only hope!'

'I know – but I can't. It's impossible. No one's seen it for hundreds of years. It's buried too deep. It's not suddenly going to turn up now!'

Shona bowed her head. 'We have to find it, Emily. We have to find a way. We can't give up.

There's too much to lose.'

'You're telling me!' Shona wasn't even the one with something to lose. I was going to lose the whole of the mermaid world, or the whole of my life as I'd known it up until now. Mr Beeston's words hadn't left my mind for a second. Neptune's law. I would see my parents on the night of the full moon, one of them for the last time ever. And I didn't even know which one.

'And before you say I've got nothing to lose,' Shona said, reading my mind as usual, 'I have. I've got *you* to lose. And I'm not prepared to let that happen. Right?'

I let myself smile at my best friend. 'Right,' I said.

We stared out at the castle. It seemed to be staring back at us, the mist curling around its base like a dark blanket, the turrets bright and harsh in the sun, the windows shining like lights.

'We can find it,' Shona insisted quietly as she swam towards me and grabbed my hand. 'Emily, you can end the curse! You just need to bring the rings back together. You'll change Aaron's life as well!'

'Maybe it'll bring harmony back to sea and land too,' I said excitedly. Before I could stop myself, I added, 'And then Neptune would change his mind and Mum and Dad could carry on being together!'

Then I stopped. My shoulders slumped and I sank lower in the water as I thought about what I was saying. What if Mum and Dad didn't even *want* to be together? The way things had been lately, they would probably be happy with Neptune's new law! And then there was of course the fact that the ring was buried so deep it would never be seen.

I was going to lose a parent. It would happen just as Mr Beeston had told us. When the full moon came, Neptune would bring my parents to me and I would say goodbye to one of them – forever. The thought was so dark and so huge, it felt as if I was falling into it, into the deep chasm that was my future. I stroked the gold band on my finger, pressed the diamond against my palm, looking for comfort, but it felt cold. It had no comfort to offer me.

'Who am I kidding?' I said, my words as heavy as my heart. 'We're not going to find the ring. We'll never stop all these terrible things happening.'

'We will NOT give up!' Shona said, swimming round in front of my face and lifting my chin just like Mum does when she forces me to listen. 'Do you hear me?' she said sternly. 'That is not my best friend talking. The one who explores shipwrecks and caves and breaks into prisons to rescue her dad! We'll find a way. Right?'

I nodded gratefully. 'OK,' I said. She was right. I couldn't give up. I couldn't just let my life slip away, lose a parent, lose half of what I was. Being a mermaid wasn't just something I did for fun. It was part of who I *was*. I couldn't lose that. We *had* to find the other ring and bring the two together. Then anything born of anger and hatred would end. The curse on me would have to be lifted, and the curse on Aaron, too. He could have a completely new life. Perhaps he and his mum could even come to Allpoints Island with us! We *had* to find the ring. It was as simple as that.

'OK,' I said again. 'We need to find out when the full moon is. That's how long we've got till the curse on me is complete. As soon as the full moon has passed, that's it. I won't be a semi-mer any more and Neptune will take back his ring.'

'And I may never see you again,' Shona said quietly.

We both looked down in silence. Below me, a couple of black and yellow striped fish darted into the boat like lovers running away together. They swam off to the other end of the boat, leaving the sea fans waving gently behind them.

Just then, a shuffling noise above us made us both glance up. Millie's face appeared at the trapdoor. 'Ah, you're awake,' she said. 'I was just going to make some breakfast. You coming?'

'We'll be right up,' I said. Conversation closed, for now.

I munched slowly on my one piece of toast. I had to make the most of it; I wouldn't get anything else till lunchtime, and even then it wouldn't be enough to satisfy the gnawing in my stomach. I didn't know if it was just hunger or the pain of missing my parents so much. Either way, it hurt.

Millie sipped her tea. 'Not the same without milk,' she murmured. 'I can't be doing with too much bergamot.' She winced as she put her cup down. 'So, what shall we do today?' she asked, almost brightly. She sounded as though we were on a package holiday and just had to decide between the pool, the beach or the trip to see the dolphins. 'I thought we might try a bit of dowsing,' she added before we had a chance to reply. 'It could help us to work out where we are.'

'What's dowsing?' I asked.

Millie closed her eyes and drew a heavy breath. Gathering her cloak around her, she held her hands up to her chest. 'Dowsing,' she said breathily, her voice husky and deep, 'is the harnessing of the senses — or, more precisely, of the sixth sense.'

'The sixth sense?' Shona said. 'I thought we only had five senses.'

'Intuition, my dear,' Millie replied, briefly opening an eye to glance at Shona. 'The ability to dowse is something I firmly believe to be within us all,' she went on. 'Most of us do not know a fraction of what we can do. For too many of us, our intuition is ignored or relegated to some backwater of the mind. But it's there. It's all there.' She fell silent, nodding gently as she breathed heavily and slowly.

Her eyes closed, she held her hands out in front of her, palms facing up. 'Dowsing is often used to find water, but it can do so much more.' She glanced at our blank faces before continuing. 'In layman's terms, it is a way of tuning into sources of spiritual power, harnessing nature's own resources just as the chakras harness the powers within our bodies.'

'Mm,' I said, not following a word.

After a few more deep breaths, her eyes snapped open and she sat up straight. 'Right then,' she said, smiling at us both. 'We just need a Scrabble set and a couple of coat-hangers and we're sorted.' And with that, she got up and went inside.

Shona and I took one look at each other and burst out laughing. 'You'll get used to her,' I said. 'Just look as though you know what she's going on about and you'll be fine.'

'But she's got a point,' Shona said.

'What? About the dowsing?'

She shook her head. 'The stuff she said about harnessing nature's energy. That's what we need to do.'

'Harnessing nature's energy?' I said. 'You're getting as bad as Millie!'

'Emily, we need to use anything we can think of if we're to find this ring,' Shona said crossly.

Millie had joined us back out on the deck before I had a chance to reply.

'It's the perfect time to do this,' Millie said, scattering the Scrabble letters on the deck and bending the wire into a new shape. 'I don't know why I didn't think of it earlier.'

'Perfect time?' I said. 'What's perfect about it?' What could she possibly see as being perfect about *anything* right now?

'Magical time,' she said with a wink. 'Spring equinox some time around now.'

'The spring equinox?' I asked, remembering what Aaron had said. The tide was at its lowest point of the year. A brief spark of hope flickered – but went out almost as fast as it had come when I remembered what he'd said next. That there would only be one year when the tide was low enough – and that time had probably already passed.

'In fact . . . ' Millie was saying as she reached into the little bag she always carried on her shoulder. She pulled out a small book. It was bound in black felt with pink and blue feathers around the edges and 'Orphalese Oracle' spelt out in fancy letters along the spine. 'If I remember rightly, this year is even *more* special.'

'Even more special?' Shona asked, her voice tight and high. 'Why is it even more special?'

'Let me check.' Millie looked through her book, licking her thumb and flicking through the pages. 'Aha! Yes, that's it,' she smiled. 'It *is* extra special! This year the full moon and spring equinox are at exactly the same time. The same day. And my word! Fancy that!'

'What?' I asked, my nerves about to crash and splinter.

'The full moon falls at midnight!'

I swallowed hard. 'At *midnight*?' I asked, my voice quivering like a freshly caught fish. 'Are you sure?'

'Absolutely!' Millie snapped. She tapped the cover of her book. 'Emily, you'd be sensible not to doubt the word of the Orphalese Oracle. Never been wrong yet, in my experience.' She tutted loudly and went back to flicking through the book, squinting and mumbling under her breath. 'Full moon at midnight,' she muttered. 'I bet that doesn't happen often.'

Happen *often*? How about once every five hundred years! This was *it*! This year — the one chance to find the ring!

'Millie, can I see?'

She passed me the book. My hands shook so much the words started to blur. But I saw all I needed to see. She was right! The full moon was at midnight on the spring equinox! My hands shook so much when I read the next bit that I nearly dropped the book. The date! It was tonight.

I handed the Orphalese Oracle back to Millie in silence. I couldn't make any words come out of my throat.

'*Very* interesting,' Millie said, oblivious to the change in mood as she smiled at us both. Then she put the book back in her bag and picked up the coat-hanger. 'Now, let's see about this dowsing.'

'That's odd,' Millie said, frowning in concentration as she waved her coat-hanger over the Scrabble letters.

'What? Has it told you where we are?' I asked, edging closer to watch over her shoulder.

Millie shook her head. 'It keeps moving over to you.' She glanced at me. 'To your hands. As though it wants to tell us something about the ring. Watch. It's telling me there's a strong connection between the ring and ... hold on. It's spelling something out.'

I watched her waggle the coat-hanger over the letters. It didn't look as if it was doing anything except twitching and wiggling in her hands.

'Something about a star,' Millie mumbled as the coat-hanger moved across the letters.

Shona hitched herself higher on the side of the deck. 'Stars? Maybe it's telling us to use the stars to find our way back.'

'No, it's definitely to do with the ring. A strong link with the ring and — hold on. It's not finished,' Millie said, following the coat-hanger's progress and reading aloud. 'Star — l — i — '

'Starlight?' I suggested.

'Could be. Wait.' We all watched the coat-hanger intensely as it moved to the letter 'n', then 'g', then 's'. After that, it stopped twitching and lay still in Millie's hands.

'Starlings!' Millie said eventually, pulling a hanky out from her bag and wiping her forehead as she put the coat-hanger down.

'Starlings?' I repeated blankly. 'What have starlings got to do with anything?'

Why? Why had I gone and done it again? Believing that Millie's so-called psychic intuition might bear any resemblance to anything that made any sense. Why?

'I don't know, love.' Millie sounded as flat as me. 'It sometimes takes a few attempts to work properly. Needs warming up, you know. Why don't you run along for now and we'll give it another go later?'

Shona and I slunk away and left her to it.

'So much for dowsing!' I said, dropping into the water beside her. My tail flickered half-heartedly to life, as weak and limp as the few shreds of hope I still had. The full moon was tonight. If we didn't find the ring, the curse would be full. By tomorrow I would have lost a parent.

'Come on, Em. Aaron said the tide would be at its lowest point for five hundred years tonight!'

'But what if he's wrong?' I said. 'The curse ends tonight. Neptune will take the ring. It's all over.' I couldn't bear it – couldn't even think through to the end of the thought. My future was a black hole, and at midnight I would slip into it.

'You have to believe him,' Shona said. Her voice was so full of hope, I couldn't help letting her enthusiasm filter across to me. My heart filled like a tight balloon.

'You're right,' I said with new determination. 'It's the only chance we're going to get and we can't afford to miss it. We've got to find that ring – tonight!'

Chapter Eleven

'Be careful,' Shona whispered as she waved me off from the porthole. 'And good luck.'

'You too,' I said with a hopeful smile. 'See you soon.'

'You're sure you don't want me to come with you?'

'I'm sure,' I said. We'd agreed I had to go straight back to the castle and tell Aaron the news. There was no time to lose. Shona was going to stay behind and fend Millie off if she came looking for us. Thankfully, she'd become so absorbed in her dowsing that she wouldn't notice any-thing for a while. I wouldn't have long, though. The last thing I wanted was for her to worry about me, on top of everything else. Or to keep a closer eye on me and stop me going out tonight. That was unthinkable! I'd just have to be careful – and quick.

I swam off in the same direction, listened to the ring in the same way, sneaked into the tunnel, and finally came up in the pool in the castle's cellar. I pulled myself out of the water and sat on the side to get my breath back. Panting and exhausted, I wondered how many more times I'd be able to get across here. My body was getting weaker by the hour. My tail was get-ting more patchy, my breathing more scratchy. *Just one more day. Please let me hold out for one more day.*

I heard a noise creak behind me, and leapt to my feet.

'Emily!' It was Aaron! Still dressed all in black, his hair was tied back in a sleek ponytail; his face shone pale and clear in the semi-darkness of the cellar.

'I've been hanging around here since you left,' he said, softly closing the door behind him. 'I was hoping you'd come back.'

'I said I would.'

Aaron took a step nearer the pool, and that's

when I noticed something. His feet – they were webbed. Of course they were. He was descended from Aurora, which meant the curse affected him too. Like me, he was stuck between the two worlds, neither fully one thing nor another.

He noticed me looking and shyly held out a hand. 'Come on, let me help you out of the pool,' he said. This time he didn't snatch his hand away. He held it out, palm upwards, fingers outstretched. Showing me. His fingers were joined at the knuckle by the thinnest wafer-like stretches of skin. His hands were webbed too. As I reached up to grab his hand, it was as though we were shaking on a deal. We were the same. We were in this together.

We sat on the side of the pool. Aaron stared as my tail melted away and my legs reformed.

'I can't even do that properly,' he said. 'My legs stick together and my toes flap about a bit, but that's all.' He looked at me wistfully. 'Just as it's been for the rest of my family, every generation.'

'Aaron, we can change it,' I said. 'That's what I've come to tell you. It's tonight. The full moon – it's at midnight!'

Aaron's eyes widened. 'Tonight? This is the year? How do you know?'

I told him about Millie and the Orphalese Oracle. I didn't mention the fact that Millie didn't always get it exactly right. She had to be right this time. She *had* to be.

'I don't believe it,' Aaron said, again and again. 'I don't believe it. Every spring equinox since I knew about it, I've hoped and wished. I've even searched for the ring, myself, and prayed the other one would somehow turn up.'

'I can't believe I ended up here,' I said, looking at the ring on my finger and smiling. I could feel its warmth smile back at me. 'I know I've had some lucky breaks in my life, but surely that's about as much of a coincidence as you can get.'

Aaron shook his head. 'It's not a coincidence at all,' he said. 'The ring brought you here.'

'Brought me to the castle?'

'The rings were meant to be together. When one is worn by a semi-mer, it wants to find the other one. While buried, the rings have no power. But when they are free, they want to be together. They're meant to be together. Its own heart brought you here.'

We fell silent, lost in our own thoughts, and maybe in our own hopes. 'Now we just have to find the pearl ring,' he said after a while.

'Not just find it. We have to find it and bring the two rings together under the full moon. It'll be too late after that. As soon as the full moon's passed, I won't be a semi-mer. I'll lose the ring again.'

'And if we fail . . . ' Aaron looked away as his voice failed.

'I lose a parent,' I said.

'So do I, Emily,' he said, his voice hardening.

'Huh?'

Aaron took a breath. 'Some years ago, life wasn't too bad here at the castle. Generations before me, it was a busy place. Years of ships wrecked on the rocks meant that occasionally the survivors found their way here. As I told you, Neptune has always installed sirens and some mermen to keep the castle isolated. So I've always at least had *some* company. Much to Neptune's disgust, there has always been love here, too. There has always been marriage, always been a determination to cross the forbidden boundaries.'

'Between land and sea?'

Aaron nodded and went on. 'But with every generation, it was the same. Just as I told you this morning, each one held the same fate. Each died young. The curse lived on from generation to generation. And still does, all these generations on.'

I didn't know what to say. I reached out to touch Aaron's arm.

He looked at my hand on his arm, then looked up at me. 'Father was the son of a ship's captain. He swore he would stop the curse before it affected my mother. No one ever knows exactly which year it will happen – only that it's always on the day of Aurora's birthday.' He glanced up at me. 'It's her side of the family that's descended from Neptune and Aurora.'

'Go on,' I prompted.

'There's not much to say. He tried to find the ring, and he failed. He searched and searched out there, but those rocks aren't kind, Emily.'

'What happened?'

'He drowned.'

'I'm so sorry,' I said quietly.

'It was three months ago,' he added, and I suddenly wondered if that was why he dressed so strangely, all in black. He was in mourning.

He turned back to face me, his eyes shining. 'That's why we've got to stop this, Emily. Even if the chances of succeeding are tiny, we have to try. We *have* to. This will be the only chance of our lives, and the only way to stop us both losing another parent.'

'Another parent? But – '

'My mother, Emily,' he interrupted. 'She's dying. It's Aurora's birthday next week. This is it.'

That was when I really understood that this wasn't just about me. It was about life and death. Literally. If we didn't find the ring, Aaron's mum was going to *die* next week, on Aurora's birthday, exactly as her ancestors had done.

'That's why she's confined to bed now. She's already ill. She only has a few days.' Aaron's voice juddered to a halt.

'We'll find the ring,' I said firmly. 'I promise.'

Aaron tried to smile, but even though he twitched his mouth up at the corners, his eyes were still the saddest I'd ever seen in my life. 'Come on,' he said, lowering himself into the water. 'I need to show you something I've just discovered. After you left, I went to see Mother, but meeting you had got me thinking. I went back to the chapel and dug around a bit more. Emily, I found something I'd never noticed before. Come and see it.'

I followed him back to the chapel.

'Through here.' Aaron guided me to the back of the chapel. At the end of the last row of seats, a few steps led down to a tiny gap, just big enough for us both to stand in.

Aaron felt around along the wall. He pushed it firmly and the wall creaked – and moved! A hidden door!

I followed him into a dark box of a room.

I looked round, blinking as my eyes grew accustomed to the darkness. Sunlight seeped in from the smallest gaps in the walls, just enough to see round the room: a small rectangle, with a long wooden bench all the way up one side, and an arched door opposite.

'I never knew it was here,' Aaron said, motioning for me to follow him. 'Look, I'll show you something strange.'

I stumbled across the dark room, my legs trembling with fatigue. Cobwebs filled every corner. I shivered as I followed Aaron to the far end of the room.

A row of paintings lined the wall, just as they lined the corridors all round the castle. 'More pictures,' I said.

Except that these were different. These weren't portraits, or pictures of battle scenes, and they weren't in frames either. They were murals, painted on the walls.

'It's all I've got. Pictures, books and maps from all round the world. That's my life. That's my school, my history, everything. But none like these.' He pointed to the first picture.

Now my eyes had grown accustomed to the darkness, I studied the painting. A deep blue sky, churning sea, and a bright white moon shining down on the castle.

'Who painted them?' I asked.

'I don't know. I bet it was my great-grandfather though,' said Aaron.

'The one who made the rings in the cabinet?'

He nodded. 'He was obsessed with the curse,

with trying to end it. The men in my family always are. These pictures seem like a clue.'

'They are,' I said, not even knowing why. The ring burned on my finger. It was the ring that knew the truth. 'They are a clue,' I repeated. 'I'm sure of it.'

'A secret clue, hidden from sight.'

'But why would someone want to pass on a message in secret?' I asked. 'If he was obsessed, why not tell everyone?'

'The only reason I can think of is so Neptune would never know.'

'But why not act on it, do something about it?'

'He probably didn't know what it meant any more than we do. But he knew it meant *something*. Look.' Aaron pointed at words scrawled all over the walls, painted around the pictures as though revealing the inner workings of the artist's mind. *'Why?' 'What is the significance?' 'How many years?'* the words said.

'Someone's been asking all the same questions as we have,' I said.

'And clearly had about as many answers as us,' Aaron replied flatly. 'Or else we wouldn't be in this position now.'

I stepped forward to study the first painting more closely. It was only then that I noticed the shadows in the sky. The swirling patterns looked familiar. A dark spinning cone in the sky.

Aaron moved to the next picture and motioned for me to follow. It was similar to the first. The same boiling sea, the sky even darker this time, the moon reflecting on to the rocks like a beam from a torch. The swirling shapes were there in the sky again. One looked like a spinning beehive, another like a dark trail from a plane that had been looping the loop.

'There's one more,' Aaron said, pointing to the third picture. It showed grey shining rocks, and the base of the castle. The swirling patterns were now just one thick black swarm: a whirlwind, its base at the tips of the rocks, in the centre of a shining white circle of light.

'I've seen these shapes!' I blurted out. 'The first night we were here! What are they?'

'I've seen them too. Usually at this time of year. It's birds. They come in their millions.'

'At this time of year? The spring equinox. But Aaron, that's proof! They *must* have something to do with the rings! And your great-grandfather knew it too.'

'I think you're right,' Aaron said. 'But the thing none of us knows is – what are they telling us?'

I wasn't aware of whether he said anything else. I was too busy staring at the words I'd just noticed among the rest, in capitals and underlined, like a title for the paintings.

My eyes glazed over, cold shivers running like electricity up and down the length of my body as I read the words: *THE STARLINGS.*

Chapter Twelve

I don't know how I got through the rest of the day. Shona and I scurried away every chance we got, to talk about what I had to do and how it was going to work out.

We swam round the lower half of the boat.

'Right, so you have to get to the castle, find the other ring and bring the two of them together,' Shona said, going over the plans for what felt like the twentieth time.

No matter how many times we repeated what I had to do, it wasn't sounding any easier.

'All in the few moments that the moon is full,' I said. 'Or it'll be too late. Neptune made his message clear enough. When the moon is full, the curse on me will be complete. I won't be a semi-mer any longer. And that means I won't even be able to touch the ring. I'll lose it forever.' *Along with everything else I care about,* I added silently.

Shona looked at me, holding my eyes with hers. 'Let's not think like that,' she said.

'I'll lose a parent,' I went on, ignoring her.

'Emily, please don't.'

'And Aaron will be an orphan.'

'Emily!' Shona took me by the shoulders. 'Concentrate. We can do this, OK?'

'OK,' I said lamely. I didn't believe for a minute that we could. The odds were just so highly stacked against us.

The sun had disappeared. This was it. A few more hours and the moon would rise into the sky. The full moon.

Millie wouldn't leave us alone. She stood on the front deck, pointing out the constellations as the stars appeared, one by one, across the vast sky.

'There's Canis Minor,' Millie said, pointing at a clutch of stars that looked pretty much exactly the same as all the others. 'And, oh, I think that might be the Corona Borealis.' She consulted her book, then looked back up at the sky. 'Yes, I think it is,' she went on, oblivious to whether anyone was actually listening. 'Well, you don't often get the chance to see that,' she said.

I smiled politely at her when she called me over, making all the right noises so she'd think I had some idea of what she was wittering on about. All I actually cared about was how I was going to get away from the boat before the moon came up. I glanced at my watch. Nearly ten o'clock. Two hours.

I tried feigning huge yawns, in the hope it would catch on and make her sleepy.

'Why don't you go to bed if you're tired?' was all she said.

Shaking my head in despair, I went to find Shona.

'What are we going to do?' I asked. 'I can't get away while she's out on the deck. We're going to run out of time.'

'Why don't you just tell her what you want to do?' Shona asked.

'I can't. She's already said again this evening she's not going to let me out of her sight. I'm not going to chance it. If only I could hypnotise her or something, like she does to other people.'

'Hey,' Shona said, a slow smile creeping across

her face. 'I might just have an idea.'

She rummaged around in her school bag. 'Ta da!' she said, producing her best B & D hairbrush. The handle was made from brass, and cast in the shape of a seahorse, the bristles soft and feathery like the prettiest horse's tail. On the back, there was a mirror, surrounded by pink shells.

'A hairbrush?' I said. 'Shona, this is no time to worry about what we look like! We've got a matter of hours!'

'I'm not worrying about what I look like!' Shona said crossly. 'Listen. I've got a plan.'

As she explained her idea, I couldn't help smiling, too. 'Shona, you're a marvel,' I said. 'It might just work.'

Millie was only too happy to oblige when I asked if she'd hypnotise me. 'It's just that I'm so tired, but I can't get to sleep,' I said. 'I need something to help me. I think your hypnotism is the only thing powerful enough to do the trick.'

She giggled and blushed. 'Oh, get away with you, pet,' she said. But she flicked her shawl importantly over her shoulder as I followed her into my bedroom.

I glanced at the chair I'd set up for Millie by my bed, hoping she wouldn't move it. It was perfectly positioned, as was the hairbrush on the dressing table. As long as she sat down without moving anything, the mirror should be in exactly the right spot to reflect her hypnotism right back on to her.

'Right then,' she began, settling herself down in the chair. Perfect! I lay on my bed and half closed my eyes. 'As you know, this is a powerful tool, so you may find you sleep even more deeply and soundly than usual,' she said. 'And you may find your dreams are more intense or elaborate. Don't worry about any of this. All that matters is you have a good long rest. Now, make yourself nice and comfy and we'll get started.'

I fidgeted around for a moment, trying to act as if I was getting myself comfortable. All I hoped was that I wouldn't get too comfortable and fall asleep.

What if it doesn't work? a voice in my head wouldn't stop asking. I did everything I could to ignore it. It simply *had* to work. There was no alternative.

Moments later, Millie was drawling in a deep, low voice about how tired I was getting. 'Imagine you are a feather,' she intoned, 'falling gradually down to the ground. With each breath, you sway a little bit lower, getting closer and closer to sleep.'

I couldn't help yawning. *Don't think about the feather, don't think about sleep,* I urged myself. *Think about what you have to do. Think about your mum, about your dad, about your one chance of getting them back together.*

That was all I needed. I was wide awake. And panicking so much it felt as if a high-speed train was racing through my chest.

'You're sleepy,' Millie drawled, even more slowly. 'Very . . . sleepy . . . ' Her voice was starting to sound as if she was drunk. 'In fact, you are so . . . very . . . sleepy . . . that you can't even . . . think . . . any more.' She took a deep breath and yawned a very loud yawn before continuing. 'All you want is to go to sleep.' A long pause. 'Beautiful sleep . . . ' An even longer pause. She yawned again. 'Peaceful . . . deep . . . '

This time the pause stretched on and on until a brief snort erupted through her nose. I waited a few more moments before daring to open an eye.

I had to clap a hand over my mouth to stop myself bursting out laughing. Millie lay sprawled across the chair, her legs spread out in front of her, her head thrown back, mouth wide open, eyes closed.

I quickly sat up on my bed. Carefully edging past Millie, I crept to the trapdoor in the middle of my floor, and lowered myself down.

'We did it!' I whispered excitedly to Shona. 'She's completely out.'

'Swishy!' Shona grinned. 'Come on. Let's go.'

We swam to the porthole and listened one more time. Nothing. This was it then.

'Wait,' I said. My tail hadn't finished forming. It was taking longer and longer. My legs had stuck together, but there were hardly any scales. I couldn't feel my legs – but I couldn't feel my tail either. It was as though there was nothing there at all. The whole bottom half of my body felt completely numb.

For a second, I panicked. What was going on? Had I become paralysed? Maybe I'd never walk *or* swim again!

Eventually, my tail formed, what there was of it. Bluey-green shiny scales at the ends, fleshy white skin almost all the way down to my knees. It felt wooden and inflexible, flicking half-heartedly in the water. My breathing was raspy. I don't know if Millie's hypnotism had anything to do with it or if it was just the curse, but by the time we swam out through the porthole, I was so exhausted I could almost have fallen asleep in the water.

Shona swam ahead, her tail splashing shiny droplets that sparkled in the moonlight. Would I ever do that again? Not that I ever swam as gracefully as Shona anyway. My heart felt as heavy as the rest of me.

'Wait,' I called, struggling to catch my breath.

Shona slowed. 'We've got to hurry,' she said. 'We haven't got long. The moon'll be up within the hour.'

'I know. I'm doing my best. I just – can't – keep up,' I gasped.

Shona swam beside me and took hold of my hand. 'Come on, Emily,' she said softly. 'You can do it. You've got me. We'll do it.'

I didn't reply. No point wasting my limited energy talking.

But however hard we swam, the castle just wasn't getting closer.

'Where's the tunnel?' Shona asked.

I shook my head. 'No good,' I said. 'Can't hold my breath. Have to go this way.'

I tried to do what I'd done the first time the ring had led me to the tunnel. Tried to let go, listen to the ring. I stroked the gold band as we swam and twisted the ring round so I could see the diamond sparkle and glint on my finger.

It was leading us there. I could feel it, even if I couldn't swim through the tunnel, even if the current was so slight I could have imagined it, even if the castle only seemed to be getting closer a millimetre at a time. We were still getting there, and the ring was doing all it could to help. Maybe it was getting weaker, like me.

Please hold out, I begged silently. *Please get us there.*

We seemed to have been swimming forever.

'I can't do it,' I cried. Tears were starting to slip down my face. 'I can't do it.'

'Emily, look!' Shona let go of my hand to point ahead. I followed the line of her finger. 'The castle!' she said. 'We're getting closer!'

She was right. In the half light, I could see it more clearly than ever. The mist lay across its middle like a belt. Above, three large turrets stood proud, serrated against the deep blue night. Its windows shone as though polished, black and dark, hiding a thousand secrets behind them.

Below the mist, rocks were emerging by the second. Huge boulders lay dotted about on the stony beach. In between them, jagged rocks were scattered everywhere, like a range of forbidding mountains. Waves thundered against them.

The sight of the castle so close spurred me on. I tried flicking my tail, but it hardly moved. My arms were weakening with every stroke, my tail growing more and more like a plank of heavy wood with every flick.

And then the moon began to rise.

First the tip, poking out through the sea, growing bigger with every moment, until it was whole. The most enormous orange ball, balancing on the water, it slowly edged its way into the sky. We'd have maybe twenty or thirty minutes till it had fully risen. It wasn't long enough.

'We're never going to do it,' I said. 'We might as well give up.'

But before Shona had a chance to reply, a voice called across to us in the darkness. 'Emily!'

I peered ahead, scanning the rocks.

'There!' Shona screeched, jabbing a finger at one of the huge jagged rocks, sharp and pointed as a witch's hat, and just as black. A figure stood halfway up its side. Aaron!

'Emily! Hurry!' he called. 'Please hurry!'

I couldn't give up! Of *course* I couldn't. It didn't matter if every single cell in my body wanted to scream with exhaustion. I had to get there.

Shona held tightly on to my hand. 'We can do it,' she said, again and again. 'I'm going to get you there.' But pulling a dead weight along in the water can't be easy for anyone, and even Shona was starting to get tired. Still the castle lay out of reach. *Come on, come on, we have to get there*. Inwardly, I urged myself on, screamed instructions and demands, begged, bribed. *Just get there. I'll do anything*.

The moon climbed slowly upwards, growing fatter and whiter by the second. Any moment, the curse would be complete and it would all be over. Neptune would be here to claim his ring – and he'd be bringing my parents to say goodbye. My chances of solving all this would be lost forever, along with everything I cared about.

I splashed through the water, clumsy and awkward like a puppy in a lake. Useless. Useless! The castle seemed to be getting further away. The moon shone down, its beam like a searchlight across the top of the ocean. I kept my eyes on the water ahead of me, hiding from the shaft of light like a fugitive. If it didn't catch me, maybe we were safe.

I glanced up at the castle. Still too far away. It looked like a cardboard cut-out against the night sky. A dark silhouette, the little figure of Aaron standing on the rocks, waving and calling to us. His voice seemed to be getting fainter.

And then something else.

As I stared, a thick black cloud came from nowhere, swirling like a shoal of black fish, then spreading out, slinking like a snake; twisting, turning up, down, circling round and round. It looked like a giant swarm of bees.

They moved as one, towards me and Shona. As they did, I saw what it was: birds. Instantly, they flicked and turned, back towards the castle. In a private dance for us, they wove with perfect grace and timing around and around the castle, gliding in slow motion, as though silently sliding down the banister of a spiral staircase; then bunching into a black ball again, spinning above the castle.

The dance went on and on as the birds whirled upwards in the shape of a genie emerging from his lamp. Then, as one, they spread out and flew towards us in a fan. An enormous flock of tiny black birds passed over our heads, chattering in a million different languages and briefly turning the sky black before they disappeared into the distance.

Seconds later, they were back, coming towards us again: more of them this time, a thick black line of them dividing the sky. They just kept coming and coming, more and more of them, to dance and swirl and break up and re-form around the castle.

'What in the ocean is that?' Shona said eventually, her voice breathless and tight.

'The starlings!' I said.

'Starlings? Are you sure?' Shona asked.

'Positive.'

'But starlings don't fly at night, do they? And certainly not out in the middle of the ocean.'

I shook my head. 'Look at the sky, Shona.' It was brightening by the second as the moon climbed higher and higher. 'This is no ordinary night.'

'You can say that again,' Shona breathed. 'What are they doing though?'

As if to answer her, the birds formed themselves into a tight, perfect cone. Pointed and sharp at its base, it twisted and whirled towards the rocks, round and round like an electric drill. Hovering over a bunch of rocks right at the water's edge, the cone spun as though boring into the ground. As it did, the ring burned on my finger, heating my hand, filling my body with warmth and emotion. And in that moment, I knew.

I turned to Shona. 'They're helping us,' I said. 'They want us to find the ring.'

They must have done it every year. They were connected to the ring, somehow, and Aaron's great-grandfather had figured out that much, too. But we had more on our side than he'd had. We had the ring. And we had the moon. I glanced up. Higher and higher it climbed.

Suddenly I wasn't tired any longer. 'The starlings!' I screamed into the air, jumping to life as though I'd been struck by lightning. 'Aaron! Follow the starlings!' That's what the paintings had been telling us. I had no doubts at all now. I pointed at the sky, jabbing my fingers again and again at the birds.

Aaron stared at the black swarm above his head. Then, as though the same flash of lightning had struck him too, he juddered into action. Clambering down the rock, he raced to the edge of the water and fell to his knees, scrabbling in the sand and round the rocks.

The moon edged up another notch, shining so strongly the sky lightened as it rose. It was almost like daylight. It was nearly there! *Please Aaron, find it, find it.* I watched him scrape at the water's edge, stopping to look up at the starlings, then back to the ground, a new spot, a different position, lifting rocks, tossing them aside, digging into the stony ground. Every time, his hands came back empty.

As we swam on, the water seemed to turn against us. Waves came from nowhere, splashing our faces, ducking me under. Eddies broke out around us. Small whirlpools. Bubbles cracking and popping like lava. What was happening?

Shona caught my eye. 'It's Neptune,' she said, her face white and thin. 'He must be on his way.'

'Emily!' Aaron screamed to us. He was waving his hands in the air. 'Look!' He pointed just below the base of the starlings' cone. It was too far away to see exactly what he was pointing at but as the moon edged even higher, I saw something glint and sparkle, just below the rocks he was standing on. As the sea withdrew even further, it shone brighter. The ring.

We'd found the ring! We'd really done it! The starlings swarmed around the rocks, their wings purple and green against the bright moonlight, before they separated, the line thinning out as they started to move away. Their job was done.

A spurt of energy drove me on. I had to get there before Neptune. Before the moon had fully risen. Before the curse was over and it was all too late. Urgent thoughts whipped at my mind like the waves whipped across my face, lashing me, crashing against each other like cymbals. *No, they won't beat me. They won't. We've got the rings. We can do it.* Over and over, I repeated the same words.

'Hurry, Emily!' Aaron called as he stepped towards the ring.

And then, an enormous wave came from nowhere, washing over me, hurling me down into the sea where I could no longer swim. I pounded back up to the surface, gasping for air.

As soon as I caught my breath, I scanned the rocks. Huge frothy waves engulfed the spot where Aaron had been standing only moments earlier.

There was no sign of him.

Where was he? What had happened to him?

'Emily!' Shona called me. She'd been thrown even further away from me. 'Hang on! I'll get you,' she cried.

Another set of waves threw me under almost immediately, dunking me again and again, only just giving me time to catch the smallest breath in between.

I couldn't keep fighting against it. I wasn't going to get there. So near, so near. But it was impossible. I wasn't going to make it.

I cried with all the energy I had left, my tears adding the smallest salty drops into the raging ocean. I stopped trying to swim, stopped trying to fight. 'You win!' I screamed at the sky, the moon, at the sea. 'I give up!'

It was all over. I'd lost everything. My one

chance to keep my parents together and carry on living with them both. My life as a semi-mer – all of it gone, taking Aaron's future with it too.

Chapter Thirteen

As I cried, I looked hopelessly out at the sea all around me. We'd never get out of this alive. Shona had drifted further away. She was still calling me. 'I'll get to you. Just hang on,' she cried.

But I could hardly keep my head above the water. When the waves weren't crashing over my head, I was sinking down into huge swells, rising up only to be thrown under again.

Then I slipped down into the biggest swell yet. All I could see on every side of me was a deep blue wall of water. It was like a well, with me at the bottom. Surely this was it. I opened my mouth to pray for my life.

But the wave didn't break. As it washed past me, I rose up on to another crest. I searched the skyline for Shona. Nothing. Where was she? I craned my neck, squinting into the distance.

I scrutinised every wave, all the way to the castle, searched every rock. And then I saw it. A boat. A small, green, abandoned rowing boat, paint peeling from it everywhere, its wood rotting and half burnt.

The thought crashed into my head as hard as the waves. The boat could save us. If only Shona could somehow get it to me. Where was she? I searched the horizon. There! I saw her head! We could do this!

'Emily!' Shona called again.

'The boat! Get the boat!' I cried. My voice was hoarse, screaming over thunderous waves.

'I can't hear you!' Shona yelled back. She was swimming back to me. A wave engulfed me before I could reply.

Gasping, pulling hair off my forehead and choking back sea water in my throat, I called back to her. 'The boat!' I cried. 'There's a boat. Find Aaron. Get him in the boat.' Another wave hit me. I choked as I swallowed a mouthful of salty water.

Shona searched the rocky beach. 'That?' she asked, pointing to the abandoned rowing boat. It was half filled with water.

I nodded. 'Just do it. It's our only hope. Quickly!'

Shona gripped my hand for a second. 'Stay here, Emily. Just stay here. You'll be fine. I'll come back for you. OK?' Her voice broke as she looked at me.

'Go,' I said. 'Hurry.'

Shona turned and swam away from me, zooming off at full speed towards the rocky beach, the abandoned boat, the boy I hoped with all my heart was still there somewhere.

I watched the moon climb ever higher. How much time did we have? Minutes? Would she find him? Did he have the ring? My head was ready to burst with questions.

I squinted across at the castle, the rocky beach. She'd made it! Shona was at the water's edge, dragging the boat into the water. Please find Aaron. Please find him.

'Emily!'

Someone was calling me. Near the rocks.

'Someone! Help me!'

Aaron! I could just see his head bobbing on the waves, his hand high in the air, curled into a fist. 'I've got it! I've got it!' he shouted. 'Someone help me!'

'Shona!' I yelled with every bit of energy I could muster. She was edging the boat from the shore. I pointed desperately to Aaron. As she turned to look, he waved his fist again. Instantly, Shona pushed the boat out, swimming across towards him. As she pulled alongside him, he clambered over the side, practically falling into the boat.

Come on, come on. All I could do now was wait here, and hope with all my might that they got here before the moon had fully risen. I looked up. Surely it was nearly there. *Hurry!*

Shona was behind the boat, pushing it along, her tail spinning furiously as the boat dipped and rolled with the waves. It kept disappearing out of sight as huge swells moved across it, rolling towards me. Each time it happened, I held my breath, closed my eyes and prayed that it would appear over the top of the next crest. And each time, thank goodness, it did.

Closer and closer, the boat edged towards me, Shona swimming, propelling it along, her tail its only engine, Aaron sitting up in the boat, one hand raised aloft in a fist. The ring was inside his fist, I knew it. *Please!* I begged silently for them to reach me soon; my body was weakening with every second. My tail had all but disappeared now. My legs felt as though they were glued together and numb. Only my feet were replaced with the tip of my tail.

My breathing scratched and tore at my lungs. I couldn't hold on much longer.

'Emily!' Shona called as I flailed about, desperately trying to stay afloat. They were here!

'You were right!' Aaron called as they edged

closer. 'The starlings, they pointed right at it. All these years I've seen them. I never knew. We never knew.' He leaned out of the boat as they glided towards me. 'Grab my hand.'

I swam towards them, as fast as I could, reaching up with my hand, holding it as high out of the water as I could. We were really going to do it! I smiled as my eyes met Aaron's. His fingers were centimetres from mine.

And then it hit me. The biggest wave of the lot. Smashing over my head, almost knocking me out, throwing me down, deep under the water, flipping the boat into the air. All I could see was a fountain of froth and bubbles, and sand swirling all around me. I swallowed about a gallon of water; my lungs were on fire.

Pushing with all the strength I had left, I kicked with what remained of my tail, clutching at water with my hands as though I could claw my way through it. Eventually, I made it back to the surface. Coughing and spluttering, I knew that was the last time I could do that. Next time I would have no strength left to pull myself up.

'Aaron,' I gasped. 'Shona!'

They were nowhere to be seen.

And then the sea really erupted, shaking and rocking like the biggest whirlpool in the world. I knew it could only mean one thing: Neptune had arrived.

I saw him in the distance, his chariot pulled swiftly along by about twenty dolphins. They charged towards us. I felt like a prisoner on death row, ready to give up completely.

'Emily!' A voice called behind me. I swivelled round. Aaron! One hand still held high in the air, he was paddling towards me on a piece of driftwood. 'The boat collapsed,' he gasped. 'This is all that's left.'

I swam frantically towards him, willing my tail to hold out just a few more moments.

'The moon,' Aaron panted. 'We've only got a minute.'

A wave washed over my head, but I shook it off. Paddling furiously, I made it to the makeshift raft and grabbed hold of it, gasping for breath. One more minute and then I'd lose the ring forever. Everything that mattered to me would slip down to the bottom of the sea with it, never to be seen again.

I could hear Neptune roaring instructions at the dolphins, waving his trident in the air.

'Now!' I said, holding my hand out. Aaron was wearing the other ring. He held his hand out to mine. The pearl glowed white. The diamond burst with brightness. It was almost blinding. The sea bubbled and boiled all around us as we fumbled to try and bring the two rings together. Come on, come *on*!

Neptune was in front of us, his face as angry as the darkest thunderstorm, his trident high above his head, his eyes burning with rage, his mouth open to shout at us. And then –

The sea stopped moving.

The mist cleared.

Neptune opened his mouth to yell at us. Our hands met.

And the rings came together.

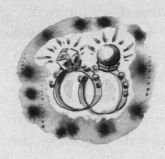

Chapter Fourteen

We'd done it! We'd really, truly done it.

We held the rings between us, each gripping the raft with the other hand. Light fizzed out from them like an exploding box of fireworks. White lights rocketing to the sky, bright blue balls of energy whizzing round and round, orange bubbles exploding all around us. I laughed with relief, tears rolling down my cheeks.

With every spark, I felt the life return to my broken body. My tail burst into action with the light, filling up, flicking the water. My tail had come back! I was still a semi-mer! We'd beaten the curse!

'Look!' Aaron arched his body; something flipped on to the water behind him. A tail! Sleek and black, it shone and glowed as it batted the surface of the sea. 'My tail,' he said, staring at it in wonder. 'I've got a tail!'

'We did it!' I cried, clenching his hand tight as we held the two rings together.

And then Neptune rose in his chariot, his figure blocking out the moon itself.

He opened his mouth to speak, to roar, to do all the things Neptune does. I squeezed my eyes shut in anticipation. What would he say? What would he do now? Surely he wasn't going to leave it like this. How could we have thought for the tiniest second that we could get away with it?

But no sound came. Eventually, I opened my eyes again, to see Neptune in the same position; his hand in the air, his body taut and tense, the sea around him motionless. He was staring in our direction, but not at us.

I turned to see what he was looking at. At first I thought it was just the mist, hovering around the castle as it always did, bunching up into a ball. But there was something inside the mist. A person. A woman. She had the most beautiful face I'd ever seen. Eyes as green as the brightest emeralds, framed by thick black lashes. Her hair was jet-black,

578

stretching down her back. She reached out a hand to Neptune, holding his eyes with hers.

'Aurora?' he said eventually. 'Is that really you?'

Aurora? The woman who broke Neptune's heart?

As she smiled back at him, her eyes brightened even more. Her smile seemed to lighten the whole ocean. 'It's really me.'

'How? How are you here?' Neptune's voice grew harder. 'Is it magic? A trick of the light? What is it? How do you come before me like this?'

'Every year at the spring equinox, I wait for you. I try to find you. I have never seen you until this time . . . ' She swept a hand in front of us, smiling down at me and Aaron as she did so. It felt like the sun coming out. 'This time, the rings have come back together, and they have brought me to you, and you to me.'

'But you left me,' Neptune replied, his voice hardening. 'You broke my heart. You cannot mend it. You can never undo the suffering you caused me!'

Aurora held a slender finger to her mouth. 'Don't say this. Never say such a thing. I would never leave you.'

'Liar! You did. You left me!'

'I was a mortal. I wished with all my heart not to be. I even tried. For you. And I drowned, trying to swim to you . . . '

Her voice was fading. The mist swirled around

her face, wrapping around her like a scarf. 'You must forgive me,' she whispered.

'Aurora!' Neptune called. Waving his trident at the sky, he cried. 'Don't go! I ORDER you to stay! Do NOT leave me!'

The mist had all but swept her away. Her image. Her spirit. Whatever it was, it had almost faded completely.

'It's gone midnight. The moon has passed its fullness. We are moving into day, towards the light, the spring, new life. I cannot stay. Forgive me,' she said, her voice as gentle as a breeze. 'Forgive me. I beg you, forgive me.' Again and again, she repeated the same words, until there was no more voice, no vision, only the wind and the moon and the night.

In the silence, we watched the mist that continued to swirl around the castle, wrapping it in fog. Neptune stared the hardest. His eyes didn't flicker.

Aaron let go of my hand. 'Look,' he whispered. Under the moon's power, the pull of the rings had loosened. Aaron slipped his from his finger. Putting it carefully on the raft, he held his hands up. In the moonlight, I suddenly realised what he was looking at. The webbing. It had gone.

Gently placing my ring next to his, I examined my own hands. They'd gone back to normal too! I laughed with pleasure, grinning at Aaron, at Shona, at –

'Gotcha!' A hand snapped up out of nowhere,

snatching the rings from the raft.

'No!' I lunged forward to grab them back, but it was too late. I dived down into the water. Fuelled with new energy, my mermaid self intact, I swam as hard as I could to catch whoever it was who had stolen the rings. But he was too fast for me. He bolted away, swimming like a lightning streak towards Neptune's chariot.

When I came back up to the surface, I saw who it was. Smiling his smarmy, creepy, nasty smile, holding out the rings for Neptune to take. Who else?

Mr Beeston.

'Neptune won't fall for any of that sentimental codswallop!' he snarled. 'Oh no, he knows what is important in life. What really matters, what — '

'Beeston!' Neptune growled.

Mr Beeston bowed low, holding the rings out in front of him as he flicked his tail to tread water. 'Your Majesty,' he said, his voice deep and intense. 'I humbly return to you what is rightfully yours. I swore my allegiance to you and I have not failed you. Finally, the rings are back with you. Once again, they may be parted and buried, safely out of trouble. And you have my word, I will never, ever let anything like this happen again.' Mr Beeston carried on bowing so low his head was practically underwater. No one else moved. No one spoke.

Then Neptune held out a hand. 'Give me the

rings,' he said.

Mr Beeston instantly swam forward to hand the rings over to Neptune. 'Your Majesty, I am humbled by your – '

'Silence!' Neptune barked, his face contorted – with rage, with pain? I couldn't tell.

I stared at him. After everything we'd done, everything that had happened, how could it go wrong so quickly? Now Neptune had the rings back, he could curse us all over again – and this time there wouldn't be a single thing we could do about it.

I sank lower in the water, my tail hardly moving. Shona swam over to join me. She took hold of my hand. 'I'll always be your best friend,' she whispered. 'Whatever happens.'

But maybe she wouldn't have that choice. None of us had any choices any more. All the choices were in Neptune's hands. Literally.

Neptune flicked his trident in the air. Instantly, three dolphins swam to the side of the chariot. He bent down to say something to them and they disappeared, returning moments later pulling something along. Another chariot, a sleigh of some kind. There were two people in it. A woman and – a merman. No! It couldn't be! But it was! Mum and Dad! Of course! Neptune said he'd bring them tonight!

I swam as hard as I could to reach the boat.

'Mum! Dad!' I cried with every tiny bit of me. But the joy I felt disappeared as soon as I saw their faces.

Of course.

They had come to say goodbye.

Here, under the full moon, on the spring equinox, the one point in the year when day meets night, earth and sea would finally be separated, and for good this time.

Mum reached out from the carriage to throw her arms round me. 'Oh Emily,' she sobbed, grasping my hair, pulling me to her so tightly I couldn't breathe. I didn't care. All that mattered was that I was in my mother's arms again. 'I looked for you everywhere. Everyone on the island has been searching. We found every last jewel that Neptune had been after, but we couldn't find the most precious one of all. You.'

Then Dad's arms were round me too. Hovering in the water next to me, he reached out to wrap me in his arms. 'My little 'un,' he said, his voice raw and broken.

'Windsnap!' Neptune bellowed. All three of us looked up at him. He was pointing at Dad. 'Come here,' he said firmly.

Dad let go of me.

'No!' I lurched on to him, gripping him round the neck with my arms. This was it. My dad was going to be taken away; I'd say goodbye to him for the last time. 'No! Please!' I begged.

Dad unpeeled my fingers from around his neck. 'It'll be OK,' he said, the quivering in his voice giving him away. He didn't believe that any more than I did. Then he looked Mum in the eye. 'I always loved you,' he said. 'And I always will, right?'

Mum swallowed hard and nodded.

Dad glanced at Neptune, who glared back at him. 'I have to go,' he said. Kissing Mum's hand, ruffling my hair, he turned and swam away.

I darted through the water to follow him. Gripping his arm, I swam alongside him. Dad tried to shake me off. 'Please, little 'un, don't make this harder than it already is,' he said.

'Don't go,' I begged. I swam to Neptune's chariot with him. 'Please!' I begged Neptune, choking on sobs. 'Please don't make me have to lose my dad again. Please. Please don't make them have to part. I'll do anything. I'll be good. I'll never get into trouble again. *Please*.' I let go of Dad and wept openly. I had nothing left to say, nothing to ask, nothing to offer, nothing to look forward to.

'Stop your crying, child,' said Neptune. 'Listen to me.' He turned to Dad, looking him harshly in the eyes. 'Windsnap,' he said. 'Do you love your wife?'

'More than anything,' Dad said. He looked round for inspiration – and found it in the sky. 'More than the moon itself.'

Nodding briskly, Neptune asked, 'And she feels the same way?'

Dad glanced across at Mum. 'I hope so.'

Mum held her hands to her chest. Wiping her cheeks with the back of her hand, she nodded vigorously.

Neptune was silent for a long time. He put his trident down on the seat in his chariot and held the rings in both hands. Juggling them in his palms, he looked back and forth between Mum and Dad. His powerful face looked different. The lines of anger streaking down each cheek seemed to have gone. His eyes looked rounder, softer. For the first time ever, I noticed how green they were.

In the darkness, rain began to fall, tiny sharp droplets plopping onto the sea all around us. Neptune opened his mouth to speak again.

'No one has to say goodbye tonight,' he said quietly. He turned to Mr Beeston. 'Beeston,' he said. 'You were wrong.'

Mr Beeston swam forward. Bowing low so his hair fell right into the water, he gabbled, 'Your Majesty, if I have failed you in any way, I – '

Neptune raised a hand to silence him. 'You acted out of loyalty. But you are mistaken. I do not know what is important in life, what really matters. Or if I do, I have only just found out.' He looked up at the mist, still swirling around the castle. The rain fell harder, bouncing off the sea all around us. 'I have only just remembered.'

Then he held the rings out in front of him. 'Come here, Windsnap,' he said. Picking up his trident, he nodded to the dolphins, who instantly swam forward, bringing the carriage and Mum to Neptune.

What was he doing? 'I will no longer hide from the truth. I will no longer attempt to bury my feelings,' he said.

Neptune called Aaron. 'You are the man of the family now,' he said to Aaron. 'I cannot undo what has been done. But I can make amends. You are free to travel, to live where you please, mix with whoever you like. I will not hide you from the world any longer. You are my fin and blood and I am proud of you.'

Aaron smiled hesitantly at Neptune. His eyes, his deep green eyes. Neptune's eyes.

'Your Majesty, sir,' he said. 'What about my mother?'

'She will be waiting for you at the castle.'

'Is she . . . ?'

Neptune nodded. 'She will be fine,' he said. 'Like

you, she has a long life ahead of her. I want you both to enjoy it.'

'You mean she's better? We're no longer cursed?' Aaron burst out.

Laughing, Neptune replied, 'I will no longer allow curses. They are forbidden – by law!'

Aaron punched the air. Then he turned and smiled the widest smile at me.

Neptune turned back to my parents. 'I am a firm ruler,' he said. 'And I always will be. No one can ever try to deny this.' Mum and Dad both nodded, waiting for him to continue.

'But,' Neptune went on, beckoning me to come to him. 'But this daughter of yours has brought something back to me which I lost many hundreds of years ago.' He fell silent.

'The rings?' I asked, hoping to prompt him, even though I should have known better than to interrupt Neptune.

'No,' he said gently. 'Not the rings. You and your family may never fully understand what you have given me, but let me tell you, it is the most valuable thing. In return, I give it back to you.' Then he reached out to Mum and Dad – and handed them the rings! The diamond one to Dad, the pearl to Mum.

Silently receiving the rings, Mum and Dad gazed at each other, at me, at Neptune.

'You represent what I have lost, and you will

represent its revival too.' He spread his arms upwards to the sky. 'It is the spring equinox,' he called, 'the day of my wedding anniversary, the day of new beginnings. Merfolk and humans will from now on live in peace together. I order it!'

I gasped and looked at Shona. Really? Did he really say that?

'Not just on one small island. It's time for the whole world to start again. We will start a new world. A new world that is not a new world at all. The world that was there all along, to anyone who was not too blind to see it.'

Then he turned back to us and frowned. 'But you must make me a promise,' he said sternly. I *knew* there'd be a catch. I knew it couldn't be that simple. Nothing in my life ever was.

'You must swear to me that these rings will never again be parted.'

Dad grinned so widely his smile almost broke his face in two. Grabbing Mum round the waist and pulling me towards him with his other arm, he replied, 'Your Majesty, that is the easiest of promises to keep.'

Neptune smiled. 'Very well. I have said all I need to say.' Holding his trident in the air, he waved it in the direction of *Fortuna*. A group of dolphins broke away and swam off towards it. 'Your boat will be fit to sail by morning,' Neptune said. 'Now go. Travel the world. See new sights. Pass the message on to all you meet.'

'We will,' Mum breathed. 'We won't let you down, your Majesty. How can we ever thank you?'

Neptune waved her words away with his hand. 'Just respect the rings and what they represent. I am giving you a great responsibility. You must show me you are ready for this. I shall be watching you.'

With that, Neptune clicked his fingers and held his trident aloft. Motioning for Mr Beeston to join him, he sat back down in his chariot.

'Look, I never meant you any harm,' Mr Beeston mumbled as he passed. Blushing and stammering, he added, 'I didn't mean to – you know. It was just duty, you understand. Loyalty. I mean, Neptune. He's the king. We're still friends, aren't we?'

'Friends?' Mum spluttered. 'When have we ever been real friends?'

Dad touched her gently on the arm. 'Penny,' he said. 'It's a new world. We have to set an example.'

Penny. He called her Penny! Things really were back to normal. Better than normal!

'Just like that?' asked Mum. 'After everything?'

Dad nodded. 'Look at all we have to be grateful for. Let's start again.'

Mum turned to Mr Beeston.

'Very well,' Mum sighed. 'We'll try. But as long as you remember you have to be loyal to us too, now.'

'I will,' Mr Beeston simpered. 'I will. Thank you. Thank you.' Then he gave me one last lopsided smile. 'No hard feelings, eh?' he said, reaching out to ruffle my hair.

I stiffened, dodging his hand. 'Mm,' I said. I wasn't ready to forgive and forget yet.

'Emily,' Dad said firmly.

'OK. Whatever.'

And then the strangest thing happened. We looked at each other, me and Mr Beeston. And for the first time in my life, I felt that we really saw each other; saw, heard and understood each other. I saw someone like me. Desperate to fit in, to please, to belong. That was all he wanted. And when he smiled at me, I didn't recoil and squirm and think about his crooked teeth and his odd eyes. I found myself smiling back. 'Yeah,' I said. 'No hard feelings.'

'That's a good girl,' he said.

'Beeston!' Neptune called again and Mr Beeston swam off to join him in his chariot. As the dolphins pulled them away, the moonlight lit a trail ahead of them.

In the silence of the night, I could hear Neptune's voice as they sailed away. 'I forgive you,' he called to the sky. 'I forgive you.'

As his words echoed through the dark night, Dad pointed up into the sky. 'Look at that,' he said. I wouldn't have thought it possible if I hadn't seen it with my own eyes. The moonlight sparkled on the sea, lighting up the raindrops that kept falling. In the distance, the castle stood dark and solid. But the mist had completely cleared. In its place, framing it with a perfect arc, every colour bright and clear, was a rainbow.

'Just go through it once more,' Millie said, blinking round at us all on the front deck. Aaron's mum was sitting on the front benches with her and Mum. She looked just like Aaron, thin and pale with jet-black hair. She hadn't said much since she'd joined us, but she'd smiled a lot. A great wide smile that infected everyone around her, just like Aaron's.

Dad leaned over a rail along the side of the boat. Aaron was in the water with me and Shona.

The sky was pale blue, wispy clouds floating lazily across it, each one tinged with pink edges. Millie had only just woken up. None of the rest of us had been asleep at all. How could we have slept on a night like this?

Mum laughed as she handed Millie a cup of tea. 'We've told you the story three times now!'

'Yes, but I still don't believe it!' Millie replied, closing her eyes in ecstasy as she sipped her tea.

'Nor do we,' Dad said, smiling at Mum as he reached for her hand. The rings shone on their fingers. 'But it's true.'

Millie took another gulp from her cup.

'We can go anywhere we like,' Mum said. 'We don't need to hide what we are.' Then she glanced at Shona. 'Of course, we'll go back to Allpoints Island first. These last few days I've realised how much everyone there cares about us. We may even stay there for good if we want to.'

'Swishy!' Shona and I shouted in unison.

'Can we go too, Mother?' Aaron asked.

'I don't see why not,' his mum replied with a laugh.

'Of course you're coming too,' Mum said, linking her arm. 'We're not letting you go that easily.'

'And if we ever get bored with Allpoints Island, we'll move somewhere else. Anywhere we like,' Dad said, his eyes shining with excitement.

'And if we don't, we'll just take lots of holidays,' Mum smiled.

'We'll visit every country, every land, every sea,' Dad went on. 'We'll show the whole world they can get on in harmony like us!'

'We will, darling,' Mum said, smiling back at him. 'And maybe we'll even bring a tutor along with us so Emily doesn't miss out on her schooling.'

'Perfect!' Dad said. 'She'll come back from her travels and still get top marks in Shipwrecks and Sand Dunes.'

Mum's face tightened. 'I was thinking more of

her sums and spellings, Jake.'

'I'll get her a new hairbrush, a whole set of hairbrushes, and an ocean chart so she can recognise all the fish in the sea.'

'Or a ruler and a dictionary,' Mum insisted.

'Oh, you two,' Millie sighed. 'You're not at it again, are you?'

Mum and Dad looked at each other and burst out laughing. 'OK,' Dad said. 'Maybe changing the world is a bit ambitious just now.'

'We'll start small,' Mum said, reaching for his hand.

Dad kissed her palm. 'Lead by example,' he said. 'No arguing.'

'Never,' Mum agreed.

'Come on,' I said. 'Let's get going. Shona needs to get back to her parents!'

We'd hooked *Fortuna* up to some ropes so we could tow it back. I don't know what Neptune had done, but the lower deck was dry and sealed up so it floated like a normal boat. 'We'll put it back to normal when we get home,' Dad smiled.

With a bit of help from Aaron's maps, we'd set a course back to Allpoints Island. Dad reckoned it would only take a few days if we took turns at pulling. He had left it to the three of us for now while he hitched on to the side of the boat near Mum.

Shona and Aaron and I pulled on the ropes as we

set off, flipping our tails to make rainbows with the water, ducking under to see the rubbery round yellow fish with big black eyes bouncing on the seabed, racing and chasing each other all the way.

As we passed the castle, we fell silent. Without the mist, it looked almost naked. Lonely, even. 'We'll come back,' Aaron's mother called down. 'Even if it's just for a visit.'

Aaron smiled up at her, then splashed me and grinned. He pulled his rope taut. 'Race you to the next wave!' he said with a grin.

Shona dived down to follow him. But I stayed close to the boat for a while. The sky was growing lighter and lighter. Up behind me I could hear Mum and Dad talking.

'I've nothing against rulers,' Dad was saying. 'But protractors. I mean, come on, does she really need one of those?'

'I tell you what,' Mum replied. 'I'll let you have the scale polish if you give me the algebra set.'

'The scale polish and a kiss,' Dad said.

'Done.'

They were quiet for a while after that.

I smiled to myself as we swam on. What lay ahead for us? Where would we go? What would the future hold?

I couldn't answer the questions spinning round in my head any more than I could stop Mum and Dad bickering about my schooling, or Shona worrying about her hair, or Millie trying to tell fortunes with coat-hangers.

It didn't matter. What mattered was what I could see around me: my best friend racing our new friend along the surf; Mum and Dad smiling at each other and joking and kissing; Millie spreading the tarot cards out on the deck for Aaron's mum.

And beyond that? Well, beyond that lay a brand new day.

Also by Liz Kessler

Philippa Fisher's Fairy Godsister

Imagine if a fairy granted you three wishes . . .

This is what happens to Philippa Fisher when Daisy, the new girl at school, announces that she has come to be her fairy godsister.

Daisy doesn't really want to be there, but she has a job to do. So she's not best pleased with Philippa.

And Philippa has to find a good way to use her three Wish Vouchers, which is easier said than done – especially when each one seems to make things worse.

A story that sparkles with magic and is all about friendship, luck and how we decide what we really, really want.